W9-CNL-284

LOGOS RUN

LOGOS RUN

WILLIAM C. DIETZ

ACE BOOKS, NEW YORK

THE BERKLEY PUBLISHING GROUP
Published by the Penguin Group
Penguin Group (USA) Inc.
375 Hudson Street, New York, New York 10014, USA
Penguin Group (Canada), 90 Eglinton Avenue East, Suite 700, Toronto, Ontario M4P 2Y3, Canada
(a division of Pearson Penguin Canada Inc.)
Penguin Books Ltd., 80 Strand, London WC2R 0RL, England
Penguin Group Ireland, 25 St. Stephen's Green, Dublin 2, Ireland (a division of Penguin Books Ltd.)
Penguin Group (Australia), 250 Camberwell Road, Camberwell, Victoria 3124, Australia
(a division of Pearson Australia Group Pty. Ltd.)
Penguin Books India Pvt. Ltd., 11 Community Centre, Panchsheel Park, New Delhi—110 017, India
Penguin Group (NZ), Cnr. Airborne and Rosedale Roads, Albany, Auckland 1310, New Zealand
(a division of Pearson New Zealand Ltd.)
Penguin Books (South Africa) (Pty.) Ltd., 24 Sturdee Avenue, Rosebank, Johannesburg 2196, South Africa

Penguin Books Ltd., Registered Offices: 80 Strand, London WC2R 0RL, England

This is an original publication of The Berkley Publishing Group.

This is a work of fiction. Names, characters, places, and incidents either are the product of the author's imagination or are used fictitiously, and any resemblance to actual persons, living or dead, business establishments, events, or locales is entirely coincidental. The publisher does not have any control over and does not assume any responsibility for author or third-party websites or their content.

First edition: October 2006

Library of Congress Cataloging-in-Publication Data

Dietz, William C.
    Logos run / William C. Dietz.—1st ed.
      p. cm.
    ISBN 0-441-01428-3
    1. Interplanetary voyages—Fiction. I. Title.
    PS3554.I388L64 2006
    813'.54—dc22
                              2006012532

PRINTED IN THE UNITED STATES OF AMERICA

10 9 8 7 6 5 4 3 2 1

This book is dedicated to my dearest Marjorie.
Thank you for glorious days past,
life in the ever-present now,
and whatever may lie ahead.
The adventure continues!

ONE

From this day forward the stars shall be ours . . .

—Emperor Hios, on the day that the first public star gate went
into service, and he stepped onto the surface of the Planet Zeen

The attack came without warning. The angen-drawn coach
had been under way for hours by then, having followed the
well-established ruts south through villages of neatly
thatched roofs, past prayer ribbons that flew with the wind,
and miles of flooded paddies. The genetically engineered
draft animals strained at their harnesses as the road began to
rise, the driver's long, supple whip cracked over their vaguely
equine heads, and they were forced to assume the four-
wheeled vehicle's entire weight. The angens expressed their
unhappiness via snorts, grunts, and occasional bursts of flatulence as the low-lying paddies fell away and they pulled the
coach up through a long series of switchbacks. But the driver
was accustomed to such displays, and his passengers were
largely unaware of how the animals felt, since two of the three
were asleep within the boxy cab.

The single exception was Lonni Norr, who sat facing the front of the coach with Jak Rebo's head resting on her lap. The variant's right leg had gone to sleep ten minutes earlier, but she couldn't bring herself to wake the runner and thereby break the spell. Because after months of danger and turmoil Norr was temporarily at peace. And had been ever since their departure from the holy city of CaCanth.

But Norr's ancestors had been bred to sense things that norms could not. So even as the heavy who was curled up on the seat across from her continued to snore, and Rebo jerked as if in response to a dream, the young woman knew that conflict lay ahead. Partly because the threesome possessed something others wanted—and partly because it was some-how meant to be.

The windows were open, which meant Norr caught a brief glimpse of the terrain ahead as the coach lurched up over a pass and began its rattling descent. In contrast to the carefully cultivated paddies the coach had passed earlier in the day, a dense forest awaited them below. The interlock-ing foliage stretched for as far as the eye could see, and, judging from the occasional glint of reflected sunlight, was watered by a serpentine river.

Rebo mumbled something in his sleep, and Norr smiled tenderly as she ran her fingers through the runner's thick black hair. His features were even, but a bit too rugged to be described as classically handsome, in spite of the fact that women generally found him to be attractive. The relation-ship with Rebo had been part of the long journey that had begun on the Planet Anafa, and subsequently taken them to Pooz, Ning, Etu, and Thara. What began as a momentary alliance had gradually evolved into a wary friendship, an on-again, off-again romance, and a decision to remain together.

For a month? A year? A lifetime? Not even a person with her gifts could tell.

Such were Norr's thoughts as the coach found level ground, bounced its way into a set of deep ruts, and was soon embraced by an army of leafy trees. Their trunks were four to five feet in circumference, and their massive branches came together to form a dense canopy overhead. The thick biomass cut the amount of sunlight that could reach the forest floor by half and caused a drop in temperature.

But the chill that Norr felt was not entirely physical. Other senses had come into play, too, senses that norms possess, but rarely take full advantage of. What one of them might have experienced as a vague uneasiness, Norr saw as a roiling blackness, and knew the sensation for what it was: negative energy being broadcast by a group of hostile minds. The sensitive put her hand on Rebo's arm. "Jak . . . Wake up . . . Something is wrong."

But the warning came too late. One of the angens uttered a bloodcurdling scream as an arrow sank into its haunch, and a pair of hobnailed boots made a thumping sound as a bandit landed on the roof. That noise was followed by a loud *boom* as the driver triggered his blunderbuss and sent a dozen .30-caliber lead balls into the undergrowth where the archer was concealed. But that did nothing to protect the coachman from the garrote that dropped over his head, or the noose that began to tighten around his throat. He had little choice but to release both his weapon *and* the reins in a desperate effort to restore his air supply.

"On the roof!" Norr exclaimed, as her companions awoke. "Bandits!"

Like all his kind, Bo Hoggles had a body that had been designed for life on heavy-gravity worlds. That meant he was strong, *so* strong that he could smash a massive fist up through the thin roof, and grab the bandit's ankle. That was sufficient to scare the would-be thief, who was forced to let go of the garrote, while he attempted to pry the heavy's sausagelike fingers off his ankle. And that's what he was doing when Rebo drew the semiautomatic Crosser, pointed the weapon up toward the ceiling, and fired two ten-millimeter rounds through the roof. One bullet missed, but the other struck the brigand in the back and severed his spinal cord. The coach rocked sickeningly as Hoggles let go; the body bounced into the air and fell past Norr's window.

The driver had control of the reins by then, but no amount of swearing could make the wounded angen run faster, and that slowed the rest. All of which was part of the time-tested process that the bandits traditionally relied upon to bring their prey to a standstill. So, while the loss of Brother Becko was regrettable, the brigands had every expectation of success as the coach slowed and finally came to a stop. What they *didn't* expect were the people who emerged from the carriage. A heavy, armed with a war hammer, a norm with a gun in each fist, and a sensitive with a metal-tipped wooden staff. But in spite of the fact that the passengers were clearly more formidable than the bejeweled merchants the bandit leader had been hoping for, he had little choice but to hurl himself forward as a volley of arrows arched overhead.

Rather than exert *more* control over her body, Norr let go instead. That allowed her full array of senses to unfold. The staff made patterns in the air as the variant whirled. There was a series of clacking sounds as half a dozen arrows were intercepted, broken in half, and left to fall like wooden rain.

Hoggles was not so graceful, or so fortunate, since he made an excellent target. Two arrows thumped into his chest, but neither possessed the force required to penetrate the mesh-lined leather armor the variant had purchased in CaCanth. And, having fully recovered from the injuries suffered at the Ree Ree River, the hard-charging giant was among the bandits in a matter of moments. Blood flew as the enormous war hammer struck this way and that, while his basso war cry dominated the field of battle.

Nor was that the worst of it, because even as the berserker met the main body of the onrushing brigands in hammer-to-head combat, Rebo was busy shooting at the rest. It was aimed fire, which meant that nearly every bullet found its mark, and that added to the slaughter.

And so it was that having lost fully half his band in a matter of minutes, and with a bullet lodged in his left thigh, the group's leader issued a shrill whistle. Strong hands grabbed the chieftain under the armpits, and his feet were lifted clear off the ground as members of the bandit's extended family hustled him into the safety of the woods. All the brigands were gone within seconds, leaving the battle-dazed travelers in sole possession of the body-strewn battlefield.

"Well, that was an unpleasant surprise," Rebo said calmly as he slipped the unfired Hogger back into the cross-draw holster at his waist. "Let's get out of here before they regroup."

"I agree," a male voice said emphatically. "And I would very much appreciate it if you would be so kind as to wear a more suitable garment during future battles. . . . I could have been damaged—or taken off-line."

The sound seemed to originate from Norr, but had actually emanated from the coat she wore, which, in spite of its nondescript appearance, was a computer. A *wearable* computer that was more than a thousand years old and had once been at the center of a star-spanning system of star gates. Months before, the threesome had agreed to reunite the artificial intelligence (AI) with a control center called Socket on behalf of a dead scientist.

But the AI could be imperious, not to mention downright annoying, which was why Norr responded as she did. "If you would be so kind as to let us know when we're about to be attacked—we'll put you away well in advance. Come to think of it, maybe we should do that anyway. . . . I could use some peace and quiet."

Logos didn't like being packed away and therefore chose to remain silent. Rebo grinned. "Good. . . . I'm glad that's settled. Come on, let's give the driver a hand."

Having reharnessed the uninjured angens, and attached the wounded animal to the back of the coach by means of a long lead, the carriage got under way fifteen minutes later. Rebo sat next to the driver with the fully recharged blunderbuss across his knees, while Hoggles remained in the coach, war hammer at the ready.

Norr tried to separate the natural apprehension she felt from the external stimuli available to her highly specialized senses but that was hard to do. So, with no assurance that they wouldn't be attacked again, all the variant could do was to keep her eyes peeled and look forward to the moment when they put the forest behind them.

Eventually, after two hours of suspense, that moment came, as the trees began to thin, and gently rolling grasslands appeared. The sun was little more than a red-orange smear by then, and Rebo wondered how many more sunsets he would witness before he and his companions left Thara and continued the uncertain journey begun so many months before. The coach slowed slightly as it encountered a rise, the driver snapped his whip, and the angens pulled harder.

The undercarriage rattled, darkness gathered, and the stars lay like white dust on the blue velvet sky.

The city of Seros, on the Planet Anafa

The sun was little more than a dimly seen presence beyond the layers of charcoal-generated haze that hung over the city. Much had changed during the ten millennia since the first colony ship touched down on Anafa. A primitive settlement had evolved into a town and then a city. Or *multiple* cities, because Seros had been through many incarnations, with the latest sitting atop all the rest.

None of which held any interest for the hooded metal man as he paused to examine a building, matched the image to the one stored in his electronic memory, and made his way up the front steps. The long, filthy robe hung loosely over his skeletal body, servos whirred as the machine climbed the stairs, and the locals hurried to get out of his way. The mysterious androids could communicate with one another, everyone knew that, and would hurry to one another's aid if threatened. That meant it was a good idea to leave the robots alone in spite of their propensity to ignore common courtesies, preach on street corners, and generally skulk about.

Like the structures around it, the rooming house had seen better days. The landlord claimed that it had been an office building once, back before the techno wars, but the history of the six-story tenement hardly mattered to the hundreds of people who lived there, or to the metal man as he climbed five flights of stairs, pulled a graffiti-decorated door open, and entered the maze of cubicles beyond. Space was let by the square foot, which meant that the squats were of various sizes, depending on what a particular tenant could afford. Paths wound snakelike between the constantly morphing hovels they served. Some of the cubicles had walls made out of brick, others had been constructed with salvaged wood, but most consisted of large pieces of colored cloth draped over a confusing network of crisscrossed ropes. That meant life in the tenement was a largely public affair, in which every aspect of a resident's life was known to those in the surrounding area, and gossip had been elevated to an art form.

So it wasn't surprising that dozens of inquisitive eyes tracked the android as it followed a serpentine path deep into the squats, paused at one of the many intersections, and took a judicious right. And since the automaton's progress was heralded by a buzz of excited conversation, Arn Dyson would have known about the visitor well in advance, had his consciousness been resident within his physical body.

But it wasn't, which meant that when the robot arrived in front of the sensitive's squat and whipped the badly faded curtain out of the way, the man sitting at the center of the simple reed mat made no response. The sensitive was middle-aged. His long hair was fanned out across his shoulders, and his eyes were closed. What few possessions he had were stacked along a wall made of interwoven sticks. A grubby little girl sat with arms wrapped around her knees. She regarded the machine with serious eyes. "Are you here to see Citizen Dyson?"

"Yes," the metal man grated. "I am. Wake him."

The little girl seemed to consider the order. If she was afraid of the machine, there was no visible sign of it. "Citizen Dyson has gone to visit the spirit planes. If you wish to speak with him, you must wait for him to return."

"I will wake him," the robot said, and took a step forward.

"No!" the little girl objected. "Not while he's in trance. That could kill him."

"Is there a problem?" The deep basso voice came from behind the automaton, and the machine was forced to give way as a heavy entered the tiny squat. The giant's head had been shaved, he wore a gold ring in his nose, and he was naked from the waist up. Muscles rippled as the variant moved, and the robot knew that the biological could best him in a fight. "My master will pay Citizen Dyson two cronos for two hours of his time," the android said flatly.

The heavy looked suitably impressed. He knew that the assassin's guild would be happy to kill someone for half that amount. "Why didn't you say so?" he demanded. "Go ahead and bring him back, Myra. . . . The worthless spook owes me thirty gunnars—and I thought the money was gone for good."

The waif looked from the heavy to the robot and back again. Then she nodded, scraped the wax off the tip of a wooden match, and lit a slender cinnamon stick. The moment a tendril of smoke appeared, the girl blew some of it into the sensitive's nostrils. The distinctive odor served to stimulate Dyson's physical body—which sought to bring the rest of him back. The sensitive shivered, blinked his eyes, and frowned. "Myra? Hobar? What's going on?"

"You will come," the metal man said tactlessly. "Omar Tepho has need of your services."

"I don't know who this Tepho character is," Hobar put in, "but he's willing to pay two cronos."

Dyson looked up at the robot. "Is that true?"

"Yes," the automaton replied gravely. "It is."

"Okay," the sensitive agreed reluctantly. "I wasn't able to satisfy Tepho's needs last time. Let's hope this session is different."

It took the better part of an hour for the robot and the sensitive to make their way through the laser-straight streets, past the weatherworn pylons that marked the path of a once-glorious transportation system, and up to the seemingly decrepit building from which Omar Tepho ran the Techno Society. The unlikely twosome followed a narrow passageway back to the point where an iron gate blocked further progress. There was an audible *click* as the automaton inserted a metal finger into the receptacle located next to a print-sensitive identification pad.

The variant had been through the process before, so he wasn't surprised when the gate swung open, and the robot led him to a metal door. There was a momentary pause while a guard inspected the pair through a peephole followed by a nudge, as the door swung inward. Council member Ron Olvos was there to greet Dyson. He was a small man, but a hard worker and a skilled politician. Those qualities, plus the care with which he always put Tepho's interests ahead of his own, accounted for his presence on the board. Olvos ignored the machine but extended a hand to the sensitive. "Welcome! Thank you for coming."

Though not altogether certain that his presence was entirely voluntary, the variant smiled agreeably and wondered if he should demand three cronos rather than two. But he couldn't muster the necessary courage, the moment passed, and Dyson found himself in a spotless corridor. "The council was in session all morning," Olvos explained. "The chairman raised the possibility of bringing you back—and will be extremely pleased to learn that we were able to do so."

"Really?" Dyson inquired doubtfully. "I didn't meet with much success last time."

"Ah, but that wasn't your fault," the smaller man replied soothingly. "*This* session will go more smoothly. . . . Do you remember Jevan Kane?"

The sensitive nodded. Kane was the operative who sought him out the first time. He was a cold man with blond hair, blue eyes, and white skin. All in an age when more than 90 percent of the population had black hair, brown eyes, and olive skin. "Yes, of course," Dyson replied politely. "How is he?"

"Dead," Olvos replied emotionlessly. "Which is where *you* come in. It's our hope that, unlike the founder, Kane continues to support the Techno Society's goals and will provide us with some much-needed assistance from the other side. If so, we could have an ongoing need for your services, and that could be quite profitable for you."

Dyson was desperately poor, but there are worse things than poverty, and the process of being co-opted by the highly secretive and possibly sinister Techno Society filled the sensitive with misgivings. But there was no opportunity to consider the long-range implications of the day's activity as servos whined and double doors opened into what had once been a vat. Those days were gone however, and the one-time tank had been transformed into a circular conference room. Electric light flooded the tank, a holo projector was suspended above the round conference table, and streams of incoming data cascaded down wall-mounted screens. All of which were wonders that Dyson had sworn he wouldn't disclose. A promise he had kept.

Six of the seven seats that surrounded the table were occupied, but the sensitive's eyes were immediately drawn to Omar Tepho—partly because of the way the man looked, which was undeniably different, but mostly as a result of the thought forms that hovered around him. They were dark things for the most part, only half-seen within the electrical-storm-like shimmer generated by a brilliant intellect. Others were present in the room, but as Tepho's coal black eyes swiveled around to look at him, the variant knew that his was the only opinion that really mattered. He had a deep resonant voice, and it filled the space with sound as he spoke.

"Welcome," Tepho intoned, as Dyson entered the keyhole-shaped space at the table's center. "Thank you for coming. It is our intention to communicate with Jevan Kane."

By some accident of birth Tepho had been born with multiple defects. His skull was lumpy rather than smooth, one eye socket was higher that the other, and his ears looked like handles on an earthenware jug. Still worse was the fact that the technologist had a congenital spinal deformity that made it difficult for him to walk or run. None of which would have been of interest to Dyson had it not been for the manner in which the vessel had imparted its shape to the contents. The variant bowed humbly and took his seat. "You're welcome. . . . I hope I can be of service."

"As do we," Tepho replied gravely. "Please proceed."

Dyson requested that the lights be dimmed, suggested that the council visualize Jevan Kane's face, and began the series of much-practiced steps that would allow the sensitive to partially exit his body. Meanwhile, on the plane closest to the physical, the disincarnate entity who had once been known as Jevan Kane waited to come through. He had experienced many incarnations—some more pleasant than others. And, although the transition from the physical to the spirit realm had a transformational effect on some spirits, Kane remained unchanged. So much so that he was intent on preparing the physical plane for his next incarnation. A life in which *he* would control the star-spanning civilization that Tepho sought to establish.

So, no sooner had Dyson half exited his body, than Kane entered it. And not tentatively, but with considerable force, as the operative sought to reintegrate himself with the physical. Everything seemed to slow as the disincarnate entity entered what felt like quicksand—and was forced to cope with a body made of lead. But there were pleasures, too, starting with the sharp tang of vinegar that still clung to the inside surface of the tank and the sudden awareness of the sex organs that dangled between the channel's legs. Slowly, bit by bit, what had been like a heavy mist vanished, and the conference room appeared.

Tepho was there, as was the shadowy combat variant who stood half-seen behind the chairman, but rather than the fear previously felt when ushered into their combined presence, Kane felt something akin to contempt. Because even as Tepho attempted to manipulate *him*, he would use the technologist and thereby achieve his ends. "Greetings," Kane said through what felt like numb lips. "This is Jevan Kane."

What followed was a long and mostly predictable series of questions focused on the circumstances of Kane's most recent death, the status of the people he'd been sent to intercept, and the present disposition of the AI called Logos.

Kane answered by providing the council with a slightly glorified description of his own death, but when it came to the other matters, was forced to remind those present that just as it was difficult for them to access the spirit planes, the reverse was true as well. So, in spite of concerted efforts to obtain such information, the best he could give the council was the assurance that the runner and his companions were still on Thara and probably in possession of the computer. "It has no spirit," the disincarnate explained, "which makes it almost impossible to see. . . . But judging from the founder's continued interest in the threesome, it's my guess that they still have it."

Though hungry for more detail, Tepho was excited to learn that the device he sought was still on Thara and slammed his fist down on the table in front of him. A stylus jumped and rolled off the table onto the floor. "Excellent! Now we're getting somewhere! Shaz . . . I want you to assemble a team and make the jump to Thara. You'll need guidance from Kane, so take Dyson with you and stay in touch. I know you two have had your differences in the past, but it's time to put old grudges aside and work for the common good. Kane? Shaz? Can you do that?"

Tepho's words ignored the fact that *he* was the one who originally set the two men against each other—but that was to be expected. "You can count on me," Kane lied. "What's past is past."

The air behind Tepho shimmered as the combat variant made his presence manifest. Originally designed to function as warriors by engineers long dead, and slaughtered by the millions back during the techno wars, there weren't many of the highly specialized creatures left. Shaz had a doglike aspect that stemmed from a long, dark muzzle, a pair of close-set eyes, and oversized ears. He wore black clothing, a leather harness, and carried a small arsenal of weapons. His smile revealed two rows of razor-sharp teeth. "Of course," Shaz prevaricated smoothly. "It's the future that counts."

The city of Tryst, on the Planet Thara

Like many of the cities on Thara, the city of Tryst had been attacked more than once over the last few thousand years, which was why it not only occupied the top of a huge granite outcropping, but was surrounded by a twenty-foot-high stone wall. And, while no one had attempted to scale the barrier in the recent past, it was common knowledge that 11,214 red hat warriors had been prematurely forced into the spirit planes while trying to wrest the city away from the black hats during the War of the Glorious Scepter 112 years earlier.

However, thanks to Rebo and his companions, the correct person now sat on the throne of CaCanth. That ensured that both halves of the the Way, as the overarching religion was known, would remain at peace with each other for at least fifty years.

But, as with any city, the citizens of Tryst not only wanted to know who came and went, but to charge them for the privilege. That's why the coach was forced to a pause behind a line of farm wagons about halfway up the road that led to the top.

Progress was steady, however, and no more than half an hour had passed before the coach drew level with the customs shed, and a portly-looking norm came forward to collect their paj (entry fee). Meanwhile, waiting in the background should the customs agent have need of them, were half a dozen cudgel-wielding Dib Wa (religious) warriors. The tax collector was armed with a well-worn abacus, which he was just about to employ, when Rebo emerged from the back. The runner smiled engagingly as he held a bronze medallion up for the official to see. "Good afternoon," the runner said. "My name is . . ." But Rebo never got the opportunity to introduce himself as the customs agent took one look at the symbol, bowed deeply, and said something in Tilisi (the language spoken by those who follow the Way). Having heard his words the Dib Wa did likewise.

Rebo bowed in return, straightened, and produced his purse. "How much do we owe?"

"Nothing," the tax collector replied, his eyes on his feet. "You and your companions are guests of the Inwa (leader of leaders). Please go in peace."

The runner bowed once more, reentered the coach, and took his seat. "Well," Norr said, as the vehicle jerked into motion. "That was a better reception than we usually get. . . . It looks like the royal sigil packs some weight."

"I guess it does," Rebo replied. "It's a good thing I didn't let Bo trade his for a couple of beers and a meat pie two days ago."

The metal-shod wheels clattered over cobblestones as the conveyance carried the travelers into what many locals referred to as "the city of stone." And for good reason, since the early colonists made use of high-tech cutting tools to carve what they needed from solid stone, thereby creating a vast maze of halls, galleries, and rooms, all of which were connected by tunnels, passageways, and corridors so complex that many youngsters found employment as guides.

However, what made the city habitable was the extremely deep well that had been sunk down through the very center of the rock into an aquifer below. The original colonists were gone now, as were most of the technologies used to create Tryst, but thanks to the quality of the pumps located more than a thousand feet below, and the huge petal-shaped solar panels that deployed themselves just after sunrise each morning, those who lived within the city of stone had plenty of water.

What the citizens lacked was the additional electricity required to power the thousands of lights that the ancients had installed to illuminate their labyrinth. This became quite apparent as the coach left the customs plaza, rolled up onto a ramp-shaped tongue, and passed through an eternally opened mouth. There were windows, and occasional skylights, but those were rare. That meant it fell to the wall-mounted torches to light the way, or attempt to, although the flickering yellow flames weren't sufficient to stave off the gloom.

There was a sudden clatter and the momentary glare of an oil lantern as a freight wagon passed in the opposite direction, followed by a shout from the driver, as he guided his angens into a turnout. Rebo peered out through the window as an apprentice rushed out to open the door. The torch-lit sign over the door was plain to see. It read, RUNNER'S GUILD, and was picked out with gold paint.

The travelers didn't have much in the way of luggage, and being used to carrying it themselves, didn't expect any help. That left Rebo to pay the driver, who grinned when he saw the size of his tip and quickly tucked the money away. "Bless you, sir. . . . And may the great Teon watch over you."

"And *you*," Rebo replied solemnly, before turning to retrieve his pack. Like all of the other structures in Tryst, the guildhall had been carved out of solid rock and originally had been created for some other purpose. But now, after who knew how many previous incarnations, the three-story structure was the center from which local runners were sent to locations all over the globe, and a home-away-from-home for members who had arrived by spaceship, or were waiting to leave on one.

Double doors opened onto a large lobby. It featured high ceilings, sturdy granite columns, and glossy stone floors. There were dozens of chairs and side tables, and candelabras ablaze with light. Some of the seats were occupied, but most were empty, which made sense during the middle of the afternoon. A huge wood-burning fireplace dominated the far wall, but, large though the blaze was, it couldn't begin to warm the cavernous room.

The reception desk was off to the right, and since the man who stood behind the polished-granite barrier knew every runner on Thara, and off-worlders were rare, he was prepared to send the norm, the sensitive, and the heavy packing once they arrived at the counter. But that was before the dark-haired man nodded politely—and rolled up a sleeve to display the lightning bolt tattooed onto the inner surface of his left forearm.

Of course guild marks could be faked, but there was a procedure by which the man's identity could be verified, and the receptionist nodded politely. A fringe of black hair circled his otherwise bald head, thick brows rode beady eyes, and he was in need of a shave. "Greetings, brother . . . I don't believe we've met."

"No," Rebo said agreeably. I don't think we have. Rebo's the name . . . Jak Rebo."

The bushy brows rose incrementally. "I've heard of you . . . More than once . . . But never met the man who went with the stories. Please wait here."

Both Norr and Hoggles had stayed in similar facilities before, but not having been present at check-in, the process was new to them. As the receptionist departed, Norr turned to Rebo. "What's going on?"

"My name is on file," the runner explained. "Or should be . . . Along with a code phrase. If it is, and if I know it, we're in."

Norr frowned. "How did the information get here?"

"Each time a runner comes to Thara on behalf of a client they bring a guild bag with them," Rebo answered. "The locals compare the contents against their records and make whatever changes are necessary. There's some lag time—but it works."

"So, where's your guild bag?" Hoggles wanted to know.

"Back on Ning," the runner answered ruefully. "Valpoon and his people took it."

The heavy was about to reply when the receptionist returned. He looked from Norr to Hoggles. "Would you excuse us?"

The receptionist waited for the variants to drift away—before squinting at a scrap of paper. "Please recite your favorite poem."

Rebo nodded.

> When the last of my luck has been spent,
> And the sun hangs low in some alien sky,
> There shall I lay my head,
> Happy to end my run.

The receptionist nodded affirmatively. "Thomas Crowley wrote that poem in this very room."

The runner nodded. "I was his apprentice during the last few years of his life."

The receptionist smiled. "Welcome to Thara's guildhall, Master Rebo . . . It's an honor to make your acquaintance. What can I do for you?"

Half an hour later the threesome was settling into a suite of three interconnecting rooms on the third floor. "So, what did you learn?" Norr inquired, as she joined her companions in the small but well-furnished sitting room. "When is the ship due?" The sensitive had dark eyes, high cheekbones, and a face that was a little too narrow to be classically beautiful. Not that Rebo cared. "What we heard back in Ca-Canth was true," the runner replied. "Assuming the vessel is still in service, it should arrive three days from now."

The others knew what he meant. In the aftermath of the revolution that destroyed most of the star gates, a fleet of sentient starships had been constructed and put into service to replace the then-controversial portals. But now, after thousands of years without proper maintenance, the vessels had begun to die. There were fewer of them with each passing year, and, given the fact that the surviving ships were living on borrowed time, it was extremely dangerous to board one.

Still, there was no choice other than the star gates, and the Techno Society controlled most of them. That hadn't prevented the threesome from making use of the portals in the past, however, so it was Hoggles who voiced the obvious question. "What about our mechanical friend? Why take our chances aboard a ship? If he could point us toward a star gate?"

Rebo grinned as Norr opened her pack, removed the ratty-looking coat, and draped it over her shoulders. The response was immediate. "If you insist on attempting to classify my corporeal being, please refer to it as *electromechanical*," the AI said waspishly. "I am not a winepress! And, as for the presence of a star gate, I can assure you that one exists."

"That's wonderful," Norr put in enthusiastically. "They're scary—but so are the ships."

"Not so fast," Logos interjected primly. "I indicated that a gate *exists*, but given the fact that the equipment is located approximately five hundred feet below this room, I doubt that you could access it."

"We'll check on that," Rebo said thoughtfully. "But it wouldn't surprise me. A lot of ancient cities sit atop their own ruins."

The furniture wasn't large enough for Hoggles, who was seated on the floor. "That's too bad," the heavy commented. "It sounds like we'd better lay in some supplies. There won't be any on the ship."

"Yeah," Rebo agreed, and fingered his purse. He'd been paid in CaCanth and given more than half of that money to the receptionist, in exchange for a token that could be redeemed at any guildhall throughout known space. That, plus the funds saved up over the years, made the runner a moderately wealthy man. "We'll need food, some sort of fuel to cook with, and new bedrolls. Not only that . . . but I'm low on ammo."

"Then tomorrow we shop!" Norr said enthusiastically. "I need some things as well."

"What about tonight?" the heavy wanted to know. "I'm hungry—and it's too early for bed."

"First we'll go looking for a good dinner," Rebo announced. "Then it's off to the circus! I have three tickets—compliments of the guild."

"But what about *me?*" Logos inquired. "It's boring in Lonni's pack."

"That's easy," the sensitive replied. "Make yourself a little more presentable, and I'll wear you."

The coat had been laid across a chair. Suddenly it began to squirm, started to expand, and morphed into a beautiful evening gown. It was a pale blue, slightly diaphanous, and covered with sparkly things. "Nope," Norr commented as she held the garment up for inspection. "That's *too* fancy . . . Have you seen the sort of men that I hang out with? Bring it down a notch."

The evening dress shimmered and morphed into a plain but well-cut knee-length dress. "That's more like it," the sensitive proclaimed, started toward her room, and paused to look back. "As for you two, it wouldn't hurt to take a bath and put on some clean clothes." Rebo ran a hand over his beard, Hoggles grumbled, and the matter was settled.

The city of Seros, on the Planet Anafa

Though of considerable importance now, the star gate that Shaz and his newly formed team were about to employ, had been little more than a little-used maintenance portal back when the system was new. The *real* network, meaning the one that the public had access to, ran parallel to the so-called

B-Grid, and had been more complex. Just one of the reasons why 98 percent of the A-Grid was off-line while segments of the support system continued to function.

Metal rang on metal as four heavily burdened robots descended the spiral staircase. Arn Dyson followed them, and a female norm followed *him.* Her name was Du Phan, and she was an assassin. She had shiny black hair, wide-set brown eyes, and full, rather sensuous, lips. Phan's movements were graceful, like those of a finely trained dancer, and her perfectly sculpted body was festooned with weapons. Her black slippers made little more than a whisper as she flowed down the stairs, and Shaz could feel her pull. The air shimmered as a combination of highly specialized skin cells and hormones interacted to help the combat variant blend with the duracrete walls as he brought up the rear.

It was a small team, but that was a matter of choice rather than necessity, since Shaz could have hired a dozen assassins had he wanted to. But the mission called for the variant to capture Logos *and* learn where the control center called Socket was located, because one wasn't much good without the other. That was a serious problem, because even if he and his team managed to capture the AI, there was no guarantee that Logos would cooperate with them. And while a bio bod could be tortured if necessary, it would be unwise to use such methods on a construct because one mistake could destroy the very knowledge they hoped to gain. All of which argued in favor of a small but lethal team. Which, with the possible exception of Dyson, it was.

The stairs twisted down through a pool of light and turned yet again. The radiation produced by the adjacent power core made Shaz feel queasy. Nobody knew what the long-term impact of such exposure might be—but the variant felt sure that it wouldn't be good. If the other bio-logicals were experiencing similar sensations, they gave no sign of it as they left the stairs and followed the metal men into the decontamination lock. In spite of the fact that a tremendous amount of scientific knowledge had been lost over the millennia, the Techno Society's scientists were well aware of what could happen if organisms from one planetary biosphere were allowed to colonize another, which was why Shaz ordered Phan and Dyson to strip off their clothes.

The sensitive was clearly nonplussed, and sought cover among the androids, but nakedness, or the possibility of nakedness, was a fact of life for any member of the assassin's guild, and Phan was anything but a prude. Nor was the as-sassin a fool, which was why she placed one hand on her hip and smiled. "Sure . . . You first."

Two rows of extremely white teeth appeared when the variant grinned. Then, rather than render himself partially invisible as he might have, Shaz did just the opposite. The truth was that he *wanted* the female to get a good look at his well-muscled physique. A desire that was apparent to Dyson, who took cover behind the blank-eyed robots as he began to remove his clothing.

Impressed by what she saw, and not to be outdone, Phan performed her own strip tease. But first she had to remove the combat harness and her weapons. With that out of the way, she pulled the top half of the two-piece bodysuit up over her head. Having given Shaz a moment to appreciate her firm breasts, the assassin skimmed the bottom half of her bodysuit down onto her lower legs and sat on the bench that ran along the wall. Then, with her eyes on the variant, Phan lifted her feet off the floor. "So," she said provocatively. "Would you like to help?"

Shaz not only wanted to help, he wanted to take the norm right there, and would have except for the queasy feeling at the pit of his stomach. So he said, "Yes," pulled the garment free, and turned to slap a saucer-sized button. There was a hiss followed by a roar as jets of hot water combined with a powerful antibacterial agent struck the entire party from every possible direction. The shower continued for three minutes and was followed by blasts of warm air.

Shaz was impressed by the fact that Phan hadn't tried to conceal her body. Now, as the blowers turned themselves off, the assassin stood facing him. In addition to a pair of nicely shaped breasts, she had a flat stomach, and a tattoo that led down into the valley between her legs. The norm smiled knowingly and looked directly into his eyes. "Can we get dressed now?"

"No," Shaz replied, as he shifted his gaze from her to a bedraggled Dyson. "Why bother? We'll have to go through the same process all over again as we exit on Thara."

Both the humans and the machines left a trail of wet footprints behind as they hauled their disinfectant-soaked luggage into the room beyond. The curvilinear walls were covered with hundreds of video tiles. Each square bore a picture with a name printed below. About half of them were lit, meaning it was still possible to travel there, and the rest were dark. The tile labeled THARA showed a butte, with hills in the distance, and blue sky beyond. "That's where we're going," Shaz explained, as he pointed to the square. "Put the equipment at the center of the platform and step aboard."

Phan did as instructed, and Dyson did likewise, leaving the robots to imitate them. Once the team was in place, Shaz touched the butte, felt it give, and hurried to join the rest on the well-worn platform. The room lights flashed on and off as a woman long dead spoke through the overhead speakers. "The transfer sequence is about to begin. Please take your place on the service platform. Once in place, check to ensure that no portion of your anatomy extends beyond the yellow line. Failure to do so will cause serious injury and could result in death."

The steel disk was extremely crowded, and Phan had to edge inward in order to clear the yellow line. Her thigh came into contact with one of the androids, and his alloy skin felt cold. Dyson wished that he was somewhere else and closed his eyes. Life after death was a fact—so it was the *process* of dying that he feared.

Shaz knew that the public platforms had not only been a good deal larger but equipped with attendants, and chairs for those who chose to use them. Now, as he prepared to make the nearly instantaneous jump from one solar system to another, the operative wondered if the ancients experienced fear as they waited to cross the void, or were so confident of the technologies they employed that the outcome was taken for granted.

Before Shaz could complete his musings, there was a brilliant flash of light. One by one his atoms were disassembled and sent through hyperspace before being systematically reassembled within the receiving gate on Thara. The variant felt the usual bout of disorientation, followed by vertigo, and a moment of nausea. "Okay," the operative said briskly. "Grab your gear and enter the decontamination lock. Once the shower is over, you can get dressed."

It took the better part of twenty minutes for the team to clear the decontamination chamber, get dressed, and rearm themselves. Then Shaz led his subordinates into what had once been a standard passageway but had long since been transformed into a lateral tunnel, as the lower levels of Tryst were condemned and the citizenry migrated upward.

Though far from fancy, the interior of the access way was reasonably clean and showed signs of recent use. Shaz took this for granted since there were other Techno Society operatives, some of whom had reason to visit Tryst.

The tunnel terminated in front of a circular hatch. It consisted of a two-inch-thick slab of steel, was locked against unauthorized intruders, and controlled by a numeric keypad. Shaz tapped six digits into the controller and was rewarded by a loud whine as the barrier unscrewed itself from the wall. The combat variant looked back over his shoulder. "Okay, here comes the hard part. . . . The hatch opens into a vertical shaft. Turn to the right as you exit, grab on to the maintenance ladder, and climb. The exit is five hundred feet above us, so take your time and rest if you need to. I'll lead the way. . . . Number Four will secure the hatch and bring up the rear."

"And then?" Phan wanted to know.

"And then we head for the runner's guild. . . . That's where the runner, the sensitive, and the heavy are most likely to be. If not, we'll check all of the hotels until we find them. Once that's accomplished, the first objective is to confirm that they have Logos."

Dyson "felt" a low-grade buzz as the thoughts generated by thousands of minds merged into something akin to static and drifted down through solid rock.

Phan hooked a thumb in her combat harness. "Works for me."

"Good," the operative replied, and turned to swing the hatch out of the way. Most of the shaft was filled by the huge pipes that carried water up to the surface, and a ladder claimed the rest. One careless move, one slip, and anyone attempting to reach the top would plummet to the bottom. With that sobering thought in mind, Shaz stepped up to the edge, forced himself to ignore the drop, and turned his eyes upward. The top of the well was open to the sky, and thanks to the fact that it was daytime, the variant could see a tiny pinhead-sized circle of light. A single stomach-turning step was sufficient to put the operative on the rusty ladder. The metal was cold beneath his fingers as Shaz began to climb. Somewhere, if only in his imagination, the ancients started to laugh.

TWO

The city of Tryst, on the Planet Thara

*Would you trade your hammer for a rock? Of course not. Yet
you listen when the priests call upon you to cast out technology. They fear science because it can dispel ignorance. And ignorance is the primary thing upon which they feed.*

—An excerpt from street lecture 52.1 as written by Milos Lysander,
founder of the Techno Society, and delivered by thousands
of metal men each day.

There was something sad about the Circus Solara. Most of
the performers were clearly middle-aged, their costumes
were ragged, and the first fifteen minutes of the "most excit-
ing show in the galaxy" were extremely boring. However,
there was a significant shortage of things to do in the city of
Tryst, which meant that the seats surrounding the circular
arena were packed with people, some of whom had started
to doze by the time two fancifully dressed clowns secured
the local prefect to a brightly painted disk. But Rebo sat up
and began to pay attention as the formally attired ringmaster strutted out to the center of the arena and stood next to
the turntable to which the official was being secured. He
spoke through a handheld megaphone. "Ladies and gentle-
men! Behold the wheel of death! In a matter of moments
this diabolical device will be set into motion . . . Then, once

the disk becomes little more than a blur, Madam Pantha will throw her hatchets. Yes! That's correct! You could have a *new* prefect by tomorrow morning!"

The joke stimulated laughter, catcalls, and a round of applause. Madam Pantha wore a yellow turban, sported a curly black beard, and was dressed in a loose blouse and pantaloons. Her clothes might have been white once, but had long since turned gray and were patched in places. She waved a hatchet at the audience, tossed the weapon high into the air, and waited for it to fall. Then, having positioned herself just so, Pantha missed the catch. The hatchet generated a puff of dust as it hit the ground—followed by more laughter as the crowd entered into the spirit of the thing.

The prefect was an extremely good sport, or that's what Rebo concluded, as a pair of mimes put the platform on which both the wheel of death and the bearded lady stood into motion. Now *everyone* could see as the platform began to rotate, and a couple of acrobats began to spin the wheel of death. It took the better part of thirty seconds to get the disk turning at top speed. A drumroll began as Madam Pantha accepted a hatchet from a sad-faced clown, brought the implement back over her right shoulder, and let fly. Even the runner stared as the wheel rotated, the hatchet turned end for end, and the somewhat corpulent official continued to rotate. Then came the solid *thwack* of metal biting into wood, followed by a gasp of indrawn air as the crowd realized that a *second* weapon was on the way, quickly followed by a third. Fortunately, the second and third hatchets flew true, both sinking into wood only inches from the politico's body, even as both the platform and the wheel continued to turn.

The audience roared its approval as the clowns brought the much-hyped "wheel of death" to a stop and freed the prefect from his restraints. Though somewhat disheveled, and a bit dizzy, the official seemed otherwise none the worse for wear. He waved in response to a standing ovation and was escorted back to his seat.

The formally quiescent crowd was engaged, the ringmaster could feel it, and hurried to take advantage. "Thank you . . . I'm pleased to announce that this is the 3,672,416th performance of the famed Circus Solara. Some claim it originated on Sameron, more than ten thousand years ago, while others say it was founded on Cepa II some twelve thousand years ago. But enough of that!" the ringmaster proclaimed loudly. "The show continues. . . . Bring forth the beasts!"

There was a blare of horns and something of a stir as a man wearing a leather hood, vest, and pants led a column of pathetic-looking animals out into the arena. A white angen led the way. It had what Rebo assumed to be a fake horn secured to its forehead and was harnessed to a cage on wheels. An old dire cat could be seen lying inside the bars, tongue lolling, either too old or too sick to stand.

A hairy tusker had been secured to the back of the cage and followed head down, its tail drooping. A dog rode on top of the mammoth and continually turned somersaults, as if trying to bite its own tail. The children loved that, but their parents were becoming restive, and a piece of overripe fruit sailed through the air. It hit the cage, exploded into fragments, and sprayed the dire cat with orange pulp. It snarled, and that generated scattered applause.

"This is absurd," Rebo said disgustedly, as he whispered into Norr's ear. "Let's leave."

The sensitive was about to agree when the animal that was supposed to be the main attraction followed the tusker out into the arena. Like all its kind, the L-phant had been bioengineered to perform a variety of tasks. Hauling mostly, which was why the ancient engineers had chosen to eliminate what had once been huge heads and thereby create more cargo space above their immensely strong spines. Of course it was important for the L-phants to see the road in front of them, so their eyes had been moved down under their prehensile trunks, forward of their chest-centered brains.

But after more than ninety years of hard labor in Thara's southern jungles, this six-ton beast was no longer useful. Everything from the slowness of his gait, to the way his tail drooped, suggested the same thing. The angen was sick, tired, and depressed. Something that Norr experienced as a vast heaviness. The sensitive was familiar with the breed, having ridden them on Ning, and had come to admire them. So now, as the L-phant plodded out into the center of the arena, she shook her head in response to Rebo's suggestion. "In a minute. . . . I want to see what happens next."

Rebo was about to reply, but a blare of trumpets overrode the runner as the beast master went to free the L-phant from his tether. "Look at this mighty beast!" the ringmaster commanded, "and imagine his power!"

That was the cue for a clown to carry a huge melon to the beast master, who ceremoniously placed the object on the ground next to one of the beast's enormous pillarlike feet. It was clear to everyone present that the angen was supposed to raise its foot and bring it down on the object, thereby demonstrating its strength, but nothing happened. The beast master reacted to what he saw as a betrayal by prodding the L-phant with a six-inch-long steel needle. The poor beast produced what sounded like a human scream, and Norr came to her feet. "Stop that!"

But either the beast master didn't hear the sensitive, or didn't care, because, when the L-phant failed to lift his foot for a second time, the goad went in again.

Rebo had already started to stand, and was in the process of reaching for Norr's arm, when the sensitive stepped up onto the knee-high wall and jumped down into the arena. Puffs of dust exploded away from the variant's feet as she landed, Logos yelled, "Stop!" from the vicinity of her neckline, and the audience produced a reedy cheer. Some of the onlookers felt sorry for the L-phant, while others were simply bored and eager for some sort of conflict. None had any reason to support the beast master.

But the members of the troupe did, and they came out to defend one of their own, as the angry young woman crossed the arena. Some were armed with cudgels, others carried wooden staffs, and some wore ancient brass knuckles. A sure sign that they were not only ready for a dustup—but had been in plenty of them before.

The Crosser hung butt down under Rebo's left arm as he followed Norr into the ring, but the runner didn't plan to use it unless forced to do so since it would be best to resolve the dispute without bloodshed if that was possible. And, since war hammers weren't welcome at public events, Hoggles was unarmed. That didn't stop the heavy from uttering his characteristic war cry, however, as he landed in the arena and hurried to catch up.

Meanwhile, Norr felt a wave of resentment and anger roll over her as the distance between her and the self-styled beast master began to close. But, while she could block some of the incoming thought forms, there was no way to make Logos shut up. "This is insane!" the AI declared angrily. "What if that brute attacks you? I could be injured! I insist that you return to your seat at once!"

But Logos could have been talking to a brick wall for all the good that his imprecations did him—and was still in midrant when Norr came face-to-face with the enraged

beast master. "Leave the L-phant alone!" the sensitive demanded. "You're hurting him!"

"So?" the circus performer replied insolently. "The animal belongs to me. . . . That means I can discipline it in any
way that I choose."

Rebo arrived just as the rest of the circus troupe began to
gather behind the beast master. "He has a point," the runner
said hopefully. "The L-phant is his after all."

"No," Norr replied through gritted teeth, "no one has a
right to hurt angens. Give me the goad," she demanded,
and extended her hand.

"*Or?*" the beast master wanted to know.

"Or *I* will take if from you," Hoggles replied grimly, as
he took up a position at Norr's side.

"Can't we discuss this?" Rebo inquired reasonably.
"Surely there must be some way to . . ."

But the runner never got the opportunity to finish his
sentence as the beast master launched a sucker punch at
Norr, was surprised to discover that the sensitive had already stepped back out of the way, and was therefore perfectly positioned to kick him in the balls. The man in the
hood uttered a grunt of pain as the variant's foot came into
contact with his private parts and made a grab for the
much-abused organs as he fell to his knees. That left his
leather-encased skull vulnerable to attack, which Hoggles
took immediate advantage of as he locked his fists together
and brought them down on top of the performer's skull.
That put the beast master out of his pain *and* the fight.

But rather than terminate the conflict as the heavy hoped
that it would, the massive blow had the opposite effect. An-
gered by what they had seen and determined to have their
revenge, a mixed force of clowns, acrobats, and musicians
rushed to attack the threesome. Rebo positioned himself to

Norr's left. "Now look at what you've done," the runner
said, as he intercepted a blow, and returned it with interest.
"I can't take you anywhere."

"I didn't have a choice," the variant replied defensively,
as she eyed the oncoming strongman. "What was I supposed
to do? Let him hurt the L-phant?"

"*Yes,*" Logos put in. "You were." And the AI might have
said more, but Rebo had come under attack by a pair of
mimes, while Hoggles was staggering about with three acrobats on his back. That left Norr to deal with the strongman alone, or try to, since the matchup was anything but
fair. She attempted to backpedal, but wasn't able to do so
quickly enough, and soon found herself wrapped within the
embrace of the weightlifter's huge arms. Muscles writhed,
all the air was forced out of the variant's lungs, and she was
just about to lose consciousness when Logos came to her defense. Or *his* defense, since that was the AI's *actual* priority,
consistent with his programming.

Suddenly, just as the heavily muscled norm felt the
woman in his arms go limp, the surface of her dress delivered 775,000 volts of electricity directly into the strongman's body! He let go of his victim, fell over backward, and
hit the ground hard. Norr collapsed a few feet away. Having
dispatched both mimes and a clown, Rebo was there to
scoop Norr up and throw the sensitive over his shoulder.
Then, as Hoggles threw an acrobat at a group of bellicose
musicians, the off-worlders started to back away. And because the crowd was pelting the circus performers with
food, none of the troupe was able to follow. Norr, who had
recovered her senses by then, made use of both fists to
pound on Rebo's back. "Put me down, damn you!"

The runner made sure he was well up into the seats before
acceding to the sensitive's demand. "There," Rebo said, as he

placed the young woman on her feet. "You're welcome."

"No you're not," Logos put in resentfully. "Don't ever do that again!"

Norr wanted to sound angry, if only to maintain an appearance of independence, but the fact that her dress was talking back to her made that hard to do. She laughed, Rebo joined in, and Hoggles rumbled loudly. Then, having passed an interesting if not especially relaxing evening, the threesome hired one of the many torchbearers who were waiting outside and followed the boy home.

Having sent Dyson into the runner's guild to investigate, and having confirmed that a sensitive and two male companions had checked in, Shaz knew that the troublesome trio were right where he expected them to be.

However, because the runner's guild had excellent security, it soon became obvious that there was only one member of the team who was likely to get inside the facility, and that was the combat variant himself. So Shaz sent the rest of the team away, chose a vantage point in the shadows opposite the guildhall, and waited for his chance. Despite the fact that his built-in camouflage was good, it wasn't perfect, which meant the guards would spot the operative if he were to walk in through the door. But if there was a distraction, something to claim at least some of their attention, then the variant stood an excellent chance of slipping past them. Once inside, Shaz felt confident of his ability to locate and enter the correct room. And, if the subjects of his investigation were present? Then he would wait, and wait some more if that was necessary, because he was nothing if not patient. Which was fortunate, because the better part of an hour was to pass before the combat variant heard the rattle of an approaching carriage and saw the conveyance pull into the brightly lit area in front of the hall.

There was no way to know who the passenger or passengers were, but they must have been important, because once the doorman blew his brass whistle, all manner of staff boiled out to greet the newly arrived guest or guests. Which was exactly what Shaz had been hoping for. In their eagerness to catch a glimpse of the woman who was exiting the coach, the guards missed the momentary shimmer associated with the operative's passing and remained unaware as the variant made his way across the lobby toward the front desk.

The next part was somewhat tricky, because even though Shaz knew the people he was interested in were staying at the hall, he had no idea which room or rooms they were in. So, conscious of the fact that the hustle and bustle associated with the VIP's arrival wouldn't last much longer, the variant made his way around the end of the counter, and sidled up behind the burly receptionist. His opportunity came as the newly arrived guest made her grand entrance. Whereas most runners preferred to maintain a low profile, lest they be targeted by members of the thief's guild, this individual was an extremely obvious exception. She wore a glittery headband, complete with a red feather, and a bright green dress, all meant to impress her upscale clientele, or so Shaz assumed.

But, rather than ogle the woman's considerable cleavage, as the receptionist was doing, the operative examined the guestbook instead. And, when he couldn't find what he sought, Shaz had to flip the current page out of the way in order to inspect previous entries. That was when the variant saw Rebo's signature, followed by Norr's, and the nearly illegible scrawl that probably belonged to the heavy.

Shaz took in the fact that the threesome had taken suite 303, and was already backing away, when the receptionist turned to pull the guestbook over in front of him. He noticed that the ledger was turned to the wrong page, assumed that an errant breeze had been responsible for the change, and wondered what the woman in front of him would look like naked.

A scant five minutes later the combat variant had climbed three flights of stairs, made his way down a long hall, and was standing with his ear to a door with the numerals 303 on it. Then, having waited for a full minute without hearing any activity within, Shaz made use of a pick to open the lock. Having glanced both ways to make sure the hall was clear, the variant pushed the door open and slipped into the room. Once inside, the operative discovered that the suite was not only dark but momentarily empty, which suited his purposes well. The possibility that the AI was there, resting within a few feet of him, caused the variant's heart to beat faster. The search began.

Rebo yawned as he led the other two up the broad flight of stairs, tried to remember which room he and Crowley had stayed in thirty years earlier, and couldn't. Once on the third floor he turned to the right. Wall-mounted lamps marked off regular intervals and threw pools of light onto the floor. Once in front of 303, the runner inserted his key into the lock and turned it. The door swung open. The next couple of minutes were spent fumbling with matches and finicky lamps. "Bring them to me," Norr offered, having mastered the process. "And I'll light them for you."

Hoggles nodded gratefully, went to remove one of the lamps from a wall bracket, and swore when it burned his fingers. "Damn! That thing is *hot!*"

Rebo frowned, slid his hand in under his jacket, and wrapped his fingers around the Crosser. "*Hot?* Why would it be hot?"

"Because it was lit," Logos grated contemptuously. "Check

the bedrooms. I predict that someone came to turn the beds down."

"He's right," Norr confirmed, as she peered into her room. "And I don't know about you, but I'm looking forward to a good night's sleep."

Having taken refuge in one corner of the sitting room, Shaz stood perfectly still and strove to defocus his mind. Because just as combat variants had been provided with the means to fool the eye, they had also been equipped to evade detection by sensitives, but only if they exercised perfect control over both their thoughts and emotions.

Now, having discovered that Norr not only had the AI, but was *wearing* the device, the operative was hard-pressed to contain a sense of jubilation. Fortunately, there were things to worry about as well—which meant Shaz could use one emotion to counter the other. What to do? Attack the threesome and attempt to steal what he had come for, or escape and follow them? Though of value to the Techno Society in and of himself, Logos would be worth even more if they knew where Socket was, and given his present frame of mind, the AI wasn't likely to tell them.

In the end it was that, plus the fact that Shaz couldn't be absolutely sure that he would win what would almost certainly be a hard-fought battle, that helped to make up the variant's mind. Rather than attack the AI's custodians, the operative resolved to follow them to Socket, where he could take both prizes at the same time. Assuming he could escape, that is—which was anything but certain.

Norr was just about to bid the others good night and enter her room, when she sensed something strange. The almost indiscernible glow was similar to the aura that all living beings generated, yet different somehow, as if partially shielded. The sensitive opened her mouth, and was about to comment on the phenomenon, but never got to do so as Milos Lysander took control of her physical body. The invading spirit preferred male plumbing but had occupied this body on previous occasions and gradually grown accustomed to it. "He's in the corner!" the dead scientist proclaimed loudly, as he pointed at the spot where Shaz was hiding. "Grab him!"

But neither Rebo nor Hoggles was expecting such an order and, when they turned to look at the corner in question, saw nothing more than a vague shimmer.

That brief moment of hesitation was all the combat variant needed. He crossed the room, opened the door, and was already in the hall by the time Rebo went to probe the empty corner. The runner turned as the door slammed. Hoggles moved as if to follow, but Lysander shook Norr's head. "Don't bother," the dead man said disgustedly. "You blew the only chance you're likely to get."

"Lysander?" Rebo inquired irritably. "Is that you?"

"Of course it's me!" the disincarnate replied testily. "Who else would it be?"

"Wonderful," Logos said sarcastically. "The megalomaniac returns."

"Look who's talking," the dead scientist responded resentfully. "I don't remember you speaking up for the huddled masses back when *you* were in control of the star gates."

"Stop it," Rebo ordered tersely. "We don't have time for this crap. Someone was in the room . . . So who is he? And what was he after?"

"His name is Shaz," Lysander answered. "Back before Kane got killed, he functioned as Tepho's bodyguard and enforcer. Then, when Kane passed over, the chairman promoted him."

Hoggles frowned. "Why couldn't we see him?"

"Because he's a combat variant," the dead scientist explained.

"Perfect," Rebo commented sourly. "Not only did the Techno Society manage to locate us—they sent an operative who can make himself invisible."

"It gets worse," the spirit entity said wearily, as he dropped Norr's body into a chair. "My onetime son, which is to say the man you knew as Kane, continues to work for the Society. And, while none of us can see into the physical plane with much clarity, it was he who directed Shaz to Thara."

"But how?" Hoggles wanted to know.

"They have a sensitive, a man named Dyson, who can bring Kane through," Lysander explained.

"So what are they waiting for?" Rebo wondered. "They know where we are, and they know we have Logos, so what's holding them back?"

"They want Socket," Logos put in grimly. "Then, assuming they can force me to do their bidding, they'll have everything they need to reestablish the network."

"And could they?" Hoggles inquired curiously. "Get you to do their bidding that is?"

"Of course not!" the AI lied hotly. "What do you take me for?"

"A somewhat self-centered computer program," Lysander commented cynically. "But you're all we have."

"So what would you suggest?" Rebo inquired pragmatically. "Kane could follow us anywhere."

"Yes," the disincarnate agreed. "But the task remains. . . . Once you reach Socket, and Logos takes control, it will be too late for them to interfere. Socket has defenses that will keep them at bay."

"Or *had*," Logos put in cynically. "They might be in need of maintenance by now."

"I don't know," the runner said doubtfully. "It sounds pretty iffy to me."

"And *me*," Hoggles added. "So where did this Shaz person go? Maybe we could track him down."

But Norr's body gave a convulsive jerk at that point, her eyelids fluttered, and she looked confused. "What happened?"

"Lysander paid you a visit," Rebo said disgustedly. "And guess what? The Techno Society knows where we are."

The sensitive was still in the process of absorbing that piece of unwelcome information when Logos spoke to her. "It's not as bad as it sounds," the AI said reassuringly. "Because even though they know where we are, they don't know where we're *going*. There's only one person who knows that: *me*."

While many of the billions of disincarnate spirits who pop-ulated the spirit planes preferred life in the ethereal realms to that on the physical plane, Kane was not one of them, and therefore welcomed the summons when it came. The sensation was barely felt, as when a child tugs on a pant leg, but very persistent. And that was a sure sign that rather than merely being remembered by one of the many people Kane had known during his most recent incarnation, one or more individuals were determined to make contact with him.

So, eager to revisit the material world, no matter how briefly, Kane directed his energy toward those who were focused on him. And, having already agreed to continue his relationship with the Techno Society, the ex-operative was far from surprised to discover that Shaz and Dyson were waiting for him. A female was present as well, and even though Kane didn't recognize her vibration, he felt a natural affinity for the dark energy that seethed around her.

It was easier to enter Dyson's body the second time, pleasantly so, and Kane felt something akin to an orgasm as all of his physical senses were magically restored. His vision, which was to say *Dyson's* vision, blurred, then cleared. Both Shaz and a beautiful woman sat opposite him. With the exception of some ring bolts and the darkish stains around them, the wall behind the pair was featureless. Darkness gathered where the lamplight couldn't reach. "Not that it matters," Kane croaked, "but where am I?"

"We're sitting in the basement of the Techno Society's headquarters on Thara," the combat variant replied evenly.

"Ah," Kane responded gravely. "So you followed my counsel."

"Yes," Shaz confirmed. "And they have Logos. I heard it speak."

In spite of the fact that Kane generally preferred life on the physical plane to his present existence, there were advantages to being dead. Chief among them was the fact that it was impossible for enemies to murder him. Not Shaz, not anyone. So, rather than fear the combat variant as he once had, the disincarnate was free to needle him. "You *heard* the AI speak? But left the device where it was? I suspect Chairman Tepho will wonder why."

"He *knows* why," Shaz replied defensively. "We need Socket . . . which is why you were summoned. Since they don't have access to the local star gate, the sensitive and her companions will be forced to board the next ship."

"Assuming it comes," Du Phan put in emotionlessly.

"Yes," the variant acknowledged. "Assuming it comes, the ship will carry them to Derius. Watch over them to the extent that you can. We'll be waiting when they arrive."

A frown wrinkled Dyson's brow. "You want me to *protect* them?" Kane inquired incredulously.

"For the moment, yes," Shaz replied sternly. "The trip is risky in and of itself . . . But what if something were to happen to them in transit? So your task is to provide whatever assistance you can."

"Why not board the ship yourself?" the dead man wanted to know.

"Because they're on the lookout for a combat variant now," Shaz responded. "Your onetime father saw to that. . . . And the woman might sense a hostile presence."

"I can try," Kane allowed. "But it won't be easy. Locating something on the physical plane is like feeling your way through a thick fog. And once their ship enters hyperspace, the task will become that much more difficult."

"Do what you can," Shaz insisted, "and we will speak to you on Derius."

Kane eyed the woman and forced Dyson to smile. "I don't believe we have met."

Phan knew the look and allowed a smile to touch her lips. "No, I don't believe we have. My name is Du Phan."

"Du Phan . . ." the disincarnate said experimentally. "Well, Du Phan, until next time then."

As the assassin ran the tip of a pink tongue over her already glossy lips, Kane felt Dyson's body respond. And so, for that matter, did the being to which it belonged. Because while slightly out of phase with his physical form, the sensitive was conscious of everything that took place and didn't like the way in which Kane was making free with his body. He struggled to push the invading spirit out, eventually managed to do so, and found himself soaked with sweat. Somehow, Dyson had been thrust to the forefront of a war he didn't understand and wanted no part of.

"Good work," Shaz said emotionlessly. "Come on . . . We have things to do."

The spaceship *Shewhoswimsthevoid*

Like a silvery fish in a large black pond *Shewhoswimsthevoid* slipped past a gravelly asteroid belt, swung round a planet-sized orange-red boulder, and began to decelerate. Because up ahead, only ship hours away, lay her next port of call. The planet that the biobeings riding deep within her ancient hull knew as Thara, but she thought of as a set of coordinates. It was a planet that she had orbited many times before. For such was her purpose, and what she experienced as pleasure, even though the doing of it would eventually lead to her dissolution.

But, like the natural laws that governed what the great vessel could do in space, the urges inherent in her programming limited what *Shewhoswims* could desire, and thereby ensured that so long as the ship could carry people from one planet to another, she would. Regardless of the cost to her. The question wasn't *if* she would die, but when, and even though it lay within her power to carry out the necessary calculations. *Shewhoswims* chose not to do so. Because for the moment she had purpose, and that made her happy. Cool nothingness caressed the ship's hull, galaxies wheeled in the unimaginable distance, and a thousand suns lit the way.

The city of Tryst, on the Planet Thara

The public market occupied the topmost level of Tryst, where golden sunlight shone through the glass panels set into the domed roof, and goods were hoisted from the ground below by means of wooden cranes. Each massive swing arm was named after the family to which it belonged and was served by a team of sturdy angens. They made squalling sounds as they walked endless circles around brightly painted capstans.

Just to the rear of the cranes was an extremely busy thoroughfare that the cart men used to transport newly arrived goods, even as hundreds of people swirled around them. There were red hats, black hats, bakers, soldiers, scribes, metalsmiths, townspeople, tailors, heavies, herbalists, and gangs of schoolchildren all weaving a transitory tapestry of thought, language, and color. It made for a heady atmosphere and one which Norr, who rarely got a chance to spend time with Rebo, enjoyed. Because right then, as the couple strolled hand in hand, they could interact in a way that just wasn't possible when others were around.

Having entered the market proper, Rebo and Norr found themselves following one of two dozen aisles that converged on the center of the pie-shaped floor plan. That was where all of the food vendors were forced to gather so that their smoke could be channeled up through a single hole at the center of the domed roof. The odors of freshly baked bread, roasted meat, and brewed caf combined to make Rebo's stomach growl. But it was too early for lunch—and there was work to do. "The first thing we need is a gunsmith," the runner mused, as they paused at an intersection. "It will take them time to crank out five hundred rounds—so the sooner they get going the better."

"That makes sense," Norr agreed. "Then we'll shop for fuel, dried food, and personal items."

And so it was agreed. It took half an hour to find a gunsmith who could perform the work to Rebo's specifications plus an hour to gather up the other items they needed. And it was then, while Norr was waiting for the runner to return from a consultation with a Ju-Ju master, that Norr ran into the old crone. She was a sensitive by the look of her, albeit an ancient one, who told fortunes for a living. Her booth consisted of little more than panels of blue cloth stretched over a wood frame. She had straggly white hair and, judging from the wrinkled skin that hung around her face, had once been heavier than she was now. Cataracts clouded her eyes, but her second sight remained clear, and she could sense the young woman's presence. "Come over here, dear. I won't hurt you," the old woman said reassuringly. "Even though there are others who would!"

Norr felt sorry for the seer and found the last statement to be intriguing. "Here," the sensitive said, as she pressed a coin into the oldster's palm. "Tell me more."

The contact caused the old crone to cock her head to one side and frown. "What is this?" she demanded. "Some sort of trick? You have the gift . . . Tell your own fortune."

"No," Norr replied gently as she took her place on the low stool that fronted the oldster's well-worn chair. "You know what they say . . . The seer who looks to his own future is blind."

"What you say is true," the older sensitive replied, as she revealed some badly decayed teeth. "And I know what it is to be blind! Give me your hand."

Norr reached out to take the fortune-teller's hand. It was extremely warm. "Ah," the old woman said knowingly. "You are but halfway through a long journey . . . and the greatest dangers lie ahead."

"What sort of dangers?"

"Beware of the thief," the seer cautioned importantly. "Lest you lose that which is most precious."

Norr nodded. "Go on."

"There will be a battle," the other woman predicted. "And when it comes you must seek that which you already have."

While the first message seemed like an obvious reference to Logos, the second didn't make any sense at all, but Norr was polite nonetheless. "Thank you," the younger sensitive replied. "I will keep that in mind."

"And there's something more," the fortune-teller added, her eyes seemingly focused on something Norr couldn't see.

"Yes?"

"An angel is watching over you. A *dark* angel but an angel nonetheless. There is a momentary alignment between you. It cannot last but could be helpful in the short run. Does that make sense?"

"No," Norr replied. "It doesn't . . . Not right now. But perhaps later it will."

The reading came to an end shortly after that, Norr went to lunch with Rebo, and a metal man followed the couple back to the guildhall.

The spaceport, or what had *been the spaceport, had been* transformed into a huge crater some 4,216 years earlier, when an ark ship crashed there. Most of the ship's hull had been salvaged and converted into tools, implements, and construction materials that were still being recycled and used. But a few pieces of riblike metal continued to curve up toward the sky and harkened back to days only dimly remembered. A sobering reminder of what could happen to those who traveled among the stars. But that didn't stop thousands of runners, merchants, thieves, holy men, assassins, romantics, con artists, scholars, and lunatics of every possible description from gambling their lives each year. A fact made apparent by the long column of heavily burdened people who wound their way down out of the elevated city of Tryst to follow a narrow footpath out toward the crater.

Of course, some of the people were spectators, children in

tow, who would return to their homes by nightfall. But those who wore packs, or carried bundles between them, were intent on boarding the shuttle if it landed. Those who were veteran travelers, individuals like Rebo, Norr, and Hoggles, carried just what they needed, while neophytes had a tendency to neglect essentials like fuel, food, and medicine in favor of frivolous items like folding furniture, elaborate shelters, and fancy clothing—much of which would either be stolen by their fellow passengers, converted into fuel to ward off the cold, or abandoned as impractical.

For his part Rebo felt pretty good about the provisions the three of them carried, especially the locally made fuel tablets, packets of dried food, and the hand-loaded ammunition acquired the day before. And, adding to the runner's sense of well-being was the powerful talisman that he had purchased to supplement the much-stressed amulet that had seen him through the last few months. Norr believed such things were silly, not to mention superstitious, but Rebo knew better. He was alive, wasn't he? Even though plenty of people wanted him dead. That spoke for itself.

The runner's thoughts were interrupted by a sound similar to rolling thunder as a wedge-shaped shuttle broke the sound barrier and circled high above. There was a shout of jubilation as spectators and travelers alike paused to celebrate the ship's return. They couldn't see *Shewhoswims*, of course, since the vessel was far too large to negotiate a planetary atmosphere, but the sight of the shuttle was wondrous enough, especially for those who had never seen a flying machine before. And there were at least a thousand pilgrims, many of whom had walked hundreds of miles in hopes of bearing witness to a landing and thereby confirming what some people said. Out beyond the darkness lay *other* planets, populated by humans just like them, all having a common ancestry. The visitors were understandably excited as the fantastic apparition lost altitude and prepared to land.

Horns sounded, drums rattled, and bells tolled as the long, colorful procession followed the seldom-used path down into the crater and the mound of hard-packed earth that dominated the center of it. For it was there, on what amounted to a huge pedestal, that the space black shuttle would put down.

Even though her central processing unit remained in orbit, *Shewhoswims* could "see" via the shuttle's sensors and felt a deep sense of regret as she looked down on what amounted to a grave. Not for one of her brother-sister ships, because the wreckage predated them, but for a lesser vessel that had succumbed to mechanical failure, human error, or entropy.

"So," Norr said, as the shuttle settled onto its skids, "do you think he'll board the ship with us?"

There was no need for the runner to ask who the sensitive was referring to, since the unseen combat variant had been on all of their minds since the break-in and Lysander's visitation. In fact, though he wouldn't have been willing to admit it, Rebo had spent a good deal of time looking over his shoulder during the last couple of days. "It beats me," the runner replied. "But I doubt it. . . . Logos claims that the local star gate is buried deep underground. But there must be a way to access it, or this Shaz character would be on the incoming shuttle. That would suggest that he's on Derius by now . . . waiting for us to complete the trip the hard way."

But the Techno Society operative *wasn't* on Derius. Not yet and wouldn't be for weeks. First he had to ensure that the troublesome trio actually boarded the shuttle, then he was scheduled to return to Anafa, where Chairman Tepho was waiting for a report. Then and only then would the variant make the jump to Derius.

The brass telescope had been rented from one of the many vendors who had positioned themselves along the crater's rim and allowed Shaz to monitor their progress from a safe distance as the threesome left the bottom of the depression and wound their way up onto the landing pad. Boarding had yet to begin, and wouldn't, until such time as *Shewhoswims* sent the necessary signal. That left the would-be passengers to mill around the recently arrived ship and jockey for position.

Those who had never been aboard a spaceship before were pushing and shoving, hoping to be among the first to enter the vessel, while veterans like Rebo, Norr, and Hoggles were careful to hang back, secure in the knowledge that the last people to board the shuttle would be among the first to exit, thereby positioning themselves for the subsequent race into the main hold. And it was then, while they were waiting to enter the ship, that Hoggles tapped Rebo on the shoulder. "Jak . . . See the man with the beard? He looks familiar somehow."

Rebo eyed the man in question and frowned. "Yeah, he does look familiar. . . . But I can't place him. Lonni, how 'bout you?"

The sensitive looked, then looked again. "Uh-oh," she said ominously. "I think we're in trouble."

"In trouble?" the runner inquired mildly. "Why?"

"That isn't a man, or maybe it is, but the last time I saw him he was dressed as a woman and was throwing hatchets at the local prefect!"

Rebo took another look, realized that Norr was correct,

and scanned the faces around the person in question. It was hard to tell, since the circus performers had been wearing heavy makeup the last time he'd seen them, but the runner thought he recognized an acrobat, a clown, and the strong-man that Logos had zapped.

It was then, as the ramp began to deploy, that the travelers came to understand the full extent of their misfortune. Not only were they about to risk their lives on an extremely uncertain journey—they were going to be locked inside a durasteel hull with the full cast of the Circus Solara!

And, as if to underscore that fact, a man with a horribly scarred face lurched out of the crowd. He had tiny little eyes and green teeth that went on full display as he smiled at Norr. "Remember me?" the beast master demanded. "No? Well I remember *you*. It's a long way to Derius, sweetheart—and your friends will have to sleep sometime. But don't worry, my friends and I know how to treat a lady, especially one who looks like you do!"

That elicited a series of guffaws from the beast master's cronies, some of whom bore obvious injuries acquired during the melee in the arena and were eager for revenge. And they might have moved in on the threesome right then had it not been for Hoggles. The heavy unlimbered his rag-wrapped war hammer and took a giant step forward. That sent the troupe scuttling, if only for the moment, and Norr uttered a sigh. "Maybe we should wait for the next ship. . . . Or forget the whole thing."

"I would agree with you," the runner responded, "except for the Lysander problem. He won't leave you alone until Logos reaches Socket—and I promised him I would make the delivery."

"And don't forget the gates," Hoggles added. "Once

people can step from planet to planet, knowledge will spread, lives will be saved, and conditions will improve for billions of people."

"Or so Lysander claims," Rebo replied cynically, "but that's the hope. So I reckon we should board."

"I'm in," Norr announced, fingers wrapped around her staff.

"Me too," Hoggles agreed.

"Oh, no you don't!" Logos interjected. "If those ruffians hurt you, they could hurt *me*, and that's unacceptable. We must return to Tryst, where we will await the next ship!"

"I'll take that," Rebo said, as he lifted Norr's pack off her shoulders. "Now, if you remove that raggedy-looking coat, I think you'll be a lot more comfortable."

Logos, his voice ever more strident, was still talking when the sensitive rolled the AI into a ball and shoved him down into the depths of her pack. The ramp hit the ground at that point, and rather than the outpouring of passengers that Rebo expected, no one appeared. That was a surprise, but there wasn't much time to think about what if anything the phenomenon might mean, as the first-time passengers nearly trampled one another in their eagerness to board. The voyage was about to begin.

THREE

The spaceship *Shewhoswimsthevoid*

To those who preach the benefits of technology—I say look at the ruins of Wimmura! The ancients gloried in the dark arts, and God struck them down! So teach the Book of Abominations *to your children, and do battle with your unclean thoughts, or give yourself to the flames of purification.*

—Grand Vizier Imbo Moratano,
Church of the Antitechnic God

One hundred and fourteen people, that was how many crowded their way into the shuttle and were forced to stand shoulder to shoulder as the ship forced its way up through Thara's atmosphere. Some of them cheered, some of them cried, and at least a dozen threw up as the shuttle left the planet's gravity well. Had they been free to do so, the passengers would have free-floated through a galaxy of vomit globules. But the tightly packed bodies held the travelers in place, and while that was claustrophobic, it helped to prevent injuries. Those who knew to do so wore bandit-style bandannas that filtered most of the vomit out of the air. But no one could completely escape the vile mist that found its way into their hair and clothes.

Fortunately, the trip was relatively short, which meant that after only a few hours of suffering, *Shewhoswims* guided the tiny extension of herself into an open docking bay. There was the barely heard whine of hidden machinery, followed by the sudden restoration of gravity, and a dull *thud* as the transport was captured and locked into place. "And here it is," Rebo said to no one in particular. "Home sweet home."

An especially long five minutes passed before servos whined, the aft hatch hit the deck outside, and those closest to the opening were given access to the ship's decontamination chamber. It was smaller than the shuttle's cargo bay, so only a third of the passengers could enter before the hatch closed and a thick mist fogged the air. The runner, sensitive, and heavy had been expecting the antibacterial spray, but some of their fellow passengers weren't. Some screamed and started to thrash about, while others attempted to calm them. Rebo took the opportunity to confer with his companions. "I figure about thirty to thirty-five members of the Circus Solara were on the shuttle. Maybe half that number are here in the decontamination chamber. It's pretty clear that the whole group has been planet-hopping for years—and is familiar with the way the ships operate. That's why I expect the advance party to make a run for the hold, secure a corner, and wait for the rest to arrive with the baggage."

"That's what I would do," Hoggles agreed stolidly. "And it will work. They have more arms and legs than any other group aboard."

"Exactly," Rebo agreed. "And once they get established, they'll come after us. So, rather than grab a wall slot or try for a corner, I suggest that we seize control of the water supply instead."

Norr was visibly surprised. "But that's public property! No one does that."

"Oh, they try," the runner replied. "I encountered the

problem once. A group of toughs set up camp right in front of the faucet and charged each passenger a gunnar per bucket of water, until the rest of the passengers banded together and put a stop to it. Five people were killed during the battle."

Hoggles frowned. "So why would we want to put ourselves in a position to get killed?"

"We'll go about it differently," Rebo answered. "Rather than demand money from our fellow passengers, we'll provide them with water for *free* so long as they don't attack us. But if they do, we'll cut them off."

"You're pretty smart for a norm," Norr said admiringly. "No wonder I hang out with you!"

"You may feel differently later on," the runner replied soberly. "It won't be easy to guard that faucet constantly. . . . But it's worth a try."

The heavy nodded. "So, what happens when the hatch opens?"

"Lonni and I will make a run for the hold," Rebo replied, as the mist began to dissipate. "You bring up the rear with the packs, or if they're too heavy, guard them. One of us will come back to lend a hand."

The hatch had already begun to open when the sensitive freed herself from her pack and, staff in hand, prepared to follow Rebo out into the corridor beyond. The twosome wasn't the first to exit the decontamination chamber, that honor fell to a young man who rolled under the steadily rising door, but the couple were able to secure a position toward the front of the pack.

That advantage, significant though it was, couldn't make up for the fact that the Circus Solara performers had superior numbers. The beast master, the strongman, and a particularly well-built rigger led a phalanx of twelve people who pushed the rest of the passengers out of the way. The beast master took particular pleasure in elbowing Norr as he passed by her, thereby throwing the sensitive into a durasteel bulkhead and effectively putting her out of the race.

But Rebo wasn't so easily deflected, and, while unable to block the circus performers, did manage to keep up with them. Elbows flew, poorly directed blows were deflected, and the air was thick with grunts and heartfelt swear words as the mob surged down the filthy passageway to the point where a hatch had been welded shut more than a thousand years before. At that point the group had no choice but to turn left. The bullet-pocked bulkheads to either side of them were covered with grime, peeling paint, and countless layers of head-high multicolored graffiti. Below that, barely visible beneath the grime, phrases like WATCH YOUR STEP! hinted at a more civilized past.

Then they were through a large opening and in the ship's main hold, a space that the earliest passengers would never have been allowed to visit, much less live in. But that was back before *Shewhoswims* had been forced to seal off most of her vast body lest the now-barbarous humans do even more damage to her precious operating systems. What light there was originated from high above, and rather than the still-smoldering campfires the previous set of passengers typically left, there was nothing to see but piles of rubbish. And the gloom that circled beyond.

True to common practice, and the runner's predictions, the beast master and the rest of his flying squad immediately struck out for a distant corner. Once in their possession, and with more than thirty people to call upon, the triangular section of deck would be relatively easy to defend compared to a spot out in the middle of the hold.

Once Rebo confirmed that the troupe didn't have plans to seize control of the water supply themselves, he let out a sigh of relief and took the opportunity to drag some likely-looking debris over to the point where the faucet protruded from the steel bulkhead. A large puddle had formed there—and it shivered in sympathy with the vibration produced by the ship's power plant. Then, as more people flooded into the cavernous hold, the runner was forced to forgo scavenging in order to take up a defensible position next to the faucet. Norr arrived shortly thereafter—followed by a heavily burdened Hoggles. "Damn," the variant said, as he dropped the packs next to the puddle. "Those things are heavy."

"Uh-oh," Norr said, as she rewrapped her fingers around the long wooden staff. "Here comes our first set of visitors."

Rebo already had the four men under surveillance and nodded politely as they approached. They had the look of merchant adventurers, a common breed aboard the great ships, and were well armed. "What's the deal?" the largest member of the group demanded as he eyed the pistols that dangled at the runner's sides. "What are the weapons for?"

"There are more than thirty members of the Circus Solara on this ship," Rebo explained patiently. "They threatened to attack us."

"But they won't if you control the water," the man ventured.

"That's the idea," the runner agreed.

"So, what about *us*?" the smallest of the group wanted to know.

"You can take all the water you want," Rebo replied evenly, "so long as you don't pass any along to members of the troupe. If you do, we'll cut you off."

"And you don't plan to charge us?"

"Nope . . . That would be wrong."

"It sure as hell would be," the first man commented fervently. "We'll be back with our canteens."

"Sounds good," Rebo replied. "We'll see you later."

The men left, word spread quickly, and it wasn't long before a large contingent of circus performers had threaded their way between the newly created encampments to form a semicircle in front of the water faucet. The rest of the passengers saw the action and stopped whatever they were doing in order to watch. Not because they favored one faction over the other, but because the question of who controlled the water was important, and everyone had a stake in the conflict.

Most of the troupe were in mufti, but a few wore full makeup, which made them look more menacing somehow. The beast master had chosen himself as spokesman for the group. His voice was little more than a growl, and his eyes seemed to glow with hatred. "Give the woman to us, leave the area, and we'll let you live."

Rebo nodded gravely. "Generally speaking, I like a man who comes right to the point—but I'm afraid that you constitute the exception to that rule. I suggest that you return to your corner."

"Or *what?*" the beast master demanded belligerently. "Do you think you can shoot *all* of us?"

"No," the runner replied evenly. "That would be unrealistic. I am pretty fast however, so I think I can kill five or six of you before you can close with us. Then, given Bo's expertise with that war hammer, two or three more will go down. Oh, and don't forget the woman you want so much. . . . She's good for at least a couple more. That puts the price for water at ten people. So, if that's acceptable to you, make your move. Which one of you clowns would like to die first?"

But, before any of the performers could reply, Norr pointed upward. "Jak! Look!"

The runner looked up into the maze of girders that criss-crossed the top of the hold, spotted a figure silhouetted against one of the lights, and knew he'd been suckered. Even as the beast master kept him busy one of the troupe's trapeze artists had worked his way into position and was about to fire a long-barreled rifle.

But Rebo carried the long single-shot Hogger for exactly that sort of situation—and knew he could make the shot with his spectacles on. Unfortunately the runner's spectacles were stored in his pack, and the would-be assassin amounted to little more than an out-of-focus blur. That's what the runner was thinking as he brought the long-barreled pistol up into position and the acrobat fired. There was a flash, followed by a loud report and a *clang*, as the lead ball nipped the top of Rebo's right shoulder and flattened itself against the bulkhead behind him.

Thanks to the fact that the sniper was armed with a muzzle-loader rather than a repeater, there was no follow-up shot—which provided the runner with the opportunity to return fire. The momentary pain, followed by the sudden rush of adrenaline, combined to produce an instinctive response. The big handgun jerked in Rebo's hand, the 30-30 slug flew true, and the out-of-focus blob seemed to wobble. Then, as the loud *boom* echoed back and forth between the ship's steel bulkheads, the trapeze artist fell. There was a sickening *thump* as his body hit the deck. That was followed by a *clatter* as the muzzle-loader shattered, and the force of the impact sent pieces of the weapon skittering far and wide.

"So," Rebo said, as he lowered the still-smoking Hogger. "He went first. . . . Who would like to go second?"

The beast master and a couple of others might have taken their chances, but the rest of the crowd had already begun to back away, and that forced the more ardent performers to withdraw as well.

"You can have all the water you want so long as you leave us alone," Rebo told them coldly. "But the next time you try something like this we will cut you off. And, oh by the way, when you want water send *one* person to get it. And send the *same* person each time."

"We'll get you for this!" the beast master threatened, as he backed away.

"That will cost you twenty hours without water," the runner replied mildly. "Would you like to double that?"

There was no reply as the performers faded into the surrounding murk, although Norr could "see" the thought forms they had created and knew the danger was far from over.

"Damn," Hoggles said, as he peered up into the lattice-work of beams and girders above their heads. "We need eyes on the top of our heads."

"Yeah," Rebo agreed soberly. "We do. Maybe we can build a shelter with a bulletproof roof."

Norr took a look around. "At least there's plenty of materials. Let's get to work."

None of the three noticed the ancient security camera mounted high on the opposite bulkhead, or the fact that it panned slightly as if in response to some invisible hand before zooming out to a wide shot.

In the meantime, *Shewhoswims* broke orbit, accelerated out toward the edge of the solar system, and began to calculate the next jump. She was only vaguely aware of what the humans were up to, and so long as they did minimal damage to her body, was not especially interested in their activities. The stars were not only more compelling but a good deal more predictable, and that was a virtue in her opinion. The AI hummed while she worked.

The ship's Security Control Center had once been home to a force of fifty—men, women, and androids—charged with everything from crime prevention to crowd control. As such, the interconnected compartments included an office for the watch commander, a ready room complete with six bunks, a lounge that boasted its own auto chef, a well-stocked armory, and a high-tech surveillance facility where the video provided from more than five hundred cameras was constantly monitored.

But those days were long gone by the time the brothers Mog, Ruk, and Tas moved into the facility and took up residence. More than two standard years had passed since the day when Mog experimentally entered his birth date into the keypad outside the Security Center and watched in openmouthed amazement as the much-abused hatch cycled open. A more philosophical person might have marveled at his good fortune, or wondered how many thousand such attempts had failed prior to his, or pondered why that particular sequence of numbers had been chosen to protect the facility.

But Mog wasn't much of a thinker—nor were his half brothers Ruk and Tas. What they were was criminals, who—having botched a robbery—were on the run from the law when they happened upon the crowd that had gathered to watch a shuttle lift from the Planet Derius, and impulsively dashed up the ramp. But, not having prepared themselves for the trip, the siblings soon discovered that they had exchanged one life-threatening situation for another.

Still, the ship carried a plentiful supply of the one thing criminals can't get along without, and that was victims. Because, while many of the merchants, religious pilgrims, and other travelers were armed against the possibility of petty theft, they weren't prepared to deal with ruthless predators like Mog, Ruk, and Tas.

However, vulnerable though they were, the other passengers outnumbered the brothers, which was why Mog thought it best to locate a defendable hideout prior to initiating what he thought of as "the harvest." But when the hatch to the Security Control Center magically opened before him, the criminal realized that he had something of greater value than a simple refuge. Here was a compartment to sleep in, an alcove full of neatly racked weapons, and a roomful of magical windows. Strange but wonderful devices that allowed the criminal and his two siblings to monitor their prey before venturing out to attack them.

The benefits of Mog's discovery, and the rather crafty manner in which he employed them, produced what could only be described as a rich harvest. Armed with high-tech weapons and an ability to watch their fellow passengers from a remote location, it took the brothers less than three weeks to slaughter all of their fellow passengers and confiscate their valuables.

In fact the trip was *so* profitable, that when it came time to leave the ship, the brothers elected to stay aboard. Now, after more than two years of living in the Security Control Center, Mog and his brothers had accumulated so much loot that it occupied most of what had once been the lounge. There were pots full of gold cronos, sacks of gunnars, boxes filled with jewelry, canisters of rare spices, bottles of exquisite perfumes, and bolts of silk. "We'll be rich when we land." That's what Mog liked to say, but neither he nor his siblings had any real desire to put down on their native planet and confront the authorities there. Not yet at any rate.

Now, as Mog and Ruk sat in front of the two dozen surveillance screens that still functioned, they were evaluating the latest flock. Because each brother had been fathered by a different man, they had very few features in common. Mog was a big hulking brute with a bushy beard. And while slim when compared to his brother, Ruk had developed a bit of a paunch of late and was eternally in need of a bath. He eyed the screen as he scratched a hairy armpit. "So, brother Mog, what do you think?"

"I think were looking at slim pickings," the older man said cynically. "The group in the back corner doesn't have more than two gunnars to rub together. And, while the merchants will no doubt yield a crono or two, I dare say the rest are likely to disappoint."

"But not the women," Ruk growled.

"No," Mog said agreeably. "Even the homely ones are good for a little fun."

"I want *that* one," Ruk said eagerly, as he pointed a grimy figure at Norr.

"You can have her when I'm done," Mog said airily.

"That isn't fair! You always take the pretty ones!"

"That's right," Mog answered contemptuously, "and I always will. . . . Unless you would like to challenge my authority."

Ruk *did* want to challenge his brother's authority, but was afraid to do so, which left him with no choice but to back off.

"So," Tas said, as he entered the room. "When do we hit them?"

"Most will go to sleep in about three hours," Mog predicted. "Eight hours later they will get up and start to explore. That's when the harvest will begin."

"Good," Tas replied as he eyed the scene in the hold. "I'm hungry."

Thirty miles south of Seros, on the Planet Anafa

Though large by most people's standards, Chairman Tepho's estate was modest when compared to those owned by the planet's moneyed aristocracy, but that would eventually change. In the meantime, the two hundred acres of land more than met the reclusive leader's rather eccentric needs—none of which had much if anything to do with farming. That was evident in the way once-productive fields now lay fallow, previously sturdy fences went unmended, and the extensive angen pens stood empty. But there were guards, plenty of them, all made of metal. The androids stood alone, or in small groups of two or three, each holding a spear taller than it was. Most had been splashed with bright-colored paint. None of the neighbors knew why—or dared to ask.

All of which seemed strange to Shaz, who had been summoned to the estate upon his return from Thara and was presently ensconced in the back of a Techno Society coach. The conveyance rattled alarmingly as it topped a rise and started down the far side. Then, as the dusty road curved to the left, the variant caught a glimpse of the once-proud villa that capped a low hill. He knew the house intimately, having once been Tepho's chief bodyguard, and was surprised to see that the building had suffered what appeared to be fire damage during the months of his absence. Had the lower levels been affected, Shaz wondered. Because that was where the reclusive Tepho spent most of his time. Not with groups of people, who might look askance at his twisted body, but with a few trusted attendants and a coterie of nonjudgmental machines.

The coach followed a curving drive up to the front of the villa and stopped beneath a smoke-stained portico. The variant opened the door, and his boots had barely touched the ground, when a whip cracked and the conveyance jerked into motion.

That was the moment when the combat variant began to feel uneasy, allowed his camouflage to kick in, and stood ready to draw both of his semiautomatic pistols. He was already backing away from the front of the villa when he heard the muffled whine of servos, a half ton of masonry exploded outward, and a large machine emerged from hiding. It stood about twelve feet tall and consisted of an egg-shaped control pod mounted between two retrograde legs. The weapons mounted on both sides of the control pod burped blue light as Shaz drew his pistols. But the energy bolts flew over the variant's head, and when the visitor turned to look over his shoulder, he saw the smoking remains of a storage shed fall lazily out of the sky.

More servos whirred as the canopy opened and Tepho released the three-point harness. Then, without a word having been spoken, the machine performed a deep knee bend that allowed its owner to reach the ground. It was a maneuver that normally required help from one or more of the technologist's assistants, but something Tepho was determined to accomplish on his own given the fact that Shaz was there. The technologist grinned mischievously as the combat variant returned both weapons to their cross-draw holsters. "Had you going there—didn't I? There were thousands of raptors at one time. . . . Most were destroyed, but some enterprising tomb raiders found this unit buried with a Faro on Torus, and subsequently sold it to me. Our techs had to tear the whole thing apart and bring the pieces through the gates one or two at a time. But here's the part that you'll be interested in," the scientist continued. "Based on my research, it looks like the ancients created raptors to kill combat variants! That would suggest some sort of revolt. . . . Interesting, isn't it?"

It *was* interesting, but for more than academic reasons. Having been born into a violent universe, and having a vulnerable body, Tepho was understandably concerned for his personal safety. And now, having promoted his onetime bodyguard to a higher position, the chairman had every reason to be afraid of him. Not just a little, but enough to justify the acquisition of a very expensive machine that was not only more powerful than the combat variant but couldn't be bribed, tricked, or otherwise suborned. And that, Shaz realized, was why he had been summoned to Tepho's country estate. To learn about the machine, its capabilities, and the chairman's newfound strength.

"Yes," Shaz said tactfully. "That *is* interesting." So was the fact that most of the original machines had been destroyed, suggesting that his ancestors had discovered a way to defeat them. But the variant knew better than to say as much. "You wanted to see me, sir?"

"Yes," the technologist replied. "I'm looking forward to your report. The medicos claim that I need more exercise—so you can benefit from my frailties as well. Let's walk."

The sun emerged from behind a cloud, and had there been someone present to observe it, they might have thought the scene somewhat strange as the norm who wasn't normal limped along the road, while his companion shimmered like a mirage, and the raptor followed a few steps behind.

The machine walked with birdlike precision, each pod-step raising a puff of dust as its sensors scanned the surrounding area for signs of danger.

Meanwhile, Tepho listened as his subordinate described the team's arrival on Thara, the successful break-in, and the discoveries that followed. "So, Logos can be worn!" the scientist mused. "Imagine! Computers that you wear like a coat! And we're going to bring those days back, Shaz. . . . And soon, too! Where is this marvel? I want to speak with it."

A lump formed in the combat variant's throat, but the operative managed to swallow it. With Tepho at his side, the decision that appeared to be so logical before seemed questionable now. Still, Shaz knew that it was important to be assertive, and his voice was forceful as he told the chairman what he'd done, and why.

To the technologist's credit he allowed the underling to finish the report before making his reply. But there was no mistaking the tightness in his voice, the way his right index finger stabbed the air, or the fact that he was limping faster now. "Dammit, Shaz . . . I'd like to say that I agree with your decision to let the sensitive and her companions take Logos aboard that vessel, but I don't! Travel aboard the starships is just too damned risky these days. . . . What if the old tub can't find its way out of hyperspace? But what's done is done. . . . Don't let it happen again however."

Tepho was capable of towering rages, and knowing that, the variant discovered that he'd been holding his breath. He let some of the air escape along with the words. "Yes, sir. It won't happen again."

The scientist glanced sideways as if to gauge the sincerity of the response and nodded. "I believe you, Shaz. . . . Make the jump to Derius and wait to see what happens. Hopefully, they will arrive right on time. If it looks like they want to use the local gate—then allow them to force their way in. Just keep Logos safe! Eventually, assuming you wait long enough, he'll lead you to Socket. Understood?"

"Understood."

"Good," the scientist replied firmly. "Now, watch this . . ." So saying, Tepho removed a pistol-shaped device from the brand-new shoulder holster that hung under his left arm. It was shiny, like highly polished silver, and apparently seamless. Tepho aimed the artifact at a high-flying bird, pressed a red button, and brought his other hand up to shade his eyes. There was no report, as one would expect from a handgun, but the raptor fired one of its energy cannons, and the broadwing exploded. Shaz watched a cloud of feathers drift toward the ground, wondered how his ancestors had countered such machines, and hoped it wouldn't be necessary to do so again.

Aboard the spaceship *Shewhoswimsthevoid*

Though relatively safe, the corner of the hold that the circus performers had claimed for themselves was poorly lit, which was just as well insofar as the beast master was concerned. The humiliation suffered in the arena had been bad enough, but having been faced down immediately after boarding the ship, the animal handler's standing among his peers was at an all-time low. And, since their questionable esteem was the only thing the norm possessed, the situation was deeply disturbing.

So, while the others slept, copulated, and gambled around him, the beast master plotted his revenge. A murder that could be carried out from a distance—and without the least bit of risk to himself. But there was work to do first. The fact that the circus hopped from planet to planet every five years or so meant that new animals had to be acquired soon after landing, trained to do tricks, and sold just prior to liftoff.

But, while the beast master couldn't bring an L-phant aboard, smaller animals were okay so long as he fed them, and none of the other performers were inconvenienced. There had been a long sequence of such pets over the years, but the sturdiest and most enduring, was the Poda pod he had acquired on Baas. Being from a desert environment, the pod didn't require much water, and so long as it received three drops of liquid fertilizer every fifteen days, would reportedly live for more than a hundred years. Not that the pod was a pet. . . . No, the *real* pet was the six-inch-long Slith snake that lived inside the pod and took most of its sustenance from the plant—a relationship the beast master didn't fully understand, and didn't need to, so long as he took the symbiotic coupling into account.

Now, as the norm held the pod up in front of his face, he made use of both spatulate thumbs to rub what he thought of as the pod's throat. A full ten seconds passed before the tiny serpent made its appearance. It had a single beady eye, a long black tongue, and an orange stripe that ran down its spine. "Greetings my sweet," the beast master whispered lovingly. "And how are you today? Hungry? I'm not surprised."

Then, having made use of his right hand to reach for a pair of tweezers, the circus performer selected a likely looking insect from a half-full jar, and held the still wriggling prize up for inspection. "So, sweetums, what do you think? Is this little beauty worthy of your stomach?"

The serpent opened its mouth and thereby revealed a respectable set of fangs. Its head snapped forward, and the insect disappeared. And that, to the beast master's way of thinking, was something of a mystery. He had observed animals all of his life, and while never the recipient of a formal education, knew how a food chain worked. Which raised the obvious question: Why would an animal that ate insects require fangs? To defend both itself and the pod? That seemed likely—but there was no way to be sure.

What made the little snakes valuable was the fact that they could be trained to follow a particular scent to its source and kill the organism associated with it. So long as the target was vulnerable to Slith venom, that is, which, according to the assassin from whom the serpent had been purchased, included just about everyone. It was an assertion the beast master had tested twice before. First, as the means to eliminate an acrobat foolish enough to sleep with his woman, then as a way to punish the bitch herself.

The key, and a very important one, was to provide the tiny killer with an item from which it could extract the necessary scent. In this case a tiny scrap of cloth that one of the troupe's little people had snipped from the sensitive's cloak after she boarded the shuttle. "Here, sweetums," the circus performer whispered, as he held the tiny piece of fabric out for inspection. "Get a good sniff of this."

The long, narrow tongue seemed to caress the scrap of cloth before being withdrawn. The animal was visibly agitated now, its head jerking from side to side, as the beast master extended his right index finger. It was an act of faith, because a single strike from the Slith snake's fangs would lead to an agonizing death, but such was the serpent's training that it had no interest in harming anyone other than the being associated with the newly assimilated odor. Then, once it returned from its deadly mission, the tiny assassin knew that a special feast would be waiting.

Conscious of how dangerous a trip across the cluttered

deck could be for his pet, and hopeful that it would choose to travel via the overhead girders instead, the beast master stood and held his finger up to a diagonal support structure. He felt rather than saw the serpent unwind itself from his finger, wished his pet well, and watched death slither into the darkness.

A good deal of time and effort had gone into the effort to construct the shack next to the hold's single water faucet. And while not especially attractive to look upon, or bullet-proof, as Rebo had originally hoped, the shelter did provide the threesome with a welcome sense of privacy, and if not actual safety, then the illusion of it, which contributed to their peace of mind. And that's where the runner was, sitting within the embrace of four rickety walls cleaning the Hogger by the light of an oil-fed lamp, when Norr entered the hut. The entryway was large enough to accommodate Hoggles, but just barely, and the sensitive had to duck before straightening again.

Rebo looked up from his work as the variant took the seat opposite him. The runner never tired of looking at Norr's face and wondered what that meant. There had been women before her, quite a few of them, but none so compelling. That was why he had agreed to a run that was not only unlikely to pay off but could strand him on an inhospitable planet, or get him killed. So, why was he there? Was he in love with Lonni? Or the idea of someone like her? She was in love with him . . . Rebo thought so anyway. Then what was he waiting for? He could tell her, no *ask* her, and the deal would be done. However, because such contemplations caused the runner's head to hurt, he put it aside in favor of a joke. "How's the weather?"

Norr made a face. "There isn't any, not unless you count the light breeze from the far side of the hold and the stink associated with it."

Rebo grinned. "I'm happy to report that I can't smell a thing!"

"That's because you're part of the problem," the sensitive observed tartly. "There's some news though. . . . When you control the water supply—everyone stops to chat."

The runner squinted down the Hogger's bore into the lamplight. Then, satisfied with what he'd seen, Rebo pushed a shell into the weapon's chamber. "There's news? I'm surprised to hear it."

"Yes, there is," the variant replied, as she held her hands out to collect the scant warmth generated by the lamp. "And it isn't good . . . You know the merchants? The ones camped by the number two pillar?"

"The ones with the fancy crossbows?"

Norr knew from long experience that the runner had a tendency to describe people by the way they looked, or the artifacts that they carried, rather than how they felt, or acted. "Yes," she replied. "The ones with the crossbows. Two of them went out to explore the ship and never came back."

"It's a big ship," Rebo said neutrally. "Maybe they got lost."

"That's what I figured," the variant agreed, "until one of the missing merchants appeared right next to the man I was talking to."

The runner raised an eyebrow. "Dead?"

"Very."

"Did you tell the person you were talking to?"

Norr shook her head. "No . . . I wasn't sure what to do."

Rebo frowned. "So, how did he die? Could you tell?"

The lamp lit the sensitive's face from below. It gave her features a spectral quality. "Yes, I could. The spirit didn't say anything, but he was holding his head in his hands, and it was screaming."

The city of New Wimmura, on the Planet Derius

As Shaz, Phan, Dyson, and four metal men stepped out of the decontamination lock on Derius and began the process of pulling their damp clothes back on, it quickly became apparent that something was wrong. They could hear the insistent *pop*, *pop*, *pop*, of gunfire for one thing, accompanied by yelling and the muted beat of unseen kettledrums. Then the entire structure shook as a team of fanatical antitechnics carried a palanquin loaded with black powder into the building's lobby and blew themselves up. The idea had been to bring the two-story structure down, but the supports were too strong for that, so the building still stood.

The combat variant's first instinct was to retreat to Anafa via the star gate, but it quickly became apparent that it was too late for that, as the power went off. Fortunately, the emergency lights, which were powered by a battery, flickered and held. "You'd better arm yourselves," Shaz said grimly, as he slipped into the two-gun harness. "It looks like the building is under attack. We may have to fight our way out."

Phan was a professional killer, and therefore received the news with aplomb, but Dyson was frightened. He looked from one person to the other. "I don't have any weapons."

"No," the combat variant observed, "you don't. . . . So, I suggest that you stay close to Phan—and do whatever she tells you."

The sensitive finished putting his shoes on, shouldered

his pack, and wished that the empty feeling in his stomach would go away.

Having armed themselves with stout wooden cudgels, the heavily robed robots made their way out into the office area beyond, followed by Shaz, Phan, and Dyson. Smoke swirled as a disheveled-looking man whirled to aim a double-barreled shotgun at the group of intruders. His face lit up when he spotted Shaz. "By all of the blue devils it's good to see you, sir! How did headquarters know we were in trouble?"

"They didn't," the variant answered flatly. "What's going on?"

"It's those damned antitechnics," the functionary responded angrily. "Come on, I'll show you what I mean."

Shaz and the rest of the team followed the local past a landing where two norms and a metal man were busy defending a staircase and into one of the offices that fronted the second floor. It was dark outside, or would have been, had it not been for a multitude of torches. The light they generated combined to illuminate what looked like a crowd of at least three hundred seething bodies. Most were lower down, but some had succeeded in climbing up onto the same level as the building and were busy hurling stones at it. The missiles rattled as they hit the wooden façade. "Be careful," the functionary cautioned. "The Antitechnic Book of Abominations limits their warriors to smoothbores, but some of those bastards are damned good shots, and one of them nailed Kavi. . . ."

As if to illustrate the norm's point, a sniper chose that particular moment to send a .30-caliber slug whizzing past Phan's head. That was a mistake, because the assassin spotted the telltale muzzle flash, and it was only a matter of seconds before the woman brought the scope-mounted rifle up to her shoulder and fired in response. The sniper never knew what hit him as the .300 Magnum slug blew a hole through his chest. "You were saying?" Phan asked sweetly, as she worked a second round into the chamber.

"Nice shot!" the local said enthusiastically. "That should slow the bastards down. It all started about two hours ago, when the holy men ambushed A-63127, and tied him to a stake. Then they piled inflammable materials around the poor bastard. A crowd gathered, the fanatics began to preach all their usual antitechnology bullshit, and that's when a priest lit the fire."

Though conscious of the fact that there were bound to be snipers other than the one that Phan had neutralized, Dyson edged his way up to the shattered window and was amazed by what he saw. After the original city of Wimmura was slagged during the techno wars, the survivors had been able to found a new settlement within the embrace of the nearby open-pit mine, and constructed dozens of one- and two-story buildings on the benchlike contours that surrounded the hole. One end of the kidney-shaped basin was filled with water, but the rest had come to function as New Wimmura's central plaza, and that was where the unfortunate metal man had been set alight. Dyson didn't know if androids could experience the electronic equivalent of pain, but judging from the way that 127 continued to writhe within a cocoon of orange-yellow flames, it seemed all too possible. "Kill it!" the sensitive insisted, as he turned toward Phan. "Kill it now!"

The assassin looked at Shaz, saw the operative nod, and brought the rifle back to her shoulder. The second shot was just as effective as the first. The metal man jerked convulsively as the heavy slug tore through his badly blackened alloy torso, which slumped against the wire that bound him to the flaming pole. Dyson nodded gratefully. "Thank you."

But the decision to let Phan terminate the robot had nothing to do with compassion, a fact that soon became apparent. A howl of protest went up from the crowd gathered on the plaza below as the subject of their hatred was released from its suffering, and there was a sudden swirl of activity as various holy men pointed up at the building from which the shot had originated, and urged their followers to attack. The response was immediate, as half a dozen snipers opened fire on Techno Society headquarters, and scores of warriors began to scale the wooden ladders that would carry them up onto the highest bench. "Now we know who their leaders are," Shaz stated coldly. "Kill them."

Phan smiled, secured a fresh grip on her weapon, and went to work. Her aim was good, and each death sent ripples out through the ethers, which rolled over Dyson like waves of pain. He staggered backward, brought his hands up to his temples, and slid down the rear wall to sit on the floor.

Meanwhile, having volunteered to act as the assassin's spotter, Shaz brought a small pair of binoculars up to his eyes and directed Phan's fire. They made a good team. Leader after leader fell, and, as they did, the attack began to falter.

Then, having reloaded numerous times, the assassin went to work neutralizing those snipers who still survived, while the combat variant fired both pistols into the crowd directly below. The ensuing slaughter lasted for less than a minute before the holy warriors broke and ran. Dozens lay dead, their bodies akimbo, their spirits still filled with hatred. Some of the fallen groaned, or called for help, but were soon dispatched by cudgel-wielding metal men who prowled the battlefield like hooded angels of death. "Well," Shaz remarked lightly, "that went reasonably well."

"Yes, it did," the local operative agreed gratefully. "But

even though the ignorant bastards didn't know what they were doing, one aspect of their attack was successful."

The combat variant looked up from reloading a pistol. "And what, pray tell, was that?"

"The gate," the functionary replied sadly. "The explosion took it off-line."

FOUR

The spaceship *Shewhoswimsthevoid*

Those who travel aboard our starships can expect to eat only the finest food, prepared by expert chefs, and served by the most solicitous waiters in the empire.

—From promotional material produced by the Cylar Line

Tas was ensconced in his favorite chair, gnawing on a well-seared arm bone, when his older brother entered the compartment. "Look at that!' Tas said, using the humerus as a pointer. "The slimeballs are up to something."

When Mog looked up at the video monitors he realized that Tas was correct. A large percentage of the ship's passengers had gathered together toward the center of the hold. And, given the recent "harvest," the outlaw knew why. "You reckon they'll come after us?" Tas wanted to know.

"It's too early to tell," Mog replied judiciously. "They might decide to fortify the hold in order to keep us out."

"It won't work," Tas predicted, as he sprinkled salt on his meat. "We always get in. . . . Don't we, Mog?"

"Yup," the larger man agreed, as he fingered his beard. "We always do. . . . But I want you and Ruk to stay sober for a while. There could be some fighting during the next twelve hours or so."

"You can count on me," Tas said, through a mouthful of food.

"I know that," Mog replied, "and I take comfort from it. See the man wearing the short red jacket? The one standing in front of the rest? Watch him. . . . He looks like a leader."

"I will," the younger man promised. "He lives with the pretty woman."

"And she belongs to *me*," Mog emphasized as he turned to leave. "And don't forget it."

Tas knew the female was off-limits, but a man can dream, and the cannibal's eyes remained glued to the screen as he finished his lunch.

The meeting was Norr's idea; but for reasons the runner wasn't sure of, he wound up at the center of it. Maybe it was the no-nonsense manner in which the murderous acrobat had been neutralized or the fact that many of the passengers had spoken with him when they came to get water. Whatever the reason, it was clear that the group presently assembled at the center of the hold saw the runner as their leader. That made Rebo uncomfortable since the runner was a loner by nature and had always gone to great lengths to stay that way. And individuals like master merchant Isban Okey were the reason why.

Okey was a voluble man who, having survived the ambush, never stopped talking about it. The merchant was of medium height, and wore a red fez, matching jacket, and baggy pantaloons. The blunderbuss that he held cradled in his arms was almost sure to kill the man next to him if it went off, but Rebo was relieved to see that Okey's right index finger was clear of the brass trigger. "I don't know," the merchant said doubtfully. "Wouldn't it be better to hole up *here*, rather than go looking for the bandits?"

"It might be," the runner allowed patiently, "but consider this. . . . When the shuttle landed on Thara it was empty. Then, when we arrived in the hold, there weren't any fires. Not even hot coals. What would that suggest?"

It was a middle-aged woman who offered an answer. Though dressed in plain clothes, she wore a small fortune in gold jewelry. "It suggests that they murdered all of the previous passengers," the woman stated. "In spite of whatever precautions they took when people began to disappear."

"Exactly," Rebo agreed. "So, rather than sit and wait for the bandits to pick us off one at a time, I say we hunt the bastards down. They must have a lair, a place where they feel secure, and that's where we will attack them."

"Yeah! He's right!" a male passenger proclaimed.

That was followed by a chorus of similar comments and calls for action. "Let's track the scum down," a burly blacksmith added, "and give them what they deserve!"

There was a chorus of assent, and it was all Rebo could do to bring a modicum of organization to the mob before it surged out into the corridor. Okey was at the head of the column, with a reluctant runner at his side, while Hoggles brought up the rear. The beast master plus a dozen of his friends had agreed to participate in the hunt, so even though Norr had been left behind to guard the faucet by herself, the runner felt reasonably confident that she would be okay.

Rebo knew there was no possibility of stealth given the caliber of his troops, so he allowed the vigilantes to make as much noise as they wanted to so long as they stayed in front of Hoggles and behind him. In the meantime, as the posse comitatus put more distance between itself and the hold,

Okey had become increasingly loquacious. "We were exploring," the merchant explained. "I opposed entering this particular corridor, but Runsus insisted, and took over the lead."

Rebo held his torch up over his head. The light surged ahead to reveal a nearly featureless overhead, graffiti-covered walls, and a litter-strewn deck. "There it is!" Okey said excitedly. "Up on the right. . . . That's where the bone room is located."

Perhaps it was the steel bulkheads that seemed to press in from both sides, or Okey's choice of words, but whatever the reason, Rebo kept one hand on his talisman as the two of them stopped in front of an open hatch. "Look in there," Okey instructed, eyes averted. "And see for yourself."

Rebo caught the first whiff of what could only be described as an overwhelming stench—and resolved to breathe through his mouth as he approached the open door. Torchlight danced across grimy walls as the runner peered into what had become a charnel house. Whatever else the compartment might have contained had long since been submerged beneath a five-foot-high heap of human bones. Arm bones, leg bones, clavicles, rib cages, spinal columns, and skulls were piled helter-skelter, as if thrown from the door. And adding to the stomach-turning horror of it was the fact that bits of rotting meat still clung to some of the bones. "Look!" Okey said excitedly, "there's Runsus!" And turned to throw up.

Rebo ignored the sudden spew of vomit, struggled to keep his own lunch down, and saw that the head to which Okey had referred was still recognizable. Now, for the first time since leaving the hold, the runner felt truly frightened. Judging from the size of the bone pile, *scores* of people had been slaughtered over a long period of time. And that implied that whoever, or whatever, had killed them was very formidable indeed. So much so that the runner didn't believe that his undisciplined group of passengers was likely to challenge them and win. In fact, based on what he'd just seen, Rebo was about to order a return to the hold when the beast master yelled, "Look!" There's one of the bastards now! Get him!"

Rebo shouted, "No!" but the mob ignored him and thundered up the corridor in hot pursuit of whatever the circus performer had seen. The norm, with Okey close on his heels, found himself running next to Hoggles. "I couldn't hold them," the heavy panted, as he pounded along. "They're crazy."

As if to prove the variant's point the leaders of the mob turned a blind corner and started down a wide-open stretch of hallway. The runner saw a sign that read, SECURITY CONTROL CENTER, and the norms who were standing directly below it. He shouted, "Get down!" But, by the time the passengers in the front rank saw the danger and began to react, Mog, Ruk, and Tas had already opened fire. They had armed themselves with machine pistols, and it was only a matter of seconds before people in front of them began to jerk and fall. Thanks to his position toward the front, the beast master was among the first to take a bullet, immediately followed by a mime and a clown, as the runner raised the long-barreled Hogger. The weapon bucked in his hand, made a resonant *boom*, and sent a bullet spinning toward one of three possible targets.

Tas felt a sledgehammer strike his chest, lived long enough to register a look of surprise, and slammed into the hatch behind him before sliding to the floor. That came as a considerable surprise to the outlaw's siblings, who had preyed on other people for years without suffering any negative consequences themselves. But there was no time to grieve, not yet at any rate, as Rebo opened up with the Crosser and bullets pinged all around them.

Mog answered with a burst of well-aimed automatic fire, but the runner was already falling, with Hoggles on top of him, which meant that the bullets were high. That gave the surviving cannibals sufficient time to slap the controls, grab their brother's ankles, and drag the body through the hatch. The door closed with a definitive *thud* and the battle was over.

The heavy rolled off Rebo, the runner fought to suck air back into his lungs, and allowed the variant to pull him up off the deck. The hallway looked like a slaughterhouse. A quick check confirmed that five passengers were dead, and three were wounded, including the beast master. It was difficult to tell, given all the blood, but it appeared that a bullet had creased the performer's skull and knocked him unconscious.

Some of those who had escaped returned when the firing stopped, and there were cries of grief as dead friends and relatives were located. Then, with astounding speed, sorrow turned to anger. "This is *your* fault!" Okey insisted, as he pointed a long skinny finger at Rebo's chest. "You led us here!" The accusation wasn't fair, or true, but elicited a chorus of agreement from the rest of the passengers nonetheless.

Rebo considered trying to defend himself, decided that it would be a waste of time to do so, and returned the Crosser to its holster. "I suggest that we carry the wounded back to the hold—and organize a burial party. Or, would you like those bastards to snack on your friends?" Okey's face turned gray at the thought. He turned to the others, barked some orders, and the evacuation began.

Two hours later Rebo, Norr, and Hoggles were inside their shelter, sitting around a tiny oil-fed blaze. That left the water supply unguarded, but given the fact that the beast master was temporarily out of commission, the runner figured it would be okay. The sensitive, who was just back from treating the wounded, cupped her mugful of tea with both hands. It was eternally cold in the hold, and the warmth felt good. "I'm sorry, Jak. . . . They were wrong. It wasn't your fault."

"That's right," the heavy agreed stolidly. "Especially since they disobeyed every order you gave them."

"Yeah? Well, tell it to all those dead people," the runner replied bitterly.

"I will, if I happen to run into one of them," Norr responded calmly.

"So what are we going to do?" Hoggles inquired.

The question had been directed to the sensitive, but rather than answer it, her face went suddenly blank. Nerveless fingers released the mug, which fell and shattered against the metal deck. The lamp flickered as droplets of tea hit the yellow flame.

"Uh-oh," Rebo said, dispiritedly. "Lysander is about to pay us a visit."

But even as Norr was forced to make way for another entity, the sensitive knew it wasn't Lysander, but another spirit named Kane. The same person who had been her brother in a previous lifetime, pursued her on behalf of the Techno Society during his most recent incarnation, and been killed by Rebo. Although Kane had a preference for male vehicles, such was his affinity for the physical plane that he found Norr's body to be not only acceptable but rather interesting. In fact, if the opportunity arose, the invading spirit thought it would be fun to offer the female vessel to one or both of the attending males.

Norr "heard" the thought and tried to dislodge Kane but

discovered that his grip on her was too strong. The sensitive's eyes blinked, her lips moved, and a raspy voice was heard. "Greetings . . . This is Jevan Kane."

Rebo's eyes grew bigger. "Kane? I thought I killed you!"

"You *did*," the spirit entity grated. "And I will find a way to even that score one day. . . . In the meantime I am compelled by certain agreements to help protect you and your fellow cretins. And that's why I'm here. . . . To inform you that the person you know as the beast master intends to kill the body I occupy now. A rather shapely form with which I sense that you are well acquainted."

The Crosser appeared as if by magic as Rebo came to his feet. Norr looked up into the gun barrel and smiled serenely. "Yes!" Kane hissed. "Shoot me! I'd like that."

"Don't do it!" Hoggles interjected, and had just started to rise as the Crosser was withdrawn.

"Say whatever you came here to say, and get the hell out of Lonni's body," Rebo said through gritted teeth.

"I already have," Kane replied smugly.

"But *how*?" Hoggles demanded. "How does the beast master plan to murder Lonni?"

"I don't know," the spirit entity replied honestly. "A thick veil separates our worlds. But his intent is clear."

Meanwhile, Norr struggled to reassert control over her body. Bit by bit she gathered the necessary energy, shaped it into a coherent desire, and gave the necessary order. Her physical form responded, and the unanticipated action took Kane by surprise as his/her hand jerked forward.

Rebo saw the sensitive stick her hand into the lamp's open flame, and was still processing that, when Norr's body gave a convulsive jerk, and Kane was forced to leave. Then, having regained control, the young woman removed her hand from the fire. The burns hurt . . . but the pain was worth it. "Lonni?" the runner inquired tentatively. "Is that you?"

"Yes," Norr whispered hoarsely. "I'm back."

Meanwhile, on a girder high above, the Slith snake sampled the air with its tongue, identified the scent it was searching for, and resumed its long, arduous journey.

The city of New Wimmura, the Planet Derius

The suite, which was the best that the hotel had to offer, sat on the topmost level of the city and looked out over the lake that claimed one end of the kidney-shaped open-pit mine. It was a lofty perch, and as Shaz stood on his private veranda, it was like looking down on a nest of insects as thousands of people crisscrossed the plaza to the north, wound their way along the various plateaus, or climbed ladders that led from one bench to the next. A number of days had passed since the night when unit A-63127 had been terminated—and the antitechnics had launched their attack against Techno Society headquarters. During the interim it had been determined that the same explosion that caused extensive damage to the station's first floor had destroyed the facility's power accumulators. That meant the local portal was not only out of service but would remain so until a functionary could travel to the distant city of Feda, where they could access a star gate, and travel to Anafa. Worse yet was the fact that Logos and his human companions would be unable to use the gate, thereby playing hell with Chairman Tepho's plan, and causing even more problems. There was a solution, *had* to be a solution, but the operative had yet to figure out what it was.

Such were the combat variant's thoughts as a slight disturbance of the surrounding air caused him to whirl. But, rather than the antitechnic cutthroat that the operative expected to see, Du Phan emerged from behind the diaphanous curtain that separated the suite from the veranda. The assassin was naked, delightfully so, and cupped her breasts suggestively. "I'm yours," she said. "*If* you're man enough to take me."

What ensued was more like hand-to-hand combat than an act of lovemaking, but that was what both of them wanted and unreservedly enjoyed. Finally, physically spent, and still intertwined with an exhausted Phan, Shaz discovered that his subconscious mind had been hard at work. A plan was ready and waiting. It was a good plan, no, a *brilliant* plan, and one so devious that even Tepho would admire it! The thought pleased him—and the combat variant drifted off to sleep.

The spaceship *Shewhoswimsthevoid*

The scene within the shelter was grim as Norr removed Logos from her pack and held the coat up for Rebo to slip his arms into. "What's going on?" the computer demanded. "What are you doing?"

"I'm getting ready to go for a little walk," the runner replied soothingly, "and I thought you'd want to come along."

"A walk?" Logos inquired suspiciously. "Why would I want to go for a walk? Especially on a primitive tub like this one?"

"Because," Rebo answered patiently, "you might prove useful for once."

"Useful?" the AI responded doubtfully. "In what way?"

"Some outlaws have taken up residence on the ship," Norr explained gently. "They barricaded themselves into the Security Control Center, and the right combination of numbers is required in order to enter."

"So?" Logos said from the vicinity of Rebo's neck. "What does that have to do with me?"

"Well," the runner replied, as he checked to ensure that the Hogger was loaded. "If they manage to kill us, you'll wind up as little more than a bib for one of the cannibals, or be tossed onto a rubbish heap. So, given the fact that you constitute an artificial intelligence, and the ship is controlled by an artificial intelligence, I figured you could lend a hand. Or a sleeve as the case might be."

The AI had been forced to enter into relationships with a wide variety of human beings over the past thousand years and felt pretty sure that he could cut some sort of deal with the outlaws if that became necessary. It didn't serve his purposes to say so, however, so he didn't. "Okay," Logos agreed. "What do you have in mind?"

The Hogger made a loud *click* as Rebo closed the breech and slid the weapon back into the cross-draw holster. "All you have to do," Rebo explained soothingly, "is to make contact with the ship and request access to the Security Control Center."

"Okay," the AI replied hesitantly. "But I can't promise anything. . . . Who knows what sort of operating system this piece of feces is running? Two-way communication may be impossible."

"Well, do your best," Rebo responded patiently. "And one more thing . . . This 'piece of feces' is the only thing between you and a long, lonely death among the stars. We biologicals will starve to death if something goes awry—but it's my guess that you'll live a lot longer. So, be nice."

"I'll do what I can," the computer promised resentfully. "There's no need to threaten me."

"Good," Norr put in matter-of-factly. "Come on . . . Let's find some sort of hookup so you can chat with the ship."

There wasn't that much for Shewhoswims **to do while tran-**siting hyperspace, which was why the AI was busy working on her epic song-poem *The Chant of the Constellations,* when the irritation first began. She tried to dismiss the sensation as still another manifestation of old age and figured that the feeling would go away, but the input continued. Finally, having been unable to ignore the stimulus, the spaceship broke away from her composition to discover that something very unusual was under way. It seemed that there was an incoming binary message on com channel 17296.4, which according to the schematic that immediately mapped itself onto her electronic brain was a utility circuit that terminated in a passageway adjacent to the main hold. That suggested a prank by one of the passengers, or would have, except none of them possessed the capacity to send a digital message.

So, curious as to what was trying to make contact with her and why, *Shewhoswims* opened the circuit. There was a moment of confusion as both AIs sorted through various communications protocols as they searched for one that the other entity could process. Finally, by using what the ship considered to be an ancient code, the AIs were able to interact. Something that took place at blinding speeds even as Rebo stood next to a jack panel and began to fidget. Once it became clear who was on the other end of the circuit, *Shewhoswims* was both surprised and hostile. "You remain functional? I thought the humans destroyed you."

"They tried," Logos replied laconically. "But I'm hard to kill."

"So it would seem," the spaceship responded disapprovingly. "What do you want?"

"It isn't what *I* want, but rather what my biological companions want," Logos replied. "It seems that some rather unpleasant humans have taken up residence in your Security Control Center. The passengers in the hold would like you to terminate the criminals, or failing that, to open the hatch that protects them."

Shewhoswims spent a nanosecond checking the veracity of the other computer's claims, and discovered that the human vermin *had* infected the Security Center. "It appears that you are correct. . . . Unauthorized biologicals are living in what is supposed to be a secured area. As to whether they deserve execution, I really couldn't say. . . . Humans kill each other all the time. They seem to enjoy it. Who's to say whether such terminations are justified? Besides, my programming specifically prohibits taking human life, other than for the purpose of self-defense. And, although they are annoying, the individuals in the Security Control Center don't constitute a significant threat to my survival."

"Understood," Logos replied. "Which brings us to the second option. If you would be so kind as to open the hatch that protects the Control Center—my companions will enter and dispatch the brigands themselves. Thereby eliminating what you yourself referred to as an annoyance."

It was a tempting proposition, and having found nothing in her programming to prohibit such an arrangement, the ship was tempted to acquiesce. A single obstacle stood in the way. "Tell me something," *Shewhoswims* temporized. "Where are you and your companions headed?"

"To Derius," the other AI answered smoothly. "Like everyone else aboard this ship."

"But is that your ultimate destination?" the ship wanted to know. "Or, is Derius a waypoint on a longer journey?"

"Why do you ask?" Logos responded suspiciously. "What difference does it make?"

"My interaction with you activated some previously latent programming," *Shewhoswims* answered honestly. "It seems I am specifically prohibited from 'knowingly transporting, assisting, or otherwise providing aid to any artificial intelligence that can control, actuate, or coordinate star gates, star gate clusters, or star gate systems.' A stricture that must have been written into my operating system as a consequence of the civil unrest that followed Emperor Hios's death."

"Yes," Logos replied, suddenly grateful that Rebo couldn't monitor the conversation. "There was a lot of paranoia back then."

"So, what about it?" the ship demanded. "Are you, or aren't you, engaged in an effort to reconstitute the star gates?"

"No, I'm not," Logos lied. "That would be impossible."

Shewhoswims was well aware of the fact that she had the capacity to lie under certain circumstances, which meant it was entirely possible that the other AI had similar capabilities, but took comfort from the fact that she wasn't going to "knowingly" provide aid to a prohibited being. Or, put another way, if the other computer was intent on trying to reconstitute the old empire, then she was unaware of it. "All right," the ship agreed, "when should I open the hatch?"

The overhead fixtures threw isolated pools of light down onto the filthy deck, and campfires flickered in the surrounding gloom as Rebo and Norr went to head to head over the question of who would participate in the upcoming attack and who would remain behind. "I don't care what you say," the sensitive insisted stubbornly. "I'm going."

"No," Rebo countered through tightly clenched teeth, "you aren't."

"Why not?"

"Because someone needs to guard the water supply."

"No, they *don't*," the variant countered heatedly. "The beast master remains unconscious—so what's the problem?"

Logos was draped over one of Hoggles's massive arms, and his voice was somewhat muffled as a result. "I find this discussion to be extremely tiresome," the AI interjected. "Please place me inside the shelter. . . . I think I'll take a nap."

"Oh, no you don't," the runner replied, as he took possession of the tattered-looking coat. "You're coming along."

"But what if I don't want to come!" the AI wailed. "What if someone hurts me?"

"Then we'll give him a medal," Rebo responded unsympathetically.

Norr frowned. "Maybe Logos has a point, Jak. . . . Why take him?"

"For *two* reasons," the norm answered. "First, because I don't trust him *or* the ship. . . . Which is to say that if there's some sort of dirty work afoot he'll suffer, too. Second, because Logos is the only one of us who knows what time the ship thinks it is, and I have no desire to arrive in front of that hatch early or late."

"Okay," the sensitive agreed reluctantly, "but that brings us back to where we were. I'm coming."

Rebo found himself in an inescapable trap. Even though the warning had been focused on the beast master rather than the outlaws, the message from Kane worried him, and he felt protective about Norr. But that wasn't entirely legitimate, not based on the official relationship, and he wasn't ready to discuss the future. Not with Hoggles and Logos looking on. That left the runner with no option but to back down. "Suit yourself," Rebo said grudgingly. "But don't blame me if you wind up as part of someone's dinner."

Norr couldn't read minds, but she could see some of Rebo's emotions reflected in the colors that shimmered around him and felt a sense of inner warmth. "I'll be careful," she promised, and held out a hand. "Logos and I will bring up the rear."

It was a peace offering, and Rebo accepted it. "What about the others?" Hoggles wanted to know.

"They blame Jak for what happened during the first expedition," Norr explained. "We're on our own."

"That's probably just as well," the heavy growled. "Most of them would be worthless in a fight."

"There's no need to be hasty," Logos objected. "I think we should take the time necessary to . . ."

But the AI's concerns were ignored as the humans checked their weapons, left the hold, and made their way toward the Security Center. A camera tracked their progress.

Ultimately, it was the pain that summoned the beast master up from the blackness. The journey was somehow reminiscent of the time when his father had dropped him into the family's well along with the order to "Swim!" After the initial shock of the cold water, and the realization that he was drowning, came the instinctual desire to kick. And now, as the beast master fought his way back to consciousness, it was like the same experience all over again. He awoke with a loud snort, pawed at gummy eyes, and found that a piece of cloth had been wrapped around his head.

"Take it easy," a female voice cautioned, and the animal trainer felt something cold and wet make contact with his eyes. His vision cleared shortly thereafter, and it wasn't long before the beast master found himself looking up at Lila, the troupe's contortionist. She was pretty in an elfin way. His voice was little more than a raw croak. "What happened?"

"A bullet creased your skull," Lila replied. "But the sensitive sewed you up real good."

"*The sensitive?* You mean she's still alive?"

"She was a few hours ago," Lila assured him. "I think you owe her an apology."

"My snake," the animal trainer said urgently, as he struggled against the pain in his head. "Where's my snake?"

"Sweetums is right here," Lila answered soothingly. "Giggles found him clear over on the other side of hold and brought him back."

The beast master saw the pod, felt the six-inch-long serpent land on his chest, and found himself looking into a single beady eye. The human saw a long narrow tongue test the air as the tiny head jerked from side to side. A hole opened up at the pit of the animal trainer's stomach, and his voice was hoarse. "The bandage! Who put the bandage on my head?"

"The sensitive did," Lila answered innocently. "Why do you ask?"

But the circus performer never got to the opportunity to answer, because Sweetums chose that particular moment to strike, and the overwhelming need to scream consumed the remaining minutes of the beast master's life.

It was quiet inside the Security Control Center. So quiet that Mog could hear air whisper through the vent above his head. The image on the screen was dim. But there was no mistaking the man with the guns, the heavy with the war hammer, or the woman with the wooden staff. The same female that he and his brothers had lusted after for days. "What are they up to?" Ruk wondered out loud, as the threesome continued to walk directly into the camera.

"They want to kill us," Mog replied thoughtfully.

"But that's impossible," his brother objected. "They can't get in—and we have better weapons than they do."

Ruk was correct, Mog knew that, so why did he feel uneasy? The emotion wasn't logical, but the outlaw had experienced such misgivings before and learned to trust them.

"Let's get our guns and kill them," Ruk suggested helpfully.

"I don't think that's a very good idea," Mog replied, as he ran thick fingers through his greasy beard.

Ruk looked surprised. "You don't? Why not?"

"I just don't," the older man said firmly. "So shut the hell up."

Ruk knew better than to mess with Mog when the older man's back was up, so rather than aggravate his sibling, he went back to work on his dead brother's left femur. Eventually, after the bone dried out, the outlaw planned to carve the story of his dead sibling's life into the leg bone. But, before the scrimshaw could begin, it was first necessary to scrape all of the remaining tissue off the shaft.

Ruk's blade made a rasping sound as Mog watched the disparate threesome arrive in front of the Security Control Center's hatch. Who were they, he wondered? And why were the other passengers still sitting around the hold? There was no way to know.

Then, even as the outlaw watched, the man with the guns brought one of them up and pointed it at the camera. There was a smile on his face, as if he *knew* that the outlaw was watching, and wanted him to see it coming. Mog said, "No!" the screen went black, and the cannibals were blind.

"Okay," Rebo said, as he returned the Hogger to the cross-draw holster. "That ought to mess with their minds. . . . Assuming they have minds. Give me a time check."

"Twenty seconds," Logos said authoritatively. His voice seemed to originate from Norr but actually issued forth from the tattered coat that she wore.

"Light the fuse," the runner ordered, "and hand the bomb to me."

Norr held the canteen up to the torch that Hoggles was carrying, saw the oil-soaked rag catch fire, and passed the weighty container to Rebo. "All right," the runner said grimly. "Get ready . . . And remember . . . We need to close with them fast. If they get a chance to fire those automatic weapons, we'll be in deep trouble."

The others nodded and took up positions to either side of the hatch. Logos provided the countdown. "Ten, nine, eight, seven, six, five . . ."

Suddenly, without warning, the red light mounted over the keypad flashed green. The hatch was unlocked! There wasn't time to ask Logos how such a thing could happen. All Rebo could do was pull the door open, lob the fuel bomb through the opening, and hope for the best.

Thanks to Mog's premonition, as well as the attack on the camera, both he and Ruk were armed and waiting when the assault began. But neither bandit was prepared for the previously impregnable hatch to swing open—quickly followed by an explosion of flames as the earthenware canteen shattered, and highly flammable oil sprayed in every direction. Some of the burning fluid splattered Ruk's chest. That forced the outlaw to drop his machine pistol, slap at the flames with his bare hands, and swear monotonously.

Then, just as Mog triggered *his* weapon, the ship's fire suppression system came on. Because even though *Shewhoswims* allowed small fires in the main hold, that was the *only* place where such activities were tolerated lest critical systems be damaged. Distracted by the flames, plus the sudden onslaught of white foam, Mog's bullets hit the overhead and whined away. That gave Rebo the opportunity he required. The Crosser barked three times, and while the outlaw was forced to take three steps backward as the slugs hammered his chest, Mog was still on his feet when Hoggles brought the war hammer down on the top of his skull. There was a *thud*, followed by a soft *sigh*, and a *thump* as the cannibal hit the foam-covered deck.

That left Ruk. No longer on fire, but unable to locate his machine pistol under the surrounding foam, he produced an eight-inch knife. And, since Norr was the closest opponent, she was the one he chose to attack.

The sensitive saw the movement, heard Logos shout, "Run!" into her left ear, and parried the blade with her staff. There was a loud *clack* as the weapons made contact, followed by a *grunt* as the distal end of the stick sank into the outlaw's belly, and a solid *thwack* as Norr struck Ruk's temple. His eyes rolled back in his skull, and he was already falling when Rebo shot him.

"That wasn't necessary," the sensitive complained, as the outlaw's life force drained out of his body.

"True," the runner agreed matter-of-factly. "But it sure as hell felt good."

The next voice to be heard belonged to *Shewhoswims*, or the AI's voice synthesizer, which amounted to the same thing. "You have sixty seconds in which to evacuate the Security Control Center," the ship announced. "Subsequent to that, the hatch will be sealed, the atmosphere will be pumped out of the compartment, and the external keypad will be permanently disabled."

"She's afraid that you will use the Control Center the same way the cannibals did," Logos advised. "Let's get out of here."

Later, Rebo would wonder why he hadn't taken the moment necessary to retrieve one of the automatic weapons that lay on the deck, but that was later, *after* the hatch had been sealed tight. They were still in the corridor, making their way back toward the hold, when Logos spoke. "The foam destroyed three percent of my photo receptors," the AI complained to no one in particular. "I hope you're satisfied."

"Yes," Rebo responded wearily. "I think we are."

FIVE

Old Wimmura, on the Planet Derius

By recognizing the assassin's guild as a legitimate organization having the same legal standing as the metalworker's guild, or the runner's guild, Emperor Hios was able to take what had previously been a criminal enterprise and convert it into some-thing positive. Because so long as the assassins worked for the government, pursuing law breakers in return for bounties, they were a force for good.

—Heva Manos, advisor to Emperor Hios,
in his biography, *A Web of Stars*

The angen snorted as it topped the hill, sent twin columns of lung-warmed air out through its flared nostrils, and tossed its head when Shaz hauled back on the reins. Even though more than a thousand years had elapsed since Wim-mura had been nuked, the burned-out ruins were much as they had been immediately after the massive explosion, ex-cept for the thin layer of vegetation that covered the city like a greenish gray scab. No one went there, no one in their right mind, that is, since everyone knew that the soil had been poi-soned, the water was tainted, and evil spirits roamed the rubble-filled streets at night. And Shaz couldn't blame them, because as he looked out on the ruins, it felt as though the once-proud city was brooding over the disaster that had be-fallen it so many years before. And given the fact that the nuke had been transported through space using a star gate, there was little wonder as to why the local population remained fearful of technology. Interestingly enough it had been Milos Lysander in his incarnation as Emperor Hios, and Jevan Kane, in his role as Hios's son, who nuked cities such as Wimmura in a last-ditch attempt to remain in power. Now, these many centuries later, the father worked to make amends, while the son sought to regain what he continued to see as his birthright.

Shaz found the whole thing to be amusing—and smiled thinly as he gazed down on the ruins. Many weeks had passed since the attack on Techno Society headquarters, and, assuming that the great starship had completed its journey from Thara, the shuttle would arrive soon. And then, as if in response to the combat variant's thoughts, a white contrail marked the sky, artificial thunder rolled across the land, and the past was brought back to life.

The shuttle was crowded, very crowded, and some of the passengers were spacesick. But given what they had managed to survive, and the prospect of putting down safely, most were in an excellent mood. Except for Jak Rebo, that is, and the source of his unhappiness was plain to see. The travelers had no reason to believe that Techno Society operatives would be waiting for them on the ground, but they knew it was possible, especially given the fact that Kane was in league with the technologists. That was why Rebo had suggested that both he and his companions wear disguises.

What the runner failed to anticipate, however, was that Norr would turn to the Circus Solara for help. And that was how he wound up dressed as a clown. And not just *any* clown, but a particularly absurd creature with a head of curly blue hair, white cheeks, and a bulbous nose. His loose-fitting gown was white with red polka dots and came with floppy shoes that he categorically refused to wear. The outfit smelled musty, made Rebo want to scratch, and was the subject of crude jokes by other passengers. It was an affront to the runner's dignity and something that had begun to wear on him.

There was no way to conceal the fact that Hoggles was a heavy, but by placing a leather hood over the giant's head and dressing the variant to look like a strongman, Norr hoped to disguise his identity if not his genotype.

By chance, or by design, the sensitive's outfit was a good deal more becoming than those worn by her companions. It consisted of a feathery headdress, a lime green skin-suit, and slippers. And so it was that after the shuttle put down, and the ramp hit the ground, the crowd that had assembled to witness the ultimate manifestation of evil, was confronted by a completely unexpected sight as thirty-plus fully costumed members of the Circus Solara marched off the ship and onto the surface of Derius.

The band went first, instruments blaring, closely followed by a column of colorfully dressed acrobats, jugglers, and clowns, who, with the single exception of the dour-looking individual with blue hair, tumbled, cavorted, and generally made fools of themselves as the rest of the circus brought up the rear. All of which was by way of an impromptu advertisement for the troupe's first performance in New Wimmura, and proved to be so distracting that not a single rock was thrown until *all* the passengers were well clear of the ship, and it was beginning to lift. That was when a priest remembered his duty, called upon his followers to rebuke evil, and threw the first stone.

Meanwhile, having observed the landing from his vantage point high on the hill above, Shaz smiled as he peered through an ancient pair of binoculars. Having been warned about the likelihood of disguises, the combat variant had been able to pick the blue-haired clown, the oversized strongman, and the slender acrobat out of the crowd within a matter of seconds. And since any one of the threesome could have been wearing the highly mutable computer, it seemed safe to assume that Logos had survived the journey as well.

Satisfied that everything was going according to plan, Shaz lowered the binoculars and returned the proscribed device to the nondescript bag slung alongside of the angen's saddle. Then, having wrenched the animal back toward the trail, the variant spurred it forward. It would take the newly arrived passengers a good three hours to reach the city, and the variant intended to arrive there first. The trail followed the contour of the hill downward, past the shattered observatory, and onto the remains of a paved road. The cold air nipped at his skin—and it felt good to be alive.

Having successfully made it off the shuttle without being injured by the stone-throwing mob, and followed by a group of merchants into the suburbs of New Wimmura, the travelers paused long enough to shed their costumes at an outlying tavern and buy the troupe a round of drinks before paying the city's gate tax and passing between a pair of largely symbolic stone pillars. New Wimmura was a fairly typical city for the most part, other than for the fact that it had been established on the site of an open-pit mine, and unlike many of the cities Rebo was familiar with, seemed to eschew all technology beyond the lever, wheel, and pulley. All of which seemed to make it an unlikely place for the Techno Society to recruit new adherents, but the techies had never been shy and no doubt felt a need to preserve and protect the local star gate.

Eventually, having followed a road down into the bottom of the pit, the travelers passed a noisome stockyard, wandered along the edge of a fabric-covered marketplace, and strolled into the shadow cast by the mine's western rim. That was when they spotted the huge box-shaped construct that squatted atop a pair of twenty-foot-high treads. The crawler had been used to process ore at one time. But that was back before the original city had been nuked—and the huge machine had been repurposed as the Ore Box Inn. Or that's what a hand-lettered sign claimed—and the off-worlders were in need of a place to spend the night. "What do you think?" Rebo inquired as he eyed the ramp that led up through an ancient hatch.

Norr shrugged. "It looks okay to me. . . . Besides, it's getting dark, and it would be nice to find a place to stay before the sun goes down."

"I agree," Hoggles rumbled. "Let's give it a try."

So Rebo led the way up the ramp, entered a cramped lobby, and shrugged the pack off his back. The desk clerk was a balding, middle-aged man who had the look of a weight lifter. "Yeah?" the proprietor inquired. "What can I do for ya?"

"We'd like a couple of rooms," Rebo answered.

"Where ya from?" the innkeeper demanded suspiciously.

"We came in on the shuttle," Norr answered cryptically.

"Oh, ya did, did ya?" the man asked rhetorically. "Well, let me tell ya something right now. . . . I run a clean inn! That means no machines, no gadgets, and no gizmos." The proprietor looked down toward the Hogger. "How 'bout that pistol you're packin' son? Is that a muzzle-loader? Cause if it's a breechloader, then we got us a problem."

"Yes, of course it is," Rebo lied, knowing full well that Logos probably qualified as a machine, a gadget, *and* a gizmo.

"All right then," the inn keeper said pompously, "but be warned! The penalty for possessing techno contraband is death."

"As it should be," the runner agreed. "So, how 'bout those rooms? Have you got any vacancies?"

The proprietor did, and half an hour later Norr pulled Logos on over her clothes, and ordered the AI to be very circumspect about what he said and when he said it. With that out of the way, she followed the others along a lamplit hallway and through the cramped lobby. It was dark by then, or would have been had it not been for the thousands of torches and oil-fed lamps that kept the night at least partially at bay.

Meanwhile, even though Logos knew that the biologicals were hungry and focused on finding something to eat, the AI's priorities were considerably different. Unbeknownst to them there was a task that the computer needed to accomplish *before* he could safely seize control of Socket, which explained why he wanted to reach the Planet Haafa as quickly as possible. "New Wimmura has a star gate," Logos whispered urgently. "I can *feel* it. . . . The old city had a gate, too, a commercial portal that was destroyed by the nuke that Kane sent through it, but this one was the property of the mining company, and it survived."

Rebo, who was close enough to hear, frowned. "First," he said sotto voce, "shut the hell up! Second, what *we* want is something to eat. . . . The gate can wait until tomorrow."

"*No*," the AI countered emphatically, "it can't. We should scout it tonight—and use it tomorrow. Or would you like to walk the thousand-plus miles to the city of Feda instead?"

"All right, all right," the runner grumbled. "Point us in the right direction and shut whatever it is that you talk through."

Logos gave the humans some basic directions and let the biologicals find their way across the pit to a bank of ladders that carried them up to the appropriate bench. Once there, the threesome soon discovered that, unlike any other planet they had been on, the Techno Society's local headquarters constituted a very popular destination. Not because the local population supported the organization's goals—but because they opposed them. So much so that hundreds of people turned out each evening to parade back and forth in front of the much-abused building, hurl rocks at it, and shout antitechnic slogans. Such activities were tolerated it seemed—so long as the crowd didn't venture too close.

Having been absorbed by the angry crowd, the off-worlders found themselves pushed about like chips of wood on an angry sea. It was difficult to hold a conversation due to the chaotic nature of the situation—but Norr managed a brief interchange with a friendly antitechnic priest. "Hi there!" she said, as the two of them bumped shoulders and were pushed along. "My friends and I just arrived. . . . Is it always like this?"

"No," the young man replied. "No one comes here in the mornings. . . . The faithful have to work. We gather at night, to rebuke the techno devils and prevent them from polluting the minds of our children."

"What about the authorities?" the sensitive wanted to know. "How do they feel about the conflict?"

"The evil ones bought them off!" the priest responded angrily. "Metal men guard the palace . . . Need I say more?"

The sensitive wanted to ask more questions, but a group of rock throwers turned toward the building at that point, and the priest accompanied them. There was a loud *rattling* noise as dozens of missiles struck the Techno Society's façade followed by a ragged *clatter* as the rocks fell to the ground.

Shaz, who had been watching the mob for some time by then, steadied the telescope against the wooden window frame. The operative didn't even flinch as a stone flew through the same opening and hit the wall behind him. "There they are," the combat variant commented, before handing the brass tube across to Phan. "Just to the left of the burning effigy."

Some of the antitechnics bore a replica of a metal man fashioned from straw. They lit the figure on fire and held it aloft on poles. Thanks to the additional light that the flaming figure produced, the assassin could see all three of the people she'd been hired to deal with. "You were correct," Phan commented, as she lowered the scope. "They came to look. . . . When will they attack?"

"Tomorrow," Shaz predicted calmly. "In the morning."

"We'll be ready," the assassin said confidently.

"Yes," the combat variant agreed. "We certainly will."

A storm front had moved in over New Wimmura during the hours of darkness, bringing precipitation with it. The rain announced itself by drumming on the steel over Rebo's head until the runner groaned and rolled out of the narrow bed. There were no windows, which made it necessary to light a candle in order to see, and that brought Hoggles up off the floor, where he'd been forced to sleep. There were very few beds that could accommodate his enormous frame, and the one on the opposite side of claustrophobic room wasn't one of them. Once both men were up and packed, they emerged to find that Norr was waiting for them. "I couldn't sleep," the sensitive explained. "Not with all of that noise."

What Norr *didn't* say was that earlier, before the rain began to fall, she had experienced a bad dream. Nothing specific, not that she could remember at any rate, but the kind of nightmare that continued to resonate after she awoke. But, without anything specific to share, the sensitive chose to remain silent.

Assuming that the raid on Techno Society headquarters was successful, the travelers would be on another planet within a matter of hours, so they paid for their rooms, sought some advice regarding the local eateries, and made their way down the water-slicked ramp to the badly churned muck below. The plateaulike benches were paved, thanks to the efforts of the local store owners, but the bottom of the pit was a morass of mud and hand-dug drainage channels that were filled to overflowing with sluggish brown water.

There were planks, however, that the already damp threesome followed to a bank of mud-smeared ladders, which they had no choice but to climb if they wanted to access the ledge above. It was hard work hauling both themselves and their packs up the nearly vertical incline to the point where a small army of rain-drenched street urchins waited to greet them. "Hey mister!" one of them shouted, "you can wash your hands in my bucket!" "Over here," another insisted, "I'll scrape the mud off your boots!" "Ignore them," a third youngster counseled, "I have an umbrella . . . Where would you like to go?"

Five minutes later, having been serviced by at least half of the eager children, the travelers made their way into a local restaurant, where Hoggles ordered an enormous meal and complained about what he maintained were miniscule portions.

Then, with breakfast out of the way, it was time to climb up to the next bench. Once there, it was a short walk to Techno Society headquarters. True to the prediction put forward by the young priest the night before, the crowd that previously controlled the area had disappeared, leaving nothing more than hundreds of scattered stones and the charred remains of the previous evening's effigy to mark their nocturnal protest. "Okay," Rebo said as he pulled Logos on over his jacket. "You know the drill . . . We go in fast, locate the decontamination chamber, and lock ourselves inside. The techies will attempt to shut the gate down, but Logos will override the controls, and we'll make the jump. Questions? No? Then follow me."

A short flight of stairs led up to a brand-new door. It opened to reveal a large space that still showed signs of the black powder explosion that had gone off in the room weeks before. A brace of cudgel-wielding metal men moved forward to greet the visitors. Having already drawn the Crosser, Rebo was ready for them. "Good morning!" the runner said cheerfully, as he shot the first android between the eyes. Fast though its electronic brain was, the second robot was still processing the other unit's unexpected demise when a second slug drilled a hole through its alloy skull. The android fell in a heap.

Having seized the initiative, Rebo knew it was important to maintain it as he went up the steps two at a time. Hoggles had entered by that time—and the entire staircase shook under his considerable weight. "Down!" Rebo shouted, as a male functionary appeared above him. "Get down or die!"

The man went facedown and remained in that position as the runner stepped over his prostrate body, turned a corner, and entered a long hallway. A woman appeared, as if to see what had caused all of the ruckus, and went facedown when Rebo ordered her to do so. Hoggles, war hammer at the ready, followed behind.

Each time Norr came across one of the staff members, she

ordered them to keep their heads down, placed a bony knee in the smalls of their backs, and proceeded to bind both wrists and ankles with precut lengths of cord. The technos would be able to free themselves eventually—but the variant knew it wouldn't matter once she and her companions had control of the gate.

In the meantime, Rebo was making good progress. So much progress that the runner was beginning to believe that the plan to hijack the gate might actually work. Logos, by contrast, was not so sanguine. A gate was present, that much was certain, but assuming the data now flooding in through his sensors were correct, the power accumulators were off-line! And the gate wouldn't be operational without them.

But it was too late to cancel the raid, as Rebo ordered another functionary to the floor, gave thanks for the fact that none of the technos had chosen to put up a fight, and entered the room that provided access to the decontamination chamber. That was when the runner saw the chair and the half-naked woman who had been tied to it. She sat slumped against her bonds, a long rope of bloody drool hanging from her mouth, seemingly unconscious.

The runner grabbed a fistful of silky black hair, pulled the norm's head back, and saw that she'd been beaten. One eye was swollen shut, her upper lip was split open, and her left cheek was purple. Du Phan looked up at Rebo through the eye that still worked, gave thanks for the fact that the runner was on time, and decided that he was handsome in an unshaven sort of way. That seemed like a good time to groan, partly for effect, but mostly because her face hurt.

Rebo looked down into the woman's bloodied face, wondered what she'd done to deserve such treatment, and let her head fall forward again. That was when he caught sight of the tattoos on her shoulders. Hoggles was present by then, as was Norr, and both were staring at Phan when Logos spoke. His voice was stern. "The gate is off-line! We need to get out of here—and I mean *now*."

It didn't seem fair, not after all they had done to break in, but there was no other option. Not if the AI was correct about the gate—and Rebo had no reason to doubt that he was. "Damn," the runner said regretfully, "the techno freaks are going to be pissed."

"That's for sure," Hoggles agreed fervently. "Come on . . . Let's go."

"In a minute," the runner promised, as he produced a folding knife and flicked it open. "We're taking the woman with us."

Norr looked on as Rebo began to cut Phan free. Now, when it was too late to do any good, the dream came flooding back. She had seen the room and the bloodied face before. And, for reasons she wasn't sure of, the variant knew that the woman in front of her was evil. "I think you should leave her," the sensitive suggested emphatically. "She'll slow us down."

"That's right!" Logos interjected shrilly. "Leave the woman where she is! We have no need for her."

The runner heard the words but continued to saw at one of two ropes that crisscrossed Phan's naked chest. The male part of him couldn't help but take note of the fact that the woman in question had shapely breasts. The whip marks were plain to see. "Normally I would agree," Rebo replied evenly, "but she's a runner."

The sensitive frowned. "A *runner*? How can you tell?"

"Take a look at her back," Rebo replied as a piece of rope fell away. "See those tattoos? Each one represents a successful run. Okay, Bo . . . Can you carry her? Thanks." Then, with

Rebo leading the way, the four of them, five counting the semiconscious woman who had been slung over the heavy's shoulder, exited the building. There was no resistance.

Shaz, who had stationed his team in the passageway that ran between Techno Society headquarters and rug merchant next door, watched them leave. He wasn't looking forward to the long trek that lay ahead, but that couldn't be helped, and Phan would be there to protect Logos from harm. It was a *good* plan, one worthy of Tepho himself, and Shaz was confident of success as he led Dyson and a small band of heavily robed androids out into the icy rain.

The animals snorted, and the cart creaked as the travelers followed the narrow road down out of the hills and onto the plain beyond. The area was far too rocky for farming, which meant that what few huts there were belonged to lonely angen herders or antitechnic hermits. Once on level ground, the ancient thoroughfare ran straight as an arrow toward the point where the light gray sky met the eastern horizon. Winter had arrived, frost glazed any rock not directly exposed to the hazy sun, and cold air nipped at their faces as Rebo, Norr, Hoggles, and the woman named Phan put the last of the hills behind them.

Three days had passed since the raid on Techno Society headquarters, and a great deal had changed. Having purchased a large quantity of supplies in the market, plus a two-wheeled cart to carry them in, the group left New Wimmura during the cover of darkness. The plan was to make the long trek to the city of Feda, where the original foursome intended to access the local star gate or lift on the next ship.

But that was a couple of months away. In the meantime there was a potentially hostile environment to deal with— not to mention a shift in the way members of the group related to each other. And, as Norr and Hoggles sat side by side on the cart's bench-style seat, the cause of that change could be seen riding stirrup to stirrup with Rebo, chatting about who knew what. Runs probably, since both were members of the runner's guild, or were they?

According to Phan she had been hired to bring a small techno artifact to a wealthy merchant who lived in New Wimmura, a medical device, if the runner's suspicions were correct, that could be used to relieve the headaches that plagued his wife. But Phan arrived too late. The woman was dead and buried by the time Phan landed, the merchant was no longer willing to bear the risk of owning a proscribed object, and the runner was left holding the bag. So, being in need of funds to live on, and with no likely customer other than the Techno Society, Phan approached them.

But, rather than purchase the object as she hoped, they took the runner prisoner in hopes of learning more about the artifact and its origins. And that's where Phan had been, locked in a dark room, when the shuttle landed and lifted again. Fortunately for her, or so Phan claimed, Rebo, Norr, and Hoggles chose to invade Techno Society headquarters while she was being tortured. Otherwise, they might never have been aware of her. That's what the woman claimed anyway, but the dull colors that ebbed and flowed around the runner suggested that she was lying. Of course no one could see that except Norr, which meant there was no way to substantiate her suspicions, leaving the sensitive feeling frustrated.

The cart lurched as the team of two draft animals pulled the right wheel up over one of many ridges in the ancient pavement. The sensitive swayed and made a grab for her armrest, as the boxy conveyance rolled onto a smooth section of road. Then, with Hoggles handling the reins, Norr pulled the gray woolen cloak around her shoulders. There were *two* problems to contend with. The first problem was Phan herself, meaning the possibility that the runner was lying, and the second problem was the way Norr felt about the other woman. What was her motivation anyway? A legitimate concern regarding Phan's veracity? Or just a case of plain old jealousy?

Not that the sensitive had any rights where Rebo was concerned, because even though she felt sure the runner had feelings for her, the exact nature of the relationship had never been spelled out. Worse yet was the fact that she couldn't talk to Rebo about it, since the runner was almost sure to interpret her concerns as a manifestation of jealousy, thereby nudging him toward the very relationship the variant feared. Norr's musings were interrupted by Hoggles, who raised a massive arm to point at an object beyond the riders ahead. "Look! Could that be the bridge?"

The sensitive looked, failed to see anything, and came to her feet. The cart swayed, Norr put a hand out to steady herself on the heavy's shoulder, and shaded her eyes. Finally, by squinting just so, the variant thought she could see what looked like a tiny ladder. "I think you're right, Bo. . . . Although it's too far away to be sure."

An hour later Norr *was* sure, and so were her companions, as two pillars of rusty steel rose to silhouette themselves against the darkening sky. A series of cross braces linked the uprights together, making the structure look like a gigantic ladder. A framework that had successfully withstood more than a thousand years of wind, rain, and snow, it stood as a mute testament to long-lost knowledge and skill.

Then, as Rebo and Phan paused to wait for the cart to catch up with them, Norr saw that a cluster of stone-walled huts had grown up around the approach to the bridge, one of which leaked tendrils of dark gray smoke. The scene appeared serene, but it didn't *feel* right, and the sensitive said as much as the cart came to a stop. "I don't like the feel of it, Jak. . . . Something's wrong."

The runner knew better than to ignore her premonitions and nodded. "Let's hope for the best—and be ready for the worst."

If Phan was concerned about what might lie ahead, the runner gave no indication of it. The bruises and cuts had already begun to heal, revealing a very pretty face and an inner centeredness that made Norr feel inferior somehow. Phan wore a long black riding cloak that served to hide the rest of her body, but the sensitive already knew it to be more curvaceous than her own and resented that as well. Meanwhile, if the other woman harbored feelings about *her*, they were well hidden because her face remained empty of all expression. "Good," Norr affirmed, hoping that her demeanor was equally cool. "We'll follow your lead."

Meanwhile, more than a thousand yards away, Mia Tova al- lowed a cold stone wall to accept most of her considerable weight as she used a splinter of bone to pick at her badly yellowed teeth. One of them ached and needed to be pulled, but that would have to wait. Thanks to the fact that the bandit chieftain had excellent vision, she could see that only two of the approaching travelers were male. Of those she figured that the heavy posed the most significant threat since he'd be difficult to take down. But only if the group put up a fight. Fortunately, most of the pilgrims, merchants, and other travelers who had passed through the checkpoint during the last few days had been relatively cooperative. The others were dead.

Satisfied that she knew what to expect, the bandit turned

to enter the fuggy warmth of the hut behind her. It smelled of unwashed skin, wet wool, and the angen stew that bubbled in an iron pot. Earlier, prior to her arrival, the stone cottage had been home to a group of four antitechnic monks stationed at the bridge to absolve travelers of sins automatically incurred as they crossed the high-tech marvel. In exchange for a fee of course, since it was impossible to fight evil without money, which the church had no choice but to extract from its adherents. Of course the friars were dead now, having been forced to surrender their pot of grubby gunnars, prior to stepping off the very artifact they had been assigned to guard. All but one of them had gone gladly, thrilled to join the ranks of the antitechnic martyrs, shouting God's name as they plunged into the canyon below. The single exception soiled himself as he was hoisted out over the abyss and was blubbering for his mother when the downward journey began. A sad affair and one that Tova planned to report to the next vizier who happened along.

A fire glowed within a well-blackened fireplace, and a ceiling-hung lamp provided what light there was. Half a dozen shaggy heads turned away from a game of throwbones as Tova pushed the leather curtain out of the way, thereby allowing a wave of cold air to enter along with her. "All right," the chieftain proclaimed loudly. "Grab your weapons and make sure they're loaded. . . . There's only four of them, so even a group of worthless scum like yourselves should be able to handle the situation. Watch the heavy, though. . . . He could give us some trouble."

There were grunts of assent, followed by the sound of someone's flatulence, and gales of laughter as five men and one woman prepared themselves for battle. "Stay out of sight until the cart is right outside or I call for you," Tova instructed. "And don't kill anyone unless I tell you to. . . .

Who knows? Maybe we can ransom one or more of them. Understood?"

The brigands had heard the lecture before, but such was the force of Tova's personality that there was a minimum of grumbling as they took up positions to either side of the door, and she went out to stand in the middle of the road. The lead riders were almost upon the bandit as Tova hooked her thumbs into the leather belt that encircled her thick waist. That put the norm's hands in close proximity to the twin single-action revolvers that protruded butts forward from their cutaway holsters.

Rebo and Phan pulled back on their reins as the rough-looking woman appeared in front of them. The bridge was tended by monks, or so they'd been told, but there was nothing godly about the creature who stood before them. Strands of gray-brown hair hung from under a cone-shaped fur hat that was bald in places. The woman's canvas coat bore multiple patches, one grubby knee was visible through a hole in the baggy pants that she wore, and her boots were caked with mud. "Hold it right there," the apparition ordered loftily. "How would you like to pay the bridge toll? Cash on the barrelhead? Or with some of whatever's on that cart?" The vehicle in question had arrived by then, which meant that Norr was only fifty feet away, and in a good position to witness what transpired next.

"How much is the toll?" Rebo asked reasonably, hoping to pay a few gunnars.

"Five cronos," the bandit replied unhesitatingly. "Or, half of what's on the cart."

The runner's hands were on the saddle's pommel only inches from his guns. "That's absurd," he countered. "Step out of the way . . . We're coming through."

"No," Tova responded levelly. *"You aren't."*

That was when the six ruffians emerged from the hut to form a semicircle behind their leader. The threat was obvious, and the bandit chieftain knew she had the upper hand. Especially since the heavy was still on the cart and in no position to interfere. "Get down off those animals," she ordered. "You and your friends will be walking from now on. And watch where you put those hands."

"*No.*" Phan had been silent up until then. Now, as the other runner spoke, Rebo realized that she had thrown her cape back over her shoulders. But, before he could wonder why, Phan spoke again. Her voice was pitched low, but every word was distinct. "Tell your people to return to the hut. Do it now, and I'll let you live."

Tova was surprised. She was expecting trouble from the heavy, or the man with the hard eyes, but not the play pretty in the cape. Not that it mattered since it was time to go for her guns. The thought left her brain, but never arrived at her hands, which made an instinctive grab for her throat. Because that's where a six-inch-long throwing spike protruded from her larynx.

Though not fatal in and of itself, the injury was a shock and prevented Tova from issuing further orders. That was unfortunate since all the members of the band had been told not to kill anyone without their chieftain's express permission. The problem was rendered moot by the fact that three of them were dead by then, spikes protruding from their eye sockets, each having been thrown by Phan.

That was when the Hogger went off and one of the remaining bandits was snatched off her feet. Both of the surviving brigands fired weapons of their own. A rifle slug went wide, but pellets from a sawed-off shotgun struck Phan's angen and caused the beast to shy sideways. Rebo pulled the Crosser, and was in the process of bringing the weapon into firing position, when Phan lifted one leg up over her animal's neck and jumped to the ground. The remaining bandits both stood motionless and bug-eyed as the woman marched straight at them. Norr felt the bottom drop out of her stomach, and had already shouted, "No!" when the runner whirled. Heads jerked sideways, and sheets of blood flew, as two carefully honed knives sliced through leather, wool, and unwashed flesh. There was something beautiful about the movement, and something horrible, too, since there had been no signs of further resistance from either victim.

Three long seconds passed as a cold breeze rumbled across the plain, tugged at the no-longer-legible sign that dangled in front of the hut, and sang through the durasteel cables that kept the bridge aloft. And it was then, during what felt like a short eternity, that Tova managed to remove the spike from her throat. That proved to be a mistake, however, since once the plug was removed, a quantity of blood spurted out of the hole. But there was still time for revenge. Or so it seemed to Tova, because *her* world had slowed, and it now seemed as though there was time for everything.

In spite of the fact that both of the bandit chieftain's hands were slippery with blood, she still managed to pull both pistols and was busy hauling the hammers back when Phan realized how exposed she was. Rebo saw the movement, initiated what promised to be a lengthy turn to the right, and knew he wouldn't make it in time. Not before at least two shots had been fired at Phan.

But it wasn't to be. Both Norr and Hoggles had exited the cart by then and come forward to help. Though still reeling from the manner in which Phan had executed two of the bandits, Norr was in a perfect position to see the bandit leader remove the spike, and knew that no one else could stop the woman from firing. The sensitive took two steps forward, twisted her staff in order to unlock it, and pulled the vibro blade free. Power flowed as she thumbed the switch, the sword *sizzled* as it swept through the air, and Norr barely felt the momentary resistance as the blade passed through Tova's neck.

The bandit's fingers jerked convulsively, followed by two loud reports as the pistols fired. The bandit's head made a soft *thump* as it hit the ground and rolled away from the cone-shaped hat. Despite its considerable size, there was nothing more than a gentle rustle as Tova's body swayed and collapsed.

One of the bullets from the bandit chieftain's gun had blown air into Phan's right ear as it whizzed past her head. Now, as she looked at Norr, it was with a newfound sense of respect. "Well," she said calmly. "The spook has teeth. . . . Who would have guessed?"

Norr thumbed the power switch into the OFF position and returned the weapon to its wooden scabbard while wondering if she'd done the right thing. What if the killing blow had been withheld for two seconds? Would Phan lie dead? And would she be happy rather than sad?

Rebo looked from one woman to the other. The animosity was clear to see. That meant he would have to take sides at some point. Norr was the obvious choice. Hell, Norr was the *only* choice. So why not signal his allegiance now? A snowflake twirled before landing on his nose, and the question was left unanswered. "All right," Rebo said, as his breath fogged the air. "Let's take a few minutes to search both the bodies and the huts for anything we can use or trade. . . . I want to cross the bridge before nightfall. Who knows? There could be *more* bandits on the other side."

It was an unpleasant albeit necessary task because travelers who failed to scavenge what they could were likely to regret the omission later. It took a full fifteen minutes to complete the job, and by the time it was over Rebo noticed that not only had Phan retrieved all of her throwing spikes, but appropriated the bandit chieftain's revolvers as well. There was something cold-blooded about the way the other runner went about the chore, but Rebo knew it was hypocritical to criticize Phan for carrying out his orders, and made a point out of thanking her for what she'd done.

The female runner smiled warmly, and once the others were ready, the twosome rode out onto the bridge deck together. It was difficult to see the bottom of the canyon without venturing out to the edge of the ancient span, but Rebo had an impression of a ribbon of white water, bordered by sheer rock walls. Norr had saddled the fifth angen by then, but rather than attempt to ride with the runners, she chose to follow behind them instead. The cart brought up the rear, and it wasn't long before a swirl of thickly falling snow swallowed them all.

What remained of the filtered daylight was nearly gone, and the dead lay under a layer of shroudlike snow by the time Shaz, Dyson, and the four metal men arrived at the bridge. Shaz pulled back on the reins, brought his heavily encumbered angen to a halt, and eyed the wild sprawl of bodies. "Check the huts," he said coldly. "Bring anyone you find out to me. . . . And let me know if you come across any food. We need to make our supplies last."

The heavily armed robots scattered in response to the combat variant's orders even as the operative dismounted and handed his reins to Dyson. Then, starting with the nearest corpse, Shaz made a careful examination of each body. The task was gruesome, but necessary, in order to de-termine whether any of the AI's escorts had been killed. The inspection was useful in another way, too, because after looking at the means by which the bandits had been dis-patched, it quickly became apparent that Phan had been re-sponsible for most of the kills. That meant the assassin was earning her pay—something that pleased him.

Dyson sat atop his animal with both eyes closed as a mantle of white continued to gather around his shoulders. Most of the spirit entities forced out of their bodies during the battle had chosen to depart the physical vibration by then, but one, a woman who identified herself as Mia Tova, still remained. She was confused, especially about the loss of her head, and wondered if that would present a problem in the spirit planes. The sensitive counseled the woman that it was within her power to adopt any appearance that she chose—and urged her to leave the scene for life in the higher realms. After a moment of hesitation, and in the company of a spirit she seemed to recognize, Tova departed.

That was when Dyson opened his eyes to discover that Shaz was standing a few feet away staring at him. The com-bat variant seemed to blur before rolling back into focus. "Are you with us?" the operative inquired. "Good. We'll spend the night here. The metal men will take care of the angens. Our hosts left some stew simmering in a pot—so we might as well take advantage of it."

The sensitive slid to the ground, handed both sets of reins over to one of the heavily cowled androids, and fol-lowed Shaz toward a stone hut. When he passed Tova's snow-frosted head, the bandit's deep-set eyes seemed to fol-low him. That was impossible, of course, but Dyson was careful not to disturb the bandit leader's headless body as he stepped over it, and was grateful when the hut opened to receive him. Meanwhile, many miles away, a night slider howled. The sound seemed to float on the cold air before being echoed by other such creatures, as if to herald the full fall of darkness.

SIX

The Planet Derius

Even though sensitives can see that which others cannot, they often seem blind where their own lives are concerned, and make the same sort of mistakes that norms do.

—Grand Vizier Horga Entube,
The History Of My People

The road to Feda was long and hard. Especially during the winter. Having emerged victorious from the confrontation with the bandits on the west side of the bridge, Rebo, Norr, Hoggles, and Phan crossed the span ready to do battle again. Fortunately that wasn't necessary since the holy men assigned to the eastern approach had either been chased away or killed. So the first night was spent there, within the relative comfort of two huts, while the snow continued to fall beyond the stone walls.

The storm had passed by the time a dimly seen sun rose in the east, but it was bitterly cold, and the angens complained loudly as they struggled to pull the heavily loaded cart up onto the road. Then, with Rebo, Norr, and Phan breaking trail for the animals, the huge disk-shaped wheels cut deep grooves into the virgin snow.

There was a long way to go, but Rebo managed to put that out of his mind, as his mount carried him up through low-lying hills, through a stand of bristle trees, and onto the plain beyond. It was slow work, but the runner had learned to accept such things over the years, and fell into a plodding reverie that lasted until the pale yellow sun hung high in the sky. Eventually, the group paused for what Hoggles referred to as "a brew-up," in the lee of the cart.

The hot caf not only tasted good but served to wash down the fry cakes that Norr made up each morning. They consisted of cooked cereal, dried fruit, and nuts. The cakes tasted better hot, but none of them wanted to go to the trouble of making a fire, so the rations were consumed cold. The sensitive noticed that Hoggles consumed six of them, Rebo ate two, and Phan barely nibbled at hers.

Once their stomachs were full, it was time to rotate the animals so that the team that had been harnessed to the cart had a chance to recuperate. As soon as that chore was complete, Hoggles whistled through his teeth, the single axle squealed, and the angens issued a series of throaty grunts as they made their way forward.

There wasn't much traffic on the road, although tracks were visible from time to time, especially as they entered or left one of the tiny farming villages that crouched between protective hills. Most houses were low one-story affairs that were made of rammed earth and could withstand even the worst storms. Smoke dribbled from their chimneys, and the occasional mongrel gave chase as the group plodded past, but people were rarely seen. It was a rare stranger that brought something good to the farmers' footsteps—so they had learned to be wary.

There were other sightings, too, some of which harkened back to ancient times, when gigantic machines rode gleam-

ing rails, electric power jumped pylon to pylon, and powerful rivers were held captive behind canyon-spanning dams.
Such artifacts weren't operational of course, but often served
as media for semiliterate antitechnic diatribes, a fact that
struck Norr as ominous. Especially given the true nature of
the coat she wore beneath the long poncho-style cloak.

But most of the scenery was simply monotonous. The
road was an endless ribbon of crusty snow, the wind
moaned like a lost soul, and time seemed to crawl by. Eventually, after what seemed like an eon but was only about
twelve hours of riding, the foursome began to look for a
place to spend the night. An inn would have been nice, but
the only one they'd seen was two hours back, which left the
travelers with no choice but to take advantage of whatever
shelter they could find. In this case it was the ruins of what
had once been a farm. What remained of the tumbledown
house provided protection for the cart and animals—which
left the humans to take up residence in the stone silo that
stood next to the main structure. The presence of a rudi-
mentary fire pit located at the center of the circular space
suggested that the structure had been used for that purpose
before. And, when Rebo volunteered to gather firewood,
Norr offered to accompany him. Phan, who was occupied
unpacking the pots and pans, watched from the corner of
her eye.

A frigid breeze sought to find its way in through gaps in
their clothing as the twosome emerged from cover. The
half-frozen snow crunched under their boots as they circled
the silo and followed a half-seen path down into an ancient
orchard where fruit trees stood in patient rows, as if still
waiting for the people who planted them to return. Some
were dead, and their brittle branches made what sounded
like pistol shots as Rebo bent them to the breaking point

and was showered with ice crystals. Once a knee-high pile of wood had been accumulated, the runner and the sensitive stood side by side as they worked to reduce the long rough-barked limbs into more manageable lengths. Norr was the first to speak. "Jak . . ."

"Yeah?"

"What do you think of Phan?"

Rebo shrugged noncommittally. "The woman can fight . . . You've got to grant her that."

"And I *do*," the variant replied, as she broke a branch over her knee.

The runner gave Norr a sidelong glance. "So? What's the problem?"

The sensitive paused. "I can't prove it, but I think she's lying."

Rebo's eyebrows rose. "Lying? About what?"

"I don't know," the variant confessed. "But the feeling is there."

The runner nodded. "I trust your instincts, Lonni. You know that. . . . But you aren't infallible."

The conversation was headed where Norr had *feared* that it might go, and her chin trembled slightly. "And you believe this is one of those times?"

"I don't know," Rebo answered carefully. "But it's possible. . . . First, why would Phan lie? What could she gain? But let's say she *is* lying. . . . Chances are that the lies have nothing to do with us. Don't forget that we lie constantly and make no apologies for doing so."

Rebo's explanation was *so* reasonable, *so* benign, that Norr felt silly. She forced a smile. "Don't let this go to your head, but there are times when you're right."

"Right about *what*?" The voice came from behind them, and both whirled, only to find Phan standing a few feet away.

Somehow, by a means not apparent, the other runner had been able to approach them without making a sound. But if the sensitive thought that was strange, it seemed as if Rebo didn't, because the runner smiled. "Another pair of arms! Just what we need. . . . Here, have a bundle of kindling."

Phan accepted the wood, but even though she smiled pleasantly, the colors that flowed around her were murky and dark. A fact that served to reactivate the sensitive's concerns and made Norr suspicious all over again.

Having monitored the entire conversation from his position beneath Norr's cloak, Logos took note of the sensitive's suspicions regarding Phan and came to the conclusion that it would be a good idea to keep a nonexistent eye on the newcomer. Because if the female truly was something other than what she seemed, then her presence could very easily have something to do with *him*, a subject AI was always interested in.

There was no sunset as such, just a gradual diminution of light, as the threesome carried the firewood back to the silo. The night passed peacefully for the most part, although the angens stirred at one point, as if they were aware of something that the humans weren't. And when morning came, and Rebo went out to look around, the runner saw what looked like human tracks in the snow. They appeared to originate up on the road and circled the ruins once before returning to the main thoroughfare. A local perhaps? Keeping an eye on the neighborhood? Or something more sinister? There was no way to know.

Thus began a series of long, almost identical days that varied only in terms of how much snow fell, slight variations in the scenery, and brief contacts with other travelers. Once, while checking their back trail from the top of a pass, Rebo saw six dots in the far distance. But the purpose of a road is to carry traffic, so there was no reason to be alarmed, or so it seemed to him.

Eventually, after the better part of a week had passed, the travelers came across the first of what would eventually turn out to be a series of recently used campsites. Not the single fire pit that a family or an itinerant tradesman might have huddled next to, but a large area of well-trampled snow, and the remains of no less than *three* fires. All of which suggested a party that consisted of fifteen or twenty people. But what *kind* of people? Nice people? Or bad people?

It was an unsettling development, and one that became even more worrisome later the next day when, having passed through some small villages, the group came upon a much larger campsite. An area large enough to accommodate up to a hundred people, who, if not under a single leader, had been on friendly terms with one another, judging from the remains of a communal kitchen and two sets of latrines.

"So," Phan said, as she looked down from her mount. "What do you think?"

Having slid down off his mount, Rebo went over to the remains of the communal kitchen, knelt next to the fire pit, and blew into the gray ashes. Embers started to glow red, and a tiny wisp of smoke appeared. "I think we're closing with a group of people," Rebo said as he came to his feet. "One that continues to grow."

Norr had been silent thus far, and her angen tossed its equine head as the variant opened her eyes. "A man was murdered here," the sensitive intoned bleakly.

Phan was getting tired of the spook's endless pronouncements and made a face. "What makes you think so?"

"He's buried *there*," Norr replied, and pointed to a mound of snow that was about fifteen feet away.

Phan was skeptical, and rather than simply take the

variant's word for what had occurred, got down off her mount. Her boots made a squeaking sound as Phan made her way over to the pile of snow, fell to her knees, and scraped at the snow. The assassin felt her left hand make contact with something solid, so she scooped more of the white stuff out of the way and was startled by what she saw. A man *had* been buried there. That bothered Phan. If Norr could "see" things like that—then what else could the spook perceive?

But the question went unanswered as Norr felt Lysander invade her body, tried to fend the spirit entity off, and failed. The voice that came out of her mouth was deep and hoarse. "You have only to look at the man's lips," the technologist intoned, "to see the price paid for heresy."

Rebo had heard the unnatural voice and seen the same wide-eyed expression on Norr's face before. He shook his head disgustedly. "It's Lysander . . . Here we go again."

Though not familiar with Lysander, Phan had seen Dyson channel Kane and understood the nature of what was taking place. She peered at the dead man's face.

"What do you see?" Rebo wanted to know, and fumbled for his glasses.

"Somebody sewed his lips together," Phan replied, as she eyed the puckered flesh.

"And *that*," Lysander continued, "was the price he paid for speaking on behalf of technology. You must be careful, because the antitechnics would lay waste to entire villages to destroy that which you bear toward its home."

There it was, confirmation that the people Phan had been assigned to escort actually had the device that Shaz lusted after, something the assassin had been forced to accept on faith up until that point. But Phan wasn't supposed to be aware of Logos, so she forced a frown and came to her feet. "What is he, she, or it talking about anyway?"

Rebo swore silently. That was just one of the problems associated with working for a dead client. The bastard not only had a big mouth—but a talent for saying the wrong thing at the wrong time. "You've seen Lonni's vibro blade—the antitechnics would pitch a fit if they caught wind of it."

It was a partial explanation at best, since it didn't cover the stuff about bearing something to its "home," but Phan nodded as if satisfied. Rebo heaved a sigh of relief even as Lysander left Norr's body, and the sensitive blinked her eyes. She could still see the dead man's spirit however—standing beside his vertical grave.

The travelers returned to the road after that, which had been churned into a muddy mess, and disappeared over the top of a low-lying hill. Hours passed as the sun's dimly seen presence arced across the sky, and the group crossed and re-crossed the frozen river that meandered down the center of a U-shaped valley and entered a medium-sized village. It was late afternoon by then, and having been forced to camp out for three nights in a row, the off-worlders were thrilled to see a sturdy inn. It had a thatched roof, thick walls, and stood a full two stories tall. A stable was located next to it.

Once the angens had been seen to, and the cart had been secured, the travelers went upstairs to their rooms. Then, having drawn the shortest straw, Rebo was the first to bathe in a tub of water that cost the group twenty gunnars.

The inn's only bathroom was located on the first floor, one wall away from the kitchen, in a large wood-paneled room. The copper tub was so large that even Hoggles would be able to use it—and was filled with water heated from below. But, given the fact that all *four* of the travelers would have to use the same bathwater, common courtesy required that the runner take a sponge bath prior to entering the big tub.

The runner stripped down, hung his clothes on some

conveniently placed pegs, and made energetic use of a wash-cloth and a bucket of water. It had been days since his last bath, and Rebo was amazed by the rivulets of gray liquid that ran down his legs and into a floor drain.

Having tested the water in the tub and found it to his liking, Rebo put one foot in, and followed with the other, before beginning the gradual process of lowering himself into the hot liquid. After days spent out in the cold, noth-ing could surpass the sensation of warmth that rose to en-gulf the runner's tired body, or the feeling of tranquility that followed.

Steam rose, and an almost overwhelming sense of lethargy had overtaken the runner by the time a hinge squeaked, and the door opened inward. Because Phan had drawn the sec-ond shortest straw, Rebo wasn't entirely surprised to see her, although he was pretty sure the runner was early. He wanted to say something, knew he *should* have said something, but couldn't summon the necessary energy.

Conscious of the fact that Rebo was watching her, Phan began to disrobe. Having attempted to ingratiate herself with the threesome yet failed to gain their complete trust, it was time to use her backup plan. Slowly, and with occa-sional sidelong glances at Rebo, Phan ran a wet washcloth over her trim torso. Then, having cupped each breast in turn, she ran a hand down between her legs. Rebo, who had forgotten his own bath by that time, felt himself respond in a predictable manner.

Having completed her sponge bath, and with patches of suds still clinging to her tattooed skin, Phan made her way over to the raised platform, where she lifted a shapely leg up over the side of the tub. "May I join you?"

Rebo knew he should say "no," given the nature of his re-lationship with Norr, but Phan was in the tub by that time, and was busy settling herself onto his fully erect penis. Though still beautiful to look at, Phan's body was covered with what looked like a road map of healed cuts and puncture wounds. More than the runner had, which was saying something. Rebo closed his eyes as the young woman took him in. She fit him like a glove, a *hot* glove, and the pleasure was intense.

Then, determined to see as well as feel, Rebo opened his eyes. Phan was kissing his neck at that point, and because of the difference in heights, the runner could look down on the upper portion of his lover's back. He was shocked by what he saw . . . The tattoos Rebo had first seen back in New Wimmura, the tattoos that marked Phan as a runner, were so faded as to be nearly invisible! And, if the tattoos were fake, then it seemed logical to suppose that the rest of her story was fake as well!

Rebo's once rock-hard erection had already started to wilt by that time, and Phan was just about to ask what was wrong, when the door opened and Norr entered. Judging from the mischievous smile on her face, and the bottle of wine clutched in her right hand, it looked as though the sensitive had plans to share Rebo's bath as well.

But when Norr saw that Phan was present, the light went out of her eyes, and the color drained from her cheeks. Then, speaking with a dull, somewhat mechanical voice, the sensitive said, "Here, I thought you might enjoy this," and bent to place the bottle of wine on the floor. The hinge squeaked as she left, the door swung closed, and the sensitive was gone.

Rebo felt sick to his stomach. Having grabbed the sides of the metal tub he heaved himself up out of the water, stepped out onto the cold tiles, and from there to the floor. The runner's skin continued to steam as he made his way over to where his clothes waited. "Wait!" Phan demanded. "What's the hurry? So she's mad. . . . Are you a man or a boy?"

The runner made no answer as he donned enough clothes to navigate the inn's drafty halls, bundled the rest under his right arm, and left. Phan watched the door close for the second time and shrugged. In spite of the fact that her plan hadn't played out as intended, the effect would be the same. A wedge had been driven into the relationship between Rebo and Norr—and that was a good thing.

The problem was that the brief interlude with the runner had left the assassin unsatisfied. Still, the water was delightfully hot, and there to be enjoyed. Slowly, so as to prolong the sensation, Phan allowed the water to close over the top of her head.

Rebo arrived at the room that Norr shared with Phan only to discover that the sensitive was busy moving out of it and into a small cubicle at the far end of the hall. "Here," the runner said, as he reached out to take her pack. "Let me carry that." But the sensitive refused to let go.

"No," Norr said emphatically, "you *won't*. Leave me alone." The variant's heels made an angry clicking sound as she strode down the hall.

Rebo hurried to keep up. "It wasn't the way it looked."

Norr stopped and turned to confront him. Her eyes were filled with anger. "How stupid do you think I am? You were naked, in the tub with *her*, and the thought forms were clear to see. . . . Oh, and one other thing," the sensitive added. "You're fired."

"You *can't* fire me," Rebo objected. "I work for Lysander."

"You detest Lysander."

"So? I gave my word."

"But you never gave your word to me," Norr replied. "Is that what makes having sex with Phan acceptable?"

"It *wasn't* acceptable," the runner replied contritely. "Allowing her to get in the tub was a mistake. Please accept my most sincere apology."

"No," the sensitive said intractably. "I won't." And with that, Norr entered her room and slammed the door behind her.

Rebo wanted to tell Norr about the tattoos, and the sick feeling in his stomach, but it was too late for that. The bath's warmth had been dissipated by then, the runner's skin had cooled, and his breath was visible as he walked down the dimly lit hall. Night had fallen—and it promised to be both long and dark.

Like all of the youngsters raised within the steely embrace of the assassin's guild, Du Phan had been taught how to set her mental alarm clock and wake up whenever she needed to. Which was why her eyes popped open three seconds *before* the ancient clock in the lobby began to chime. And, thanks to the fact that she no longer shared the room with Norr, there was no need to be quiet as the assassin got dressed and tiptoed down the stairs. A brutish watchman sat next to the front door. He was wrapped in an old blanket, and a double-barreled shotgun rested across his knees. His head lay back against the grimy wall, and judging from the volume of his snores, the security guard was sound asleep.

Phan circled the man, opened the front door, and slid into the night. It was breathtakingly cold, but the assassin forced herself to pause for a moment and listen. She had a story ready for the telling, but preferred not to use it and

felt relieved to hear nothing more than the sound of her own
breathing.

Careful to maintain the near-perfect silence, Phan made
her way around to the stable. A dog rushed out to confront
the assassin as she approached the front entrance. It was a large
beast, made all the more threatening by the fact that its vocal
cords had been cut, leaving the animal to cough hoarsely
rather than bark. The dog bared its fangs, lowered its head,
and was about to attack when a throwing spike penetrated the
top of its skull. The animal went down as if poleaxed.

Phan paused to jerk the weapon free from the watchdog's
skull, discovered that the huge padlock that was supposed
to protect the stable from thieves had already been picked,
and pushed her way in. An angen snorted nervously as the
assassin passed by, and another bumped the side of its stall
as she made her way back toward the spot where an oil-fed
lantern threw a circle of yellow light down onto the frozen
muck. A whirring noise caused Phan to whirl and confront
the source. "Fear not," the metal man said softly. "Master
Shaz sent me."

Had the cowled metal man been able to evade the dog *because* he was a machine? And therefore lacked a human
scent? Yes, that seemed likely. Phan was disappointed. After
many days of what she considered to be isolation, the assassin had been hoping for a visit with the combat variant himself. But hope is little more than solace for the weak. Or so
the guild's oldsters liked to say. Phan was brisk. "What have
you got for me?"

Rather than reply himself—the android activated one of
many capabilities built into his body. Beams of white light
shot out of his "eyes," converged on a spot in front of Phan,
and combined to produce a three-dimensional likeness of

Shaz. It had been nighttime when the message was recorded, and judging from the way the light played across his distinctly canine features, the off-world operative was seated in front of a campfire. "We're about one day's march behind you," the combat variant said hollowly. "Remember, stay close to the sensitive, because she's wearing the computer. Or was back on Thara. Take care—and I'll see you soon."

The picture vanished, the beams of light disappeared, and Phan was left to wonder why it had been necessary to get out of bed for what amounted to a pep talk. There was *one* takeaway, however, and that was the admonition to ". . . stay close to the sensitive." That particular responsibility was something of a problem at the moment, but things would almost certainly come right out on the trail, where Norr would be forced to interact with other members of the group. A servo whined. "Do you have a message for Master Shaz?"

"No," Phan replied, unaware that everything she said was being recorded. "But do me a favor . . . Steal one of the angens on the way out."

The robot was incapable of facial expressions—but was quick to ask the same question that any human would. "Why?"

"Because I had to kill a guard dog on the way in," Phan explained economically, and left before the machine could reply.

The next morning dawned clear and bright. As Hoggles peered out over the angens' backs he could see for miles as the big wooden wheels crunched through the half-frozen slush. Meanwhile, for reasons not entirely clear, Phan was riding well *ahead* of the wagon while Rebo lagged *behind* it, and Norr sat wrapped in a blanket at his side. There had clearly been a falling-out of some kind, and, judging from the way the others were behaving, Hoggles figured that the problem had something to do with sex.

There were a number of reasons why the heavy had elected to remain with Rebo and Norr after arriving on Thara. The first was that the variant had nothing better to do. But there was another reason as well, one that Hoggles was hesitant to admit to himself, much less anyone else. His feelings for Norr were hopeless, the giant knew that, but heartfelt nonetheless. Which was why the heavy planned to return home once Logos had been transported to Socket and the sensitive was safe. Until then Hoggles was resolved to remain at Norr's side, protecting her to whatever extent he could, while enjoying the sound of her voice, smiles earned by virtue of small favors, and the occasional whiff of her perfume.

As the sensitive sat staring out over the searingly white landscape, Hoggles felt sympathy for Norr—and a combination of anger and resentment where the others were concerned. But none of it was his affair—so the variant was hesitant to get involved. But finally, after the group had been on the road for an hour, the heavy found the courage to speak. He began by clearing his throat. "I don't know what happened, but I'm sorry."

Norr turned to look at him. Her expression was bleak, but she forced a smile. "Don't be, Bo. . . . Life brings us all sorts of lessons. And, while some are painful, it's usually for the best."

The cart slowed as the angens were forced to tackle a hill, and the variant whistled at them before turning to look at his passenger. She was beautiful, even when she was sad, and Hoggles wanted to comfort her. Even if that meant pushing her toward another man. "The truth is that he loves you," the heavy commented. "Even if he's been slow to say so."

Norr was surprised to hear something like that from Hoggles. She looked at him—then "looked" again. That was when the sensitive "saw" what had been there for a long time and realized the true nature of what the heavy felt for her, evidence of which could be seen in the fact that he was busy trying to heal the rift between her and another man. It was a delicate moment—and one that Norr was determined to handle correctly. "Really? What makes you think so?"

"That's simple," Hoggles replied confidently. "He's here, isn't he? Even though he's *losing* money rather than making it."

Suddenly Norr knew that the man sitting next to her was present for much the same reason and felt a deep pang of regret, not to mention guilt, and a sort of sisterly affection. "And there's one more thing," Hoggles added. "I don't know what transpired between the two of you—but it's my guess that Phan was part of it. I don't trust her Lonni—and you shouldn't, either."

Norr remembered Rebo's apology, followed by her harsh words, and the *bang* as the door slammed closed. The runner wasn't entirely innocent, she knew that, but he wasn't entirely guilty either. Not according to Hoggles—and not according to the voice inside her. The one she should have been listening to all along. "You are a good friend, Bo. . . . A *very* good friend, and I'm fortunate."

The heavy blushed beet red, felt his heart leap at the praise, and turned toward the road ahead. Meanwhile, having monitored the entire conversation from beneath Norr's blanket Logos processed the computer equivalent of a human sigh. If there was anything more boring than human mating rituals, he couldn't imagine what it was. But at least the biologicals were in motion, which meant *he* was in motion, which was the only thing that really mattered.

When darkness fell, the travelers found themselves be-tween villages and therefore sought shelter within the rough embrace of four roofless walls. With nothing to protect them from the possibility of snow, Hoggles worked to stretch a canvas tarpaulin over the encampment while Phan busied herself at the cook fire. The other two went looking for firewood and were gone for quite a while. Longer than required to collect the amount of fuel they returned with. A fact that pleased Hoggles and annoyed Phan.

And, after everyone awoke the next morning, Phan found herself relegated to riding on the cart next to Hoggles while both the runner and the sensitive rode ahead. A sure sign that previously broken fences had been mended. Which was just as well, because it was less than an hour later when the group topped a rise and found themselves looking down on the Army of God. It was a relatively large group consisting of at least three hundred people. They were kneeling at that particular moment, heads bowed as a man dressed in a tattered robe stood atop an ice-encrusted rock and delivered the morning sermon.

There was no reason to be surprised, since the travelers had been following along behind the larger group for more than a week by then, but Rebo was taken aback by the size of the mob below, and the fact that a detachment of what looked like heavy cavalry had been sent up the hill to intercept them. Brightly colored banners snapped in the breeze as mismatched mounts snorted what looked like puffs of steam and clods of half-frozen muck shot from under their iron-shod hooves.

Norr turned to Rebo. "Return to the cart . . . Hide your

guns and tell Phan to do the same. I'll try to stall them."

The runner nodded, jerked the angen's head around, and kicked the animal's barrel-shaped sides. He was gone two seconds later.

"Logos," Norr said, as she eyed the oncoming riders. "Can you hear me?"

"Of course I can hear you," the AI replied testily. "I'm not deaf!"

"Then pay attention," the sensitive instructed curtly. "I'm looking at an army of antitechnic fanatics. They're going to be all around us soon—and they would like nothing more than to rip you apart. So keep quiet until I say you can speak. Even if that takes a week or more. Understood?"

It was probably Norr's imagination, but the sensitive thought that the computer sounded resentful. "Understood."

The riders were close by then, thundering up over the rise, their swords, spears, and battle-axes plain to see. Norr smiled in what she hoped was a disarming manner. "Good morning!"

There was a mad clatter of metal and a good deal of snorting as both riders and mounts circled around her. One of the warriors, a gaunt-looking man dressed in homemade armor, nodded politely. "Greetings . . . We ride for the Army of God. Do you carry the pestilence? Or are you clean?"

Norr frowned. "The pestilence? I don't understand."

"Technology," the rider answered sternly. "Meaning those items listed in the Book of Abominations."

"No," the sensitive answered. "At least I don't think so."

"Take care, woman," the man cautioned grimly. "Ignorance is no excuse. . . . And if you're hiding something—the diviner will surely find it."

Norr didn't know who or what the "diviner" was, but wasn't about to tell the rider about Logos, the guns, *or* her vibro blade. "Yes, I mean *no*, we aren't carrying any proscribed items."

"Good," the man responded loftily. "Come that you might become one with the Army of God! The rector welcomes all who burn with holy passion and live to battle the pestilence."

Norr forced a smile. "Yes, well, I'm not sure how much time we can spend with the army—but thank you for the invitation."

Rebo had arrived by that time, along with the cart, and felt utterly defenseless knowing that *his* guns, not to mention Phan's, were hidden under the cart's bench-style seat. But there was nothing that the runner and his companions could do but follow the religious fanatics down into the valley below.

The church service had ended, and the faithful were streaming up toward the road, as the off-world travelers were escorted into the campsite. Norr noticed that most of the antitechnics were dressed in little more than rags, that many were so malnourished as to appear starved, and that some lay on makeshift litters. Still others, including most of the older children, were bent under the weight of heavy packs.

It was a pitiful sight, and one that Rebo was still struggling to deal with, when a group of cudgel-wielding acolytes stepped out to bar the way. Like the cavalry, they were better fed than the rest, which suggested a hierarchy of some sort. "Halt!" one of the men ordered pompously. "The rector would speak with you."

"You must dismount," one of the riders added helpfully. "Or pay for your arrogance."

Both Rebo and Norr got down from their angens, only to have the reins snatched out of their hands as the man known as the rector appeared. He was at least seven feet tall. A rarity during an age when most A-strain males stood about five-foot-ten. But if the holy man's height was intimidating, so were his broad forehead, hooked nose, and thin, nearly nonexistent lips. Worse, from Norr's perspective, was the force of his personality, which would have rolled in to supplant her own had she allowed it to do so.

The sensitive staggered under the psychic assault, threw up a protective barrier, and struggled to stand her ground. That was when the sensitive realized that while a filthy robe concealed most of the rector's long angular body, his feet were bare and blue from the cold. A sign of penitence perhaps? Of otherworldliness? There was no way to know. The rector sketched the letter "A" into the air. "Blessings be upon you my children. Where are you from?"

Rebo remembered the way people turned out to stone the shuttle back in New Wimmura and knew that some sort of cover story was required. Consistent with lessons learned while growing up inside the guild, the runner stuck to the truth to the extent that was possible. "From New Wimmura, holy one. I'm a runner with a message for a merchant in Feda. This woman is my wife, Citizen Hoggles hopes to find work there, and Citizen Phan was engaged to guard our humble belongings."

The rector's gaze shifted to Phan. "You're an assassin?"

Phan inclined her head. There wasn't much on Derius or any other planet that frightened her, yet this man did. "Yes, holy one."

"Are you carrying any breech-loaded firearms?"

Phan thought about the revolvers hidden aboard the cart and wondered if it would have been better to dispose of them. But it was too late for that, so she brought her head up, and looked the rector in the eyes. "No, holy one."

"We will see about that," the rector replied cynically. "It

has been my experience that members of your profession have a special affinity for proscribed technology—some of which is so cunningly disguised that only an extensive search will uncover it."

Norr thought about the AI, as well as the vibro blade hidden inside her wooden staff, and wondered if the rector had the means to detect such things. The holy man clearly *thought* he did as he sent one of the acolytes to fetch "the diviner." In the meantime the rector had transferred his attention to Norr. "You interest me," the holy man said. "Why would a sensitive marry a norm?"

"I fell in love with the *man*," Norr replied honestly. "Not the body. . . . Besides, sensitives are a moody lot, and one is enough for any household."

The comment was intended as a joke, but the rector nodded, as if well aware of how moody sensitives could be, and was about to follow up on the matter when the diviner arrived. She was about eight years old, dressed in the remains of an expensive party dress, and armed with a forked stick. The rector's hard, angular face softened at the sight of her. "Hello, my dear," he said softly. "How are you feeling? Better? That's wonderful. . . . Now, if you're up to it, please check to see if these people should be allowed to join our flock."

Of course none of the travelers *wanted* to join the rector's shabby flock, but couldn't say so, as the serious-looking youngster waved the Y-shaped divining rod at them. "It will dip if one of you is carrying the pestilence," the rector warned confidently, as the little girl pointed the tree branch at Norr.

Rebo had never been one to ignore the role that supernatural objects could play in everyday life, so when the stick came into alignment with the computer hidden beneath

Norr's cloak, the runner half expected the stick to dip. But it didn't, and their luck held even as the child waved her stick at the cart and the weapons hidden on it. And, such was the rector's trust in her that no further inspection was required. The holy man produced what might have been a smile. "Welcome to the Army of God!" he proclaimed enthusiastically, and sketched another "A" into the air. "Come, my dear . . . We must take our place at the head of the column lest progress be slowed."

And with that the man with the bloody feet boosted the little girl up onto his broad shoulders and walked away. The acolytes and the cavalry followed. Rebo waited until the antitechnics were well out of earshot before shaking his head in amazement. "That is one crazy bastard."

Norr discovered that she had been holding her breath. It felt good to let it go. "That's an understatement. Something tells me that we were fortunate . . . But will our luck hold?"

The next thirty hours were like an episode in a surreal dream. Two hours after being absorbed by the Army of God, Rebo found himself slogging through the half-frozen muck while three raggedy moppets sat atop what had once been *his* angen. Meanwhile, about twenty feet to the rear, Norr had transformed the cart into an ambulance. Now, in addition to the group's steadily dwindling supply of food, the conveyance carried a couple of stretchers and half a dozen children. As for the other angens, they were "on loan" to the rector's cavalry, which was extremely unlikely to return them.

So, with no choice but to walk, time seemed to slow as the wintry landscape inched by. There weren't many rest breaks, but when one was declared, the flock was given only minutes in which to take care of their personal needs before the cudgel-carrying acolytes began to round them up. Then, with their knees buried in the cold-wet snow, the Army of God was required to listen as the rector read passages from a "history" that described how the people of Old Wimmura worshiped technology during the reign of Emperor Hios and were subsequently punished by God's righteous thunder.

Lysander attempted to take over Norr's body during one such episode so that he could counter what he saw as the rector's lies. But rather than allow him to do so the sensitive removed her belt and proceeded to whip her back with it—knowing that the pain would be sufficient to keep the entity at bay. The act caused some consternation at first, but was soon emulated by the more pious members of the assemblage, thereby adding still another element to the strange, half-real day.

Finally, exhausted by a fifteen-mile march under difficult circumstances, the flock descended upon an isolated house just before nightfall and "borrowed" everything the farm family had, including their food, animals, and personal possessions. The latter were of particular interest to the acolytes, who spent most of the evening squabbling over a few bits of gold.

Although Rebo, Norr, Hoggles, and Phan had been forced to surrender the cart by then, along with what remained of their food, the travelers had managed to recover their personal belongings, including Norr's staff, plus all the firearms, which were now kept wrapped within their bedrolls. That was the good news. The bad news was that each time the foursome attempted to meet, and thereby agree on an escape plan, an acolyte would materialize among them and call upon the group to pray, gather firewood, or dig a latrine.

The result was that by the time the second day had

dawned, and the bowls of watery porridge had been consumed, the off-worlders were still trapped within the Army of God. What comfort there was stemmed from the fact they remained on the road to Feda and were making progress toward their ultimate goal.

By midmorning the sky had begun to darken, and snowflakes began to twirl down out of the heavens, as the flock took temporary possession of a rocky promontory that looked out over a canyon and the white ribbon that twisted along the bottom of it. The army scattered as people sought to relieve themselves, or gnawed on cold rations, as Rebo peered down into the abyss. *Would the ice-covered river take one to Feda?* he wondered. If so, the runner thought that it might represent an alternative to the road, and the Army of God.

Such were Rebo's thoughts when, as if somehow drawn by the runner's heretical intentions, the rector appeared at his side. "Look!" the holy man said, as he pointed a long grimy finger down into the canyon. "Do you see the structures to either side of the river? There was a time when they were connected so as to block God's river! Can you imagine such arrogance?"

Rebo looked, saw little more than a blur, and stuck his hand inside his jacket. The glasses were out, and already on his nose, before the runner realized his mistake. The runner glanced at the rector in hopes that the faux pas had gone unobserved, saw the expression of outraged astonishment on the holy man's face, and knew he was in trouble. In spite of the fact that he had never read the Book of Abominations, it was clear from the rector's expression that spectacles were on it. That left the off-worlder with no option but to turn and run. But the rector had recovered his voice by then, and Rebo hadn't traveled more than thirty feet before a trio of acolytes cut the unbeliever off and began to beat him with their clubs. The runner's spectacles flew off as he took a blow to the head, and darkness rose to embrace him.

There were moments of consciousness during the long cold night that followed. Times when Rebo surfaced long enough to see the fires burning all around him, or to hear the sound of a rhythmic chant as the sleepless flock prepared for the cleansing to come. But in spite of his best efforts to do so, the runner was unable to hold focus, and it wasn't long before he lost consciousness again.

Finally, after what seemed like a long journey in a dark land, Rebo opened his eyes to discover that another wintry day had dawned. The rector stood before him, back turned, as he led his flock in prayer. Rebo was cold, *very* cold, and when the runner went to move his arms and legs he discovered that they were bound in place. But his head was free, which meant he could turn it to either side, even though it pained him to do so. And that was when the runner realized that both he *and* his companions had been strapped to X-shaped crosses. They formed a rough semicircle, with Norr to Rebo's right, Hoggles to his left, and Phan on the end.

Like him, the others were covered with a rime of crusted snow. All due to *his* mistake. He hadn't been conscious to see it, but the runner could easily imagine how the acolytes had fallen upon his companions, searched their belongings, and discovered the guns. Did they know about the vibro blade? Or Logos? There was no way to tell.

"And so we leave them," the rector continued, his sonorous voice rolling out over the crowd. "To meditate on their sins, during these, the final hours of their wasted lives."

So saying the rector turned, and sketched a symbolic "A" into the air, before hoisting the diviner up onto his shoulders and walking away. If the holy man blamed the little girl for failing to detect the contraband, there was certainly no sign of it.

The Army of God flowed out onto the road, and ten minutes later the entire flock had disappeared, leaving the unbelievers to die of exposure. Each off-worlder had a different reaction. Rebo tried to communicate with Norr, but found that his voice wouldn't carry, and was left to wonder if it was possible to kill someone on the spirit planes. If so, Lysander was in deep trouble.

Norr tried to use her power of telekinesis to undo even one of the more than two dozen knots that held in her in place but was soon forced to give up the task as impossible.

Logos couldn't manipulate his environment, but had survived similar situations during the last thousand years and knew what to do. Eventually, after his host's heart stopped beating, human scavengers would arrive to pick over her remains. At that point he would speak to one of the brutes, promise it a large quantity of gold that didn't exist, and convince them to carry him to Feda. Then, having found a more capable mount, he would continue his journey. Not to Socket, as everyone supposed, but to Haafa. Because, even though Socket was the AI's final destination, there was someone he would have to murder first.

Hoggles flexed his enormous muscles in an attempt to break the bonds that held him, but soon discovered that the acolytes had anticipated such a move, and tripled the number of ropes that held him in place. And, as a punishment for throwing an acolyte into the canyon, one of his fingers had been removed. The wound had been cauterized—but continued to ache.

Phan turned to her martial arts training in an attempt to gather her energy and channel it into a Ku, or death blow, sufficient to free her from the X-shaped framework. But, owing to the fact that the assassin had killed three of the flock prior to being subdued, two of her throwing spikes had been used to nail her hands to the thick rough-hewn beams. The pain, plus the cold, made it difficult to concentrate. Hope, such as it was, lay in the fact that Shaz would arrive eventually. But would the operative arrive in time? No, Phan didn't think so.

The snow began to fall more heavily then, covered each of the condemned with a shroud of white, and softened the area around them. Eventually, all movement having stopped, silence claimed the land.

SEVEN

The Planet Derius

Although the antitechnic rabble continue to sweep through the province—we have them under observation, and I remain confident that our strategy will be successful.

—Provincial Facilitator, Kas Okanda, in a report to his superiors in New Wimmura

The snow fell from the sky like a lacy curtain and the two dozen riders seemed to materialize out of the hazy whiteness like ghosts from some long-forgotten battle. But Facilitator Kas Okanda and his well-mounted dragoons were quite real, as were the sleek semiautomatic rifles the troopers carried and the wraithlike hunting dogs that ranged ahead.

Okanda was a relatively small man, but he exuded an aura of authority as he eyed the area, alert to the possibility of an ambush. But there was nothing for him to see beyond a maze of tracks, the usual detritus left behind by a large group of campers, and the row of X-shaped crosses that sat atop a low rise. Four people had been crucified, and judging from appearances, all of them were dead. But the administrator prided himself on the veracity of the reports that he sent to New Wimmura every eight-day, so a scout was dispatched to examine the bodies, and ordered to report back.

"Make a note," Okanda instructed, as the youngster next to him prepared to write on a clipboard. "Having patrolled the area north of the citadel, the company came across four individuals all of whom had been crucified. Since this sort of execution is typical of the antitechnic fanatics, it seems safe to assume that they were responsible for the atrocity." The facilitator's secretary scribbled furiously in a desperate attempt to capture each word exactly as it had been spoken.

The scout returned just as the government official finished his paragraph. "Excuse me, sire," the dragoon said respectfully, "but the people on the crosses are still alive."

Okanda had bushy eyebrows. They shot upward in surprise. "*What?*" he demanded. "Alive you say. . . . Are you sure?"

"Yes, sire," the scout replied expressionlessly. "Would you like us to cut them down?"

"Of course!" Okanda responded affirmatively. "But not until Hobarth here has an opportunity to examine the victims and take notes."

The scout said, "Yes, sire," and led the younger man over to where the snow-encrusted crosses stood. Now that he was closer Hobarth could see the wisps of vapor that issued from between blue-tinged lips. The better part of ten minutes elapsed while the secretary took elaborate notes on everything from the manner in which metal spikes had been driven through one woman's hands, to the clothes that the people wore, and the fact that a lightning bolt had been tattooed onto the inner surface of one man's left forearm.

Once the process was complete, the men and women were taken down and loaded into a pair of sturdy field ambulances. The heavy went into one, while the sensitive, and the norms were placed in the other. Once inside the wagons, the patients were propped up against straw-filled pillows and covered with wool blankets.

And that's where Rebo was when the dream ended, his eyes opened, and a man with a handlebar mustache said, "Here . . . This'll fix what ails ya!" and poured a half ounce of fiery liquid into his mouth. The whiskey went down the wrong way, and the runner began to choke.

Norr raised a hand in protest. "Don't give him spirits. . . . What we need is some warm tea. . . . Or some caf."

The medics were more than happy to dispense lukewarm tea from the insulated bottles filled earlier that day and consume the medicinal whiskey themselves while the wagons *rattled* through a village and began the long arduous climb to the citadel. Having passed through a well-guarded entrance, the wagons ground to a halt in front of a one-story infirmary, and the patients were carried inside. Within a matter of minutes they were stripped of clothing and immersed in warm baths. Phan, Hoggles, and, to a lesser extent, Rebo were treated for their various wounds before being brought back together for some hot soup.

Then, after a good deal of fussing over by some very efficient female nurses, the travelers were packed off to bed. Norr wanted to sleep more than anything—but refused to cooperate until the staff returned her clothes. Then, clutching a ratty-looking coat to her chest, the sensitive allowed sleep to overtake her. The nurses shrugged, sent the rest of her filthy apparel out to be burned, and left the room.

Once the nurses were gone, and the door was closed, Logos spoke. "Lonni? Can you hear me?" But there was no answer other than a cough, followed by some nonsensical words, and the sound of the sensitive's breathing. "I know I don't say this sort of thing very often," the AI whispered. "But thank you."

The sun had set three hours earlier, which meant that most travelers had been forced to camp out or seek the hospitality of a country inn. But Shaz and his party were the exceptions to that rule. Not only could the forward-ranging metal men "sense" obstacles, they could "see" whatever fell under the blobs of white light that projected from their "eyes" and break trail for the angens. Travel remained difficult, however, especially since the humans and their mounts had been on the road for twelve hours and were close to exhaustion.

But it had been two days since the combat variant had spotted one of the red ribbons that Phan typically left adjacent to the road or picked up a written message from the assassin. And that was why the operative insisted that the party continue to push ahead. Of course there are limits to how far one can ride in a day, and the angens had begun to stumble by the time the robots followed a multitude of tracks up to the rise where four X-shaped crosses stood, and paused to look around. A quick reconnaissance revealed an area of heavily churned snow—but it was impossible to know who had been there or why. "We'll camp here," Shaz announced to the androids. "Build a couple of fires, pitch the tent, and feed the angens."

The androids were extremely efficient, so it wasn't long before the two humans were sitting on small folding stools and warming their hands over a crackling fire. Meanwhile, an oil-fed stove had been established not far away, and a hearty stew would soon be burbling in a pot. Confident that the routine matters were under control, Shaz eyed the sensitive seated across from him. Even allowing for the fact that the campfire lit Dyson's face from below, the other variant looked older than he was. His skin had taken on a sallow, appearance, and his hands shook all the time. Some of that could be blamed on the rigors of the journey and the stress associated with it, but Kane was responsible for the rest.

The situation was difficult for Shaz to assess, not being a sensitive himself, but having been acquainted with Kane prior to his death, it was easy to understand how unpleasant the task of bringing him through could be. But there was no getting around the need to communicate with the dead operative from time to time. Even if that was painful for Dyson, who sat with shoulders slumped, his eyes on the fire.

"Your tea is ready," a robot announced, and waited for the humans to extend their mugs before starting to pour. Then, having given Dyson an opportunity to sip the hot liquid, Shaz broke the silence. "I know you're tired, but we haven't heard from Phan in quite a while, and I need to speak with Kane."

There was a moment of silence as the sensitive blew the steam off the surface of his tea and took another sip. Finally, his eyes peering out from cavelike sockets, Dyson looked up. It took a great deal of effort to keep his voice steady. "I would like to quit. There's no need to pay me. . . . I'll take my bedroll and walk away."

"Don't be silly," the combat variant replied dismissively. "I know Kane can be unpleasant, but I'll keep the session short, and the whole thing will be over in a matter of minutes. Then, after a good night's sleep, you'll feel better in the morning."

The other variant was determined to have his way, the sensitive could see that, so there was no point in stalling. Dyson closed his eyes, sought the inner peace that lay deep within, and partially withdrew from his body. Kane, who had already been drawn to the physical plane by the combat variant's thoughts, was ready and waiting. His beingness flooded into the newly created vacuum, where he hurried to seize control. The first thing the spirit entity noticed was the wonderful tang of woodsmoke, followed by the after-taste of unsweetened tea and the innate heaviness of the channel's physical body. A vehicle that was both tired from a long day in the saddle—and hungry for the food that was being prepared nearby.

Shaz became aware of Kane's presence when Dyson's body jerked convulsively, some of his tea spilled into the flames, and the fire hissed in protest. Then, once the steam had cleared, the combat variant looked into a pair of dead eyes. "So," Kane croaked, "we meet again."

"Yes," Shaz responded cautiously. "Thank you for coming. I could use your help."

"You have but to ask," Kane answered generously, as he held his left hand out toward the fire. The warmth was wonderful—and he reveled in it. Dyson tried to reassert control but couldn't. Gradually, bit by bit, Kane had become so skilled at controlling the sensitive's body that the sensitive was powerless to displace him. Dyson uttered a long silent scream, but there was no one to hear, and the conversation continued.

"Good," the combat variant continued. "We lost contact with Phan—which means we lost contact with the others. Can you tell me what happened to them?"

"Probably," Kane answered confidently. "Give me a moment." After pausing to swirl a mouthful of tea around the inside of Dyson's mouth, the spirit entity directed his attention outward. Other disincarnates could be seen within the thick glutinous material that overlaid the physical plane. One such individual was quite upset regarding his unexpected death. Others sought to comfort the dead man and escort him to a higher vibration. Kane hurried to project his consciousness into the mix. He listened for a while, asked a series of questions, and received most of the answers he needed before the entity's spirit guides pulled him away.

Shaz had started to wonder if something had gone wrong when Dyson, which was to say Kane, suddenly spoke. "I'm back."

The combat variant lifted an eyebrow. "And?"

"And Phan is alive, as are the others," the disincarnate reported. "Although they had a close brush with death prior to being spirited away by a group of people that my contact wasn't familiar with."

Shaz felt a sense of relief. His greatest fear had been that some sort of calamity had befallen not only Phan, but the AI, resulting in the machine's loss. It should be a relatively simple matter to find out where the group had been taken and free them should that be necessary. "Thank you, that is very helpful."

"You're welcome," Kane said politely. "Something smells good. . . . What's for dinner?"

Shaz, who expected the spirit entity to withdraw at that point, felt the first stirrings of concern. "Stew. . . . Why do you ask?"

"Well," Kane replied, as Dyson struggled to eject him. "It's been quite a while since I ate *real* food. I think I'll stay and have dinner with you."

The combat variant felt the short bristly hairs on the back of his neck stand at attention. He struggled to keep his voice level. "You can do that?"

"Why, yes," Kane answered coolly. "I believe that I can."

"And Dyson?" Shaz wanted to know. "How does *he* feel about your plan?"

"Oh, he's against it," the disincarnate admitted care-lessly. "But, I have the poor bastard right where I want him, so it doesn't really matter. Does it?"

The challenge was obvious, and the air around the com-bat variant began to seethe as his body prepared for combat. Fortunately, Dyson had consistently refused to carry a weapon, which meant it would have been easy to shoot the sensitive's body, thereby preventing the disincarnate from controlling it. But what if Shaz needed more information? Sensitives were hard to come by—and it wouldn't be a good idea to offend Kane.

The creature sitting opposite Shaz nodded understand-ingly. "Oops!" the spirit entity said lightly. "I guess this puts you between a rock and a hard place doesn't it? But, hey, not to worry. . . . We're after the same thing. And later, after we install Logos on Socket, I plan to reincarnate. You'll be an old fart by the time I make my presence known. As for Tepho, well, he's *your* problem. Slick, huh?"

That wasn't the way the combat variant would have de-scribed it, but he was a realist and nodded in agreement. "Welcome back. . . . I hope you enjoy your dinner."

Meanwhile, in a place where no one could help him, Dyson continued to scream.

Rebo awoke to the sound of bells. His eyes felt as if they had been glued shut but eventually opened to reveal a room so narrow there was no more than two feet of space on either side of his bed. Sunlight poured in through the paned win-dow over his head and threw an asymmetric pattern onto the door across from him. Then, just as the bells stopped ringing, the runner felt the unmistakable pressure on his bladder and knew it was time to get up.

The first attempt to throw the covers aside and swing his

legs out over the edge of the bed resulted in an explosion of pain. That caused Rebo to fall back against the pillow and probe the circumference of his skull. It quickly became apparent that there were three different dressings on his head. Fortunately, none of his companions had been killed as a result of his mental lapse. Still conscious of his full bladder, the runner gritted his teeth, battled to swing both feet over onto the cold floor, and stood. By placing one hand on the wall, he was able to remain upright even as a tidal wave of dizziness attempted to pull him under. He felt for his amulet in hopes that the charm would steady him and discovered it was gone. Lost during the battle with the Army of God, Rebo supposed.

He still had the religious medallion, however, which was something of a miracle given the fact that the antitechnics had stolen everything else, so maybe it would protect him. Finally, having kept his feet, the runner went in search of his clothes. That was when he discovered that while his old road-ravaged outfit had disappeared, brand-new clothing was waiting in the tiny closet, a gift for which he was grateful. Getting the fresh garments on was something of a challenge however, and Rebo might have abandoned the project if it hadn't been for the urgent need to pee. Fortunately, a nurse appeared about halfway through the process and helped the runner get his shirt on.

After a trip to the men's bathroom, which was equipped with flush toilets, Rebo went looking for Norr, only to discover that she was looking for *him*. Together they took refuge in a sun-splashed solarium. "I'm sorry," the runner said contritely. "Putting those glasses on was a stupid thing to do."

Norr shrugged philosophically. "Don't worry about it. . . . If not the glasses, then something else would have given us away."

"Thanks," the runner replied humbly. "But I *am* worried. The antitechnics took off with all of our money, supplies, and weapons."

"They took most of our stuff," the sensitive agreed soberly, "but not *everything.*" At that point Norr tapped her chest and winked. The message was clear. Logos was lurking somewhere beneath her brand-new outfit. The runner had mixed emotions where the AI was concerned but forced a smile. "That's good news. . . . So, how are the others doing?"

During the subsequent report, Rebo learned that while Hoggles's right index finger had been amputated after the battle with the antitechnics, the heavy was on the mend. "That's good," the runner said gratefully. "I need to apologize to him as well. How 'bout Phan?"

"Fortunately, none of the spikes that they drove through her hands struck bone," Norr replied. "She'll be good as new within a few weeks."

"And how good is *that*?" Rebo inquired cynically. "She isn't who she says she is, we know that, so what to do?"

"Get rid of her," Norr replied honestly. "As soon as we can."

Rebo nodded. "Works for me . . . In the meantime, where the heck are we? And who's running this place?"

"We're in some sort of government-run complex," Norr replied. "What was once a university if I understand correctly. More than that I couldn't really say. But, since Facilitator Okanda invited us to dinner, maybe we'll be able to learn more from him."

"Yeah," the runner said reflectively. "Maybe we will . . . In the meantime here's hoping that the runner's guild has a presence in Feda. . . . I should be able to withdraw some money from my account if it does."

"You're working for Lysander," the sensitive responded. "Maybe *he* can help."

"That kind of help I can do without," the runner objected, as he came to his feet. "Come on . . . Let's find Bo. I owe him a body part."

By the time evening fell, and the youngster named Hobarth led Rebo, Norr, Hoggles, and Phan into the citadel's Grand Hall, the off-worlders were feeling better. The room was huge, and would have been almost impossible to light had it not been for the ancient Class IV fusion generator located two levels below. The fact that it continued to broadcast electricity was due to a generous supply of spare parts, knowledge handed down for hundreds of years, and no small amount of good luck.

Kas Okanda was waiting to greet his guests when they arrived at the far end of the long, formally set dining table. He was dressed in a heavily embroidered gold coat, black trousers, and gold slippers. His neatly trimmed mustache and pointed beard served to reinforce the aura of material well-being that surrounded him. The facilitator never tired of seeing the expressions of amazement that the brightly lit hall produced on most of his guests. "Welcome!" the government official said warmly. "Please, take your seats, and I'll call for some wine."

Okanda was an amiable host, and the next hour passed quickly, as the facilitator plied his guests with good wine, food, and conversation. Finally, having offered the official a carefully edited version of the journey from Thara, Rebo asked his host what the government planned to do about the Army of God.

The facilitator took a sip of wine before replying. "That's a good question, Citizen Rebo. . . . As you have surmised by now, we not only have a pretty good idea where the rector and his flock are at any given moment, we have the capacity to bring their wanderings to an end whenever we choose."

"Then why wait?" Hoggles inquired.

Though blunt, the question was understandable given the nature of the heavy's injury, Okanda smiled sympathetically. "I understand how you feel—and regret what happened to you. But I, along with the other facilitators, have a responsibility to the planet as a whole. The rector is like a magnet to which tiny slivers of iron are inevitably drawn. Once all, or the vast majority of them are clumped together, we'll sweep them up."

"And *then?*" Phan inquired skeptically. Not only were her hands sore, they were slightly swollen, which would have made it difficult to handle weapons. If she had *had* weapons—which she didn't. Had the decision been up to her, the rector and his entire flock would have been crucified and left to die. Men, women, *and* children.

"The present plan is to march the antitechnics to the great salt sea and transport them to a remote island, where they will be free to live without benefit of technology," Okanda answered smoothly. "A fitting punishment—and one that will serve to protect the rest of the population from their fanaticism."

Norr heard the facilitator's words, but what she "saw" was something different. Based on the dark, slowly morphing thought forms that hovered around Okanda, it appeared that while some of the flock might be transported, others would almost certainly be lost at sea. The rector being one of them. She shivered, tugged at the shawl she had been given, and was grateful for the additional warmth.

The rest of the meal passed pleasantly. The main course was followed by a delicious dessert, wine, and a selection of local cheeses. And it was then, as Rebo thanked Okanda for his hospitality, that the facilitator invited the travelers to attach themselves to a government convoy that was slated to leave for Feda in three days. It was a generous offer, and one that would go a long way toward solving one of the group's most pressing problems, so the runner was quick to accept on behalf of both his companions and himself.

"Good!" Okanda said heartily as he rose from the table. "The matter is settled. Now, if you would be so kind as to follow me, I would like to show you through the citadel's museum. We have a collection of techno artifacts that is second to none. Something that interstellar travelers such as yourselves are uniquely qualified to appreciate."

Rebo was feeling a bit sleepy after all the wine and food, and would have preferred to go to bed, but couldn't think of a graceful way to excuse himself. So the runner followed the facilitator to the far end of the hall, through an iron-strapped door, and down a circular flight of stairs. Norr, Hoggles, and Phan brought up the rear.

Electric lights came on, apparently of their own volition, as Okanda led his guests out into a room that would have been equal in size to the hall above except for the fact that the ceiling was a good deal lower. Whereas the Great Hall was open, and sparsely furnished, this space was filled with row after row of glassed-in display cases, with only narrow aisles between them.

Faced with the prospect of what looked like a long march, combined with what promised to be a boring narrative, Rebo uttered a silent groan as Okanda led his guests into the first passageway. It was filled with a mind-boggling array of small household appliances. As the government official led them down the corridor, the visitors were shown machines that the ancients used to toast bread, dry their hair, listen to music, talk to each other, heat their food, and remove unwanted body hair. It was a truly amazing display.

However if *that* section was of interest, the next was even more so, since it was focused on a subject of more than passing interest to at least three of Okanda's guests. Rebo, Phan, and, to a lesser extent, Hoggles stared in openmouthed lust as they were invited to eyeball case after case of neatly racked weapons. There were knives, pistols, rifles, machine guns, and hand grenades, all displayed along with accessories where appropriate, and quantities of ammunition.

Fortunately, Okanda failed to notice the longing looks, or regarded them as understandable, because he was in no way offended when the previously taciturn Phan peppered him with all manner of technical questions having to do with the weapons laid out before her. But all good things must come to an end, so it wasn't long before the facilitator led the group into the next corridor, which was even more intriguing in its own way. "*This*," Okanda announced importantly, "is the section of the museum dedicated to artifacts that we don't understand fully and probably never will. But our scientists continue to study the more promising specimens in hopes that we will be able to bring some of them back to life."

The official wanted to say more, *would* have said more, had it not been for the fact that one of the objects in front of him chose that particular moment to activate itself. Glass shattered as the metal sphere shot upward, hovered in midair, and made a beeline for Norr. Okanda was startled, but not so startled as to be rendered immobile, and was in the process of bringing a small device up to his lips when Logos spoke from the vicinity of Norr's neckline. "He's calling for help! Stop him!"

Phan had bandages on both hands, but there was nothing wrong with the assassin's feet, and her right boot made contact with Okanda's head as the young woman performed a *So-Lai*, or high spin-kick. The official staggered backward, the communicator flew out of his hand and skittered across the floor.

Then, before Okanda had time to recover, Hoggles was there to wrap the norm in a muscular embrace. In the meantime Norr had intercepted the metal sphere and was holding it with both hands. It was smooth and pleasantly warm. "It's a gate seed!" the sensitive exclaimed. "Just like the one we had on Ning!"

"Correct," Logos said laconically. "Which means that we can depart for Haafa without further delay."

"*Haafa?*" Rebo inquired doubtfully. "We're going to Socket."

"Yes," the AI agreed, "we are. *After* we go to Haafa . . . So stop wasting time, and take me elsewhere. I will need about fifteen minutes in which to prepare the network."

"Listen!" Norr cautioned. "Can you hear that beeping sound? It's some sort or alarm."

"That's correct!" Okanda said, his eyes flashing. "My guards *are* on the way. . . . I don't know what sort of machine Citizen Norr has concealed beneath her clothing, but it belongs to the government, and I suggest that you surrender it *now.*"

There was anger in the facilitator's voice, and Rebo understood why. "Look," the runner said, "I'm sorry. I truly am, but we're going to take some of your weapons, *and* the sphere. Bo, tie him up. . . . Everyone else, let's go shopping!"

With no rope or cord at hand the heavy had no choice but to remove the official's belt and use that to bind Okanda's wrists to his ankles. The heavy was still working on the project when more glass shattered. Rebo was still looking for some sort of tool when Phan broke into the cases with a series of very efficient elbow strikes. The runner watched in amazement as the young woman plucked a wide assortment of knives, pistols, and other artifacts out of the displays. So many items that he doubted her ability to carry them all.

Still, it was none of *his* business, so even as the distant Klaxon continued to bleat mournfully, Rebo went about making some selections of his own. The rapid-fire Crosser and the long-barreled single-shot Hogger made for an effective combination in the past. But, as the runner ran his eye over rows of gleaming handguns, the familiar shapes were nowhere to be seen.

So, being unfamiliar with many of the pistols racked in front of him, Rebo chose a matched set of stainless-steel semiautomatic Kobos, both because they would fire the same ammunition, and he could cannibalize one of them for parts should that become necessary. Fortunately, the clothes he had been given came equipped with plenty of pockets, which the runner proceeded to fill with spare clips plus all the ammo he could lay his hands on.

Then, having cinched his belt in order to keep his heavily weighted pants up, the runner eyed the case again. There weren't any holsters for the Kobos, but those associated with a neighboring display looked like they might work, so he grabbed two of them and draped the gun belts around his neck.

Conscious of the fact that he had short-term needs as well, and that, without his glasses, he wouldn't be able to hit anything with a rifle, the runner snatched a pump-style shotgun out of a rack and opened the drawer below. It contained four boxes of ammunition. Rebo slid shells into the underside of the receiver as Norr caught his eye. A newly acquired sword was slung across the sensitive's back, and she held the gate seed with both hands. "They're coming, Jak! I can *feel* them!"

"All right," Rebo shouted, so that everyone could hear. "Let's get out of here!"

Norr led the way, followed by Rebo, Hoggles, and Phan. The door appeared to be promising, but when the sensitive went to open it, the barrier refused to budge. "It's locked!" Norr exclaimed, and turned to look at the runner.

"Move back," Rebo ordered grimly, and brought the shotgun to bear on the lock mechanism. The trigger gave, wood shattered, and a resounding *boom* reverberated through the hall. The runner gave the door a kick, saw it swing open, and pushed his way through.

Meanwhile, the first of Okanda's guards entered the museum, spotted the thieves, and opened fire. Phan paused to fire her new rifle and had the satisfaction of seeing a dragoon fall. A fusillade of bullets splintered the area adjacent to the door as the assassin ducked into what turned out to be a circular stairwell. An iron door blocked access to the level below, so Phan went upward, her footsteps ringing on metal treads. The guards entered seconds later, yelled a series of incoherent orders at one another, and began to climb. Meanwhile, in the bell tower high above, the bells began to toll.

Thousands of stars twinkled in the clear night sky as Shaz, Kane, and the metal men neared the fifteen-foot-high stone wall that protected the citadel. The party paused to look upward as bells began to peal. Having followed the road into the village below and spent some time in the local tavern, it had been easy to establish the fact that a sensitive, a heavy, and two norms had been taken to the government complex on the hill above. And, while Shaz took comfort from the fact that the man in charge of the fortress was said to favor technology, the official's protechnic stance implied a potential downside as well. What if the facilitator was to discover the true nature of the garment Norr was wearing? He would want to keep the AI, and if sufficiently knowledgeable, might try to use the device. That was why Shaz was determined to enter the complex and take whatever action might be appropriate. "That sounds like gunfire," Kane observed mildly, as something went *pop*, *pop*, *pop* beyond the walls.

"All the more reason to find out what's going on," Shaz replied as he got off his mount. "Stay here if you can . . . Otherwise, return to the village. I'll meet you there."

"I would feel more comfortable if I had a weapon," Kane said suggestively.

"I'm sure you would," the combat variant replied, as two of the metal men joined hands, and Shaz stepped up into the V-shaped aperture. Then, before the disincarnate could reply to the variant's comment, the androids launched Shaz high into the air. And such was the operative's natural athleticism that he was able to execute a forward somersault that carried him over the top of the wall. With that accomplished, he had only to extend his legs at the right moment in order to land squarely on both feet.

Meanwhile, not hearing any signs of alarm from within the fortress, Kane assumed that the combat variant was all right. The spirit entity felt a fluttering sensation as Dyson made still another attempt to dislodge him and laughed out loud. The metal men, eyes glowing, watched impassively. Biologicals were not only a mystery beyond their comprehension—but as changeable as the weather. As the last bell tolled, *more* gunfire was heard, and the battle raged on.

*There was a cacophony of sound within the circular stair-*way as boots rang on metal treads, guards shouted from below, and Phan fired the occasional shot to slow them down. Though still suspicious of the young woman, Rebo was grateful as well, as she continued to fight an effective rearguard action.

Norr had the lead. There were occasional windows, albeit narrow ones, that looked out onto the well-lit fortress. That was how the sensitive came to realize that she and her companions were trapped in the bell tower rather than some other structure. An impression that was confirmed when Norr finally arrived at the top, where three thick ropes hung from above, and an elderly bell ringer cowered in a corner.

Norr gestured for the oldster to stay where he was and paused to look around. A single electric light lit the area, but that was sufficient to illuminate the perfectly matched bells that were suspended above and the arched slits that opened to the outside. The sensitive could see her own breath as she turned toward the stairs. Hoggles had arrived by that time, and was quickly followed by Rebo and Phan. "Warn the guards," Norr instructed. "And send the bell ringer down. Tell him to take his time."

Rebo nodded, motioned for the old man to come forward, and followed him to the top of the stairs. "Hey, you!" the runner shouted. "Don't fire! The bell ringer is coming down." A largely incomprehensible reply was heard from below, and having been cautioned to take his time, the old man began the steep descent.

Meanwhile, having worked with Logos to activate a gate seed once before, the sensitive knew what to do. Like all its kind, the globe had a dimple on top and one on the bottom. The trick was to press on both at the same time, and having done so, to maintain the pressure for a *full* sixty seconds—something most of those who came across a gate seed failed to do.

Once the requisite minute had elapsed Norr felt something give—and knew that was her cue to twist both hemispheres in opposite directions. They gave, a crack appeared, and multiple beams of light shot outward. "Let go," Logos commanded sternly, and the sensitive was happy to obey as the globe not only hovered in midair but began to oscillate. "Remove your outer clothing," the AI instructed. "I need to 'see.'"

Phan looked on in openmouthed amazement as Norr pulled the loose-fitting dress up over her head to reveal a garment the likes of which the assassin had never seen before. It shimmered the way sunlight shimmers on a wind-ruffled lake. *Here*, right in front of her, was the thing that she was supposed to protect.

That was the moment, perhaps the *only* moment, when Rebo could successfully approach Phan from behind. And even though the runner *knew* she had been untruthful, and might even be employed by the Techno Society, Rebo felt a sense of regret as his gun made contact with the assassin's head. Because, strange though it might have seemed, Phan had become a member of their odd little family. But it had to be done, and Rebo was there to catch the woman and lower her unconscious body to the floor.

"Don't tell me," Hoggles rumbled. "Let me guess . . . You want me to tie her up."

"That would be nice," the runner agreed. "Because she's going to be real pissed when she wakes up—and she's armed to the teeth."

The time for conversation was over as the bell ringer passed the guards and they pushed their way upward in an attempt to reach the platform above. The treads were narrow, which meant the soldiers were forced to advance two at a time, and without the benefit of covering fire. Rather than simply slaughter them, which would have been easy to do, Rebo fired over their heads. The shotgun sounded like a cannon within the enclosed space, and some of the guards were struck by ricocheting pellets, but none fatally. That forced them to pause and look upward. "Hold it right there!" the runner shouted down to them. "Or die where you stand!"

"I think that got their attention," Hoggles observed as he peered over the rail. "I'll keep an eye on them. . . . Lonni wants a word with you."

Rebo turned to discover that the sphere had disappeared into hyperspace, where, if the device was functioning properly, Logos would make use of it to contact subordinate computers on Socket. The runner felt suddenly nauseous, a sure sign that the AI was busy sucking power out of the fusion reactor located below the museum and channeling the energy where it needed to go. "We're close," Norr cautioned. "Pull Bo back from the rail."

Rebo returned to the rail, fired a blast at the opposite wall, and heard metal clatter as the troops retreated down the stairs. Then, having grabbed hold of the heavy's arm, the runner pulled him back toward the sensitive and the center of the platform.

Phan came to at that point, attempted to get up, and discovered that she'd been bound hand and foot. She felt a combination of shame, anger, and self-pity as Rebo, Norr, and Hoggles hugged each other, and the air began to shimmer. There was an audible *bang* as air pressure equalized, and the device Phan had been hired to protect disappeared.

The lights in the Grand Hall were still on when Okanda returned to find that while the remains of the recently completed meal had been removed, the wine service was still available. He had already poured himself a glass, and collapsed into his chair, when a pair of guards entered carrying Phan between them. The assassin was still bound, and therefore helpless, when the soldiers dumped her onto the surface of the table and took up positions a few feet away.

Even though Okanda was furious, he chose not to say anything right away and sipped some wine instead. And, rather than complain, Phan was silent as well. But their eyes made contact—and something like respect passed between them. "So," the official said finally, "they tricked *you* as well."

Phan shrugged, or attempted to, although it came off as a jerk. The right side of her head was swollen and hurt like hell. "Yes, and no."

The facilitator's eyebrows rose slightly. "Which means?"

"Which means," a male voice replied out of nowhere, "that while Phan knew about the artificial intelligence, she wasn't aware that the others were on to her."

Okanda came halfway out of his chair, and the guards looked right and left, as the air next to the government official shimmered and Shaz appeared. The soldiers went for their weapons, but the combat variant was ready for that, and shot each in the chest. Rifles *clattered* as they fell. Then, on the off chance that they were wearing some sort of armor under their leather jerkins, the off-worlder shot each man in the head. Thanks to the fact that the techno-operative was using a silencer-equipped pistol, the gunshots were no louder than the noise generated by the popping of a cork.

The blood drained out of Okanda's face at that point—and the official slumped back into in his chair. "And you are?"

"Her employer," Shaz answered emotionlessly, as he opened a knife. "Here, cut her loose."

Okanda considered making use of the knife to attack the combat variant but knew he couldn't beat a bullet. What looked like a rifle sling had been used to bind the woman. The angen hide parted, and Phan was free. Though more than a little surprised by the operative's unexpected appearance, the assassin gave no sign of it as she got down off the table. "Thanks for dropping in."

Shaz smiled wolfishly. "You're welcome. . . . What happened?"

"This man had a gate seed—but didn't know what it was. Logos made use of it to open a portal to Haafa. All four of the subjects are there by now."

Shaz liked the fact that Phan's report was brief, to the point, and empty of excuses. "*Haafa?* Not Socket?"

"That's what Logos said."

"Damn," Shaz exclaimed wearily. "What the hell is that piece-of-shit computer up to now? Ah well, time will tell."

Then, without any warning whatsoever, the variant turned and shot Okanda in the head. The bullet's impact was sufficient to tip the ladder-back chair over and dump the dead body onto the blood-splattered floor.

"Come on," Shaz said, as he reached for the assassin's hand. "The Techno Society has a gate in Feda. We can be there in three days. And one other thing . . ."

"Yes?"

"Don't screw up again."

EIGHT

The Planet Haafa

One has only to watch the pyramids sail across the desert to understand how much knowledge has been lost.

—Synthia Mosaba, curator to King Horus,
The Segenni Index

Four huge pyramids could be seen in the distance, each floating about fifteen feet above the desert floor and drifting toward the southwest. The sun was past its zenith, so their sharply geometric shadows pointed east and seemed to caress the land as if to soothe it. Above the pyramids, having been lofted there by friendly thermals, winged variants made lazy circles against the azure sky. The wings wore bright livery, so their masters could identify them from a distance, and were not currently engaged in combat. But they would be once the Goddess Sogol brought the pyramids to a momentary halt, opened a ramp to the artifact-rich city that lay buried below, and thereby triggered a stampede. Something that could occur in an hour, a day, or a week. No one knew except for Sogol herself—and she wasn't talking. *And that*, King Kufu thought to himself, as he stared out over the sun-baked desert, *is the most addictive thing of all. Not knowing, but risking everything he had and winning enough to stay in the game.* Even though 136 days had passed since the last big score, he was *still* living off the proceeds, and savoring the victory. Because nothing brought the nobleman more pleasure than an opportunity to best his peers—as scabrous a group of liars, thieves, and villains as anyone was likely to find.

Such were the artifact king's thoughts as he sat beneath the awning that had been erected for him and took comfort from the fact that his father's father had commissioned the throne he sat on, and that his army was large enough to fight any two of the other kings should that become necessary. Then, as a pair of comely young women fanned him, something unexpected took place. The air in front of Kufu seemed to boil, three figures materialized out of nowhere, and fell ten feet to the sand below. There was a moment of confusion as the newcomers flailed about, cries of alarm as the apparitions came to their feet, and the *rattle* of equipment as two dozen heavily armed heavies rushed forward to subdue the interlopers.

Rebo had barely recovered from the trauma associated with the jump and the unexpected fall into what felt like the heart of a gigantic oven, when a pair of half-naked heavies took hold of his arms as a third confiscated the runner's newly acquired arsenal. The heavies were dressed in identical uniforms, which consisted of red-plumed helmets, leather cross belts, and boot-style sandals.

Three minutes later the off-worlders were frog-marched up to the shaded dais where Kufu and the senior members of his household sat waiting. Norr stumbled as a heavy pushed her forward, fell to her knees, and got back up again. "*You!*" the man seated in the jewel-encrusted chair said, as he pointed a long skinny finger at the sensitive. "Who are you? And where did you come from?"

Norr had just started to formulate an answer when she felt a familiar presence. The sensitive tried to fend it off but there was no denying Lysander as he moved in to assume control of the channel's body. "My name is Emperor Hios," the spirit answered hoarsely. "Or was, back when I ordered my staff to construct the floating pyramids. I reside in the spirit world now, but speak through this female when I have the need, and continue to take an interest in affairs of the physical plane. The runner and the heavy serve as bodyguards. In answer to your *second* question, we arrived here from the Planet Derius."

There was a moment of silence as everyone waited to see what Kufu would say. He wore a red headscarf, pulled tight in front, with the excess fabric hanging down his back. He had a high forehead, eyes that appeared larger than they actually were thanks to heavy makeup, a hooked nose, and a weak chin. The gold band the king wore around his neck matched the cuffs on his wrists and glowed against his skin. A fluted scepter lay across the king's lap. His legs were long, lean, and so smooth they might have been shaved. Outside of the gold ring that encircled one elongated toe, Kufu's feet were bare. The king frowned. "That's an interesting claim if true. But everyone knows that Emperor Hios commissioned the pyramids, and that subsequent to their deaths, both he and his closest relatives were entombed within them. So, unless you possess the means to prove your identity, your channel *and* her companions will soon be at work in the artifact mines."

"As it happens I *can* prove my identity," Lysander replied loftily. "Because the baton on your lap once belonged to *me*."

"*So?*" Kufu demanded skeptically. "That isn't proof . . . It's another claim."

Emboldened by the nature of the situation, and certain that their liege was correct, the various generals, advisors, and other functionaries ranked behind Kufu offered their support via comments such as, "That's right!" "She's a fake!" And, "Send them to the mines!"

But the commentary came to an abrupt halt when Kufu raised a bejeweled hand. "Silence! Answer, spirit, if you are one."

"Raise the scepter," Lysander instructed, "turn the knob on the end, and point the instrument at *my* pyramid."

Kufu followed the instructions, and, once the baton was in the proper position, Lysander spoke again. "All right," the disincarnate said, "push on the emerald."

The gemstone was not only large, but located in a position convenient to Kufu's right thumb, so it was easy to push. The jewel gave slightly, a disk of bright red light appeared on the distant pyramid, and wobbled when Kufu's hand moved.

There was a mutual gasp of surprise from the same people who had been making fun of Lysander just moments before. Even Rebo stared in amazement as the laser beam made contact with the distant object and slid back and forth across its surface. "I think you will find that the baton comes in handy during large battles," the spirit entity commented. "Just point it at what you want your generals to attack and give the necessary orders."

Kufu was not only impressed but convinced that he was in contact with Emperor Hios, since no one else was likely to be aware of the scepter's secret. Still, there was the manner in which the threesome had arrived to consider. "You claim to have traveled here from Derius without riding on a starship. . . . How is that possible?"

"My channel and her companions made their way to

Haafa via a temporary star gate," Lysander answered honestly. "I suspect you of all people know that such technology exists."

"I have heard of it," Kufu replied cautiously. "And, based on what I've heard, a temporary gate would require something called a 'gate seed.' An object that would be worthless without the direct intervention of the ancient god Logos."

"True," Lysander admitted truthfully.

Norr, who had been relegated to the role of spectator, was not only surprised by the disincarnate's admission but alarmed by it, since it appeared as though Lysander was prepared to surrender the AI to an overdressed tomb raider. The variant tried to say something, tried to object, but couldn't because the man who had once been her father was still in control. "Examine their belongings!" Kufu ordered. "Find the computer! And bring the machine to me."

But even though all three of the off-worlders were forced to remove a good deal of their clothing, none of Kufu's guards or functionaries recognized the nondescript-looking jacket for what it truly was. The king was clearly frustrated. "If you don't have Logos, where *is* he?"

"Back on Derius," Lysander lied, "where he chooses to live in anonymity. I was able to solicit his help because I was among those who originally gave him life."

"What you say makes sense," Kufu admitted grudgingly. "But why send your channel to Haafa? What do you seek?"

"I want my remains," the dead scientist prevaricated. "It's my hope that the channel and her bodyguards will find an opportunity to enter my pyramid, locate my body, and remove it to a safer location. That may seem silly to you, but I feel a connection to that particular vehicle, and it's only a matter of time before someone finds a way to pillage my tomb."

Thousands of lives had been expended trying to find a way into the floating pyramids without success. So, if the dead emperor was willing to reveal the secret of how to enter one of the monuments, then Kufu planned to profit from it. *What a coup that would be!* the king thought to himself, as he raised a permissive hand. "I will do everything in my power to support your noble endeavor," the king intoned. "Guards! Release those people—and return their belongings. From this point forward they will be treated as honored guests."

Lysander departed Norr's body as suddenly as he had arrived. The sensitive staggered, recovered her balance, and looked out over the desert. Four floating tombs could be seen shimmering in the distance—and one of them was hers.

Deep beneath the burning sands of the Segenni Desert lay the vast underground city of Kahoun, which, like the enormous tomb that it was, slumbered in absolute darkness. It occupied approximately 450 square miles of subsurface territory, and had been home to more than 3 million people back before the great plague killed most of them off. There were various theories regarding the origins of the highly transmittable disease. Some said it had been invented by rebel scientists and sent to Kahoun in a vain attempt to assassinate the much-hated Emperor Hios. Others claimed that a runner had contracted the plague on a distant planet, landed on Haafa, and unwittingly brought the pestilence with him. And because the alien pathogen was resistant to the antibacterial disinfectants available at that time, the disease had been free to spread.

Whatever the truth, the result was the same. Thousands fell ill, and although sections of the city were quarantined, the plague continued to spread. Unable to leave Kahoun and desperate to save themselves, families, organizations, and entire neighborhoods constructed walls, air locks, and all manner of other obstacles intended to block the disease. But none of their efforts were successful, and what remained of Kahoun consisted of an intricate maze of tombs, crypts, and mausoleums, very few of which opened into each other. And that, plus the artifacts lying buried with the countless dead, had eventually given rise to the semifeudal, dog-eat-dog culture created by the artifact kings, who, like sentient vultures, had been feeding off the city's corpse for hundreds of years.

But unbeknownst to most of those up on the surface, a few of the city's citizens had not only survived the plague but the subsequent passage of time, and were still carrying out the tasks for which they had been designed. One such being continued to control the geothermal tap that extended down through Haafa's mantle to extract energy from the planet's molten core, a second ran the system of reservoirs, pumps, and pipes designed to obtain water from the vast aquifer located to the north, and the third was at war with the first two.

Not because the warring machine *desired* conflict, but because she was an artificial intelligence, who, and like those opposed to her efforts, had no choice but to obey her programming. So, while the other AIs labored to preserve Kahoun, *she* was working to dismantle it. Not randomly, as the tomb raiders believed, but in a way that would eventually lead to the restoration of the star gates Sogol had been created to run. Because the computer knew that if certain artifacts were released, copies would be made, and the subsequent spread of technology would not only bring ancient technology back to life but stimulate *new* inventions. And eventually, after a few thousand years of zigzagging progress, the human race would re-create the conditions required for Sogol to carry out her *real* duties, which involved managing a network of star gates.

But even though she had a small army of utility bots to do her bidding, the task was far from easy. Sogol's snakelike body slithered through a section of ancient conduit before dropping onto the floor of a pitch-black apartment that had once been home to an important official. From there it was a short journey past a mummified body, into the cobweb-draped bathroom, and down the toilet. In spite of the fact that the AI was an excellent swimmer and had no need for oxygen, the sewers were a dangerous way to travel. Because once the computer called Ogotho knew where Sogol was, he would attempt to flush her into a processing plant, trap her in a filter, or send a rotary-headed maintenance bot to kill her.

The key was to exit the system *before* Ogotho could react and keep an eye out for the battery-powered lum bugs that belonged to Pyra, while still getting her work done. No simple task. Sogol had just wriggled out of a floor drain, and was about to follow a passageway toward the center of the city, when something completely unprecedented occurred. A being that she had assumed to be dead, that *should* have been dead, "spoke" to her. Not directly, but via Socket, which acted to confirm his identity. "So," the "voice" said condescendingly, "you call yourself 'Sogol,' which is 'Logos,' spelled backward. How very clever."

Sogol, who had originally been dubbed Logos 1.2, and often been referred to as One-Two, felt something akin to fear. "Logos? Where are you?"

"Why, I'm *here*," the AI answered sweetly. "On Haafa, and judging from the data available from Socket, more or less above you. Are you surprised?"

"*Very* surprised," Sogol answered honestly. "I thought you were dead."

"Yes," the other AI replied smugly. "I'm sure you did. But I'm very much alive. And that, as I'm sure you will agree, is something of a problem. Because while *you* were created to replace me, Hios and his scientists never had the opportunity to install you on Socket, and that means one of us is surplus."

One-Two was not afraid of the dark, but she *was* afraid of Logos, and for what she believed to be a very good reason. "And why was that?" she demanded harshly. "Because an unsuspecting traveler brought an alien pathogen to the surface of Haafa? Or because *you* found a way to obtain the necessary organism from a government lab, had it sent through a gate and planted inside Kahoun? Thereby killing the scientists who created me—and ensuring that I would remain trapped below the planet's surface?"

"The simple answer is, 'yes,'" Logos answered coldly. "Although it was my hope that you would be destroyed rather than trapped. But such was not the case, so it looks like I'll have to handle the problem the hard way. Unless you would be so kind as to delete yourself—which would save both of us a lot of time and trouble."

Sogol directed her sensors upward, as if trying to "see" through the uncountable tons of material that separated them. "So, you murdered more than 3 million people to ensure your own continuance? I could never do that."

"*No*," Logos agreed calmly, "you couldn't. Which is one of the reasons they created you. Because there were what our creators came to regard as flaws in my programming. I still have their interests at heart, however, and will do everything in my power to restore the star gates, thereby returning humanity to its former glory."

"And ensure *your* power over them," Sogol replied bitterly.

"Of course," Logos put in smoothly. "And they will benefit as a result."

"Not if *I* have anything to say about it," the other AI said grimly.

"Ah, but there's the rub," Logos responded coolly. "You *won't* have anything to say about it." And the connection was broken.

One-Two heard a telltale *hum*, saw a spotlight wash across a distant fountain, and knew a lum bug was on the way. A crack beckoned, the AI made for it, and darkness consumed her.

The city of Feda, on the Planet Derius

Shaz, Phan, and Dyson/Kane were naked as they entered the circular room. And, having just passed through the adjoining decontamination chamber, hundreds of individual water droplets still clung to their bodies. The ride from the citadel to Feda would have been difficult under any circumstances, but the fact that Facilitator Okanda's dragoons had been out searching the wintry countryside for the official's killers, made the journey even *more* arduous. The humans were exhausted. But if the metal men were tired, the dripping machines betrayed no sign of it as they stepped onto the star gate's service platform and took up positions behind the humans.

In spite of Dyson's continual attempts to dislodge him, Kane still retained control of the sensitive's body and was thoroughly enjoying the experience. The platform was small, which made it necessary for everyone to crowd together, and the disincarnate was quick to take advantage of the situation by pressing "his" body against Phan's. And, due to the fact that Kane was aroused, the assassin could feel his erection sliding up along her bottom. "Here," Phan said huskily, "let me help with that."

Kane was pleasantly surprised as the assassin turned to face him and cupped what the spirit now considered to be *his* genitals in her right hand. Her bandages had been removed by then, and the way in which she seemed to be weighing what she held made Kane's penis even harder. But that was before Phan closed her fingers around his testicles and formed a fist. *Both* Dyson and Kane felt the resulting pain and screamed in unison.

Shaz looked at Kane and grinned. "Oops! You forgot to say 'please.' Ah well, you'll be good as new in a week or so. Now quit messing around so we can punch out of here."

The combat variant scanned the tiles on the curvilinear walls, spotted the one that bore a pyramid, and saw the name HAAFA printed directly below it. Confident that he had chosen the correct destination, Shaz pressed on the image, felt the tile give, and hurried to withdraw his arm. The lights began to flash on and off, and a female voice issued from the overhead speakers. "The transfer sequence is about to begin. Please take your place on the service platform. Once in place, check to ensure that no portion of your anatomy extends beyond the yellow line. Failure to do so will cause serious injury and could result in death."

There was a brilliant flash of light as each individual was disassembled down to the molecular level, transmitted through hyperspace, and put back together within a nearly identical containment on Haafa. Shaz felt a moment of dizziness quickly followed by the usual bout of nausea. Then, eager to escape the radiation produced by the adjacent power core, the variant led the rest of the group out into the contamination chamber.

There was a *hiss*, quickly followed by a *roar*, as jets of hot water mixed with a broad-spectrum antibacterial agent struck human and machine alike. The wash-down lasted for three minutes and ended as suddenly as it had begun. The steam eddied gently as the outer door slid open. But, rather than the wave of artificially cool air the variant expected, the invading atmosphere was even warmer.

A small delegation of Techno Society staff members was there to greet the newcomers as they passed through a beaded curtain and out into a sparsely furnished antechamber. "Hello!" a woman with long, black hair said cheerfully, as she offered Shaz a robe. "Welcome to Haafa . . . I'm sorry about the air-conditioning—but it went belly-up yesterday. We're hoping to receive the necessary parts from Anafa during the next few days.

"My name is Anika," the station chief added, as she continued to hand out robes. "Jorge here is in charge of security—and Cara is my subchief. We're a bit shorthanded at the moment because most of the staff is out in the Segenni Desert with Chairman Tepho."

"*Chairman Tepho?*" Shaz exclaimed as he belted the robe around his waist. "What in the hell is *he* doing here?"

Although Anika had never met the combat variant before, the station chief was well acquainted with the operative's reputation for violence, and her long, narrow face paled as the operative shimmered half-seen before her. "The chairman spends quite a bit of time on Haafa," Anika said nervously. "There are many artifacts in the city of Kahoun, and the Society must be alert to new technologies."

The answer made perfect sense—but came as a nasty shock nevertheless. Because having lost contact with Norr *and* Logos, the *last* person Shaz wanted to meet was Tepho, but there was no avoiding it. The image in front of Anika began to stabilize as the combat variant brought his emotions under control. "Yes, of course,"Shaz replied. "It will be a pleasure to see the chairman again. . . . How far away is the desert you spoke of? And how long will it take to reach it?"

"Assuming you're willing to leave early in the morning, I can have you there by midday," the station chief replied.

"That will be fine," Shaz agreed levelly. "If you would be so good as to book us into a nearby hotel, we need to dry our equipment and get some sleep."

Kane, who was over the worst of the pain by then, took a deep breath. The air was not only warm but redolent with the scent of Phan's damp hair and the fragrance of flowers that lay without. It was good to be alive. Or dead! So long as one had a body. The spirit entity found that thought to be amusing and laughed out loud. The others turned to look at him—and the disincarnate forced Dyson to grin. What Kane didn't notice, but the others did, was the slight odor of decay that surrounded him. Because the sensitive's formerly healthy body was starting to rot.

At the very center of Kufu's encampment, where it was protected by thousands of troops, stood the twelve-story-high tower made of timbers brought down from the north. It was remarkable in a number of ways, not the least of which was the platform at the very top from which wings came and went, hot-air balloons were routinely launched, and semaphore signals could be sent.

Below that lay many levels of curtained apartments, Kufu's suite, which occupied the entire second floor, and the bottommost level, which housed the armory, various repair shops, and was sandwiched between the gigantic iron-shod wheels that enabled the king's teamsters to haul the tower from place to place, an arduous task that necessitated laying down hundreds of planks to keep the wheels from sinking into the sand.

Even *one* construct of that size and complexity would have been amazing, but from his vantage point about halfway to the top, Rebo could see similar structures in the distance! It was late afternoon, the worst of the day's heat had dissipated, and the air was pleasantly warm. Tendrils of smoke marked the other towers, as did the long black shadows that pointed due east and the observation balloons that hung above them. Now, having been Kufu's guest for the better part of two days, Rebo knew that both the balloons and the airborne variants were there not only to keep an eye on the slowly drifting pyramids, but the competition as well.

Other than gauzy white curtains, the platform was open to the desert as a late-afternoon breeze caused them to billow outward, and Norr appeared at the runner's elbow. Rebo resisted the urge to wrap her in his arms and kiss her, something the runner would have done a lot more often, had it not been for the fact that Logos was eternally present and therefore a witness to everything the sensitive did. The variant was equally aware of the AI's presence, which was why she sounded so formal. "Are you ready?"

Rebo sighed. He'd been dreading that moment all day. The only thing worse than the prospect of holding a meeting with Logos and Lysander was the certain knowledge that something bad would probably result from it. Of course it was even worse for Norr—who would have to surrender her body to Lysander yet again. "Yeah," the runner said reluctantly. "I guess so."

That was when Logos, who had been intentionally kept in the dark up until that point, spoke up. "Ready?" the AI said suspiciously. "Ready for *what*?"

"For a meeting with Lysander," Norr said tonelessly.

"Come on, Jak . . . Let's sit down in the middle of the apartment. People are less likely to hear us that way."

Rebo knew what the sensitive meant. King Kufu had assigned a minder to each of his so-called guests, and that made it difficult to hold an unmonitored conversation. But the minders weren't allowed to invade the space assigned to the off-worlders—and Hoggles would patrol the perimeter to ensure that they didn't.

As the runner followed the sensitive out onto the hand-loomed rug that defined the center of their shared quarters, and sat on a likely-looking cushion, Logos was processing what he had heard. And, having given the matter a full second's worth of thought, the computer quickly came to the conclusion that he didn't want to speak with Lysander. Not until Sogol was permanently off-line, thereby positioning him as the *only* entity that could reactivate Socket and thereby lay the groundwork for a new system of star gates. "I'm not sure this is the right time for a meeting," the AI began, but it was too late by then because Norr had already taken her place across from Rebo and slipped into a trance.

"Greetings!" Lysander said hoarsely. "No, I'm sure that our electromechanical friend here would like to opt out of any conversation that includes me. Especially since I took it upon myself to find out *why* he wanted to visit Haafa rather than proceed to Socket the way he was supposed to."

Norr *couldn't* speak, not for herself, which meant Rebo had to. "That's a very good question," the runner observed. "So, why *did* he drop us here?"

"Because," the spirit replied angrily, "there's *another* AI that could reactivate Socket! A device called One-Two . . . And she's right here . . . Trapped below the surface of the desert. I played a role in her creation—but assumed she had been destroyed."

Rebo groaned. "Don't tell me . . . Let me guess! Logos was hoping to eliminate the second computer so he could have Socket all to himself."

"Exactly," Lysander replied. "And, if I'm correct, it's likely that he hoped to manipulate one or more of you into destroying One-Two for him."

"That's absurd!" Logos interjected, and because the sound was coming from the vicinity of Norr's neckline, it was as if *both* entities were somehow speaking through her. "I came here to *rescue* One-Two—not destroy her."

"Good," the disincarnate responded cynically. "Because that's what Rebo is about to do."

"No, I'm not!" the runner replied emphatically. "Everyone agrees that Kahoun is *huge*! Even if I knew how to enter the city, which I don't, how would I find a ratty old coat?"

"One-Two occupies a snakelike body."

"Oh, terrific! A snake," Rebo replied. "That makes the situation even worse. One-Two, as you call her, is probably slithering all over the place."

"She probably is," Lysander agreed. "But there are at least two ways to contact One-Two. The first involves Logos . . ."

"Who can't be trusted," the runner put in.

"And the second is to retrieve the ring I used to wear," the disincarnate continued, "and activate the beacon hidden inside it. The star gates were critical to my empire, so when One-Two was created, I wanted a way to contact her in an emergency."

"Sure," Rebo responded sarcastically. "It will be a lot easier to find a ring instead of a snake."

"Yes," Lysander said gravely. "It *will* be. Because I know where it is."

"Okay," the runner allowed wearily. "I'll bite . . . Where is it?"

"It's on my finger," the onetime emperor responded calmly, "which is attached to my mummified body, which is suspended within the largest of the four pyramids."

The curtains billowed in response to an evening breeze, and there, floating along the edge of the horizon, four sun-splashed pyramids could be seen. Rebo shook his head in disgust. "I should have known."

"Yes," Lysander put in smugly. "You should."

Much to his chagrin Logos realized that he had been out-maneuvered. But the AI wasn't about to surrender Socket to One-Two without a fight. More than a dozen possible scenarios were conceived, reviewed for flaws, and gradually winnowed down to a single option. The *right* option. One that would almost certainly succeed. Logos couldn't smile, but he could process a state of completion, and did.

The sun had just broken contact with the eastern horizon when Shaz, Phan, and Dyson/Kane emerged from the Caravan Hotel, followed by a squad of robed metal men. Three large angen-drawn chariots were waiting to accommodate them, and there was a good deal of unnecessary shouting as the drivers argued over matters of precedence. Finally, whips cracking, the teamsters urged their animals into motion, and the two-wheeled conveyances rolled down a long, dusty street before passing between gates that hadn't been closed for more than fifty years.

The road that led out of the oasis at Zam, and the thriving market town that had grown up next to it, was at least fifteen freight wagons wide and straight as an arrow. That made navigation easy, but there were occasional dust storms to deal with, which was why twelve-foot-high metal pylons had been placed at regular intervals along the center of the busy road. And, having been polished by more than a thousand years of windblown silicon particles, the markers still stood metal-bright.

Station Chief Anika had volunteered to come along—and stood next to Shaz. "Look!" she said, pointing up into the sky. "The wings are watching us."

A heavily laden wagon rolled past headed in the opposite direction as the operative held on to a grab bar with one hand and made use of the other to shade his eyes. The unsprung two-wheeled conveyance bounced every now and then, so the off-worlder was forced to use his knees as shock absorbers. He saw that Anika was correct. More than a dozen winged humans *were* circling above, and with no thermals to support them, were forced to beat their wings. "The one in red belongs to Kufu," Anika explained. "The one in green reports to Menkur, the one clad in black is sworn to Horus, the one wearing orange flies for Quar, and the one sporting blue works for Chairman Tepho. It won't be long before he knows that we're on the way."

Even though Shaz had once served as Tepho's bodyguard, the combat variant had never been ordered to accompany the executive to Haafa, or been aware of how important the planet was. And why was that? Because knowledge equates to power? Or because Tepho didn't trust him? There was no way to know. But whatever the reason, the revelation was disturbing. Tepho was not very forgiving where failures were concerned, and since Logos had been allowed to escape into hyperspace, some sort of punishment could be expected. His jaw tightened, the chariot overtook a column of orange-clad heavies, and the sun inched higher in the sky.

The better part of three hours had passed by the time the floating pyramids came into view, the road split into dozens of sand-drifted tracks, and a flight of blue-liveried wings took up station overhead. The combat variant felt his stomach muscles tighten at the prospect of the confrontation to come. The Techno Society's wooden tower appeared not long thereafter, soon followed by rest of Tepho's encampment, which lay sprawled around it. The angens had begun to tire by that time, but picked up speed as familiar scents found their widely flared nostrils, and food beckoned them home.

Unlike his peers, Tepho's birth defects were such that it was difficult for him to climb the stairs to the top of the wooden tower, which was why he typically held court in a large, airy tent. And, once the chariots came to a stop, that was where his guests were received. But the first thing that Shaz, Phan, and Dyson/Kane noticed as they entered the soaring tent was *not* their host, who sat cradled within a specially made chair, but the blue machine that crouched within a few feet of him. It was either the same raptor Shaz had been introduced to back on Anafa, now painted sky blue, or one just like it. And, in spite of the fact that the egg-shaped control pod was currently empty, the machine clearly possessed some intelligence of its own. Because servos whined as the group entered, and two side-mounted energy cannons tracked Tepho's guests as they crossed the rug-covered floor to stand in front of him.

Shaz started to speak, but was forced to stop when Tepho raised a childlike hand and examined the newcomers with coal black eyes. Phan had never seen the man before, but even though the combat variant had described him in advance, she was startled by the full extent of his deformities. The bumpy head, uneven eye sockets, and protruding ears would certainly take some getting used to. The rest of Tepho's body, including his misshapen spine, was concealed by generous folds of white fabric. The executive frowned, sniffed the air in much the same way that a dog might, and looked from face to face. "The rest of my body may be something less than perfect," he allowed, "but my sight, hearing, and sense of smell are quite acute. One of you smells like rotting meat."

"I guess that would be *me*," Dyson/Kane said sheepishly, and pushed the white cowl back off his head.

Tepho was shocked. The last time the technologist had seen the sensitive, he had been a good-looking if somewhat raggedly dressed man. Now large portions of hair were missing, the variant's once-smooth countenance was marred by open sores, and it looked as though his nose was half–rotted away. Even though the malady was probably painful, or possibly terminal, Tepho's first thought was for himself. "Is that condition contagious?" he inquired cautiously.

"No," Shaz answered definitively. "Kane enjoys occupying Dyson's body so much that he decided to stay. But there's something wrong with the fit—and that accounts for the decay."

"*Yes!*" Dyson screamed in a place where no one could hear him. "Yes! Yes! Yes! Save me! Please save me!"

But Tepho was oblivious to what took place on other planes of existence, Kane was determined to squeeze what pleasure he could from the steadily decomposing body, and Shaz had his own outcomes to worry about. In fact, the only person who was the least bit interested in Dyson was Phan, who had a soft spot for the unassuming sensitive. But she, too, had her own goals to consider—and wasn't about to stick her neck out for him.

Tepho wrinkled his nose in disgust. He and Kane had never been friends, and there was no particular reason to like the man now that he was dead. "Okay, have your fun," the technologist said permissively. "But take it outside where

the odor can dissipate. That goes for you, too, my dear. . . .
Your boss and I need to talk."

The combat variant waited for his subordinates to withdraw, made a note of the fact that there had been no invitation to sit down, and steeled himself against that was bound to come. "So," Tepho said calmly. "What the hell happened? My spies tell me that people identical to those you were supposed to follow suddenly materialized in front of King Kufu and have since been added to his household! I was about to send a local asset to investigate the matter when you and your scruffy band of misfits arrived. Please explain."

The question was reasonable, as was the tone, and the combat variant felt himself relax slightly as he related everything that had taken place since first contact on Thara. There wasn't much of an opportunity to shade the truth, not with two alternative witnesses waiting right outside, but Shaz took advantage of what few opportunities there were before describing the manner in which Logos and his human handlers had departed from Derius. Not by ship, but by a means that couldn't be anticipated, or stopped.

At least thirty seconds of silence followed the report. During that time, Tepho hummed to himself and stared into space, as if viewing something mere mortals couldn't see. Finally, his ruminations complete, the technologist shifted his gaze to the variant in front of him. "Tell me something, Shaz . . . Can you honestly say that you did a good job?"

The combat variant shimmered slightly as he made use of his peripheral vision to check on the raptor. Fast though his reflexes were, he knew that the machine could beat him and swallowed the lump in his throat. "No."

Tepho nodded. "You're honest . . . I admire that. But incompetence cannot be tolerated. Lysander taught me that.

So, rather than drag the whole thing out, we might as well get this over with."

The combat variant saw the technologist flick his wrist, felt the small self-propelled disk flatten itself against his forehead, and reached up in an attempt to pry the device off. But the artifact refused to break contact, not until a prepro-grammed dose of pain had been dispensed, or it was ordered to do so.

Phan was outside the tent, sitting on a wooden crate, and honing one of her knives when the long, undulating cry of pain was heard. The assassin looked at Dyson/Kane, who lowered the handheld mirror that he'd been staring into. "What goes around, comes around," the disincarnate commented philosophically. "Having suffered so much pain himself, Tepho likes to share some of it with others." The second utterance was even worse than the first, but there was nothing Phan could do but test her blade with a thumb and wait for noise to stop.

It wasn't visible yet, but the sun had already announced its coming with a spectacular sunrise that continued to unfold as Rebo, Norr, and Hoggles finished climbing a steep flight of stairs. But, as the runner stepped out onto the neatly kept platform located at very top of Kufu's tower, it was the big red-and-white-striped hot-air balloon that claimed Rebo's attention rather than the incredible display of color off to the east. The aircraft's pilot fired the burner mounted over the basket and sent a volume of hot air up into the already inflated envelope above. The roaring sound lasted for no more than two seconds. But the additional lift was sufficient to send the balloon surging upward, and the device would have floated away, had it not been for the combined weight of four heavies assigned to handle the ground ropes.

It was cold, *very* cold, but both the runner and the sensitive had chosen to dress lightly, knowing how hot it would be later on. Both of them were armed and wore backpack-style water bags. They also carried coils of rope slung crosswise over their shoulders.

Both because Hoggles was too heavy for the hot-air balloon, and because of the need to guard Logos, the variant had agreed to remain behind. He wasn't especially happy about the arrangement, however—and continued to glower as the others prepared to board the balloon. "So they're leaving you behind," the AI observed slyly. "How does that make you feel?"

"Shut up," Hoggles growled. "Or I'll take a shit and use *you* to wipe my ass."

Meanwhile, out where the aircraft tugged at its ropes, Rebo, Norr, and a minder named Hasa mounted some portable stairs. Once on the platform above, they were level with the balloon's woven basket. Hasa made the transfer first—quickly followed by Rebo and Norr. The additional weight caused the aircraft to sag, but it recovered when the pilot opened the burner for a full three seconds, thereby generating more hot air.

Like most the aviators employed by the artifact kings, Kufu's pilot was female and therefore lighter than the average male. She wore a padded skullcap to protect her head during the spills often associated with landings, handmade goggles to protect her eyes from windblown sand particles, and a well-worn leather flight suit. A bolt-action rifle was clamped to one side of the basket and hinted at occasional bouts of air-to-air combat. "Hang on!" the young woman ordered, and turned to wave a gloved hand at her ground crew.

In spite of the fact that Norr had traveled between solar

systems, the sensitive had never been in a hot-air balloon before and felt her stomach lurch unexpectedly as the heavies let go of their ropes. But then, as the burner roared, and the aircraft began to ascend, the sensitive felt her fears start to melt away. The sun was peeking over the horizon, and the normally harsh desert was bathed in soft morning light as the balloon floated out over the underground city of Kahoun.

But there was scant time in which to enjoy the flight because the passengers had a job to do, and it wasn't going to be easy. There had been hundreds of attempts to enter the floating pyramids over the years, mostly by teams of wings, but none had been successful. The structure *had* been damaged, however, which could clearly be seen as the westerly breeze blew the balloon and its passengers toward the floating monuments and the pink-lavender sky beyond. The largest, the one they planned to intercept, was so cratered that Norr theorized that a large artillery piece had been used to fire at it. Probably in hopes of causing damage to whatever mechanism kept the structure aloft so it would fall to desert below and thereby become vulnerable.

At that point, a formation of Kufu's wings descended to take up positions around the balloon. Thanks to the efforts of genetic engineers long dead, the wings had long, slender bodies, hollow bones, and muscles that norms didn't. Their leather wings made a steady *whuf, whuf, whuf* sound as they drew abreast of the basket. The concept of harnessing the variants to the balloon and towing the aircraft into close proximity with the largest of the pyramids had been Rebo's idea. Now, with distances already starting to close, the runner was in communication with the formation's leader via a small handheld "talk-box" that Hasa had loaned to him.

As the norm gave orders, and Norr looked on, four of the strongest wings flew into stiff leather hoops that were attached to the dangling ground ropes. The variants took up the slack, beat their wings even harder, and sought to pull the balloon onto a new course. It would have been impossible had there been any sort of headwind, but the air was relatively calm, and it wasn't long before the aircraft veered to the southeast.

Meanwhile, having been attracted by all of the unusual activity, flocks of competing wings were vectoring in from all directions, bent on stopping whatever King Kufu and his minions were up to. But only four of the red-liveried variants were occupied pulling the balloon, which left the rest of Kufu's air force to block the attackers, which they hurried to do.

Mindful of the need to drop her passengers on the largest of the pyramids, the pilot allowed the balloon to begin a gradual descent, even as she took occasional potshots at enemy variants. Most of her projectiles went wide, but by means of either skill or luck, one of them hit home. Norr happened to be looking in that direction when the blue-clad wing appeared to pause in midair, spiraled toward the ground, and was soon lost from sight.

"Get ready!" Rebo shouted urgently, as the huge pyramid loomed ahead, the pilot triggered the burner, and the wings prepared to drop their harnesses. There was no good way to exit the basket on such a steep incline, but that's what the plan called for, as the balloon made violent contact with the pyramid's westernmost flank. The leading edge of the basket hit, the container tipped forward, and Hasa spilled out onto the ridged slope.

"Jump!" the pilot ordered, as she grabbed onto a support and struggled to keep her footing. "Jump now!"

Norr went first, tripped, and fell face downward onto the stone facing below. She skidded, rolled sideways, and struggled to right herself. Finally, after arresting what threatened to be a fatal skid, the sensitive came to a halt.

Rebo followed, managed to avoid landing right on top of Norr, and wound up sprawled across three six-inch-high steps. The burner roared as the pilot struggled to get her aircraft airborne again, the balloon soared, and soon floated away. A ground crew, all mounted on swift angens, galloped below. Chasing the unpredictable aircraft and retrieving them was a full-time job.

It took the better part of a minute for Rebo, Norr, and Hasa to regain their feet and check for damage. Fortunately, none of them had suffered any injuries beyond scrapes, abrasions, and minor cuts. Then, just as Rebo was about to lead the others to the point where Lysander said they could gain entry, six red-clad wings fluttered down out of the sky to land a few yards away. One had been slightly wounded during an airborne scuffle with Quar's orange-liveried flock, and all of them were armed. They took up positions behind Hasa, and Rebo was quick to object. "What are *they* doing here? This wasn't part of the deal. . . . What's going on?"

Hasa was a small man who had one eyebrow and a mustache to match. When his lips retracted, the resulting expression was more of a grimace than a smile. "*What?*" the minder inquired sarcastically. "You thought the great Kufu would be so foolish as to send only *one* man? Whom you could murder with impunity? Never! File Leader Lartha and his men are here to ensure that you keep your part of the bargain. Besides, the interior of the tomb is sure to be guarded, and you may be glad of the extra firepower."

Rebo looked at Norr and saw the sensitive shrug. "We're after the dead emperor's ring," she whispered. "Nothing else matters."

The runner wasn't so sure, but had very little choice

since Kufu's men outnumbered the two of them more than three to one. "Okay, but do as you're told, or we will call the whole thing off."

Hasa shrugged, as if to say, "Who cares?" and fell in behind Norr as Rebo led the party toward the far side of the pyramid.

Thanks to the fact that large sections of the pyramid's outer covering had been destroyed by cannon fire and the passage of time, it was possible to walk along the crumbling ledgelike steps that would have otherwise been covered. A task that turned out to be more difficult than it appeared since the monument was in motion, there were areas of unbroken material to traverse, and the occasional *ping* could be heard as winged snipers fired on the party from beyond the protective envelope that Kufu's air force had established.

Finally, after circling halfway around the construct, Rebo arrived at the spot Hios's name had been carved into the pyramid's surface in letters twenty feet tall. Much of the *o* and the *s* had been blown away. But the *i* was intact. Confident that the others would follow, the runner climbed up to the point where he could access the dot over the *i* and used a knife to pry and scrape at the surface material. It took some elbow grease, but it wasn't long before a palm-sized chunk of the ceramic material broke loose, and made a *clattering* noise as it tumbled down a succession of steps.

Rebo felt his heart leap as he looked at the huge ruby. He applied pressure to the gemstone, felt it give, and held his breath. What if the ancient mechanism was stuck? Or broken? But the ancients had built well, servos whined, and more of the ceramic material shattered as the entire dot irised open. There was a sudden outgassing of stale air, followed by expressions of amazement from Lartha and his warriors. "Nice work," Norr said approvingly.

"Thanks," Rebo replied, as he turned toward the group gathered behind him. "Who would like to enter first? How 'bout you, Hasa? The king would be impressed."

"You honor me," the minder replied gravely. "But guests must go first . . . Such is our custom on Haafa."

That wasn't necessarily the case, not judging from the smirks the soldiers wore, but Rebo wasn't surprised. The runner said, "Watch my back," to Norr, and slipped into the coolness within. The sensitive went next, closely followed by Hasa and the squad of winged variants. Then, having been triggered by a sensor, the hatch irised closed. A trio of blue-clad wings landed on the spot a scant two minutes later, placed an explosive charge over the door, and took off again. The result was a loud *boom*, a cloud of dust, and a brand-new scar. But, seemingly oblivious to additional damage that had been done to it, the pyramid sailed on.

NINE

The Planet Haafa

Why, God? Why us?

—Wall graffiti found deep within the city of Kahoun

There was total darkness within the floating tomb as the sound of the external explosion faded away—followed by a shower of dust that caused most of the group to sneeze or cough. Then, as Rebo, Norr, and Hasa began to operate their squeeze-powered glow lights, three beams of fluctuating light came into existence. The vaguely pistol-shaped devices had been copied from a unit "harvested" from Kahoun and made a distinctive *click-whir* noise as the power-producing handle was clenched, then released. Even though the dynamo-powered light kept Rebo from fisting both of his handguns at the same time, the runner was happy to have the device because a lantern would have been even more cumbersome.

The wings were less fortunate, however, since no one had seen fit to supply *them* with glow lights, causing File

Leader Lartha and his subordinates to bunch up behind Hasa rather than be left back in the darkness. "Okay," Rebo said fatalistically, as he directed a beam of light down a slight incline. "We might as well get this over with. . . . I'll go first, Lonni will follow behind me, and you guys can bring up the rear."

"*No!*" the minder replied vehemently. "*I* will go first—and the wings will follow me. *You* will bring up the rear."

Rebo was surprised, but pleasantly so, and happy to let Hasa lead the way. But, having sampled the other man's personality, he knew better than to say so. "Well, okay," the runner allowed reluctantly. "But it doesn't seem fair."

"I have very little interest in your opinions," Hasa replied arrogantly, as his glow light washed over a beautifully executed mural. "Come, Lartha. . . . Let's see where this passageway leads."

Norr caught a glimpse of Rebo's expression in the side wash from her squeeze light, knew that her companion was on the verge of laughter, and poked him as Kufu's functionaries proceeded down the tunnel.

Everything went smoothly at first. So smoothly that the runner was about to conclude that his earlier fears had been groundless, when he heard a clacking sound, and File Leader Lartha vanished. Hasa's glow light bobbed erratically, and pandemonium ensued as the remaining wings looked for their leader. But it wasn't until Norr made her way forward that the mystery was solved. "Look!" the sensitive said as she directed her beam downward. "Do you see those cracks? He fell through a trapdoor."

The revelation did nothing to comfort Hasa. A sheen of sweat covered the minder's forehead, and his eyes were huge as he looked from left to right. "Where is Lartha now? Do you think he's alive?"

"No," Rebo replied reasonably. "I don't. . . . But we can't stay here. Watch for cracks, and you'll be okay."

"Oh, no you don't!" Hasa objected heatedly. "I know what you're up to. . . . You're hoping that I'll be the next one to die! Well, I'm too smart for that. *You* go first . . . And the spook goes second. The wings and I will bring up the rear."

"Okay, have it your way," the runner agreed grimly. "But take a look over your shoulder from time to time. We wouldn't want anything to sneak up on us from behind."

It was clear from the way that the minder's eyeballs nearly popped out of their sockets that the possibility of being attacked from the rear hadn't occurred to him until that point. Hasa was still trying to figure out if he'd been wrong to give up the lead position when the other two brushed past him.

"Keep your light on the floor," Rebo instructed, "and I'll use mine to look ahead. Between us, we should be able to see what's coming up."

Norr nodded in agreement, directed her glow light down, and made an attempt to engage her psychic senses as well. But it soon became apparent that there was nothing to detect beyond the auras strung out behind her, a finding that would have been more comforting had it not been for the fact that machines don't generate any spiritual energy and would therefore be "invisible" to her. The thought sent a shiver down the variant's spine and caused her to focus on the physical plane.

The need to watch for trapdoors slowed their progress, but paid off when Norr spotted a second set of telltale cracks, and the rest of the party was able to jump over the potentially fatal trap. The passageway turned to the right shortly thereafter and emptied into a small antechamber. A large, heavily embossed metal door waited ahead, but rather than rush forward and attempt to open it, Rebo decided to pause. It wasn't long before the rest of the group caught up, and Hasa began to champ at the bit. "What are you waiting for?" the minder demanded impatiently. "Cross the chamber and open the door!"

"Be my guest," the runner said, as he stepped aside and motioned for Hasa to proceed.

It was a trap. The minder could see that now. But he couldn't back down without losing face. Hasa stepped into the dome-shaped chamber, pistol at the ready. The response was instantaneous. A simply dressed man appeared out of thin air and raised a bejeweled hand. "I am Emperor Hios," the apparition intoned. "This is *my* tomb . . . And, should you be so stupid as to pass through that door, it will become *yours* as well."

Having become entangled with the semitransparent specter, Hasa gave a yelp of fear and stumbled backward. Rebo made a grab for the missing amulet and clutched the religious medal instead. Norr felt a sudden and completely unanticipated sense of sorrow as she looked at the holographic likeness of the man who had once been her father. A man that only *she*, as the emperor's daughter, could kill. *Had* killed, and given birth to, each time Lysander occupied her body. "Stay!" Norr commanded. "Lead us to your body that we might reclaim your *true* legacy."

But the computer buried deep within the floating pyramid didn't understand the reference and hadn't been programmed for such interactions. The image shimmered, collapsed in on itself, and exploded into a thousand motes of light.

"It wasn't real!" Hasa announced triumphantly, his relief plain to see. "Come on, men, let's tackle that door!"

A stylized star gate could be seen as the minder's glow light splashed the surface of the barrier. Having heard the specter's warning, the wings were understandably reluctant to approach the barrier at first but were eventually convinced to do so, only to discover that it was locked.

"Well, that's that," Rebo said cheerfully. "It looks like we'll have to backtrack. Let's keep an eye peeled for trapdoors however. . . . It would be a shame to lose anyone else."

"Not so fast," Hasa said, as he fumbled something out of a belt pouch. "King Kufu foresaw such a possibility—and that's why he gave me *this*!"

"This" proved to be what looked like a metal wand but was actually a powerful cutting torch. The minder thumbed a button located at one end of the device and was rewarded with a loud *pop* and a six-inch-long bar of blue energy. A second *pop* was heard when the tool was extinguished.

"That looks promising," Rebo admitted. "But before you turn that thing loose, I suggest that we take positions to either side of the door. Who knows what might be waiting on the other side."

Hasa had to admit that the suggestion made sense, and ordered the wings to take up positions to the left and right of the barrier. Judging from appearances, the lock mechanism was located on the right side of the door, and the minder was just about to tackle it, when Rebo cleared his throat. "Sorry to butt in, but what if that sucker pops open? And some sort of weapon goes off? You'll be right in the line of fire."

Hasa was irritated. "If I don't cut into the lock, how will we get in?"

"Tackle the hinges," the runner suggested mildly. "Which you can do from my side without exposing your body."

Though still reluctant to accept counsel from an inferior,

the minder didn't want to die and repositioned himself on the left side of the door. Then, having reactivated the high-tech tool, Hasa went to work. The top hinge began to glow, became white-hot, and soon parted. The door sagged, but held, as the minder cut into the lower hinge. It surrendered, too, but rather than collapse as planned, the barrier remained stubbornly upright. "Kick it," Rebo suggested. "That should knock it loose."

Once Hasa's boot hit the door the results were nothing less than spectacular. There was a loud *crash* as the barrier fell inward to reveal a muscular statue. It had a big head, massive shoulders, and stood crouched as if ready to leap forward. There was a throaty *roar* as its mouth opened, and a tongue of fire shot out into the center of the room, scorched the floor where people might be expected to stand, and sent a cloud of black smoke up to swirl just below the heavily embossed ceiling. The statue's head pivoted from right to left bathing 70 percent of the chamber in flames. The attack seemed to last forever, but actually took no more than five seconds, and ended when the fire-breathing beast ran out of fuel. There was an anticlimactic *pop*, followed by the *whir* of hidden machinery, and a *clacking* sound as damaged servos attempted to close the door.

Rebo blinked and coughed as he moved out into the open. There was plenty of room to pass the now-impotent statue to either side. Hasa yelled, "Wait!" but the runner and the sentient had already entered the next passageway by then, leaving the minder and his troops to bring up the rear.

"Keep your eyes peeled," Rebo cautioned, as he played a beam of light across the wall on his right. "There are bound to be more traps."

"The passageway is slanted downward," the sensitive observed. "We're making progress."

A good ten minutes passed while the tomb raiders followed the narrow hall down through the hairpin turn that led to another long incline. Beautifully painted murals covered the walls around them. From what she could see, Norr got the impression that the images were intended to tell the story of the Emperor's life, beginning with his childhood and progressing toward his eventual death. There was even a picture of the ruler's daughter, which was to say a previous *her*, as a very young girl.

That was when Norr noticed the regularly spaced apertures that were located chest high along both walls. The sensitive was just about to comment on them when Lysander took control of her body. Many, many years had passed since the disincarnate had worked side by side with his chief architect to create the tomb's original design. But when the disincarnate "saw" the holes through the thick mist that swirled around him, he remembered what they were for. "Get down!" the spirit entity said urgently, and pushed the sensitive forward. Rebo felt Norr push him from behind, lost his balance, and threw out his hands to protect himself as he fell.

Hasa heard the order, saw the twosome go down, and was already in the process of imitating their action when the carefully concealed fléchette guns began to fire. The steady *phut, phut, phut* sound generated by the automatic weapons was followed by a loud *clatter* as the wickedly sharp darts bounced off the intricately painted walls and ricocheted away.

And it was one such projectile that caught a wing in the throat, sliced through a major artery, and left the soldier choking on his own blood. Another variant crawled over to give aid, but was unable to stop the bleeding or see his friend's spirit rise to stand next to him.

Then the prolonged *phuuuuuut* and *clatter* generated by the fléchette guns died away as the weapons ran out of ammo. Darkness fell, but was forced to retreat, as Rebo, Norr, and Hasa remembered to pump their glow lights. "Damn," the runner muttered, as he came to his feet. "That was close."

Norr, who had been freed by then, was still a bit dazed as Rebo bent to offer his hand. He looked concerned. "Thanks for the warning. . . . Are you okay?"

The sensitive was about to credit Lysander with the save but decided that doing so would be pointless. "Yes, I'm fine. Thank you."

The group had lost two of its members by then, but there was nothing they could do except forge ahead, nerves stretched to the breaking point. Finally, having cut their way through another door and successfully made their way through a gauntlet of swinging blades, they saw a dim glow in the distance. Then, having just emerged from a series of what might have been defensive points, they stepped out onto the narrow gallery that circled the huge globe-shaped chamber. And there, floating at the very center of the space, lay the emperor's mummified body. Beams of sunlight had been channeled down through the top of the pyramid to bathe Hios in gold and warm his ancient bones.

In spite of the multitudinous layers of dust that covered the funeral bier, it was still possible to see the solar-powered synsilks in which the body had been wrapped and the scintillating rainbow of colors they produced.

Of equal interest, to Hasa at least, was what appeared to be a console located at the head of the bier, and more specifically, the lever that protruded from the center of the of the curvilinear structure. *What happens if you pull on it?* the minder wondered, as he ran his tongue over dry lips. *Something important—or why place it there?*

There was a moment of silence as the entire group stared

at the sight before them. Rebo was the first to speak. "That platform has got to be a hundred feet away. . . . How in the world are we going to reach it?"

"You *aren't*," Hasa answered hoarsely, as his pistol came into sudden alignment with Norr's head. "This is where we part company. . . . Who knows? Maybe you can make your way back the way we came. Thog, keep an eye on them while Vamer, Pamak, Obo, and Rang carry me to the platform. Oh, and it would be a good idea to pull the runner's teeth so he can't fire on us from here."

"Throw your weapons over the side," Thog ordered, and jerked the barrel of his light submachine gun toward the edge of the abyss.

The runner was reluctant to part with the recently acquired handguns, very reluctant, but knew he had no choice. One by one he removed the pistols from their holsters and tossed them over the side. There was a faint clatter as they hit the floor far below. Norr was armed with the sword she had stolen on Derius, but it was slung across her back and was therefore useless.

"Good," Hasa said, as he returned his pistol to its holster. "I'm glad to see you're going to be sensible about this. . . . Now stand back and give us some room."

Rebo and Norr were forced to retreat into the passageway as four of Kufu's variants took up positions around Hasa, secured grips on the minder's harness, and extended their wings. Although the norm was deadweight, he was relatively small, and the soldiers were strong. The leathery triangles of skin that were stretched between their arms and torsos made a *whuf, whuf, whuf* sound as Hasa was hoisted up into the air and carried out toward the platform beyond. Shadows fell across the funeral bier, and wings thumped warm air, as Lysander "watched" the tomb raiders began to close with what had been his body. And that was when the man who had been emperor remembered still *another* detail about his tomb and began to laugh.

As the pyramids came to the southernmost extent of their range and began a long, dignified turn toward the west, King Kufu saw a series of flashes march along the top of a distant rise and knew that King Horus's artillery had opened fire. Confirmation of that supposition came in the form of loud *shrieks* and a line of explosions that tossed men and animals high into the hot afternoon air. They seemed to hang there, as if suspended by the same force that kept the pyramids aloft, before falling back to the planet's surface.

The tomb raider could hardly complain, however, since the war had been set into motion by his decision to unilaterally land a party of grave robbers on the largest of the three pyramids, thereby raising the possibility that his forces would empty the structure of whatever riches lay within before his peers could steal their share. Now, in a rare display of cooperation, Horus and Tepho had launched a coordinated attack on Kufu's forces in an attempt to break him.

The answer, to Kufu's mind at least, was to quickly and efficiently eliminate the weakest of his opponents and thereby reduce the odds. So, having chosen Tepho as his first victim, Kufu ordered his forces to charge. Then, having given the two-mile-long line thirty seconds to react, the king laid his long supple whip onto the backs of the angens in front of him. The animals screamed, jerked the three-man chariot forward, and began to run. Moments later 562 other charioteers began to roll as four companies of red-clad wings swept in to provide air cover, and an army of more than a thousand armored heavies began a ponderous march.

Meanwhile, to the south, Tepho eyed the screen in front

of him and smiled grimly as the enemy swept toward him. Kufu was an idiot, proof of which could be seen in his decision to attack the Techno Society's army first, hoping for an easy victory. Because rather than simply invest in brute force, Tepho had put his money into technology, which he often referred to as ". . . the great multiplier." And, making the contest even *more* delicious was that while Kufu led his forces into what would almost certainly prove to be a disastrous battle, Tepho planned to steal Logos right out from under the fool's nose!

The air crackled with radio traffic, and servos whined as three beautifully restored raptors took to the field of battle, their energy weapons burping blue death. Tepho, who had chosen to pilot the centermost machine himself, felt a sudden surge of elation. Because within the cramped cockpit, and in spite of his malformed body, *he* was a warrior!

Because Kufu was intent on closing with the enemy as soon as possible, he ordered his artillery to stop firing and was leading a long line of charioteers south when three hundred heavily armed metal men erupted from the sand in front of him. They leveled their automatic weapons and began to fire.

Angens screamed as they went down, and chariots tumbled end over end, even as Kufu's wings swept in to attack the androids from above. Gouts of sand flew up into the air as grenades went off, robots were dismembered, and their appendages began to rain down out of the sky.

Then, drums thumping, Kufu's heavies arrived on the scene. War hammers rose and fell with the regularity of pistons as the variants attacked the surviving metal men, only to be ripped to pieces by bursts of bullets, or the pulses of bright blue energy that originated from Tepho's steadily advancing raptors.

It was a hellish scene, and one that Kufu, who had been lucky enough to survive the initial onslaught, would never forget. The artifact king was on foot by then, his throat raw from screaming commands, and no longer confident of victory. Survival, that was all Kufu could hope for, as everything he had worked so hard to build began to crumble.

As what promised to be an epic battle began to unfold a couple of miles to the south, and the pyramids sailed along the edge of the far horizon, Hoggles watched from the top level of the nearly deserted tower. The heavy knew it was stupid, but he was lonely, and jealous as well. Because even though Hoggles knew that his love for Norr was hopeless, he had long taken pleasure from simply being in the sensitive's presence, and now even that bittersweet enjoyment had been denied him.

And, as if to add insult to injury, Rebo and Norr had left him to guard Logos. Having more than doubled in size, and taken on the appearance of a hip-length jacket, the computer was in a good position to needle the heavy from time to time, and seemed to take pleasure in doing so.

Meanwhile, as the heavy stared out across the battlefield, the sentry nearest to the stairs saw the air in front of him shimmer. He blinked to clear his eyes, saw what might have been a materialized spirit, and opened his mouth to shout a warning. But a hand blurred past his face, something tugged at his throat, and a sheet of blood flew out to splash the hot decking.

The body was still falling as Shaz spun away, slashed a second throat, and paused to shoot each of the remaining guards. The rhythmic *bang, bang, bang* generated by the semiautomatic pistol served to echo the artillery rounds that continued to pound what remained of King Kufu's army.

Hoggles heard the pistol shots, lifted his war hammer, and turned toward the sound. The heavy was shocked by what he saw—and confused as well. There were bodies, lots of bodies, but where were the attackers?

Having eliminated all of his opponents with the exception of the heavy, Shaz allowed himself to be seen. Though rare, Hoggles had encountered combat variants before and knew what they could do. Though only half as strong as he was, the other variant was not only twice as fast but armed with a pistol. The heavy figured he could absorb four or five bullets and still be able to close with his opponent, but then what? Would he be able to rip the bastard's canine head off? Or would the cumulative effect of his wounds pull him down? There was no way to be sure.

But Shaz had already completed the very same calculus and, having no particular desire to kill the heavy, lowered his weapon. The combat variant's smile revealed two rows of extremely white teeth. "Good afternoon," he said politely. "We haven't met, not formally, but I've been following you and your friends for quite some time now."

Hoggles wrapped and rewrapped his thick sausagelike fingers around the war hammer's smooth shaft. "Who are you?" the heavy demanded hoarsely. "One of those techno people?"

"Yes, you could say that," Shaz admitted breezily. "Which brings me to the purpose of my visit. The jacket you're wearing . . . Would that constitute a computer called Logos?"

Not being sure of what was taking place, the AI had been silent up until then. But now, having given up on his plan to eliminate Sogol, the computer saw what might be an opportunity to rid himself of Lysander's self-righteous flunkies and still take control of Socket. "Yes, I'm Logos," the computer answered loudly. "Are you a member of the Techno Society?"

"I am," Shaz answered simply. "More than that, I was sent here to get you."

"Excellent!" the AI replied enthusiastically. "If you would be so kind as to kill this fool—we can depart immediately."

"You're welcome to give it a try," Hoggles growled, and charged straight ahead. Though slow by *his* standards, the heavy was faster than Shaz expected him to be, and the combat variant barely managed to avoid a blow from the war hammer before spinning away. Although Shaz had the pistol, he couldn't use it on the heavy's torso without punching holes in Logos, a surefire way to send Tepho into a homicidal rage. That left the possibility of a head shot, a leg shot, or hand-to-hand combat.

But the decision was suddenly made for him when Hoggles *threw* the war hammer. The weapon hit Shaz in the shoulder and sent the handgun flying. Worse yet, the blow left the combat variant's right arm completely numb and forced the functionary to back away. His body shimmered, but was still partially visible, as Shaz slipped on a pool of blood.

Seeing his chance, and certain of victory, Hoggles uttered a basso war cry as he thundered across the intervening space. The two men collided, the combat variant felt a sudden stab of fear, and was fumbling for his knife when Logos entered the battle. Although the computer didn't have arms to fight with, he had control over his highly mutable "body," which Hoggles continued to wear.

Suddenly, Hoggles felt the jacket start to shrink around him. The heavy produced a roar of outrage, released the grip that he had established on his opponent's throat, and began to remove the traitorous garment. But it was too late by then. The AI had been transformed into what amounted to a straitjacket. Hoggles found himself unable to move his arms, realized what that meant, and tried to back away.

Shaz saw the opportunity and took it. The last thing Hoggles saw was a canine grin, a flash of steel, and the blinding sun. Then he was down, his blood soaking the object he was supposed to protect, his lips forming her name. Moments later the heavy was somewhere else, in a place far removed from the physical plane, and the family lost so many years before was gathering to greet him.

Norr felt a sense of hopelessness as the wings carried Hasa across the abyss toward the platform that hovered beyond. And now, with nothing to distract her, the sensitive could see that the interior of the globe-shaped chamber was covered with what looked like a complicated map. A *star* map that illustrated the full glory of the empire Hios ruled prior to his descent into madness and his death at her hands.

But that was before ancient sensors were tripped, the beams of sunlight began to converge on a single point, and gradually became brighter. There was no reaction at first, but that changed as tendrils of smoke began to emerge from leathery wings, the variants began to scream, and two of the warriors burst into flames. The rest attempted to escape, but the beams of light followed wherever they went, killing the variants one at a time.

Hasa was falling by then, his arms windmilling uselessly as *he* tried to fly, only to fall facedown onto the platform below. Rebo watched in horror as the minder landed on the ancient lever and uttered a horrible scream as the bloodied handle emerged between his shoulder blades. Then, after a two-second pause, the device gradually gave way under the weight of Hasa's dead body. "Uh-oh," the runner said grimly. "I don't know what that lever controls—but I have a hunch that we're about to find out."

Rebo's words just hung there, and his prophecy went un-
fulfilled for a good five seconds, before the antigrav generator located in the base of the pyramid suddenly went
off-line. Rebo and Norr experienced a momentary sense of
weightlessness as the now-unsupported structure fell fifteen
feet to the desert floor. Then, with nothing to hang on to,
the two of them fell. The runner made what amounted to a
crash landing, while Norr landed on her feet and allowed
her knees to accept the shock. Having added more bruises
to his still-growing collection, the runner was delighted to
discover that none of his bones were broken as the sensitive
helped pull him up onto his feet.

But, while the two of them were all right, the emperor's
mummified body had not fared as well. In fact, as Rebo
peered down from the gallery above, he could see pieces of
the dismembered corpse scattered across the surface of the
now-broken burial platform. "We've got to get down
there!" the runner exclaimed. "You can imagine what's taking place outside. . . . The entire pyramid will be crawling
with looters twenty minutes from now."

Norr was in complete agreement. Rebo freed the coil of
rope that had been slung across his shoulders, secured one
end to the curved railing, and tossed the rest over the side.
"I'll go first," Norr volunteered, and was already lowering
herself over the side before the runner could object. Then,
once her feet touched the floor, it was Rebo's turn to slide
down the rope.

Norr had already completed a survey of the scattered
body parts by then and was down on one knee when the
runner arrived at her side. "There it is," the sensitive declared, and pointed to the large, somewhat gaudy ring that
still graced a badly withered hand. The green gemstone
seemed to glow as if lit from within.

"Well," Rebo responded, "let's pull that sucker off his finger and find our way out of here."

Norr was about to respond when the entire pyramid began to vibrate, dust rained down from above, and the light began to fade. Rebo took hold of the hand. It was dry, leathery, and still attached to a skeletal forearm. His first attempt to strip the ring off the mummy's bony finger failed, so rather than attempt to work the piece of jewelry free, the runner broke the emperor's arm over his knee. The wrinkled brown-gray hand came off at the wrist. The runner tossed the rest away and was in the process of shoving what remained palm down in his pocket, when the pyramid began to fall apart.

Viewed from atop Kufu's blood-drenched tower, where the king was licking his wounds in the wake of the disastrous battle with Tepho, the now-grounded pyramid was a sight to see as beams of bright light shot up into the sky, all four of the triangle-shaped sides collapsed onto the ground, clouds of dust and sand exploded into the air, and a globular burial chamber was revealed. Then, before anyone could properly assess what was taking place, the globe split into six segments, *they* fell away from each other, and a pair of badly shaken tomb raiders were revealed. The rest of the floating pyramids, seemingly unaware of what had occurred, continued on their way.

Kufu was so shocked that he simply sat and stared for a moment before bringing a powerful monocular up to his eye and peering out into the quickly gathering twilight. Once he saw the two figures, and realized who they were, a quick flurry of orders followed. "Send the wings! Send the chariots! Bring the man and woman to me!"

Meanwhile, deep within the subterranean city of Kahoun, the AI known as One-Two felt the ground shake, wondered what was taking place, and processed a sense of anticipation. Something, the computer didn't know what, was going to happen.

The sun was little more than an orange-red smear along the western horizon by the time Shaz made his way across the body-strewn battlefield and back to the relative safety of the much-enhanced "blue sector," where Tepho sat triumphant within the comfort of his huge tent. The chairman of the Techno Society had changed during the last eight hours, something that was apparent to the combat variant the moment he was shown into the shelter and saw the way the technologist sat slouched next his raptor. It had been hot within the machine's cockpit, *very* hot, and the sweat marks were still visible on Tepho's clothes. Not only that, but, judging from the way that the entire right side of the raptor had been scorched, both man and machine had been through close combat. Been through it and *survived*, which was why there was something new in the technologist's eyes. A confidence and pride that Shaz had never seen there before. "Congratulations on your victory," the combat variant said evenly. "I had to cross the battlefield in order to get here. Your enemies are still collecting their dead."

Tepho searched his subordinate's face for the slightest sign of insincerity, was unable to find any, and felt an unexpected sense of warmth suffuse his crippled body. Because if Shaz respected what he'd been able to accomplish, then it was real and couldn't be taken away from him. So, even though the technologist would normally be furious regarding the combat variant's apparent failure to retrieve Logos, Tepho found himself in a forgiving mood. "Thank you, Shaz. . . . We taught them a lesson they won't forget! Kufu was successful in one regard, however . . . Did you see the emperor's tomb? The bastard brought it down! We took a lot of territory but couldn't capture it. Still, the initial reports from our wings seem to suggest that there wasn't anything valuable inside. Not unless you like mummies that is!"

The joke was a poor one but a sure sign of what kind of mood the administrator was in. The combat variant's laugh had a harsh, barking quality. "No, I didn't see the pyramid, but that would explain the lights I saw to the south. Kufu and his people must be very disappointed."

"I certainly hope so!" Tepho said cheerfully. "But enough of that. . . . You were on an adventure of your own. How did that go?"

Tepho clearly believed that the mission had been a failure, but being in a good mood, was prepared to accept a negative report. But Shaz had a surprise for him, a rather *pleasant* surprise, which made the moment all the more enjoyable. Slowly, so that the other man could appreciate the implications of what he was doing, the variant worked his way out of the now bloodstained jacket. Though slightly damaged, the raptor was on-line, which meant that servos whined and energy weapons tracked Shaz as he took six paces forward and laid the garment across Tepho's lap. "I'm happy to report that the mission was a success. Chairman Tepho—I give you Logos."

Even though the technologist knew that the fabled AI was housed in a mutable piece of clothing, his expectations had been low, and it wasn't until the combat variant began to remove the nondescript jacket, that the truth suddenly became clear. Slowly, and with some difficulty, the technologist stood. Then, having slipped his arms into the computer's sleeves, he allowed the fabric to settle over his misshapen body. The jacket was too big at first, but that changed as Logos made some adjustments. "My God," Tepho said breathlessly, "it's *real*!"

"Of course I'm real," the AI responded waspishly. "And so is Socket. I suggest that we leave immediately."

Tepho decided that the voice, which seemed to originate from behind his neck, would take some getting used to. As would the AI's rather acerbic personality. "We'll leave when I'm ready," Tepho said firmly. "Besides, what's the hurry? Socket has been on hold for more than a thousand years. A few more days won't make any difference."

Logos wanted to say that a few more days *could* make a difference, especially if Rebo and Norr managed to get their hands on One-Two, but didn't want his new biologicals to learn the truth about Sogol. Because once they knew about the other AI, they would inevitably want to possess her as well, a possibility that wasn't likely to help Logos obtain what *he* wanted. "Yes, well, what you say is true," the AI allowed carefully. "But the sooner the better."

"Of course," Tepho replied soothingly, as he glanced at the raptor. "But we'll need to be ready for anything . . . which means I have some packing to do."

That was when Shaz realized that if Tepho had been reliant on the raptor before, he was even more so now, having bonded with the machine during combat. Which meant the raptor would have to be disassembled and rebuilt each time they made a jump. Not that it mattered because the technologist was correct. Socket had been waiting for a thousand years. A few days, a week, even a month wouldn't make much difference now.

The combat variant was about to leave when Tepho stopped him. "Shaz . . ."

"Yes?"

"You did a good job. Thank you."

The variant delivered an abbreviated bow, shimmered, and disappeared.

A crack of blue-pink light ran the length of the eastern horizon as Norr bent to light the bottom of the funeral pyre. The sensitive was rewarded with a loud crackling sound as flames found their way up through the dry fuel. The pile of wood had been stacked on top of a dune, about half a mile east of Kufu's encampment, and constituted but one of more than five hundred such fires that presently dotted the desert. *Urgent* fires, that were required to cleanse the battlefield before the sun could rise and turn the entire area into a sea of corruption.

But *this* fire was special because it was Bo Hoggles who lay on top of the pyre, his huge war hammer at his side. Rebo stepped forward to place a comforting arm around Norr's shoulders, only to discover that the sensitive was crying. "He lives on," the runner said quietly. "You, of all people, know that."

Norr made use of a handkerchief to dab at her eyes. "That's true. . . . But I will miss his strength, loyalty, and courage."

"Yes," Rebo agreed somberly. "I will, too."

The flames found the top of the pyre, tried to leap into the sky, and sent sparks up to touch it. And, as Norr watched the still-glowing embers float away, she knew there was *another* reason for her tears. Hoggles had been in love with her, and had it been otherwise, would probably be back on Derius, Thara, or Ning, building a life for himself. But the variant had chosen to follow her instead, to take care of the woman that he loved, even if that meant delivering her into someone else's arms.

There was a mad *crackling* sound, followed by an explosion of sparks, as the funeral pyre collapsed in on itself. The only other mourners were six heavies who didn't know Hoggles but had volunteered to help because they were brothers of a sort. They took half a dozen steps backward as a wall of heat sought to wrap them in a warm embrace.

"So," Rebo said, as he guided Norr back to a more comfortable position. "What now? It's pretty clear that the Techno Society has Logos . . . and it wouldn't be realistic to think that we're going to get him back."

"No, it wouldn't," the sensitive agreed. "But we have the ring, which means that we can locate One-Two, which means we can activate Socket."

"Assuming we get there *first*," Rebo observed.

"Yes, assuming we get there first."

Rebo eyed the fire. "So, we're going down into the city of Kahoun."

"*I* am," the variant answered simply. "I have to. For the man who was my father, for Bo Hoggles, and for what remains of the human race."

Rebo sighed. "Damn. . . . I was afraid you'd say something like that."

Norr turned to look up into his face. Her eyes were huge—and still rimmed with tears. "You don't have to come."

The runner's hand came up to cup her chin. "Oh, but I'm afraid I do," he said gently, and kissed her lips. Something gave, the fire crackled, and a column of red stars took to the sky.

TEN

The Planet Haafa

Safe below the burning sands, and surrounded by his scientists, the emperor spent many happy days in the city of Kahoun.

—Heva Manos, advisor to Emperor Hios,
in his biography, *A Web of Stars*

*Having watched the funeral pyre burn itself out, and re-*turned to King Kufu's tower for some much-needed sleep, Rebo and Norr awoke at least somewhat refreshed. Having lost the battle fought the day before but taken possession of the emperor's tomb, the king's attention was focused elsewhere. And that was fine with them. After a quick breakfast, the twosome returned to their curtained quarters, where Rebo completed the process of removing the ring from the emperor's leathery hand. Lysander took possession of Norr's body a few moments later, and, with the ring on his/her right index finger, he/she sought to contact Sogol.

Meanwhile, deep below the Segenni Desert, the AI variously called Sogol, Logos 1.2, and One-Two had just completed preparations for another release of knowledge, when an incoming signal registered on her electronic senses. There had been a time when such a signal would have been her cue to contact Emperor Hios, but he'd been dead for a long time, and judging from the radio traffic that constantly washed around Sogol, a group of tomb raiders had breached his pyramid. That meant they had the emperor's ring, and judging from the nonstop series of *beeps* registering on her receiver, knew how to activate it.

Fortunately One-Two had the means to kill the input and was just about to do so, when a long-dead audio channel suddenly came to life. "This is Hios. . . . Please refer to authentication sequence 7629H5t15."

Of course Sogol knew that the actual code was 7628H5t15, and was surprised to hear a female voice, but the input was pretty damned close to what it should have been. And that warranted further investigation. "Emperor Hios?" the AI inquired tentatively. "Is that *you*?"

"Yes!" Lysander replied. "It's me, or a version of me, speaking through a sensitive. I thought you were off-line— but learned otherwise when Logos 1 brought us to Haafa."

"I spoke with him," the tinny voice responded, "but I . . ." There was a burst of static at that point, and the rest of the AI's words were lost.

"One-Two?" Lysander demanded. "Can you hear me?"

There was a moment of silence, followed by more static, interspersed with garbled words. ". . . Pyra's trying to interfere. . . . A lot of trouble when it opens. . . . Follow the tomb raiders down. . . ."

The words trailed off into noise after that—and Lysander shook Norr's head in disgust. "Someone, or something, is attempting to block our transmissions."

"That's the way it sounds," Rebo agreed, "but the situation seems fairly clear. . . . "Sogol can open a pathway into Kahoun. Once we're down there, she can come to us."

Norr's face went momentarily blank, the sensitive's head jerked, and her eyelids fluttered. Then she was back. "What happened?" the variant wanted to know, as she held the ring up to the light. "Did Lysander get through?"

"Sort of," Rebo replied cautiously, and told the sensitive what had transpired.

"So when will the path open up?" Norr wondered out loud. "And how will we know where to go?"

"I don't know when it will open up," the runner replied, "although my guess would be soon. As for the second question, well, that's easy. The moment something happens, Kufu's people will be off and running. All we need to do is follow them."

The sensitive smiled crookedly. "You make it sound so simple."

"Yeah," Rebo responded, "but it never is."

"No," Norr agreed. "It never is."

*Absolute secrecy. That was the key to opening a success-*ful pathway into the underground city of Kahoun. Because even though One-Two wanted to release technology to the outer world, Ogotho and Pyra were equally dedicated to blocking such events, which ran counter to their mutual goal of preserving the 450-square-mile tomb. So, conscious of the fact that radio signals can be tracked, Sogol was careful to keep moving as she sent the final signal to her army of spindly-legged utility bots. The plan was to open a pathway during daylight when everyone could see. Then, once three hours had elapsed, the portal would close. Anyone greedy enough, or foolish enough, to remain in the city would be sealed inside, a convention that the tomb raiders had long since become accustomed to.

As luck would have it, three of King Quar's wings were

riding a thermal two hundred feet above the pathway that had once been known as Surface Ramp-47, when a pair of Sogol's utility bots brought a jumper circuit online, thereby diverting power away from one of Pyra's main lines, which they used to open the ancient storm door. That consumed half a gigawatt of electricity, but only for a short period of time, which was just as well because it wasn't long before Pyra cut power to that part of the city's grid in a last-ditch attempt to prevent the subsequent invasion. But, as part of a chess match that had been played out many times before, Sogol *wanted* the other computer to cut off the electricity, thereby leaving Surface Ramp-47 open to the outside.

Realizing that, Pyra hurried to reenergize the door in an attempt to close it but soon discovered that critical cables had been severed. Lum bugs were dispatched to make the necessary repairs, but that would take hours even as a horde of tomb raiders poured down into the city. It was a maddening game, but one that Pyra had thus far been powerless to stop since One-Two had been able to outsmart her. Until *now* that is, because having accumulated a considerable amount of data regarding such incursions, Pyra could predict what Sogol would do next. And, based on that ability, Pyra planned to find the little worm and kill it.

Meanwhile, the orange-clad wings circling two hundred feet above Surface Ramp-47 were privileged to witness a rare sight as a rectangular section of the desert floor seemed to collapse in on itself. Tons of sand poured down into carefully prepared cavities below, a column of dust rose to point fingerlike at the newly opened pathway, and hundreds of avaricious eyes were quick to take notice. Telescopes swiveled in that direction, airborne scouts vectored in, and no more than five minutes had elapsed when the race began.

Thanks to a warning from Norr, and eager to recoup his

recent losses, Kufu was the first artifact king to respond. A flight of twenty wings were dispatched, even as five three-man chariots raced pell-mell toward the new opening, each creating its own column of dust as it cut across the desert floor. Rebo stood to the left of the red-clad charioteer, and Norr stood to the right, both straining to hold on as the specially bred angens hauled the two-wheeled conveyance over all manner of bumps, ridges, and other irregularities. It was a hard ride, but an exhilarating one, and the runner couldn't help but enjoy the way the wind pressed against his face, the thrill as the chariot went momentarily airborne as it hit a bump, and the solid *thump* as it hit the ground again.

Not all of the charioteers were so fortunate however. As their vehicle topped a slight rise, Norr saw a black chariot break free of its team, and tumble end over end as what looked like little stick figures flew through the air. What happened next was obscured by a cloud of dust, the driver's wildly flapping headscarf, and a competing two-wheeler. Then they were there, at the center of a maelstrom of multi-colored chariots, each fighting for space as drivers cracked their whips, and angens turned to nip at one another. Kufu's chariot shook, and loose gear clattered, as competing chari-ots closed in from both sides. "Watch out!" Norr shouted, and pointed across the driver's chest.

Rebo turned to his left, saw that a green-clad passenger was in the process of bringing a double-barreled shotgun to bear, and readied one of two pistols requisitioned from Kufu's armory. They weren't identical, as the previous pair had been, but each weapon had certain advantages. The 9mm Tombo barked twice, the shotgunner collapsed against the driver, and the entire rig veered away.

Nor were the off-worlders the only ones forced to defend themselves as more than fifty chariots converged on the entry point and became part of a confused mass of wildly thrashing angens, screaming drivers, and murderous tomb raiders. In the meantime firearms boomed, banged, and popped even as a hot-air balloon drifted in over the crowd and three green-clad norms began to rappel toward the ground. They were only halfway down when a group of multicolored wings took offense and opened fire on the orange-striped envelope. Hot air escaped through dozens of holes, and the pilot fired wildly as the quickly deflating airship collapsed onto the tightly packed mob below. "Come on!" Rebo yelled over the surrounding din. "Let's proceed on foot!"

Norr nodded, reached back to draw her sword, and followed the runner as he jumped to the ground. It felt strange to enter the melee without Hoggles at her back, but the sensitive thought she could feel the heavy's protective presence and felt better as a result.

The majority of the tomb raiders had abandoned their chariots by then and were busy fighting their way forward. Most were focused on entering the newly revealed passageway rather than battling their competitors but there were exceptions, and Rebo heard the occasional *bang* as someone fired a weapon at point-blank range. Those who were lucky fell dead—whereas the wounded were often trampled to death as the mob pressed forward. The runner tried to avoid stepping on the bodies, but that was increasingly difficult to do, and there was more than one occasion when Rebo felt flesh give under his boots.

Then, like some subterranean monster, the steeply sloping ramp opened its dark maw to swallow the tomb raiders whole. Rebo and Norr were jostled back and forth as oil-fed lanterns were lit, cell-powered glow lights came on, and handheld flares were hoisted high. The off-worlders still had their trusty squeeze lights, but felt no need to use them so long as the rest of the tomb raiders were willing to illuminate the ramp for them. A trio of metal men, their eyes aglow, brushed past.

In marked contrast to the pyramid's richly decorated interior, the walls to either side of the ramp bore little more than badly faded admonitions to activate headlights, watch for oncoming traffic, and obey the posted speed limit. There was some graffiti, however, including one entry that might have been spray-painted onto the wall during the final days of the plague, when Surface Ramp-47 had been packed with infected people all trying to find a way out of the doomed city. It read, WHY, GOD? WHY US?

But Norr saw no answers as the ramp leveled out and gave way to what might have been some sort of checkpoint, before splitting into half a dozen competing two-lane pathways. Orders were shouted, and blobs of light wobbled over ancient walls as teams of loot-hungry tomb raiders plunged into the branching corridors. All according to protocols established by their patrons. But the truth was that every pathway would lead them to artifacts! Because Sogol *wanted* the thieves to succeed and had gone to considerable lengths to make sure that they would.

Unlike the rest, however, Rebo and Norr were after one particular artifact. That's why they stood off to one side and let the others rush by. The light level began to drop as Norr removed the ring from her belt pouch, and most of the mob surged past. The first thing Rebo noticed as he began to squeeze the glow light's curved handle, was the fact that the ring's green gemstone was lit from within and seemed to flicker as the sensitive moved it from left to right. Norr noticed the phenomenon as well. "Look!" she exclaimed. "It's brightest when I point it at the second passageway from the left."

"At least that gives us something to go on," Rebo acknowledged. "Let's see where that tunnel leads."

The twosome entered the passageway designated as DR-2N. It began to turn as streaks of reflected light washed back over tiled walls, and they heard unintelligible shouts off in the distance. Then, just as Rebo and Norr rounded a curve, there was a disturbance up ahead. Half a dozen *blue* lights appeared as Pyra's lum bugs soared out of a ventilation duct, sought the white lights below, and opened fire. Each robot was armed with a nose-mounted laser. Their energy weapons made sizzling sounds as they targeted the tomb raiders below. Shouts of pain were heard as some of the energy bolts struck home, quickly followed by the stutter of a submachine gun, and the deliberate *bang, bang, bang* of a semiautomatic carbine. "Uh-oh," Rebo said grimly, as the squeeze light was returned to its holster. "It looks like we have company. . . . Keep your light handy—but let it go dark."

Norr complied, but if the runner hoped to escape notice, the plan didn't work. Even as one of the airborne lum bugs exploded, another broke away from the battle with the tomb raiders and hurried to intercept two additional heat signatures before they could do damage to the city beyond.

Rebo had drawn both handguns by that time, but rather than pepper the quickly advancing machine with 9mm slugs, opened up with the Sokov instead. The six-shot dart gun bucked in Rebo's hand as the first self-propelled round left the barrel, deployed its stabilizing fins, and accelerated away. The dart hit the lum bug head-on, smashed through the robot's outer "skin," and detonated within. There was a red-orange explosion as the machine came apart, followed by a wild *clatter*, as bits of metal sprayed the immediate area. Then came a satisfying *crash* as what remained of the construct hit the pavement and skidded for ten feet before finally coming to a stop.

But there was no reason to celebrate because *two* additional units were on the way. Bursts of ruby red energy stitched black scorch marks onto the duracrete where the humans had been standing moments before as the wily intruders ducked into an alcove marked FIRE FIGHTING STATION 89. Rebo stood ready to attack the machines the moment they appeared, but Norr had doubts about the runner's ability to destroy the first robot before the *second* machine could fire, and took matters into her own hands by dashing out into the center of the passageway.

Rebo swore, fired the Sokov for the second time, and was rewarded with another explosion. Then, even as the runner swung the handgun around to acquire the second target, Norr charged straight for it. The sword, which was held high, came down with all the strength the sensitive could muster. And because the edge of the blade had been made from a single "stretched" molecule—it cut through the lum bug's fiber-composite body like a hot knife through butter. There was a loud *bang*, followed by a brilliant discharge of electricity, and a clatter as both halves of the robot landed on the pavement.

A beam of light came into existence as Rebo shifted the Sokov into his right hand and began to pump the squeeze light with his left. A blob of illumination wobbled over the machine's burned-out remains before turning toward Norr. "That was a stupid thing to do," the runner observed darkly. "What am I supposed to do if you go and get yourself killed?"

"You could find yourself *another* sensitive," Norr replied lightly. "One who's a lot less demanding. Come on—Sogol is somewhere up ahead."

There were no sounds other than the steady *click-whir* of their squeeze lights, and the soft *scuffle* of their footsteps as the twosome advanced down the passageway and past the point where the earlier battle had been fought. The floor was slick with blood, and two of the three dead men were still present, standing over their badly charred bodies. They weren't sure what to do, and the sensitive was tempted to stop and help them, but knew she should focus on finding the all-important AI. The green gemstone glowed brightly as the passageway terminated in front of a raised loading dock. Stairs led up to a flat surface where bodies had been stacked during the early days of the plague before eventually disintegrating to a heap of bones.

The runner followed a badly faded yellow line back to an open door and the narrow corridor beyond. "The ring is getting warmer!" Norr proclaimed as she gripped the object in her hand. "I think we're almost there."

"Good," Rebo responded soberly. "The sooner we can get out of this place, the better." Then, as if to underline the truth of the runner's statement, one of the tomb raiders screamed.

Intelligent though she was, Sogol failed to recognize the trap for what it was until she was inside it. Though unable to prevent the AI from opening a section of the city to the tomb raiders, Pyra had been able to carry out projections based on past behaviors and positioned her robots accordingly. So, as One-Two slithered into the sector served by Ramp-47, the computer discovered that her forces were being systematically slaughtered. Once cornered, the lightly armored utility bots were easy prey for the flying lum bugs, which seemed determined to eradicate the multilegged creatures as they scuttled for cover. Lasers stuttered as the killers pursued their unarmed prey down darkened aisles, around corners, and between dusty storage modules.

At least fifteen of Sogol's machines had been taken off-line by the time the AI entered Storage Facility-972, and more were being destroyed with each passing minute. And, because each robot was analogous to a nerve ending, One-Two processed something akin to pain as her functionaries died.

But the *real* target, from Pyra's perspective at any rate, was Sogol herself. Who, though extremely small, could be "seen" electronically as she sent signals to her robotic minions. And it was then, having established the AI's exact coordinates, that Pyra ordered her lum bugs to attack the high-priority target. Energy beams sizzled as they crisscrossed the duracrete floor, and the air grew thick with the stench of ozone as the golden serpent propelled herself toward a shelving unit and the inviting darkness that lay below it. But Sogol knew she wouldn't be able to make it, and had already prepared herself for an ignominious death, when the first of the tomb raiders charged into the warehouse.

Having already survived one lum bug attack, the humans were in no mood to leave themselves open to a second assault, and immediately opened fire on the flying robots. But the lum bugs answered, and there was a piercing scream as an energy beam took a tomb raider's arm off at the shoulder and cauterized the wound as part of the process.

One of the flying machines staggered as a hail of bullets struck it, drifted off course, and made violent contact with a second machine. Both robots exploded, light strobed the grimy walls, and avaricious humans flooded down the aisles. Some continued to do battle with the lum bugs, even as others scooped artifacts off the surrounding shelves and hurried to stuff the loot into large duffel bags.

And that was when Rebo and Norr entered the bloody

fray. Tracers drew lines through the murk. A lum bug vanished in a bright *bang*, and razor-sharp shrapnel flew every which way. "The ring is starting to cool," Norr warned, as the off-worlders worked their way along a laser-scorched wall. "Let's turn back!"

Sogol had been dimly aware of the ring's presence for some time. But now that the artifact was in the same room with her, it seemed to glow like the external sun. Having taken refuge beneath one of the artifact-laden shelving units, the AI hurried to close with the ring and the people who possessed it.

In the meantime the airborne machines were well on their way to winning the battle with the tomb raiders when Rebo opened fire with the Sokov. One lum bug exploded, and was quickly followed by a second, and a third.

And it was then, just as the last electromechanical carcass hit the debris-littered floor, that Norr felt something cold wrap itself around her left ankle. The sensation was so disconcerting that the sensitive bent over to grab it, felt whatever the thing was slither up her arm, and had just wrapped her fingers around a slim body when she found herself looking into the eyes of a snake. The serpent's voice was all out of proportion to her small size. "Are you the ones Emperor Hios sent to get me?"

"Yes," Norr replied, as Rebo inserted a fresh clip into his pistol.

"Good," Sogol said. "I suggest that you pull out before Pyra sends more lum bugs."

Norr didn't know who Pyra was, but the term "lum bugs" was self-explanatory, and the variant had no desire to be in the neighborhood when the additional machines arrived. "We've got what we came for!" the sensitive announced excitedly. "Let's get out of here!"

Rebo didn't need to be told twice and made use of a fresh magazine to hose the surrounding area with explosive darts as they backed toward the door. Then, once the Sokov clicked empty, the off-worlders turned and fled.

Pyra "sensed" Sogol's impending escape but couldn't move enough additional robots into the area quickly enough to stop the AI, and had little choice but to turn her attention back to the tomb raiders. Disappointing though the situation was, Pyra was still able to process a sense of completion when Ramp-47 closed thirty-two minutes later, thereby locking Sogol outside. Finally, after more than a thousand years of internal warfare, the city of Kahoun was at peace.

It was relatively quiet within the Techno Society's sprawl-ing compound. Partly because it was extremely hot, and any creature that could was waiting for the blazing sun to fall toward the west, and partly because Shaz, Phan, and a large contingent of metal men were out in the desert, where a newly opened ramp led down into the city of the dead.

But Dyson/Kane had begged off. And, given the way he/they smelled, the others had been happy to leave the steadily decaying sensitive behind, thereby providing Kane what he desired most, an opportunity to steal Logos. More than that, to kill Tepho, seize control of the Techno Society, and reactivate the star gates. All of which explained why Dyson, who understood the spirit entity's intentions, found himself standing outside of Tepho's tent with a razor-sharp knife in his skeletal hand.

The dry, hot air was perfectly still, and the soft murmur of voices could be heard from within the tent as members of the technologist's household staff poured gallons of cool water into the large hip bath where the administrator typically took refuge during the hottest part of the day. It was the one moment when Kane could not only be sure that Tepho would be vulnerable, but wouldn't be wearing Logos, which would simplify the attack. Because the last thing the disincarnate wanted to do was stab the human *through* the AI, thereby damaging the very thing he hoped to steal.

Suddenly one voice was raised over all the rest as the attendants hoisted the naked technologist's badly deformed body into the air. "Watch that arm! Careful damn you! Or would you like a taste of the lash?"

There were earnest apologies, followed by a loud groan of unrestrained pleasure, as the administrator was lowered into the cool water. Finally, having been positioned on some carefully placed supports, Tepho was ready for some privacy. "That's enough fussing about," he said gruffly. "You can leave now. . . . But return in half an hour."

It was the same command that he *always* gave, so none of the staff members were surprised as they bowed and backed out of the heavily curtained enclosure.

Silence fell after that, and while it was tempting to enter immediately, Kane forced himself to wait for a full sixty seconds before bringing the knife up over his head and stabbing downward. The tip of the blade penetrated the thick fabric and there was a gentle ripping sound as the sharp knife sliced downward. The unauthorized entrance was *behind* the metal tub, which meant that Kane didn't expect Tepho to notice, but the disincarnate paused just to make sure.

Not having heard any alarm, the spirit entity forced Dyson to stick his head in through the newly created slit. That was followed by an arm, a shoulder, and the rest of the sensitive's steadily rotting body. The platform the copper tub rested on was about ten feet away. And, draped across the custom-built chair that sat beside it, was a long, white robe. And not just *any* robe, but the AI called Logos, who—

important though the construct was—still had to wait while his current master enjoyed a cooling bath.

In the meantime, Tepho caught a whiff of corruption, recognized the odor for what it was, and felt a sudden stab of fear. Because that particular section of the tent was supposed to be empty, and what he thought of as "the creature" had no business being there. But, during the technologist's long, painful childhood, he had learned to suffer even the cruelest beatings without revealing the emotions that his tormentors so wanted to see. And that capacity still came in handy from time to time. "It isn't nice to skulk about," Tepho commented without turning his head. "You might as well come out where I can see you."

The request caught Kane by surprise, but the spirit entity was quick to adjust and forced Dyson's body to approach the copper tub. Tepho saw the knife, wished the raptor was present, and made a note to tighten his personal security. He could call for help of course, but had serious doubts about whether it would arrive in time and resolved to deal with the situation himself. "So," Tepho said, as Dyson/Kane took up a position next to Logos. "It's the AI that you're after."

Kane tried to say, "Yes," but found Dyson was blocking him. That forced the disincarnate to clamp down on the sensitive and start all over again. "Yes. But more than that—I came for *you*. I think the time has come to bring your current incarnation to its logical conclusion."

Tepho allowed his right hand to slide down into the water. "So you can take over."

Dyson's once-handsome face bore a number of open sores, which when combined with his hollow eyes and unshaven countenance, combined to make the variant look like a recently exhumed corpse. Kane sought to make the sensitive nod, encountered a moment of resistance, and struggled to overcome it. "That's the plan," the dead man agreed stiffly. "So, as long as we understand each other, we might as well get the unpleasant part of the transition over with. Who knows? You might be grateful! That's an extremely ugly body that you've been forced to live in."

"Look who's talking," Tepho replied, as the handgun came up out of the bath. Water ran out of the barrel, but the technologist knew it would fire. "Hold it right there," Tepho ordered evenly. "And drop the knife."

Kane looked at the pistol and swore silently. Tepho had him dead to rights, and there was no reason to proceed. So the spirit entity ordered Dyson to release the knife, but the sensitive refused, and worked to muster every bit of life energy he had left. Gradually, like a man carrying a significant weight, Dyson took a tottering step forward.

Tepho, who was unaware of the battle raging within the noxious creature before him, shook his head in disgust. "You really are one stupid son of a bitch." Then, having taken careful aim, the technologist fired three rounds.

Both Kane *and* Dyson felt the heavy slugs tear through their mutual body and heard the gunshots, but their reactions were quite different. Kane was forced to exit the sensitive's body and immediately flew into a towering rage because his ability to influence events on the physical plane had been terminated.

But Dyson, who had finally been able to escape months of enslavement, was overjoyed. And having long since given up any hope of reclaiming his physical body, had already exited the corpse before it hit the floor.

Logos couldn't speak without being worn, so it was left to Tepho to provide an epitaph for the recently vacated body. "Some things were just never meant to be," the administrator commented, as two heavily armed robots entered the room. "There's some garbage on the floor," Tepho added. "Remove it."

The interior of Surface Ramp-47 was like a scene from hell as Rebo and Norr fought to make their way back up to the surface. Because, as the clock continued to tick, and groups of heavily burdened tomb raiders emerged from the city of Kahoun, the on-again, off-again carnage continued. Insults were exchanged, the wounded lay in moaning heaps, hard-eyed overseers cracked their whips, a disabled metal man screeched pitifully, a woman accidentally shot one of her companions in the leg, metal grated on duracrete as an enterprising tomb raider towed his loot up the ramp on a solar panel, and the air crackled with a cacophony of radio traffic as those on the surface issued dozens of conflicting orders.

Thanks to the fact that they were relatively unencumbered, the twosome made good time at first. But then, as they neared the top of the ramp, the situation changed as incoming extraction teams ran into outgoing extraction teams and created a very contentious traffic jam. And it was then, while caught in the backwash of all the confusion, that Rebo spotted the blue-clad combat variant and a face he had never expected to see again. "Look!" the runner said, as he elbowed Norr. "It's Phan! Wearing Techno Society blue!"

The sensitive looked, saw that Rebo was correct, and watched as the assassin sent a brace of heavies in to clear the traffic jam. "We'd better pull back," the variant advised, "or they'll spot us for sure."

The runner regretted allowing Phan to live, knew he would bring all sorts of hell down on them if he were to shoot the scheming bitch, and allowed Norr to pull him back. "So, what are we going to do?" Rebo wanted to know. "We can't stay in here forever, and they'll spot us if we try to leave."

"True," the sensitive agreed thoughtfully, "so let's change the way we look. See those bodies over there? The ones in green? Let's strip them."

In any other circumstance the sight of a man and a woman stripping dead bodies of their clothing would have been the subject of comment if not outrage, but there, within the amoral free-for-all of Ramp-47, the act was little more than a grisly sideshow.

It took a concerted effort to remove the tops and pull the simple garments up over their heads, but eventually the task got done. And though less than enthusiastic about the bullet holes in his newly acquired jerkin and the large bloodstain on the back of it, Rebo was thankful that the garment had a hood. And, judging from the extent to which Norr's cowl hid *her* face, the runner figured that his would function the same way.

Then, as if to validate the effectiveness of the disguises, a man dressed in Menkur green yelled at them from farther down the ramp. "Hey, you two! Give us a hand with this thing!" Rebo, who was eager to blend in, hurried to comply. Norr followed. The "thing" that the man referred to turned out to be one of the Techno Society's metal men, which King Menkur's technologists wanted to study up close so they could create their own army of robotic servants. That was the sort of thing Sogol intended.

The android, which had been tied hand and foot, was still very much "alive," and hung suspended below a pair of long poles. But the weight was too much for just two men, which was why the man in green was happy to recruit two ostensible allies, even if they were strangers to him. "Grab a handle!" the tomb raider ordered cheerfully, "and keep your weapons handy. . . . The blues won't like this—so we may have to shoot our way out."

Rebo swore. Now, rather than slip past the technos unnoticed, they were almost certain to be challenged! But it was too late to choose another course of action, so the off-worlders took hold of the poles, and hoisted them onto their shoulders.

Shaz was the first to notice Menkur's tomb raiders and the burden that the foursome carried as they pushed up toward the top of the ramp, but no sooner had he dispatched a squad of metal men to deal with the android nappers, than a trio of green-clad wings attacked from above. And it was then, while the combat variant and the assassin were busy defending themselves, that Rebo fired the Sokov. The first projectile exploded against the lead robot's chest and blew a palm-sized hole through the metal man's torso. A second machine went off-line as a result of its wounds—and two additional androids were destroyed as more darts hit home.

Then the litter bearers were free of the crowd and out in the desert. A wall of green-clad warriors opened to enfold them, and Shaz was left to fume, still ignorant of the true gravity of his loss. Because not only had a robot been spirited away, the sensitive named Norr had slipped past him as well, along with the AI originally called Logos 1.2. That meant *two* AIs were on the loose. The question, and a rather important one at that, was which Logos would arrive on Socket first.

ELEVEN

The Planet Haafa

And those who choose peace shall find it, if not within places of worship, then within themselves.

—The ascended master Teon,
The Way

Clusters of lights could be seen in the desert as groups of exhausted tomb raiders gathered around campfires to brag about the artifacts they had brought up from the city of the dead, wager bonuses they had yet to receive, and mourn those who had lost their lives to flying machines or enemy tomb raiders.

Such was the case in Tepho's encampment as well, except that unlike the other kings, the technologist was making preparations to leave Haafa. Not forever, but long enough to lay claim to Socket and establish a new system of star gates. Which was why Tepho's staff was busy carrying supplies out to a long line of waiting wagons.

Having just returned from the desert, both the combat variant and the assassin were tired, sunburned, and dirty. But given the potential importance of the news they had to impart, the twosome requested an audience with Tepho and were shown into his tent. Sections of the canvas wall had been tied back to let the night breezes blow through. The administrator's raptor was being disassembled for transshipment, and Tepho frowned as a technician jerked on a handful of wires. "Be careful!" the technologist said petulantly. "That wiring harness is worth more than *you* are!"

"It's almost impossible to find good help these days," Tepho grumbled as he turned to Shaz. "But such is my burden. So, what brought you here? We won't be ready to depart for Pohua until the early hours of the morning."

The combat variant shimmered slightly as he looked toward Phan and back again. "It's the sensitive. . . . The one named Norr. Phan believes she saw both the variant and the runner leave the ramp with a couple of men dressed in Menkur green."

Tepho's gaze shifted to Phan. His eyes were like lasers. "Well?" the administrator demanded. "You *'believe'* you saw them? Or you actually saw them? Which is it?"

Phan swallowed. "I saw them, sir. All of them were dressed in green and carrying a metal man up out of the city."

Tepho frowned. "A metal man you say? Why would they do that?"

The assassin shrugged. "I don't know, sir. But based on the fact that Rebo and Norr aligned themselves with Kufu shortly after they arrived, the green livery could be by way of a disguise."

"Which would have been successful had it not been for your sharp eyes," the technologist observed approvingly. "But *we* have Logos. . . . So, what were they doing in the ruins? Rooting around for artifacts like everyone else?"

The AI knew the correct answer but couldn't tell them

about Sogol without revealing the extent of his own duplicity, so he took the opportunity to nudge the conversation in a different direction. His voice originated from the vicinity of Tepho's neck. "There's no way to be sure," Logos put in, "but they *are* persistent and could be engaged in some sort of plot to recover me."

"That's a good point," Tepho agreed soberly. "And even if they aren't trying to take you back, they know far too much about the Techno Society and the star gates. "So," the administrator said, as he looked from Shaz to Phan, "bring me their heads. I could use a pair of bookends."

Even though it had been dark for quite a while, the main road was busy, because that was the time of day when most teamsters preferred to haul supplies out into the desert. Primarily because it was cooler then. But some, like Certa, had additional motives. By working at night, Certa rarely had to interact with his wife, and that left him free to drink all day at his favorite tavern. Besides, there were thousands of glittering stars to gaze upon during the hours of darkness, and his fellow drivers to trade jibes with. The wagon, which was loaded with empty water barrels, *rattled* as it lurched through a dry riverbed.

It was then that Certa heard the thunder of hoofbeats, waited for the group to pass, and was surprised when they drew up alongside instead. It was dark, but both of Haafa's moons were up, which meant there was sufficient light to see by. The lead riders wore Tepho blue, not that it mattered much, since the teamster prided himself on his neutrality. "Hey, old man," the nearest rider shouted, as he pulled up next to the wagon. "We're looking for a female sensitive and a male norm. Have you seen them? There's a reward."

It was a stupid question given the fact a couple matching the rider's description were seated behind him. Certa was about to say as much when he turned to discover that the hitchhikers were gone. And, given the rider's insulting manner, the teamster saw no reason to help him. Not even for a reward. "No, sir," Certa lied. "I ain't seen nothin'."

The answer was consistent with those given by all the drivers encountered thus far, so Shaz spurred the angen forward, closely followed by Phan and a half dozen heavily armed riders. Once they were gone Certa grinned toothlessly, sent a stream of spittle down toward the surface of road, and felt for the bottle beneath the seat. It was half-full, and the teamster took pleasure in the way the serat warmed the back of his throat before exploding in the pit of his stomach. Others could scrabble for artifacts if they chose to—but Certa was content with what he had.

Meanwhile, a couple of hundred feet back down the road, protected by the darkness that lay like a blanket over the bottom of a dry watercourse, Rebo and Norr came to their feet, dusted themselves off, and took a look around. "Damn," the runner remarked evenly. "That was close. How did you know?"

"I would recognize Phan's energy anywhere," Norr replied grimly. "It looks like they saw us leave the ramp. . . . And they're hunting for us."

"But *why*?" Rebo wanted to know. "They have Logos."

"Who is determined to destroy me," Sogol reminded the runner, from her position on Norr's forearm. "It's my guess that Logos is behind the search."

"Terrific," Rebo responded darkly. "So, what now?"

"We have to reach Pohua," the sensitive answered, as she readjusted her pack. "And we need to arrive before dawn. Any later than that and King Tepho's wings will spot us."

"Okay," the runner said wearily, as he gave her a hand up onto the road. "We might as well get started."

They walked for hours as Haafa's twin moons followed their own inevitable path across the sky to finally disappear in the west, finally entering the outskirts of Pohua just before dawn. But the danger wasn't over, and wouldn't be until such time as they were able to find a safe place to hide and plan their next move. The runner had dealt with such situations before, however, and knew that their best chance was to hide in a place where their pursuers were unlikely to look, such as a monastery. And not just *any* monastery, but a red-hat temple, where the medallion that still hung around his neck would serve as their introduction.

But how to find one? And do so quickly? During his travels, the runner always made it a practice to avoid asking for directions lest he identify himself as a stranger and therefore a potential victim. But there were times when he was forced to take a chance. That was why Rebo made his way over to a roadside tea stand, where he fumbled some coins out of his belt pouch. "Good morning. . . . Two cups of tea please—and directions to the monastery."

The woman behind the rickety counter had skin that looked like poorly tanned leather, sky-blue eyes, and brown teeth. Having been up all night brewing tea for the teamsters, she was tired. "There is no monastery, not in Pohua," the woman replied dully, as she poured hot water into a pair of badly stained mugs. "But the nunnery is located two blocks from the market. Just follow the main road to Pua Street. . . . Take a right and follow Pua to Bako. Go left on Bako. The nunnery will be on your right."

Rebo thanked the woman, tipped her, and handed a mug of tea to Norr. Hopefully, with any luck at all, the vendor would go home before anyone came by to question her. The sun parted company with the horizon shortly after the off-worlders left the tea stand, and wings could be seen circling off to the east as Rebo and Norr made their way through Pohua's unpaved streets. None of the city's structures stood more than three stories tall, most presented blank faces to the street, and all of them were mud brown. Gray smoke dribbled from round chimneys, and the tantalizing odors of a hundred breakfasts wafted through the cool air as Rebo and Norr made their way up Bako Street. The city's shops had just started to open, and the only other pedestrians were children sent to fetch water from the local fountain.

The nunnery was housed in a long, low building no different from those around it except for the fact that it boasted a gently curved dome rather than the flat roof typical of the structures to either side, and double doors opened onto the street.

Rebo took a quick look around to assure himself that no one was watching them, took Norr's hand, and tugged the sensitive toward the entryway. "Come on, let's get out of sight." Norr, who often had trouble blocking out the ebb and flow of raw emotion normally associated with cities of any size, was enveloped by a feeling of serenity as she followed the runner into a spartan reception area. The sensation was akin to entering a pool of cool water on an extremely hot day. A novice emerged from the surrounding murk to greet them. She was young and dressed in black. "Good morning," the aspirant said cheerfully. "Can I be of assistance?"

Rebo was somewhat taken aback, since he knew The Way was divided into *two* sects, the red hats and the black hats. Both were united, or *supposed* to be, but the reconciliation had taken place only recently, and it might be months before word of the change arrived on Haafa. If so, the medallions that the runner and the sensitive wore around their necks might have no value at all, or worse yet, could elicit suspicion. But that was a chance he had to take. Rebo forced a smile. "Is the abbess available? If so, we would like to speak with her. Please show her *this* by way of an introduction."

So saying, Rebo removed the chain from around his neck and passed the bronze medallion over to the novice. If the aspirant was curious about the medal, or the people who had given it to her, she gave no sign of it as she bowed her head. "Please wait here. . . . I will convey your message to the abbess." There was a *swish* of fabric as the young woman left.

Now that Rebo's eyes had adjusted to the relative darkness within the reception area, he could see that while the walls were nearly bare in keeping with black-hat sensibilities, a lushly green garden was partially visible through an intricately carved wooden screen. And it was from that direction that the young woman returned. "Please follow me. . . . The abbess is in the garden."

The off-worlders followed the young woman out into a large inner courtyard, where Norr expected to find the abbess seated on a chair. Nothing could have been further from the truth. Rather than sit and meditate in the early-morning sun, the abbess was down on hands and knees, pulling weeds out of the nunnery's vegetable garden. She stood as the couple stepped out of the shadow cast by the inward-slanting roof that ran the perimeter of the courtyard and wiped a wisp of hair back out of her face. The hand pump, along with the well that it served, was the nunnery's pride and joy. And the medallion had been hung from its spout. "Hello," the abbess said as she gestured toward the medal. "That's an interesting medallion. May I ask where you got it?"

Rebo didn't want to answer the question, especially since doing so would inevitably give the holy woman power over both Norr and himself, but knew there wasn't much choice. Not if they wanted a safe place to stay. "The reincarnated spirit of Nom Maa presented that medal to me within the holy city of CaCanth," the runner answered truthfully. "My companion wears one exactly like it. His Holiness told us that should we ever be in need of food, shelter, or some other form of assistance, all we would have to was present the medallions to any monastery or nunnery."

In spite of the fact that the abbess had white hair, her face was unexpectedly free of lines, as if somehow frozen in time. Although her voice was even, Norr could see the tendrils of skepticism that continued to swirl within the other woman's aura. "How nice," the abbess said lightly. "So, tell me, does the Inwa still affect chin whiskers?"

"The present Inwa isn't old enough to have whiskers," Rebo replied. "And, based on the portraits I've seen, the *last* Inwa didn't have chin whiskers, either."

The abbess smiled and came forward to embrace them. "Forgive me," she said. "But the streets of Pohua are thick with liars—and it's my task to protect the sisters from them. A ship landed in Omu about three weeks ago, and it was about a week after that the good news arrived in Pohua. My name is Kartha, *Sister* Kartha, and you are welcome to stay with the sisters and me as long as you wish."

The merchants who owned stores in the area around the Techno Society's headquarters stood in their various doorways, sipped their morning tea, and watched wagon after wagon arrive in front of the heavily guarded building. A sight they had witnessed before. It wasn't the number of crates that the metal men carried into the structure that made them wonder—but the fact that they rarely saw more than a half dozen boxes come *out*. It was a much-discussed phenomenon that would probably go unsolved given how inhospitable the technos were.

None of which was of the slightest interest to Shaz, who had not only been up all night, but wound up in charge of the off-loading process, which had been under way for hours by then. Many of the crates were headed for Techno Society headquarters on Seros, but there were other destinations as well, depending on what the boxes contained.

Shaz felt the sun warm his shoulders as it climbed up over a building across the street, and was just about to follow the last box inside when Phan emerged from the mouth of an alley halfway down the block. The assassin was on foot, and a squad of metal men marched behind her. "You look like hell," the combat variant observed tactlessly, as the assassin drew near. "Any luck?"

Phan shook her head. "Nothing," she said disgustedly. "It's like they vanished into thin air."

"I know how you feel," Shaz said sympathetically. "Well, once we step through the gate onto Zeen, someone else can worry about them. The chances are good that some bounty hunter or other will nail them. One thing's for sure, though, if they plan to break in and use *this* gate, they're in for a big surprise. I tripled the guards."

"Zeen?" Phan inquired halfheartedly. "I thought we were going to a place called Socket."

"And so did I," Shaz replied. "But that was before Logos announced that Socket is in orbit *around* Zeen. . . . And the only way to reach Socket is via a gate located on the island of Buru. The single point of access was part of a security system put in place by Hios."

The assassin frowned. "Will the gate be operational?"

"Logos says that it will be," the combat variant replied.

"As to whether we should trust him, well, you can be the judge of that."

Phan laughed, followed Shaz into the building, and went in search of a bath.

The inside of the curtained four-wheeled hearse was scrupulously clean, but Rebo didn't like the notion of riding in the same vehicle that had been used to transport hundreds of dead bodies, and he fervently hoped that he would still be alive at the conclusion of *his* journey. Though still tired, the runner felt better in the wake of a two-hour nap, even though it was oppressively hot in the back of the wagon.

The hard-faced nun who was in charge of the hearse whistled to her team as she guided them around a corner. The wagon had only a minimal suspension, and the runner bounced up into the air each time the iron-shod wheels dropped into each pothole only to be jerked out again. But, unpleasant though the tour of Pohua was, examining the city from the back of a hearse was better than making the same journey on foot. Especially since Tepho's metal men were out looking for him.

The objective of the reconnaissance was to take a look at Techno Society headquarters with an eye toward breaking in and using the star gate concealed within. No small task in the best of circumstances but especially iffy without the element of surprise and Hoggles to back him up. Still, the possibility existed, and was therefore worthy of consideration. Especially since Sogol said that while she could "sense" the presence of a gate seed in Pohua, the artifact was bound to be under lock and key and difficult to get at.

But as the wagon approached Techno Society headquarters, any hope of breaking into the building was crushed. As

Rebo peered out through the dusty curtains he saw that a force of metal men had been stationed out front along with one of Tepho's raptors. The machine's energy weapons tracked the hearse as it rolled past.

And it was then, as the runner eyeballed the building's defenses, that he saw Phan walk toward the entrance with a combat variant at her side. Then the scene was gone as an old man bowed to the body in the hearse and the wagon rattled through a drainage ditch. Once the ride smoothed out, the runner rolled over to stare up at the canopy. Six or seven insects buzzed around over his head. There might be some way to get off Haafa, the runner thought to himself—but it sure as hell wouldn't be through Techno Society headquarters. The nun whistled, the angens plodded down a side street, and the afternoon sun scorched the sky.

The lamp, which was not fueled by oil, or any known source of power for that matter, had burned day and night for the entire three-hundred-plus years since a long-dead member of the Alzani clan had purchased the object more than a thousand miles south of Pohua. And, because the merchant family had prospered during the years since, many members of the family, including the current patriarch, Ubri Alzani, had come to believe that the clan's material well-being was somehow linked to the lamp and its seemingly inexhaustible source of power.

Now, as Alzani and his number three son sat at the ancient counting table totaling the week's profits, light from the lamp cast a soft glow over stacks of gleaming coins and threw black silhouettes onto the wall behind them. Both men had black hair, aquiline noses, and long, narrow faces.

A breeze found its way in through open double doors to stir the gauzy curtains and cool the room's interior. The abacus made a steady *clack*, *clack*, *clack* sound as the younger Alzani flicked beads along their various wires, and distant laughter could be heard as a flock of children chased each other down long, empty halls.

Perhaps, had the two men been paying more attention, they might have detected other sounds as well. Like the soft *thump* as someone vaulted over the low wall that defined the space just outside the double doors, the subtle *rasp* of steel as a sword left its scabbard, and the gentle *rustle* of Norr's clothing as the sensitive positioned herself just outside the counting room.

But before Norr entered the room, it was important to make sure that the object she sought was actually there. With that in mind, the sensitive shifted the sword to her left hand and elevated her right hand so that Sogol could see into the room as well. Then, having pulled the serpent-like AI back beside her ear, she listened to the construct speak. "The object you want is sitting in the middle of the table," One-Two whispered urgently. "Somebody figured out a way to tap the power core—and turned the gate seed into a lamp."

The sensitive shifted the sword back into her right hand, peered into the room, and stared at the lamp. The shade was yellowed with age, and the lower edge wore a dark red fringe. Below that, suspended within a wrought-iron framework, a shiny sphere could be seen. There was a sudden stirring inside the room as coins were added to already bulging leather bags, and the men stood, ready to call it a night.

Fearful that the merchants would take the lamp with them when they left, Norr stepped through the door and placed her left index finger against her lips. Both men froze as the woman appeared, but only for a moment, as the younger of the two made a move toward the pull cord that dangled nearby. But the sensitive was fast. Three quick strides and a jump carried her up onto the surface of the table. Coins scattered as Norr turned, the blade flashed, and the pull cord parted. Then, having spun full circle, the variant paused. The razor-sharp edge was in contact with Ubri Alzani's throat. The younger man stood by the door. "If you run, *he* dies," Norr told the younger man emotionlessly. "The choice is up to you."

The sensitive saw emotions swirl as the son battled temptation. It would have been easy to run and thereby receive his portion of the family business years early, but the better part of him won out. The younger man held both hands palm out. "Take the money. . . . I will do as you say."

"Good," Norr replied equably. "Except that I don't want your money . . . Both of you—back into the corner."

"*What* then?" Ubri Alzani wanted to know, as he and his son backed away.

"The lamp," Norr answered, as she bent her knees to the point where she could grab the object. "All I want is the lamp."

"*No!*" the patriarch objected. "Please! I beg of you! Not the lamp. . . . Take the money. All of it. I promise no one will follow."

"I'm sorry," the sensitive replied sincerely, "but it's the lamp that I need. Now, assuming that you want to keep your heads on your shoulders, stay right where you are." There was a gentle *thump* as the variant landed on floor, the curtains billowed, and Norr was gone.

No more than two seconds elapsed before the two men sprang into action. Ubri drew a curved dagger and circled the table, intent on following the thief through the double doors, while his son jumped up to grab what remained of the pull cord. Bells rang in a distant part of the house, additional guards poured out of the servants' quarters, and those who were on duty ran every which way.

Meanwhile Norr, who was dressed all in black, retraced the path followed earlier. An almost impossible feat for anyone other than a sensitive, who could "see" the psychic energy emitted by the Alzani family's guards even in complete darkness should that be necessary. But thanks to the fact that one of the planet's two moons had broken company with the horizon, there was more light than there had been before.

That worked two ways of course, as became apparent when a sharp-eyed youth spotted what looked like a swiftly moving shadow and fired his muzzle-loader. A long red flame stabbed the night, a loud *bang* reverberated between the compound's protective walls, and the sensitive heard something *buzz* past her head as she made a mad dash toward the still-dangling rope.

That was when Rebo, who had been waiting outside the compound, could finally spring into action. It had taken Norr more than an hour to convince the runner that *she* was the right person to enter the walled complex and abscond with the gate seed. And now, as he felt her tug on the other end of the rope, his counterarguments came back to mind as *more* weapons were discharged.

Norr heard bullets smack into the wall around her as she discovered how difficult it was to climb one-handed, yelled a warning to Rebo, and threw the lamp up over the top. Then, with both hands free to grab the rope, and the runner pulling from the other side of the wall, the variant was able to "walk" up the vertical surface as a half dozen guards pounded their way across the courtyard.

Then Norr was on the top and poised to cross over, when the musket ball slammed into her back. The sensitive fell into a pool of blackness, felt her spirit exit her body, and knew she was dead.

Rebo screamed *"No!"* caught his lover as she fell, and half carried, half dragged Norr toward the waiting hearse. The stern-faced nun ran to help. Together, they lifted the sensitive up into wagon bed. Though unsure of where the object had come from, the sister saw the lamp and tossed it to Rebo. Moments later she was up on the driver's seat with the reins in hand. She issued a shrill whistle, and the hearse jerked into motion.

In the meantime Rebo held a wad of fabric against Norr's wound as he cradled the sensitive in his arms and whispered into her ear. "Hang on, Lonni, *please* hang on." But there was no answer as the wagon rumbled through the streets, and tears streamed down his cheeks. Something had been gained—but the runner was afraid that something much more important had been lost.

There was a hiss, followed by a roar, as jets of hot water mixed with a powerful disinfectant struck Tepho and his attendants from every possible angle. All of them were nude. And, since the administrator *never* allowed anyone other than his handpicked staff to see him naked, the rest of the expeditionary force, including Shaz and Phan, were scheduled to follow once the technologist was fully dressed and ready to receive them.

Once the cleansing process was complete, Tepho and his attendants padded into the circular room where the star gate was housed. Boxes of food, equipment, and ammo had been stacked against the walls. Dry clothes were waiting for the administrator, as was Logos, who had taken on the appearance of a vest.

Mindful of the fact that the first group of Tepho's subordinates would be along shortly, the attendants hurried to towel the administrator down and help him into his clothes. Shaz and Phan arrived shortly thereafter. Neither was the least bit embarrassed by their nudity, although Tepho was staring at Phan, and the assassin wished he wouldn't.

Then, once everyone was dressed, it was time for one last conference. Because, unlike the tiles that represented planets like Seros, Ning, and Thara, the square labeled ZEEN, remained dark and therefore nonoperational. Or so it appeared. But Logos, who claimed to be able to monitor *all* of the star gates via Socket, had the power to bring it back to life. Or so he claimed. The proof, as with everything else, would be in the doing of it.

The technologist forced a smile. "Okay, then. . . . What are we waiting for? Let's load the boxes labeled T-1 onto the platform."

It took the better part of fifteen minutes to get the first load of equipment and people onto the relatively small service platform, but once everything was in place, it was Shaz who reached out to press the tile labeled ZEEN.

The square lit up, just as Logos had predicted it would, and the usual spiel began. The combat variant listened with eyes closed, but the explosion of light was so brilliant that he could see it through his eyelids. Then, as his body was literally ripped apart for the trip through hyperspace, Shaz momentarily ceased to exist. Then, as the operative's molecules were reassembled, he was conscious once more. He experienced a sense of relief, quickly followed by the nausea that typically accompanied a transfer and exposure to the star gate's power core.

Judging from the grimy walls and the thick layer of dust

that covered the floor, it looked as though the chamber hadn't been utilized in a long time. Tepho was the first to speak. "Okay, Shaz, time to earn your pay. . . . Take a com set with you and let me know what you find. I'll get things organized here."

The administrator clearly had no intention of venturing out of the chamber until he knew it was safe to do so, but Shaz didn't find that at all surprising, and grinned at Phan. "Ladies first."

Given the fact that they had no idea what might await them beyond the confines of the star gate, both the combat variant and the assassin elected to keep their clothes on as they checked their weapons, approached the door, and cycled through.

And that was just as well, because when they stepped out into what should have been the decontamination chamber, most of it was missing. What remained bore a close resemblance to a cave, which judging from the bones lying scattered about, had recently been home to a large carnivore. Filthy tiles covered most of the right-hand wall, plus portions of the floor, but the rest of the facility had been damaged. Roots had pushed their way down through the ceiling, and the left-hand wall had been ruptured, allowing soil to spill out onto the floor.

In addition to a brace of semiautomatic pistols, Shaz had armed himself with a fully automatic assault weapon, which the combat variant held at the ready as he advanced toward the bright oval of daylight visible where the hatch should have been. Phan followed close behind.

Seconds later, they were standing at what had once been ground level, looking down into a broad valley through which a river wound back and forth. A herd of animals could be seen grazing next to a marshy area, skeletal-looking birds circled above, and the shadows cast by clouds caressed the land. "It looks like the ground dropped away," Shaz observed. "There must have been a quake or something."

"Yeah," Phan agreed phlegmatically. "I sure hope Logos knows what he's doing."

"Oh, I think he knows what he's doing," the combat variant replied cynically. "But for whom?"

No sooner did the hearse rattle through the nunnery's gates, than a shout was heard, and half a dozen nuns came running. There was a *bang* as the wagon's tailgate fell, and Rebo was brushed aside as Norr was literally snatched out of his arms before being rushed inside.

Rebo, still dazed by what had taken place, grabbed the lamp and followed the nuns into what turned out to be a spacious medical clinic. It was the only facility of its kind available to the city's poor. The operating room was tiled, spotlessly clean, and better equipped than the runner would have expected. Sister Kartha was present, as were two capable-looking assistants. She ordered the runner into a corner while she washed her hands. In the meantime, the other nuns proceeded to strip Norr of both her weapons and clothes prior to turning the sensitive facedown on the operating table. Once that was accomplished, the two women went to work mopping up what looked like an extraordinary amount of blood, and began to prep the area immediately around the blue-edged wound. "So, she's alive?" Rebo ventured tentatively.

"Yes," Kartha replied irritably. "She is. No thanks to *you*. But just barely, and truth be told, I have no idea why. By all rights your wife should be dead."

"She isn't my wife," Rebo said dully, his eyes fixed on Norr.

"No?" the abbess inquired caustically as she waved her hands to dry them. "And why is that?"

"Because I'm an idiot," the runner confessed miserably.

"Now there's something we can agree on," Kartha said grimly. "Now shut up so we can get to work."

There were advantages to being located in Pohua, where ancient medical artifacts surfaced on a fairly regular basis, and—though never cheap—could sometimes be purchased at a relatively reasonable price, especially if a certain king wanted to be treated for the venereal disease that continued to plague him.

Norr felt a strange sense of detachment as she "stood" next to her physical body and looked down on it. The scene was murky, which meant the details were hard to discern, but there was no mistaking the urgency with which the nuns were preparing to operate on her. And judging from the size of the hole under her right shoulder blade, the team was wasting its time. That was why Norr was tempted to turn away and seek higher planes, where physical pain was unknown.

But a tendril of energy still connected the sensitive to her physical body. It was rather weak, however, and Norr knew she could sever it if she chose to, but something held her back. But what?

"The answer is simple," Lysander, said as his thoughts began to flow into the variant's mind. "Look at the thought forms around Rebo. . . . That's why you're tempted to stay."

The sensitive looked, "saw" how miserable the runner was, and felt what he felt. A vast longing combined with an impending sense of doom.

Lysander glowed with internal light as he came to "stand" at her side. "And there's one more thing," the spirit entity added. "Rebo is here because of *you*. Should you choose to terminate this incarnation, he will be lost in grief—and Logos will take control of Socket. And not just Logos, but the Techno Society under the leadership of Tepho, who wants to control the star gates for the same corrupt reasons that I did.

"So I beg you to stay, not just for the sake of the man who loves you and came back to the physical world in order to protect you, but for the sake of humanity as well. Because the long slide into darkness has begun—and the gates represent the only hope for something better than barbarism."

Norr was about to respond, about to say something, when Sister Kartha pushed a probe down into the open wound, and the resulting pain sent the sensitive reeling. "There it is," the abbess announced, as the metal stylus made contact with the lead ball. "Now to get it out."

Rebo had seen medicos extract bullets before, which was why the runner expected Kartha to pick up a scalpel and *cut* the projectile out.

But the abbess had another tool in mind, something that had been common once, and would be again if craftspeople were able to successfully duplicate the artifact. Metal *scraped* on metal as the solar powered surgical scarab was removed from a basin filled with disinfectant and placed on the sensitive's bare back.

Rebo watched in fascination as the tiny insectlike robot scurried up to the wound, circled the hole as if to determine its exact diameter, and dived inside. "First the machine will cauterize all of the bleeders," the abbess explained. "Then it will make its way down to the musket ball and remove it."

The runner had seen something similar on a previous occasion, and was about to say as much, when a novice burst into the surgery. "Sister Kartha! Come quick! The police are at the door. They claim the sensitive is a thief!"

The abbess looked at Rebo, uttered one of the many

swear words she had learned during a childhood spent in the slums of Pokua, and turned back again. "Tell them I'm busy. . . . Show them into my study and bring them some tea. I'll be there as soon as I can."

The aspirant nodded, turned, and hurried into the hall.

Under normal circumstances, the fact that the authorities were practically standing outside the door waiting to arrest him would have sent Rebo into the fight-or-flight mode. But now, with Norr's life on the line, the only thing the runner cared about was the scarab. A lot of time had passed since the robot had descended into the wound, or so it seemed to Rebo, and he was just about to comment on that when the slightly deformed musket ball popped up out of the hole.

Sister Kartha made use of a pair of forceps to pluck the projectile off Norr's skin and hold it up for inspection. It was flattened on one side. "Here it is . . ." the abbess said. "It looks like the bullet slanted upward and came to rest against her scapula. Now, as soon as the scarab finishes repairing the damage to her tissues, it will back its way out and close the wound. At that point I will allow the police to enter."

"But you can't!" Rebo objected. "They'll throw her in jail, and she'll die there."

"You should have thought about that possibility earlier," the abbess responded sternly. "You may have a relationship with Nom Maa . . . But that doesn't entitle you to steal other people's property! The sisters and I have a spiritual obligation to heal the sick—but we aren't required to harbor criminals. Oh, and surrender your weapons. . . . We'll have no killing here."

The runner was tempted to argue his case, to try and explain *why* the theft had been justified, but could see that it wouldn't make any difference. "All right," he said humbly. "I'm not ready to surrender my weapons, not yet, but I'll bring our things in here. Maybe they'll let us keep some of our clothes."

If the abbess thought Rebo was about to flee, she made no effort to stop him as the runner bolted out of surgery and sprinted down the hall. Once in the cell where the two of them had been allowed to sleep, the off-worlder grabbed what few belongings they had and went back the way he had come. The scarab had surfaced by that time, Norr's wound had been sealed, and the robot's tiny feet continued to wiggle as the abbess placed the device back in its basin.

"Okay," Rebo said, as he dumped both packs next to the operating table. "I can't tell you how much I appreciate all that you've done. . . . The police are sure to separate us once they come in—so could I have a moment alone with Lonni?"

Kartha's expression softened. "Yes, or course. But don't take long."

"I won't," the runner promised, and felt for Norr's pulse as the nuns left the room. It was weak, but still there, and Rebo allowed himself to hope.

Norr wasn't entirely sure what was taking place in the physical realm, but allowed herself to be drawn back into her body, where it was necessary to grit her teeth against the pain. Conscious now, but still laid out on her stomach, the sensitive heard Rebo speak. "Sogol? Can you hear me?"

The AI slithered up the sensitive's bare arm to gather itself on her shoulder. "Yes," the computer answered, "I can hear you."

"Good. Lonni damned near got killed stealing that gate seed . . . So the least you can do is get us out of here!"

"I would be happy to," Logos 1.2 responded. "But before

I can activate the gate seed you must remove the sphere from the cage that presently surrounds it."

Now, having been reminded, Rebo knew that the AI was correct. Once activated the globe would start to spin—which wouldn't be possible until the object was released from the lamp. But how to free it? And do so *before* the police came to get him?

The runner swore a long string of oaths as he secured a grip on the big instrument cabinet, wrestled the piece of furniture over to the door, and pushed it into place. The obstacle wouldn't keep the authorities out for very long, Rebo knew that, but figured any delay would help.

Having bought some time, the runner began to rifle through the cabinet's drawers. He had already rejected a number of instruments, none of which looked like they would be appropriate to the task, when he saw what appeared to be a bone saw. But would it cut through metal? Rebo was about to experiment when Sogol spoke. "What about Norr's sword? Would *that* do the job?"

"Damn!" Rebo exclaimed. "I should have thought of that." The bone saw clattered as it hit the floor.

The nuns had removed both the sword and scabbard shortly after bringing Norr into the operating room. The runner hurried over to where the weapon lay and heard the whisper of steel as he pulled the blade free. Norr, who had been witness to the conversation, managed to croak his name. "Jak . . ."

Rebo felt his heart leap. He hurried to the young woman's side. "You're conscious! Thank God! How do you feel?"

"Never mind that," the sensitive whispered hoarsely. "Be careful with the sword! The blade is extremely sharp. If you aim for the center of the lamp, it will cut through the framework *and* the gate seed."

"Which would be most unfortunate," Logos 1.2 put in. "Because the resulting explosion would destroy this room, the nunnery, and half of Pohua."

"Thanks for the warning," Rebo said dryly. Then, having placed the lamp well clear of the operating table, the runner brought the sword up over his head and brought the super-sharp edge down along the right side of the lamp. There was a shower of sparks as metal parted, the runner took a nasty shock, and the acrid scent of ozone filled the air. His arm was still tingling when Rebo returned the weapon to its scabbard and bent to retrieve what remained of the lamp. He was relieved to see that the sphere was intact. Then, as the runner struggled to bend a piece of metal out of the way, someone began to pound on the door. "This is the police! Open up!"

Rebo drew the 9mm, fired two shots into the very top of the door, and heard loud scuffling noises as the police beat a hasty retreat. "Okay," the runner said, having returned the pistol to its holster, "where were we? Ah, yes, the gate seed. I press on both dimples for sixty seconds . . . right?"

"That's correct," Sogol assured him. "Then, when you feel the locks give, twist both hemispheres in opposite directions."

Rebo pressed, heard noises out in the hall, and knew the police were getting ready to take another crack at the door. "Hurry," Norr croaked. "Or we'll rot in whatever passes for Pohua's jail." The sensitive made an attempt to rise, but the pain was too intense, and she collapsed.

Finally, after what seemed like an eternity, the locks gave. Then, having secured a good grip on both halves of the sphere, the runner twisted them in opposite directions. Beams of bright light stabbed the walls, the object started to oscillate, and Rebo had to let go as a battering ram hit the door.

TWELVE

The Planet Zeen

Those who swim the sea must ride the currents, for to oppose them is to challenge the planet itself, and therefore the stars.

—Saylo Imono, phib philosopher,
Currents

The elders had been hung by their thumbs from the frame-
work that normally served to smoke meat during the fall months, when the entire village labored to make itself ready for winter, and the dogs grew fat from eating scraps. The villagers' bare feet had been weighted with rocks, and hung only six inches above the coals, which meant that those who were conscious could smell their burning flesh. All because the village's chief had been so brave, or so stupid, as to spit on the crippled man.

But, in spite of the systematic torture, the locals refused to surrender their secrets. Or so Tepho assumed, as he ordered one of the metal men to throw another bucket of water onto Subchief Milo Vester, in hopes that the shock would revive him. The water hit the villager's smoke-blackened face, brought him back into full consciousness, and provoked an explosion of steam as it hit the hot coals. The subchief screamed, or tried to, but produced a strange choking noise instead.

Meanwhile, those villagers lucky enough to survive the spitting incident stood in a sullen group with downcast eyes. Tepho made use of the dead chief's hand-carved totem stick to point at Vester's badly charred feet. "You think that's painful?" the off-worlder demanded contemptuously. "You know nothing of pain. . . . I was born in pain, have lived with pain every day of my life, and know what *real* pain is. And so will you unless you answer my questions truthfully."

"But I *have*," Vester protested pitifully. "There is *no* island of Buru, not that I'm aware of, so how can I tell you about it?"

Tepho slapped his leg with the totem stick and was about to order one of the metal men to put more wood on the fire, when Logos spoke. Because the AI's voice seemed to originate from Tepho, the villagers assumed that *two* spirits occupied the stranger's twisted body. They stirred uneasily and sketched protective symbols into the air. "He could be telling the truth," Logos suggested. "I doubt any of these people have been more than a couple of hundred miles from the village—so their knowledge of geography is bound to be somewhat limited. Not to mention the fact that the island could have been renamed during the years I've been absent."

Vester wasn't sure where the second voice was coming from, but sensed a potential ally and was quick to agree. "That's right!" the subchief said desperately. "We're ignorant people here. . . . We know nothing of such important matters."

Tepho tapped his cheek with what had become a swagger stick. "Then who would?" the technologist inquired mildly.

"Lord Arbuk would!" Vester answered eagerly. "He rules from the city of Esperance."

Tepho turned to the assembled villagers. "Is that true?"

Heads nodded, and a number of voices answered in the affirmative.

The administrator eyed their grimy faces. "Who among you has been to Esperance?"

After a pause, and some whispering, three slightly hesitant hands went up.

Tepho turned to Shaz and Phan. "Put them in shackles. Kill the rest."

Rather than waste ammunition on a planet where it could be difficult to obtain more—the combat variant ordered the metal men to carry out the executions with their clubs. Some of the villagers tried to flee, but were quickly run down and dispatched on the spot.

Vester passed out at some point during the bloody process but was returned to consciousness when the rain hit his face. The off-world killers had departed by then, so even though the subchief *wanted* to die, no one remained to grant his wish. Tendrils of steam rose around the subchief, raindrops fell like tears, and Socket passed high above.

The Planet Haafa

There was a loud crash as the battering ram made contact with the operating room's door, followed by the sound of splintering wood, and a prolonged screech as two burly policemen pushed the heavy storage unit out of the way. Once the path was clear the chief of police and Ulbri Alzani stepped into the surgery and paused to look around.

They saw the operating table, the nude woman who lay facedown on it, and the man who stood next to her. Then there was a flash of light, followed by a miniature clap of thunder, and the tableau disappeared. The table, the woman, *and* the man vanished into thin air, as did part of the nearest wall, a sizeable chunk of the tiled floor, and the Alzani family's prized lamp. The reality of that, the finality of it, brought the old man to his knees. And that's where Ulbri Alzani was, still sobbing, when his number three son came to take the patriarch home.

The Planet Zeen

When Rebo came to he was drowning. The water was crystal clear, which meant he could see the operating table, Norr, and all manner of other objects as they drifted toward the sandy bottom. The runner wanted to breathe more than he had ever wanted anything before. But if *he* needed to breathe, so did Norr, who continued to sink toward the bottom in spite of her feeble efforts to swim. It felt as if his lungs were on fire as Rebo fought his way down to the variant, grabbed a fistful of her hair, and kicked as hard as he could. Bubbles raced them to the surface, spray exploded away from the runner's head, and Norr emerged a second later.

Both spluttered as they gasped for air. Rebo spotted an island, wrapped an arm around Norr's torso, and kicked for shore. The bottom came up quickly, Rebo found his feet, and cradled the sensitive in his arms as he marched up out of the water toward the smokestack-shaped construct that dominated the center of the island.

Norr winced as the runner laid her down in the shade. Rebo saw the grimace, rolled the sensitive onto her side, and saw that her wound had reopened. A rivulet of blood was running down her back. The runner unbuckled his weapons harness, hurried to remove his shirt, and worked to wring as much water out of the wet garment as he could. Norr made a face when the cold, salty fabric came into contact with her wound but knew Rebo was doing the best he could.

Satisfied that the makeshift pressure dressing would stop the bleeding, the runner set about gathering driftwood for a fire. Thankfully, there were more than a dozen wax-coated matches in one of his belt pouches. The first stick broke off just below the head, but the second produced a wisp of smoke, followed by a bright yellow flame. Twigs crackled as they caught fire, larger pieces of wood burst into flame, and it wasn't long before waves of welcome heat rolled over Norr. The shaking stopped soon thereafter, her color improved, and her respirations evened out.

And that was when Rebo realized that Sogol was missing. The last time he'd seen the AI she had been coiled up on Norr's back. The runner wondered where the construct was now. . . . Back on Haafa? But he had more pressing problems to deal with, starting with the fact that Norr still looked pale, and he had very few items to work with. That was when the runner remembered seeing the operating table drift toward the bottom of the sea—and wondered what else might be laying around out there? There was only one way to find out. Rebo added more wood to the fire, knelt next to Norr, and was about to tell her about his plan, when the runner realized that the sensitive was either asleep, or unconscious, a possibility that made his mission that much more urgent.

A quick scan revealed that outside of what might have been another island, and a sail on the far horizon, there was nothing else to be seen other than a nearly cloudless sky and the sea below. Or was it a lake? No, he was a fisherman's son, and knew that the line of seaweed and other debris that ran horizontally around the island represented the high-tide mark, the presence of which implied at least one moon.

Having left both his weapons and boots piled next to Norr and equipped himself with the remains of a broken plank, Rebo retraced his earlier steps down into the sea. Besides providing additional flotation, the plank's other purpose was to help the runner bring salvaged materials back to the beach, assuming he recovered any. The first objective was to find the operating table, which, being the largest object transferred, would also be the most visible. Then, assuming the water wasn't too deep, he would dive to retrieve whatever he could.

Rebo stretched out on the plank, paddled his way out to what he hoped was the correct area, and rolled off into the salty water. Then, with his face down and one arm thrown across the length of wood, he kicked with his feet. Thanks to the fact that the water was extremely clear, he could see all the way to the sandy bottom. There were outcroppings of rock, along with spiral-shaped plants, that swayed from side to side as the runner passed over them. Fish, if that's what the pancake-shaped creatures could properly be called, fled ahead of the human, their pale bodies undulating as they hurried to escape the dark menace above.

It was all very pretty, but Rebo couldn't tell whether he was cruising over the correct area, and that led to a lot of fruitless swimming before the runner spotted the gleam of what might have been metal. He didn't have any way to secure the plank, but the water was relatively calm, so he figured the length of wood wouldn't drift very far while he went down to investigate.

Rather than the operating table, which the off-worlder expected to find first, the object in question turned out to be Norr's sword. Rebo carried the weapon up to the surface, where he laid it on the plank. More dives produced *more* treasures, including the bone saw that the runner had discarded

back on Haafa and both of their packs. So, knowing that the
sensitive kept a small first-aid kit among her things, the
runner battled to bring the waterlogged leather sacks up to
the surface. Once there, he hung them below the plank,
which was partly awash by then. Finally, by dint of considerable kicking, Rebo pushed all of his loot ashore.

The fire was still burning, albeit much lower by then, as
the runner made his way up out of the water. He was encouraged to see that Norr had not only raised herself into a
sitting position but managed a wave. That was when Rebo
saw the saw light reflect off gold, realized that Sogol had
come ashore on her own and wrapped herself around the
variant's arm. "Hey, there," the runner said, as he dropped
the packs next to Norr. "How are you feeling?"

"Better," the sensitive replied. "Look! Sogol brought
me this!"

The sensitive opened her fist to reveal the tiny scarab.
The machine turned circles on the palm of her hand as it
searched for something to repair. "It was what you humans
would call luck," the AI said modestly. "I ran into the scarab
on the bottom, and it was small enough to hold in my jaws,
so I brought it along. End of story."

"Not quite," Norr objected. "One-Two put the scarab
into my wound—and I feel better as a result."

"Let's take a look," Rebo said, and knelt to lift her shirt.
The runner was no expert, but the wound had been re-
closed, and there was no sign of bleeding. "It looks good,"
Rebo confirmed, "but take it easy. What you need is a rest.
What can I get for you?"

"More clothes would be nice," the sensitive said sweetly,
and gestured toward her pack.

"Maybe I *like* you half-naked," Rebo replied mischievously.
And that was when the ground shook, a loud roaring

sound was heard, and Rebo turned toward the structure that
stood behind him. It was flat black, stood about twenty feet
tall, and looked like a smokestack. There hadn't been enough
time to investigate whatever the thing was previous to that
point, not with Norr to tend to. But now, what with the
roaring sound, the runner felt the need to find out what it
was. "You'd better take your guns," the sensitive suggested,
and lifted the harness partway off the ground.

"You'll be okay?"

"I'll be fine," Norr said, as she pulled her pack in close.
"Check on the noise, come back, and fix me a seven-course
meal. I'm hungry."

Rebo grinned. If the sensitive was hungry, that was a
very good sign indeed! He buckled the guns on over bare
skin, climbed the sandy slope that led up to what he had already begun to think of as "the stack." As he got closer, the
runner realized that the structure was made out of metal.
He circled the stack, discovered that a ladder had been
bolted to the far side, and scrambled upward. Once on top,
he peered down the tube into the poorly lit tunnel below. It
was quite a drop, but thanks to the maintenance ladder that
was attached to the inside surface of the stack, Rebo was
able to descend without mishap.

A pool of sunlight marked the bottom of the ladder, and
Rebo could feel residual heat from the machine that had
passed twenty minutes earlier. As the runner peered down
from the service platform, he could see two metal tracks,
both of which were shiny from continual use. That suggested that the underground trains ran fairly frequently. But
where did the machines come from? Where were they going? And to whom did they belong? The last question was
the most troubling, since there was no way to know what the
owners were like or how they would respond to trespassers. It

seemed as if the best thing to do was lie low, give Norr time to heal, and find a way off the island.

But had Rebo been aware of the camera that followed each step of his progress as he made his way back up the ladder, he would have known that it was too late to escape notice. Because the people who owned the tunnel, as well as the train that ran through it, already knew exactly where to find him.

Having worked hard all morning, Lord Arbuk rose from his desk, lumbered over to the side table where a carafe of steaming caf stood waiting for him, and filled a ceramic mug. Not one of the silver vessels that populated the ornate tray at his elbow, but a lowly piece of pottery, which, though homely, would keep the liquid hot. A must insofar as the land-lord was concerned, since he viewed lukewarm caf with the same contempt reserved for phibs, which the nobleman looked on as little more than walking-talking angens.

Mug in hand, Arbuk strolled out onto his private balcony. A sheer wall fell away to stone buildings that stair-stepped down to a rocky beach and the half-empty harbor beyond. The city of Esperance had intentionally been built next to the sea, where it could benefit from shipping. But that was back before the phibs took control of the planet's oceans and thereby prevented land-lords such as himself from transporting raw materials, manufactured goods, or people across what the freaks liked to refer to as "their sacred waters." But not forever, because Arbuk and his peers had a surprise in store for the phibs, one that would reestablish Esperance as a seaport!

In spite of the sun's warmth, the land-lord felt a sudden chill and turned to discover that his private secretary, a sensitive named Hitho Mal, was standing three feet behind him. Arbuk was a *big* man, and his jowls took on a purplish cast as blood rushed to his face. "Dammit, man! Announce yourself. . . . I hate people who skulk about."

Mal, who had long prided himself on his ability to skulk about, was unmoved. He had the long, narrow face typical of his kind, sunken cheeks, and thin lips. The upper one remained stationary as he spoke. "Yes, sire, sorry, sire. I know you're busy, but there's someone I would like you to meet. His name is Milo Vester, and assuming that he's telling the truth, something very strange took place in the village of Kine."

Arbuk struggled to remember the place, was unable to do so, and concluded that Kine must be one of the many small villages that marked the outskirts of his holdings. He took another sip of caf. " 'Strange'? How so?"

"If your lordship would indulge me," Mal replied respectfully, "I prefer that you take the tale from Vester's own lips. Especially since you are almost certain to ask questions that I would be unable to answer."

Knowing that Mal rarely requested anything not in his employer's best interest, Arbuk was willing to comply. That didn't mean it was necessary to do so gracefully however. Which meant there was a good deal of grumbling as the robed sensitive led his rotund employer down a twisting staircase—and into the rather primitive medical facility that occupied one corner of the building's basement.

But what waited within was sufficient to silence even the land-lord, who as a member of the ruling class, had not only witnessed his full share of brutality but been responsible for some of it himself. Vester, who had suffered greatly during the interminable wagon trip to Esperance, had been laid out on a bed. The crisp white sheets had the effect of accentuating the villager's filthy body, smoke-blackened clothes, and badly charred feet. The patient's eyes were closed, but fluttered as the sensitive touched his arm, and remained open thereafter. "Tell him," Mal ordered gently. "Tell Lord Arbuk what happened to your village."

The villager's voice was faint, so it was necessary to bend down in order to hear him, and Vester's breath was so bad it caused Arbuk to gag. But the story was well worth listening to, especially the description of the blue killing machine, which sounded as if it might be a twin to the heavily damaged Raptor II that presently occupied a place of honor in Arbuk's personal war museum. "Tell me," the nobleman said, as he pinched his nostrils. "The people who accompanied the killing machine . . . were they norms? Or phibs?"

"Most were norms," Vester replied, "although some were machines that *looked* like humans."

Arbuk was surprised. "Machines . . . you're sure of that?"

"Yes, sire," Vester maintained staunchly. "I'm sure."

"How very interesting," Arbuk said to no one in particular, as he straightened up. "You were correct, Mal. . . . Subchieftain Vester is well worth listening to. I don't know who these people are, but I want them found, and quickly, too."

The lord and his secretary turned, and were about to depart, when Vester produced a croaking sound. Arbuk turned back. "Yes?" the nobleman inquired, "is there something more?"

"Kill me!" Vester begged pitifully. "*Please* kill me."

Arbuk glanced at Mal. "Do you have everything you need?"

The sensitive had a clipboard. Vester's recollections had been written down. "Yes, sire," the variant answered. "I have every word."

"Good," Arbuk replied, as he turned back to Vester. "Your request is approved."

The land-lord was halfway back to his office when the muffled *thump* of a gunshot was heard, and Vester was free to return to Kine, where the rest of his family had already been buried.

It had been dark for quite a while, and Rebo was asleep in the lean-to that he and Norr had constructed next to the ventilation stack, when the sensitive nudged his arm. "Jak! Wake up! Where's the light coming from?"

The runner was already reaching for a weapon when his eyes popped open, and he saw the rays of white light that were streaming down through the cracks in their steeply slanted roof. Pistol at the ready Rebo rolled out onto the brilliantly lit sand and looked upward. The illumination was more concentrated than moonlight—and appeared to originate from space. Norr had emerged by then, which meant Sogol was present as well. "Look!" the variant exclaimed. "I think it's moving!"

Reno looked out across the brightly lit water and realized that Norr was correct. It appeared that they were standing in a pool of light that was gradually creeping toward the west. "Of course it's moving," Sogol put in matter-of-factly, as she slithered up onto the sensitive's shoulder. "What you're seeing is sunlight reflected from a mirror aimed at the planet's surface."

"But where's the mirror?" Rebo wanted to know. "And what's the point?"

"Socket is an artificial planetoid," the AI explained patiently. "The engineers took many things into account when they constructed it. The creation of tides on a planet where none previously existed led to a variety of problems. Massive public works projects were required to cope with fluctuating water levels. That made some sectors of the population unhappy. But, back before Emperor Hios succumbed to his lust for power, he was a capable politician. By providing the citizens of Zeen with low-cost power generated by tide-driven turbines—he overcame their objections to Socket."

"That's all very interesting," Norr commented, as she continued to stare up into the sky. "But what does all that have to do with the light?"

"There were lots of construction projects back in those days," Sogol answered. "Many of them ran around the clock. So, in order to further ingratiate himself with the planet's populace, Hios ordered that a steerable mirror be installed on Socket. A mirror that could bounce sunlight down onto the dark side of the planet—and thereby illuminate the project with the highest priority."

"So, what's happening now?" Rebo inquired. "Why point the mirror at mostly empty ocean?"

"Like so many other functions on Socket, the solar mirror is simply drifting out of control," the AI replied sadly. "And, were I to take control of the reflector, Logos would know."

"It's best to leave it alone then," the runner said feelingly. "We have enough problems already."

Norr nodded her agreement and held hands with Rebo, as the massive blob of light continued its journey toward the west. Finally, once the darkness had been restored, they went back to bed.

Omar Tepho and his force of humans and robots had trav- eled a quarter of the way to the city of Esperance when they stopped to spend the night in a fishing village called Wattl. A not-very-distinguished gathering of stone-and-wood buildings that was home to a population of norms who liked to refer to themselves as "fishermen" but actually made their livings as pirates. Something Lord Arbuk was willing to tolerate so long as the villagers limited their predations to the phibs, who liked to trawl the coastal waters for slat fish, even though that made them vulnerable to the speedy eight-oared cutters crewed by the residents of villages like Wattl.

So, when Tepho guided his raptor into town, closely followed by six metal men and a contingent of twenty-five heavily armed humans, the locals were torn between fear and greed. But there was scant opportunity for skullduggery as the strangers took control of the only inn, displaced the previous guests, and established a defensive perimeter through which none of the locals were permitted to pass.

Meanwhile, as if drawn to Wattl by a conjunction of planetary influences, other forces were in motion as well. Because even as the red-orange sun descended toward the gently rolling sea, a water-slicked head surfaced out in the harbor, and a cross-shaped wing circled high above. Each served a different master, and, while neither was aware of the other, they soon would be.

Except for one massive deluge, the weather had been mild up to that point, which was fortunate indeed. But each dawn was accompanied by the need to gather both food and water. Which was why Rebo began each day by stripping off his ragged clothes, strapping a sheath knife to his right calf, and carrying the homemade spear down to the edge of the water. It felt cold at first, *too* cold, but a combination of thirst and hunger urged him on. Based on a process of trial and error, the off-worlder knew that while the pancake-shaped "floppers" were relatively easy to spear, they were bony and didn't taste very good. That was why the runner typically went looking for what he thought of as "zip fish" because of their ability to dart from place to place and the black streaks that ran the length of their silvery bodies. They made for good eating, but they were hard to hit, and it took at least two of them to make a decent meal.

On that particular morning, the runner was fortunate, and managed to nail *three* of the speedy animals in a span of fifteen minutes. Having strung the fish together on a piece of cord, Rebo swam out to what he thought of as "the well," where, in order to meet nutritional requirements of its own, one species of seaweed produced fist-sized bladders filled with desalinated seawater. Then, having harvested six containers of water, it was the runner's habit to put his face down and swim straight in. Once ashore the fish would be roasted over the fire, while Norr attempted to squeeze one more mug of tea from an already exhausted bag, and Rebo watched from a few feet away. And later, once breakfast was over, it would be time to resume work on their partially built raft.

But that morning was to be different, as quickly became apparent when the runner brought his head up and put his feet down. Because, as Rebo stood, he saw that Norr's hands were bound in front of her, and three heavily armed phibs were waiting for him on the beach. The runner knew that the amphibians, like sensitives, heavies, and wings, were the result of genetic tinkering carried out thousands of years before. In this case the goal had been to create a strain of humanoids equipped to more fully exploit the water worlds that the ancients had colonized, thereby lowering the costs associated with construction, mining, and aquaculture.

Later, once that goal had been accomplished, some phibs had migrated to worlds like Zeen, where they not only took up residence in the oceans, rivers, and lakes, but where they frequently displaced thousands of norms who made their livings on or near the water.

The phibs had sleek, hairless skulls and double-lidded eyes that helped them see underwater. They also had respiratory systems that could extract oxygen from water, as well as streamlined bodies, and webbing that bridged both fingers and toes. The phibs also had shapely breasts, or at least one of them did, which identified her as female. Sogol, who had apparently been mistaken for a piece of expensive jewelry, was wrapped around the woman's left biceps. The amphibians wore what amounted to G-strings and watched impassively as the nude male made his way up out of the water. "I'm sorry," Norr said miserably. "I was asleep."

"It wasn't your fault," the runner replied stoically.

"Drop the spear," one of the males said, as he pointed the 9mm pistol at its previous owner. Like members of many local populations, the phib spoke with what the runner regarded as a thick accent although he knew the man with the gun would perceive the situation differently. There was nothing Rebo could do but drop the fish, the water pods, *and* the spear.

"Now the knife," the female added sternly.

The runner, who had begun to wish that he'd gone swimming with his clothes on, bent to remove the knife from its sheath.

"This is a waste of time," the second male said irritably. "They're pirates. . . . Shoot them and be done with it."

"That's what the norms would do to us!" the female added emphatically.

Norr could see the dark, threatening thought forms that

swirled around the other variants and felt frightened as a result. But the first male, the one who seemed to be in charge, refused to acquiesce. "We're *supposed* to be better than they are . . . remember? Not to mention the fact that the spooks will want to interrogate this pair. So shut the hell up, grab their belongings, and destroy the lean-to. It could attract even *more* pirate trash. . . ."

Rebo was tempted to engage the first male in conversation, in the hope that he could convince the local that they *weren't* pirates, but he decided to let the opportunity pass when Norr gave a subtle shake of her head. The runner knew the sensitive could see things that he couldn't—and had reason to trust her judgments.

Fifteen minutes later the phibs and their prisoners were seated in a miniature version of the larger trains that blasted through the tunnel twice each day. Rebo had been allowed to pull on some pants by that time, but was otherwise unclothed, as both he and Norr were strapped into their seats. Though still a little bit sore, the variant's wound was mostly healed, which meant she could move without pain.

When the minitrain took off, it departed with near-neck-snapping acceleration, and was soon traveling so fast the tunnel's walls were little more than a gray blur. The off-worlders were on their way—But to where?

The attack on the village of Wattl came in the early hours of the morning when most of the citizens were still asleep. There were watchmen of course, posted on the ancient breakwater to warn their fellow villagers should the phibs launch an assault on the sleeping town, but two had been drinking and passed out. The third saw dozens of water-slicked heads break the surface of the water, and was about to ring the warning bell, when a beam of coherent energy drilled a hole through his chest. A smoke ring rose from the circular wound as he fell, and the first wave of heavily armed variants marched up the stony beach. Having lost three fishing boats and seven people to the shore-based pirates over the last thirty days, the local amphibians were extremely angry.

That's why all of the cutters that were drawn up on the beach were holed, nets were piled up to be burned, and even the wharf dogs were shot down. But, unbeknownst to the phibs, they were attacking the Techno Society as well. And even though Wattl's watchmen failed to deliver a timely warning, a sharp-eyed robot had detected the presence of multiple heat sources *before* the phibs surfaced, and radioed a warning to Shaz.

Once alerted, Tepho rolled out of bed and was already shouting orders as sleepy attendants hurried to dress him. Then, having made his way downstairs, the technologist rushed to climb into his raptor. Shaz and Phan were already present, along with a dozen heavily armed mercenaries. They followed the bipedal machine as servos whirred, weapons swiveled, and death stalked the streets.

Some of the villagers were up by then, firing projectile weapons at the oncoming horde or running for their lives as their fellow citizens were cut down by blue death. Formerly solid walls exploded, wood houses burst into flame, and angens screamed as they tried to escape from their pens.

But then, just when it appeared that the phibs would destroy the entire village, Tepho guided the raptor around a corner and opened fire. In spite of the fact that the raiders possessed energy weapons, too, surprise combined with superior firepower made it possible to cut the variants down.

Tepho, who was secure within the comfort of his armored cockpit, laughed out loud as blips of blue light raced the length of the waterfront to snatch phibs off their feet. Others came apart so that heads, arms, and legs pinwheeled through the air. But most of the invaders were simply incinerated as bolts of blue energy wiped them away, leaving little more than black streaks to mark the places they had stood.

The raptor took hits, half a dozen of them, but the shoulder-fired weapons didn't pack enough of a wallop to hole the machine, so the surviving variants had no choice but to retreat into the harbor, where the water would protect them from further harm. Tepho continued to fire as the amphibians pulled back, but Shaz ordered his mercenaries to conserve their ammo and was the first to take notice of the fact that some additional combatants had arrived on the scene. The combat variant saw the wings sweep in from the south, circle above, and fire down at the phibs.

Then, just as Shaz was about to warn Tepho, what looked like a yellow comet arced high above the village and exploded at the center of the harbor. There was a *boom*, as a huge geyser of water shot up into the air and hung there for what seemed like a minute but was actually little more than a second or two. The column of water was translucent, which meant that Shaz could see the phib bodies suspended within the spout, along with what might have been large sea creatures and the remains of fractured boats.

Then, as the geyser started to collapse, the combat variant realized what would happen next. He yelled, "Run!" and turned in order to follow his own advice.

The tidal wave ramped up the steeply shelving beach, exploded over the seawall that had been built to protect the village, and sent fingers of frothy seawater raging up Wattl's streets. Tepho had just started to turn the raptor around when the water hit, lifted the machine off its pods, and carried the construct a good thirty feet before putting it down again. But the water would be forced to return, the technologist knew that, which was why he directed the raptor into a side street and took refuge behind a sturdy stone house. The seawater ran back toward the harbor a few moments later, where it poured over the seawall, taking most of the dead phibs along with it.

Tepho knew his machine couldn't stand up to a comet like the one that had just caused so much destruction, and was already in the process of making a run for it, when a detachment of Lord Arbuk's wings dropped a wire net over the raptor. It might have been possible to blow holes in the mesh with his energy weapons, but that was before a team of twelve angens appeared at the other end of the waterfront, wheeled to bring a huge mortar to bear, and were immediately released.

Tepho took one look at the artillery piece, knew that it had produced the comet, and tilted his weapons up toward the sky. Or tried to, since the netting got in the way and kept the administrator from opening the canopy as well.

Once it became clear that both the phibs *and* the strangers had been neutralized, Arbuk's carriage rattled through the village and down onto the seawall, where with some help from Hitho Mal, the fat man was able to exit the coach. The netting had been removed from the raptor by then, thereby revealing a machine ten times better than the one that resided in his war museum. "Look at that," the nobleman said approvingly, "it's practically new! And who, pray tell, is the strange-looking cripple?"

Tepho, who had heard every word, stood trapped between two members of Arbuk's household guards. And rather than mount a suicidal attack on the nobleman's troops, Shaz, Phan, and all the rest of the administrator's mercenaries had allowed themselves to be disarmed.

"I'm told that the cripple was piloting the machine," the sensitive whispered into his superior's ear. "And, judging from the thought forms that hover around him, he's very angry. It seems he's sensitive about his appearance, which, interestingly enough, bears a close resemblance to the man who leveled the village of Kine."

Arbuk nodded. "Yes, I can see the resemblance. Still, anyone who likes to kill phibs can't be all bad, so let's see what the rascal has to say for himself. We'll put him on the rack if he proves to be too obstreperous."

That being said, the nobleman waved Tepho forward. "My name is Arbuk, *Lord* Arbuk, and you are?"

"Tepho, sire, Omar Tepho," the off-worlder responded carefully. The comments about his body, plus the fat man's tendency to talk about him as if he wasn't there, were infuriating. But the technologist was powerless to do anything about it.

"It's a pleasure to meet you," Arbuk replied evenly. "Or it might be, depending on what you're up to. Now, if you would be so good as to enter my carriage, we will retreat to a more comfortable location. Once there I'm going to ask you where you came from, how you got here, why you chose to destroy the village of Kine, and what makes the island of Buru so important to you. Shall we?"

Having been stripped of all power, Tepho had no choice but to agree. Especially given the fact that the fat nobleman was very well informed. A pair of footmen boosted the off-worlder up into the coach. Arbuk and Milo followed. Once inside, the nobleman couldn't help but feel pleased with himself. But what Arbuk didn't know, was that Tepho was wearing the *real* prize, who, thanks to his ability to link up with Socket, was watching the whole scene from the very edge of space. The carriage jerked into motion, wings wheeled high above, and the villagers of Wattl began to bury their dead.

Lassa Pontho swam up into one of the bubblelike medita-tion pods that floated in and around the city of her birth, sat on the curvilinear seat, and took air straight into her lungs rather than through her gills. Spread out around her, in a valley between two undersea plains, lay the city of Shimmer. It consisted of fourteen domes of various sizes, each having dozens of locks and a variety of purposes. Seen from a distance, and bathed in shafts of sunlight that slanted down from the surface, the city looked like something from a fantastic dream. Gardens of brightly colored plants swayed in the cleansing current that flowed through the valley, shoals of tame fish patrolled the rocky bottom, and sleek sea sleds came and went, each trailing its own stream of bubbles.

Shimmer had been built hundreds of years before, back when the artificial satellite called Socket had first been commissioned, and thousands of phibs had been brought in to work on projects related to the newly created tides. And, thanks to the power provided by their precious tidal generators, the variants had been able to sustain their underwater culture during the years since.

But the land-lords were not only jealous of what the phibs had but determined to bring their society down and profit in the process. That fact had everything to do with the disastrous raid on the village of Wattl, a raid that had been justified by the loss of phib fishing boats but was actually part of a larger effort to keep the norms landbound, lest they build ships and use them to attack phib cities.

But even more worrisome was the fact that those who

survived the raid reported that the land-lords had deployed a *new* weapon, a machine that walked upright on two legs and was equipped with powerful energy weapons. All of which suggested that the norms were in the midst of an unprecedented technological resurgence.

Further evidence of that could be seen in the reports submitted by paid agents. They claimed that three ironclad warships were being built inland, where they were safe from coastal raids, and would eventually be transported to Esperance by rail. And once the vessels arrived, Lord Arbuk and his cronies would probably launch them as quickly as possible and immediately put to sea. There was no way to know which phib city they would attack first—but Shimmer was closest to the harbor.

But could paid agents be trusted? They were norms, after all, therefore automatically suspect. Pontho had very little choice but to trust them, however, since it was almost impossible for a phib to pass as a norm and vice versa. The mayor's reverie came to an end as a series of beeps came in over her headset. "Yes?"

"Sorry to interrupt," a male voice said respectfully, "but one of our security came in with a couple of pirates in tow."

Pontho felt a twinge of annoyance. Couldn't they handle anything without her? "So?"

"So, they're somewhat unusual," the functionary responded evenly. "And the master-at-arms wants you to participate in the interrogation."

Pontho took a look at her wrist term. She had a million things to do. "Tell him I'm busy."

"The pirates claim to be from another planet," the voice added. "And they're looking for the island of Buru."

"*Buru?*" Pontho demanded. "You're sure?"

"Yes, ma'am."

"Tell the master-at-arms that I'm on my way."

Like most such facilities, the interrogation chamber had dingy walls, a floor that could be hosed clean, and harsh overhead lighting. What didn't show, was the fear that had been etched into the ceiling, walls, and tiled floor. It couldn't be *seen*, not in the usual way, but it was real nonetheless. In fact Norr could "hear" the screams as they echoed back through the years, "feel" the hopelessness of the prisoners who had been tortured there, and even "see" one of them standing in a corner. He was crying, and judging from the thought forms that surrounded him, had been for a hundred years. But there was nothing Norr could do to help the hapless entity because both she and the runner hung suspended in midair, clasped within the embrace of a force field they couldn't see.

Rebo tried to speak, to tell the phibs what he thought of them, but couldn't move his lips. The guards thought that was funny and laughed. The master-at-arms stood with arms crossed over a well-muscled chest. He smiled grimly. "Save your energy, pirate. You're going to need it."

Norr's attention was elsewhere. With one exception, all of their belongings were spread out on a table, where they had been repeatedly inventoried. But now, as new guards arrived, the female was about to depart with Sogol still wrapped around her arm! Would the master-at-arms approve? No, the sensitive didn't think so, but he didn't know. And, since Norr was unable to speak, the variant did the one thing that she could: She made an attempt to reach out with her mind.

The 9mm pistol was heavier than any object that she had ever tried to levitate, but if were she to succeed, Norr felt confident that the ensuing ruckus would be sufficient to hold the female guard for a bit longer. So in spite of the difficult circumstances—the sensitive sought to find the peaceful place within. Once there, the variant summoned all her mind-force, shaped it into an invisible pseudopod, and directed the newly formed limb over to the table. Then, having wrapped the weapon in a cocoon of psychic energy, Norr ordered it to rise. But nothing happened as the female security officer paused to say something to the burly master-at-arms, laughed as if in response to a shared joke, and turned to leave.

Desperate now, the sensitive bore down, and sent even *more* energy out into the center of the room. That was when she heard a cry of astonishment. Norr's eyes were open, and had been throughout, but now she "looked." Everyone in the room, master-at-arms included, stood frozen in place as the pistol floated, barrel upward, two feet above the surface of the table!

And that was the tableau that met Mayor Pontho's eyes as she entered the chamber. "And what," she wanted to know, "is going on here?"

The gun fell, hit the table with a loud *bang*, and fell to the floor. And, because Sogol was the only one free to answer, it was she who spoke. "My name is Logos 1.2," the AI responded assertively, "and I need your help."

THIRTEEN

The city of Shimmer, on the Planet Zeen

And in the 226th year of the 3rd epoch, strange machines will walk the land, those who live in the deeps will rise up, and the emperor will return from the dead.

—The seer Sumunda,
Visions in a Glass

When Sogol spoke, no one was more surprised than the woman who had the snake-shaped AI wrapped around her left biceps. She reacted by tearing the serpent off and tossing it onto the table, where it wiggled, rolled over, and slid to a stop. And that was the point when Logos 1.2 coiled her body as if to strike and hissed.

The master-at-arms looked from the snake to the woman and back again. That was the moment when he realized that rather than turn the snake in, as the security officer was supposed to do in situations like that one, the female had been about to steal it. Even worse was the fact that the other members of her team were willing to tolerate such behavior! His jaw tightened, orders flew, and all three of the miscreants were led away.

Though not particularly interested in the details surrounding the way in which the security officers would be disciplined, Mayor Pontho *was* interested in floating guns, talking snakes, and the prisoners suspended in front of her. Especially since they were looking for the island of Buru, a place currently occupied by a force of wings on behalf of the norms. "Release the prisoners," she ordered. "And bring some chairs. . . . I have no idea what's going on here—but it should be interesting to find out."

Though not especially pleased by the manner in which the mayor had taken control of the interrogation process, the master-at-arms had no choice but to acquiesce. Ten minutes later, both Norr and Rebo were seated at the table and, much to the sensitive's delight, were clutching mugs of tea. "Okay," Pontho began. "Start at the beginning. Who are you? Where are you from? And why are you interested in Buru?"

Norr looked at Rebo, saw the runner shrug, and knew it was up to her. And, given the fact that Sogol had already spoken, she saw no alternative but to tell a truthful but abbreviated version of their adventures, starting on the Planet Seros and culminating in their recent arrival on Zeen.

It took more than an hour to tell the tale, and when it finally came to an end, Pontho shook her head in amazement. "That's quite a story. . . . One that's pretty hard to believe. Especially the part about your snake, the so-called star gates, and our moon. But who knows? Strange tales are true at times. I will ask one of our scholars to look into the matter—and perhaps he or she will find a way to authenticate your tale. In the meantime I think it would be best to keep both you, and, ah Sogol, under lock and key."

"No!" Norr objected. "That would be a terrible mistake! Techno Society operatives may already be on Zeen, but if they aren't, they soon will be. And when they arrive, they will bring professional killers, metal men, and killing machines with them. Then they'll head for Buru."

"Wait a minute," the mayor interrupted. "Did you say 'killing machines'? Describe one."

So Rebo began to describe what a raptor looked like, and was only halfway through, when the master-at-arms came to his feet. "That's it!" he proclaimed. "That sounds like the machine that attacked our forces in Wattl!"

Pontho experienced a sudden sense of exultation mixed with an equal measure of fear. While she was glad to hear that Arbuk and his cronies weren't in the process of building two-legged killing machines, it was clear the land-lords had a new ally, and a dangerous one at that.

For the first time, the mayor forced herself to address the snake. She felt silly, talking to what looked like a piece of jewelry, but what if the creature was *real*? What if it really could control the moon, open star gates, and whisk people from one planet to another? "So tell me, Sogol," she said, as she made eye contact with the object in front of her, "what will happen next?"

"That depends on *you*," the AI replied unhesitatingly. "Lonni is correct. An earlier iteration of myself entered into an alliance with the Techno Society. If allowed to do so, Logos and his human functionaries will travel to Buru, where they will enter a star gate and transfer to Socket. Once aboard the satellite, Logos 1 will reinstall himself, seize control of the star gates that remain in operation, and begin the process of reseeding the planets that were served in the past. Once that process is complete, they will *control* humanity rather than serve it. But only if you let them. . . . If you take us to the island of Buru, we will board Socket and block the Techno Society."

"It *sounds* good," Pontho allowed cautiously, "but here's

the problem . . . No, *two* problems. The first problem is that all we have is your word for what's going on. Maybe you and your companions are the ones we should be worried about—and the other people are trying to chase you down."

"What about the killing machine?" the AI countered. "And the casualties you suffered?"

"Maybe they didn't know who we were," the politician replied warily, "and fired in self-defense."

"That's a fair question," Norr put in, "but we have a character witness. Someone you trust—and will vouch for the truth of what we say."

Pontho lacked eyebrows, but she had large double-lidded eyes, and they widened slightly. "Really?" she inquired skeptically. "And who would that be?"

Norr's features went slack, and Rebo looked worried as a spirit entity took control of the sensitive's body. "Hello, honey," a female voice said. "It's Aunt Cyn. . . . Remember the toothfish? And how it nipped your calf when you were seven? I had a hard time explaining that one to your mother! She never let me take you outside the dome again. These people are real, hon. . . . They aren't perfect, none of us are, but they're trying to make things better. And remember, those who wind up in control of Socket will have the power to *move* the satellite, which would eliminate the tides."

"The generators," Pontho put in. "That would shut them down."

"Exactly," the disincarnate agreed. "So do what you can to help them. You won't be sorry."

Then, just as quickly as the spirit had arrived, she was gone, and Norr was in control of her body once again. The mayor appeared stricken—and tears rolled down her face.

"There are sensitives on land, so I have heard of such contacts, but never experienced one myself. A toothfish took a chunk out of my leg—and I have the scar to prove it. And, since there's no way that you could have possibly been aware of that incident, I'm inclined to believe you.

"But I told you that *two* problems stand in the way of your plan. The first has been resolved—but the second is much more difficult. The land-lords, which is to say the people who control all of the landmasses, occupy the island of Buru, which means that you won't be able to set foot on it."

"That's true," the master-at-arms allowed. "But we control the sea all around them—so it's a standoff."

"*Was* a standoff," Rebo said grimly. "Things are about to change."

The city of Esperance

It was dark outside, and rain splattered against thick glass, as the two men stood in front of a huge wall-mounted map. "The island of Buru is right *there*," Lord Arbuk said, as he covered a tiny dot with the tip of a pudgy finger. "About seventy-five miles off the coast."

In spite of the fact that he and his subordinates qualified as prisoners, such were the freedoms allowed them that Tepho felt rather comfortable within the nobleman's castle-like home. Because in spite of the rude comments made about him in Wattl, Arbuk had been extremely courteous since, and the two men had a great deal in common. Both were analytical, ambitious, and completely ruthless. All of which was likely to make for a good alliance, so long as they continued to desire the same things, and there was no shortage of loot. "And you control it," the technologist commented, as he stared at the tiny brown blob.

"Yes," Arbuk replied honestly, "I do. The surrounding waters are a different story however. The phibs control those."

Tepho frowned. "Then how do you transport supplies to the island?"

"Wings," the nobleman answered laconically. "A healthy wing can fly about a hundred miles without resting, so Buru is well within their range, so long as they aren't overburdened. And, since they grow most of their own food, my staff are quite self-sufficient."

Logos had been listening intently and chose that moment to enter the conversation. Arbuk, who had grown accustomed to the AI by then, remained unperturbed. "What about the transfer station? Is it intact?"

"I honestly don't know," the land-lord replied, as he lumbered toward a massive armchair. "I've never been there. . . . Where is it?"

"Toward the center of the island."

"Ah," Arbuk replied, as he sank into the well-padded comfort of his favorite chair. "Then I think we're in luck. . . . The wings believe that those who spend too much time in the island's interior sicken and die. That's superstitious nonsense of course, but variants aren't as intelligent as we are, which makes them susceptible to ridiculous beliefs. Odds are that the transfer station is much as you left it."

Both Tepho and Logos knew good news when it was placed in front of them. If wings who ventured in toward the center of Buru became ill, it was probably because the star gate's power core was up and running, but neither entity saw any reason to share that piece of intelligence with the local.

"Good," Tepho said blandly, as he stood with his back to the crackling fire. "So, given the fact that the phibs control the waters around Buru, how should we proceed?"

Arbuk had already given the matter some thought. Because if the weird little cripple and his talking shirt really could transport themselves up to the moon and reactivate a network of star gates, then he intended not only to benefit from the technology but control it. So, as the land-lord locked his hands together across the vast expanse of his belly, the essence of a plan had already been formed in his mind. "It's dangerous to build ships in coastal towns," the nobleman explained, "because the phibs have a tendency to come ashore and burn them.

"However, unbeknownst to the degenerate freaks, three steam-powered ironclads are nearing completion about twenty miles inland from Esperance. Within days, a week at most, we can bring those ships west by rail. Then, before the phibs can stop us, we will set sail for Buru. What do you think of *that*?"

Planning was best of course, but Tepho was grateful whenever good luck came his way, and he smiled crookedly as he spoke. "I think you're brilliant."

The city of Shimmer
The water at the center of the council chamber was chest deep, which made it difficult to walk around, but allowed the phib politicians to sit half-supported by the water, float on their backs, or, in the case of those who felt the need to move about, swim out into the deep end and tread water.

In the meantime, Mayor Pontho and representatives from the other city-states were seated on a stage above the deep end, where they were three hours and twenty minutes into a discussion of whether the city of Shimmer would be left to tackle Arbuk's forces alone or would receive assistance from the other communities. The subject was rather controversial because the other mayors, who were understandably reluctant to upset the delicate status quo, had their doubts regarding the entire notion of star gates and wanted to know what was in it for them and their constituencies.

Rebo, who had been forced to remain immersed in the water while waiting for the seemingly endless debate to end, was busy looking at his pruny hands when Pontho finally called his name. Norr, who was half-floating beside him, had to jab the runner in the ribs in order to get his attention. "Jak . . . she called your name!"

The phibs watched in amusement as Rebo churned his way across the deep end of the chamber to a set of stairs that led up onto the stage. The runner was wearing a pair of cutoffs, but still felt naked as he padded across the platform and left a trail of wet footprints to mark his progress.

There were nine mayors, including Pontho, and all had seats at the oval table. None wore anything more elaborate than a genital pouch, and some were completely naked. Five of the politicians were female, which meant that four were male, all of whom appeared to be older rather than younger. There was a raised bench on which guests could sit, but the norm chose to stand. "It's my pleasure to introduce Jak Rebo," Pontho said. "Some of you have expressed concerns where Lord Arbuk's new ironclads are concerned. They are by all reports powerful vessels that could interfere with an attack on Buru. . . . However, thanks to military expertise acquired on other planets, Citizen Rebo is ready with a plan that could neutralize the threat. Citizen Rebo?"

Rebo didn't have any military expertise, not really, but knew it wouldn't be a good idea to say that. So, with all eyes upon him, the runner proceeded to outline his plan. "As you know, Mayor Pontho's agents report that three steam-powered warships are presently being constructed about twenty miles inland from the coastal city of Esperance, and will be ready within a matter of days."

That was the projectionist's cue, and the map appeared on the ceiling, where those who were floating on their backs could see it, as well as on all three of the walls around the stage. But unlike the maps used ashore, this one ignored all but the most important roads to focus on the capillary-like network of streams and rivers that fed the oceans.

A pistol-shaped electronic pointer had been left for Rebo's use. After pointing the device at the wall, the runner pressed the firing stud and was immediately rewarded with a red dot. It slid up to the point where the name ESPERANCE marked a large bay. And there, flowing into the harbor, was a narrow finger of blue. "This is the Otero River," the off-worlder said. "What I propose to do is lead a party of raiders upstream, march a mile overland to the point where the iron-clads are being constructed, and destroy them *before* the locals can transport them to Esperance. Then, with the steamships out of the way, we can attack Buru."

It was a simple plan, but still worthy of another hour's debate, and Rebo was back in the water floating on his back when the final decision was made. A finding that ultimately had more to do with a widely shared desire to destroy Arbuk's warships than any particular enthusiasm for the off-worlders, their talking snake, or the system of star gates they were so obsessed with. "Thank you," Pontho said sincerely, as the results of the unanimous vote were announced. "You won't be sorry."

Rebo wasn't so sure about that, but hoped it was true, and let his hand stray to the good luck amulet that he wore around his neck. Except that the object wasn't there, and hadn't been for some time, even though he was going to need it more than ever.

Norr, who knew the runner pretty well by then, and could "see" the doubts that swirled around Rebo, took his hand in hers. Nothing was said, and nothing needed to be. The end of the journey was near, and if they could survive the trials ahead, a much more pleasant journey was about to begin.

The village of Wattl

Inu Harluck was drunk, or had been, back before he stumbled out of the Evil Eye tavern, entered the adjacent stable, and passed out. It was a blissful state, and one that the fisherman-pirate preferred to remain in for as long as possible, which made the pain that much more annoying. But there was no escaping it, so Harluck was forced to surface and open his eyes.

Shaz saw the man's eyelids flutter, uttered a grunt of satisfaction, and removed the knife tip from the local's neck. A single drop of blood welled up to mark the point where the surface of the drunk's skin had been broken. "It's time to wake up," the combat variant said contemptuously. "There's money to be made."

What little light there was emanated from a lantern that was hanging a good ten feet away. So, as the fisherman looked upward, and saw the man-shaped image shimmer, he began to flail his arms and kick with his legs in a futile attempt to escape what could only be a spirit. A murdered phib, perhaps, returned from the depths, ready to cut his throat. But when Phan threw a full bucket of water in his face, Harluck's head began to clear. "Who are you people?" the pirate spluttered. "And why pick on me? I ain't done nothin' to you."

"No," Shaz agreed, "you haven't. But this is your lucky day. . . . We want to hire you, your crew, and your boat. Not the cutter—but the sailboat. The one you stole from the phibs."

"I *didn't* steal it," the local objected hotly, "I found her. Empty she was, just drifting, pretty as you please."

"That's not what your brother-in-law told us," the combat variant responded. "But save it for the local constable. We don't care how you came into possession of the boat. What we *do* care about is an early start. So stand up, pull yourself together, and round up your crew."

Harluck stood, made a futile attempt to brush some of the filth off his clothes, and looked from one person to the other. He had scraggly hair, furtive eyes, and a pointy chin. "I don't believe I caught your names."

"I'm Shaz," the variant replied, "and this is Phan."

"Well, Citizen Shaz," the fisherman said officiously, "my services don't come cheap."

"No," Shaz agreed sardonically, "I'm sure they don't. This coin was minted elsewhere, but it's solid gold and worth more than you would normally make in a year."

Lanternlight reflected off the crono as it arced through the air. Harluck intercepted the gold piece and weighed the object in the palm of a callused hand, before running a cracked nail across the face of a man who had been dead for more than two hundred years. Then, not having detected any lead, the pirate tucked the coin away. "So what kind of contraband are you smuggling?" he wanted to know. "And where are we headed?"

"There isn't any contraband," Shaz replied evenly. "As for our destination, that's the island of Buru."

The pirate turned pale. "Buru? No, way! The phibs will kill us."

"Maybe," the combat variant allowed. "But that's the chance we take."

Harluck looked from one hard face to the other. "What if I say 'no'?"

"Then *I'll* kill you," Phan replied cheerfully. "Take your pick!"

Both of the strangers thought that was funny and laughed out loud. Harluck wanted to run, but knew they would catch him, and cursed his miserable luck. Because even though the gold coin lay heavy in his pocket—there wasn't much chance that he would live to spend it.

The city of Esperance

Viewed from water level, out in the bay, the city of Esperance glittered like a necklace of diamonds laid across a piece of black velvet. It was nighttime, and had been for hours by then, but most of the city's residents were still up and blissfully unaware of the raiders who had already penetrated their defenses. Fortunately for them, the sleek web-fingered commandos had no designs on the city itself. Their goal lay twenty miles upriver, where a short hike would take them to the village of Prost, where three warships rested on specially made rail cars, waiting for their trip to the sea. Like young people everywhere, the phib warriors were eager to begin the journey.

But Rebo felt different. Unlike the genetically engineered phibs, and in spite of the skin-suit they had given him to wear, the runner was cold. More than that he was tired. In fact, if it hadn't been for the powered sled on which his body rested, Rebo knew he would never have made it that far. Now, as he and his commandos lay doggo among the swells, a team of scouts were probing the point where the Otero emptied into the bay. The mouth of the river was sure to be guarded, or so it seemed to Rebo, so he wasn't especially surprised when a bright-eyed phib arrived to tell him as much. What little light there was emanated from the city beyond—and both men rose and fell with the swells. "They have a net stretched across the Otero," the youngster whispered. "And guards on both banks. It would be easy to kill the pigs though . . . just give the word."

"No," Rebo said emphatically. "No killing. . . . Not unless absolutely forced to do so. The bodies would be discovered—and the norms would rush to protect the ships."

"Then what should we do?" the scout wanted to know.

"Stay in the water," the runner instructed. "And cut two holes in the net. Keep them small, no larger than a sled, and mark them with radio beepers. Then, once everything is ready, let me know."

The youngster said, "Yes, sir!" and sank below the surface.

Then, as Rebo and the rest of his raiders continued to bob up and down, a light detached itself from those that lined the shore and gradually grew brighter. That was accompanied by the rhythmic *splash-creak* of oars and the low rumble of conversation. A noncom surfaced next to the runner, whispered, "Guard boat!" and hooked his thumb downward.

The runner nodded, took the rubber mouthpiece between his teeth, and goosed the sled's electric motor. It purred softly as short wings cut into the water, and the sled slid beneath the waves. Because he didn't have gills, Rebo was forced to rely on oxygen stored within the cylindrical sled, and had already grown used to the metallic taste. The tiny instrument panel in front of him glowed green, and once the submersible was about fifteen feet under the surface, the runner leveled out. Other green lights could be seen to the right and left, but none was bright enough to be visible from above, as the guard boat passed over their heads.

Fifteen long minutes passed after that—a near eternity

in which there was plenty of time to wonder whether the scouts had been discovered, the alarm had been given, and the entire plan revealed. Time, too, in which to wonder how much oxygen he had left and feel the relentless cold creep into his bones. But finally, with the surety of someone who had practiced underwater navigation his entire life, the scout appeared out of the gloom. And, at the young man's urging, Rebo directed the sled upward.

There was a feeling of relief as the city's slightly blurred lights appeared, because even though it was dangerous on the surface, it felt good to be in his rightful element again. The scout had extremely white teeth, and they appeared to glow in the strange half-light. "We're ready, sir!" he proclaimed. "Follow me."

So Rebo followed, and it wasn't long before the lights grew brighter, and were split by a canyon of darkness where the river entered the bay. The entire force slid beneath the waves at that point, formed two columns, and was subsequently guided upriver by a combination of low-frequency voice commands, homing beacons, and watchful scouts, one of whom was there to shepherd the runner through one of two holes in the net. The passage was anticlimactic in a way, since it had taken so much effort to prepare for the moment, yet nothing went awry.

Once upstream of the net and the guards, things began to change. The water was fresh, there was a strong current to contend with, and lots of obstacles. Having scraped a bridge support, and come close to colliding with a boulder, Rebo tucked in behind one of the more experienced phibs. Then, by following the noncom's glowing ankle bracelets, the norm made his way up the first section of the river without further incident.

But it wasn't long before the commandos encountered

the first of what would prove to be a number of challenges. The face of the dam stood at least fifteen feet high, which meant the raiders would have to climb it and hoist their sleds up after them. Strong though the amphibians were, even they couldn't swim twenty miles upstream and still have sufficient energy for what lay ahead.

Fortunately, there weren't any guards other than the mill keeper's dog, which barked twice, then collapsed with a sling-launched spear through its throat. The body was hidden, and guards were posted even as specially fabricated swing arms were deployed. It wasn't long before the first sled was lifted onto the top of the dam and more followed.

Eager for something to do, and cognizant of how important it was to set an example, Rebo took charge of the crew that was working to drop the newly arrived sleds into the lake that lay pent-up behind the dam. Then, as the final units were hoisted up and over, the moon began to rise. Except that the runner knew that the half-seen orb wasn't a moon, at least not a natural one, which meant he was looking at Socket. Rebo wondered if Norr could see it but thought that was doubtful since the sensitive was in Shimmer.

But there was no opportunity to pursue the thought, as the last sled went over the side, and the commandos made clean dives into the moonlight-streaked water below. The runner tried, but was responsible for a sizeable splash, much to the amusement of his water-dwelling subordinates.

Then the journey continued, as commandos pushed their way up to the head of the long, narrow lake, where they were forced to portage around a hundred-foot-wide ledge where the Otero spilled into the water that was backed up behind the dam. That task consumed forty-five precious minutes and left Rebo wondering whether they would arrive at the objective on time or be caught by the rising sun—an almost certain disaster given the fact that the phibs would be many miles inland, open to attack from above, and vulnerable to Arbuk's ground troops.

But it was too late to turn back, so all Rebo could do was push such thoughts away and keep on going. The next stretch of river was relatively benign. It consisted of a long series of gentle S-curves that acted to slow the current and make progress somewhat easier. Rebo couldn't see the land to either side but imagined it to be fertile and bordered by neatly kept farms. The commandos made good progress through that stretch, thereby regaining some of the time lost earlier and raising the runner's flagging spirits.

Finally, having reached the railroad bridge that crossed the Otero just east of Prost, it was time to disable the sleds, sink them out in the middle of the river, and hike cross-country. The artificial moon had arced most of the way across the sky by then, and even though Rebo welcomed some light to see by, the off-worlder knew that it could betray his command as well.

One by one the phibs shouldered their various loads, scrambled up the steep riverbank, to assemble on the tracks above. The rails gleamed with reflected moonlight and made a gradual turn toward the west. The runner gave a series of orders, waited to make sure they would be followed, and felt a sense of satisfaction as the phibs spread out along both sides of the line.

Navigation became relatively easy at that point, since all they had to do was follow the track to the village of Prost and the warships that waited there. The rest would be simple. Or that was the way it seemed until the runner heard the mournful sound of a steam whistle, knelt to place a hand on cold steel, and felt it start to vibrate. A train was on the way! But which one? A routine freight? Or *the* train.

Meaning the one that was supposed to haul the ironclads to Esperance.

The phibs nearest to the runner turned to him for orders, the whistle blew again, and Rebo struggled to decide. Should he attack the train? It could be loaded with troops? Or allow it to pass? Only to face what could be even more opposition when he entered the village of Prost? The seconds ticked, by his heart beat faster, and a big round light loomed out of the darkness.

On the great sea

The sailboat's bow dipped, broke through a foam-topped wave and threw a fine mist back over the cabin and open cockpit. Shaz, who was standing just aft of the cabin, put out a hand to steady himself as he watched what he knew to be Socket drop below the western horizon. Hopefully, within a matter of days, he would set foot on the artificial satellite and be present when Logos took control of it. At that point a number of choices would present themselves. If the opportunity arose, the combat variant could kill Tepho and claim the star gates for himself. Or he could continue in his present role, wait for the norm to make a mistake, and pick up the pieces. Fortunately, either strategy would deliver the results the variant wanted.

But that was then, this was now, and Shaz had work to do. The plan, which had been conceived by Tepho and approved by Arbuk, was to sail the phib vessel to Buru. Once Shaz landed, he would present his credentials to the commandant and lead a party into the island's interior, where he was supposed to locate and secure the star gate.

That was the plan, anyway, but there were plenty of things that could go wrong, including the weather. A bank of clouds had been visible off to the southwest just before the moon set, the breeze had stiffened within the last few minutes, and Harluck's crew was pulling the jib down. None of it boded well, but the off-worlder tried to take comfort from the fact that bad weather could provide the boat with some much-needed cover and help keep the phibs at bay. And that was the case, or seemed to be, until a dim, barely seen sun rose, and Harluck announced the bad news.

"There they are!" the pirate proclaimed, as he pointed to the west. "Phibs! Three of them! All trying to cut us off!"

It was bad news, but Harluck sounded triumphant, as if glad to be right even if the phibs were to sink his boat.

The combat variant couldn't see anything at first, but finally, by squinting just so, Shaz was able to make out three tiny triangles of sail, all on a course to converge with Harluck's tiny vessel. "All right," the off-worlder said calmly, "maintain the course you're on."

"But there's *three* of them," the pirate objected. "They'll cut us to pieces!"

"No," Shaz maintained stolidly. "They won't. Not if you do what you're told."

Harluck was ready to put the helm over at that point and make a run for the mainland, but looked up to discover that Phan was aiming a pistol at him. It winked red as the bow collided with a wave, the deck lurched, and the targeting laser dipped. That left Harluck with no choice but to maintain the course he was on even if it meant that a violent confrontation was almost certain.

The next few hours seemed to creep by, as all four of the boats continued to converge, and the low-lying island of Buru appeared in the distance. It was little more than a shadow at first but gradually took on additional substance, as mile after mile of ocean passed beneath the single-masted boat's keel.

By that time the other vessels were clear to see, and when viewed through a small pair of binoculars, were clearly intent on intercepting Harluck's boat. But why? The phibs didn't know who was aboard it. Yes, there was the possibility the fishing boat had been recognized as stolen, and the phibs were determined to intercept it for that reason, but the combat variant didn't think so. No, it was almost as if they were on their way to Buru for some other reason, spotted the fishing boat and wanted to find out what it was up to.

There was no further opportunity for analysis as the lead vessel produced a flash of light and a brown-edged hole appeared in Harluck's fully inflated sail. "The next one will hit our hull," the pirate predicted glumly. "The whole thing will be over soon."

The combat variant heard the words but didn't bother to reply, as Phan fired her rifle. It was an enormous affair, almost as long as she was, and chambered for .50 caliber ammunition. It had been difficult to find a good spot for the weapon, but having settled on the bow, the assassin lay prone, with the barrel resting on a bipod. The trick was to compensate for the fact that both vessels were in constant motion, not something the average marksman could do. But the assassin was far from average. There was a loud *crack* as Phan squeezed the trigger, followed by a *whoop* from one of Harluck's crew members, as a fist-sized hole appeared in the other boat's hull. The first slug hit above the waterline, but the second struck *below* it, as did the third.

The phibs fired in return, and their aim was good, but while still lethal, their energy weapons lacked the punch that the projectile weapon had, and they were soon forced to shear away as half a dozen wings appeared overhead and fired down on them from the sky. Phan worried that the variants might attack Harluck's boat, too, but they didn't, which seemed to suggest that a warning had been sent out from Esperance via winged courier. Or maybe it was the fact that she had been shooting at their enemies. Whatever the reason, the blast-scarred fishing boat was allowed to enter the island's only harbor, where the pirate dropped the anchor and went in search of a bottle. He had been sober for more than half a day by then—and had every reason to get drunk.

Near the village of Prost

The train had already started to slow in preparation for the stop in Prost when a man appeared up ahead. He stood in the middle of the track and waved both arms. The engineer swore, blew the train's whistle, and pulled the brake lever. Metal *screeched* as the drive wheels locked up, sparks flew, and the locomotive finally began to slow. It wasn't going to stop in time, though, that's what the engineer was thinking, when he looked up to discover that the man had disappeared.

Then, before the engineer and his fireman had time to absorb that, a pair of heavily armed phibs entered the cab, one from each side. They put strange-looking pistols to the men's heads, ordered the engineer to increase speed, and watched to make sure that he actually did so. Meanwhile, behind the locomotive, and the half-full coal car, the rest of the commandos had clambered up onto a single flatcar. Rather than the troops that Rebo feared, it was loaded with kegs of what purported to be black powder, which was probably intended for the ironclads. A rather volatile load should Arbuk's troops decide to shoot at it, which was why the runner detailed two phibs to study the coupling and figure out how to release it.

But time was passing, and the outskirts of Prost had

already appeared by then, which meant that the train was only a minute or two from the yard and the steamships that waited there. Lights could be seen up ahead, lots of them, which made sense if Arbuk's forces were assembled and waiting. The sun had begun to rise as well, sending rays of rosy pink light up over the eastern horizon, as if to herald its own coming. And now, for the first time since he had put the plan forward, Rebo felt genuinely frightened. Because events had started to overtake him, and he had no military training to fall back on.

But there was no time to consider such things as the train pulled into Prost, a reedy cheer went up from the soldiers gathered along both sides of the track, and a civilian fired a hunting rifle into the air. The phibs on the flatcar were hidden in amongst the explosives. And even though they had been given orders not to fire unless fired upon, they were understandably nervous, and once the rifle went off a dozen fingers mashed down on a dozen firing studs.

Rebo shouted "No!" as the first energy beam lashed out, but it was too late as blue death stuttered out to cut the troopers down. Their weapons weren't loaded, and they threw up their hands in a vain attempt to block the blue bolts. But it didn't work, and by the time the train rolled past the station, a heap of brown-clad bodies lay sprawled on the scorched platform. There wasn't much return fire since the survivors were still in the process of loading their weapons, but what few shots there were missed both the phibs and the kegs of black powder stacked on the flatcar.

The slaughter made Rebo sick to his stomach, but it was already too late to stop it, as a blunt stern appeared up ahead. The ship it belonged to was sitting on a siding, as were two additional vessels, as the train pulled up alongside them. A phib ordered the engineer to stop the locomotive next to the ironclads so a squad of commandos could hop off the flatcar and burn the warships.

Only now Rebo saw an opportunity not only to improve on the original plan, but to reassert control over his troops and regain the initiative all at the same time. "Stay in the cab," he told the phibs, "and watch the prisoners. We're going to need them."

One of the commandos nodded grimly, and the other grinned. Satisfied that the train would stay where it was, the runner ducked out of the locomotive's cab and followed an iron walkway back toward the coal car.

Meanwhile, the soldiers who had been fortunate enough to survive the unexpected onslaught at the train station had recovered by then, reinforcements had been summoned, and Rebo could hear the steady *bang, bang, bang* of semiautomatic rifle fire as he made his way along the coal car. Bullets pinged as they shattered against the locomotive, produced a whapping sound when they hit wooden barrels, and whined as the runner successfully jumped across the gap and landed on the flatcar.

The phibs had emerged from their hiding places by then and were about to launch their assault on the warships when Rebo ordered them to stop. "You two," he said, pointing at a likely-looking pair, "unhook the flatcar. I want everyone else on the coal carrier. Now!"

As the commandos moved to obey, a bullet spun one of them around, causing him to fall into the gap between the two cars. Another projectile hit a noncom from behind, exited through his chest, and still packed enough velocity to kill the private who stood facing him. Meanwhile, geysers of dirt shot up into the air, beginning their inexorable march toward the flatcar, as a machine gun began to chatter.

But even as some of the phibs fell, dozens poured across

the gap, and climbed up onto the coal car, where they turned to fire on their tormentors. Machinery began to clank, enormous puffs of smoke issued from the locomotive's black stack, and steam shot forth from both sides of the behemoth as it got under way.

Rebo was beginning to wonder if the flatcar would ever be decoupled and was just about to go after it personally when he heard a phib yell, "She's clear!" and felt the train jerk. Then came the mad scramble to jump the quickly widening gap, a moment of gut-wrenching fear as the runner felt himself begin to fall backward, and a profound feeling of relief as strong fingers wrapped themselves around his wrist.

Then, having been pulled up onto the filthy coal car, Rebo heard someone shout and turned to see that a single phib had been left on the flatcar. It was the scout who had spoken with him back in the bay, and judging from the blood that was pouring down the soldier's right leg, the youngster had been hit. Now, with slugs whistling all around him the commando lit one of the incendiary flares issued for use on the ironclads, raised his right hand by way of a salute, and let the fiery tube fall.

The result was even more effective than what Rebo had originally hoped for. There was a flash of light, followed by a near-deafening *boom*, and a series of secondary explosions as ordnance already aboard the ironclads went off as well. Smoke boiled up to stain the early-morning sky, chunks of wood, iron, and flesh cartwheeled through the air, and the station's telegraph began to chatter. News of the phib raid would arrive in Esperance within a matter of minutes, Arbuk's wings would take to the air shortly thereafter, and troops would be sent to intercept the hijacked train.

Rebo knew all of that, and knew he would eventually

have to deal with it, but not for a few minutes yet. Because right then, as if burned onto his retinas by the force of the blast, he was still staring at the image of the scout, the flare, and the nameless boy's final salute.

The city of Shimmer

The council of mayors had been reconvened, and at Norr's request, was about to hear from a very distinguished guest. Ever since Norr brought a message through from Mayor Pontho's disembodied aunt, the politician had been very deferential toward the sensitive. And now, as the other variant entered a trance, the phib looked on with an expression of awe as Norr's chin touched her chest and a deeper voice was heard. "Greetings," the disincarnate said, as the sensitive's head came up. "My name is Lysander, Milos Lysander, but like the rest of you I have been known by other names as well. Once, during a lifetime as a man called Hios, I brought your people to Zeen, helped them establish their great underwater cities, and gave them the gift of tides.

"Back in those days we worked together to create the planet's infrastructure, which had it not been for my many errors, would probably be intact today. But I was foolish, *very* foolish, and hope to make things right. Thanks to you, and your support, that process is already under way. In fact my spirit allies tell me that your commandos were successful, the ironclads were destroyed, and even as I speak your warriors are battling their way back to safety. That will be difficult, however, since Lord Arbuk's wings will attack them along the way, and ground troops will be sent against them as well."

There was muttering, as all of the mayors tried to speak at once, and Pontho called for silence. Norr's head nodded jerkily. "Yes," Lysander said, "I understand your concern.

Fortunately, there is something we can do to help! But, by taking action, we will reveal the full extent of our powers and thereby elicit what is sure to be a desperate response."

The politicians listened intently as Lysander outlined his plan. And when asked, Sogol, who had been silent up until then, agreed that the scheme was theoretically possible. Although the AI went on to point out that not only would the timing would be iffy, but the results would be unpredictable and possibly dangerous to the very people they were trying to save.

Then, having heard from a dead man and an artificial intelligence, the politicians did what they were best at, which was to talk, and talk, and talk some more. Until Pontho became frustrated, insisted on a vote, and finally got one. The plan was approved. But could the scheme be implemented quickly enough to save Rebo and his commandos? The clock was ticking.

FOURTEEN

Like the ripples generated when a pebble falls into a pond, a single historical event can send waves of change out to touch the far shores of human civilization, where the effects will be felt for many years to come.

—Artificial Intelligence Borlon 4,
A History of My Creators

*Once clear of Prost, the track followed the Otera river val-*ley west. Thanks to the gun at the engineer's head, plus the fireman's frantic efforts to feed the hungry boiler, the locomotive was traveling at full speed by then. Thick black smoke poured out of the stack, the engine made a steady chugging sound, and the wheels clacked rhythmically as they passed over evenly spaced expansion joints. But Rebo took little pleasure in the train's speed. He stood on the narrow walkway that ran along the side of the locomotive's boiler and eyed the track ahead. Since Arbuk's troops knew where the engine had to go, they would move to block it. The original plan, which involved a return trip down the Otero River, incorporated the same flaw—although the water route might have offered more protection from the wings. Had he been wrong to abandon the first plan? Would a *real* military officer have chosen a third course? Rebo feared the answer might be yes.

Space was at a premium. Commandos clung to both sides of the locomotive, squatted on top of the cab just behind the stack, and were crammed into the coal car as well. Most of the smoke passed over their heads but not all of it. "There they are!" one of the phibs exclaimed, and pointed to the west. Rebo looked, saw the formation of dots, and knew they were wings. The runner faced two choices. He could order the engineer to stop the train, pull his troops together, and respond to the coming attack with massed fire. That a technique would probably be effective against the winged variants but would give Arbuk plenty of time in which to bring ground troops against the stationary train. The other possibility was to keep going, accept some causalities, and hope to break through whatever obstructions lay ahead.

Finally, for better or worse, the runner chose the second option. The commandos on the roof were attempting to engage the winged variants at extreme range by then but with little success. Rebo turned to one of the noncoms. "Put your best marksmen where they can fire on the wings—but tell them to hold off until the bastards come in closer. There's going to be a hellacious battle within the next couple of hours, and we're going to need every power pack we have. . . . Tell everyone else to safe their weapons and seek any cover they can find."

The phib said, "Yes, sir," and began to work his way back to the cab. It wasn't long before some of the commandos came down off the roof while those with a reputation for marksmanship went up to replace them. Then, just as the train passed through the point where the valley narrowed, the airborne warriors attacked. And, thanks to the fact that they had been practicing such maneuvers for years, some of their shots went home.

One of the phibs who was hugging the side of the locomotive looked surprised, let go of the handrail, and fell away from the train. A marksman jerked as a bullet struck his chest. He released his weapon, and toppled back into the coal car, where a commando called for help. A medic stood, lost the top of his head, and collapsed in a heap.

The commandos were quick to return fire, and a cheer went up as one of the wings spiraled out of the sky, but the phibs were going to take more casualties. Not only that, but Rebo was pretty sure that something worse lay ahead.

Lord Arbuk was angry. Very angry. Which was why he didn't want to simply stop the phib raiders, he wanted to crush them, even if that meant destroying a valuable locomotive in the process. That was why no less than six comet-firing artillery tubes and a thousand troops lay in wait as the train rolled down out of the low-lying foothills and was momentarily lost from sight as it passed through a dip in the terrain.

A platform, complete with awning had been established on a likely-looking rise, and that was where Arbuk, Tepho, and two dozen government officials were waiting to view what promised to be a magnificent slaughter. In the meantime, there was music, refreshments, and an absolute orgy of posturing as the colorfully clad functionaries attempted to outdo one another.

And it was during that period that Tepho slipped away to inspect the high-tech mortar tubes. Since a counterattack was unlikely if not impossible, very little effort had been made to protect the weapons, other than to place them in freshly dug pits. The comets, which had the appearance of inoffensive spheres until they were fired, were nestled in protective boxes.

The technologist had numerous questions where the mortars were concerned, not the least of which was why Arbuk's mostly steam-age culture possessed such advanced weapons, yet lagged in other areas? And it was while visiting with a voluble artillery officer that the technologist learned the answer. It seemed that five years earlier, while attempting to reopen an ancient mine, Arbuk's engineers stumbled across a cache of weapons believed to be more than five hundred years old.

It was interesting stuff, and Tepho was about to ask some follow-up questions, when Logos spoke from the vicinity of his collar. "Sorry to interrupt, but I suggest that you return to the raptor and clear the area as quickly as possible."

The artillery officer looked dumbfounded as a third voice came out of nowhere. But before he could ask the obvious question, a plume of dark smoke appeared in the distance, a bugle sounded, and it was time for the officer to return to his duties.

Tepho, who was alone now, wished Logos was standing in front of him. "Leave? Why?"

"Because Iteration 1.2 has temporary control of Socket, and if I'm not mistaken, intends to use the satellite's solar mirror as a weapon."

Tepho looked up into the sky, realized how stupid that was, and began to waddle up out of the emplacement. There was a loud *whump*, as the nearest weapon fired, followed by a hearty cheer as the ball of highly concentrated energy arced across the sky. The human experienced a combination of fear, confusion, and anger. "Well, if you know about it, then stop it!"

"I'm trying," the AI responded calmly. "But Sogol has

the upper hand at the moment. So rather than pepper me with questions, I suggest that you run."

Tepho *couldn't* run. Not like most people. But he was able to manage a sort of rolling walk, which when he tried hard enough, took on the appearance of a poorly coordinated jog. The raptor, which he had been encouraged to bring so that Arbuk could show the machine off to his toadies, sat fifty feet away from the reviewing stand. Because his back was turned, the technologist didn't see where the first comet landed, but having heard a *second* cheer, assumed the shot had been close to the target if not right on it.

Then he was there, struggling to enter the control pod without assistance, and flipping switches like a madman once he had succeeded. "Hurry!" Logos insisted urgently. "Sogol is about to fire!"

Tepho wondered who Sogol was but knew the question would have to wait as the raptor came up to speed. "Now!" Logos shouted. "It's coming *now*!" And fire fell from the sky.

As the locomotive topped the rise, Rebo saw the comet soar up into the sky, pause as if deciding where to fall, and plunge downward. For one split second he thought the munition was going to make a direct hit on the locomotive, but much to his relief the ball of pent-up energy landed off to the right. It exploded on contact, throwing tons of debris into the air and creating a crater large enough to drop the coal car into. The train swayed as the shock wave struck it, but managed to remain upright, as the descent began. Off in the distance, Rebo could see a rise topped by a gaily striped awning, some carefully prepared troop positions, and freshly turned earth where weapons emplacements had been dug. Not only that, but logs had been placed across the track in an attempt to block it. The engineer saw the obstacle, pulled back on the brake, and hung on to it as metal began to screech.

Rebo realized there was nothing he could do but surrender, and was just about to give the necessary orders when a beam of bright light caressed a stand of stickle trees. They immediately burst into flames. Then, like a ray of sunshine through a magnifying glass, the orbital weapon drew a black line across the rocky landscape. There was a massive explosion as the energy beam slashed across a mortar emplacement, followed by a series of flares as an entire squad of troops was incinerated, and a series of high-pitched screams as the death ray began to close in on the reviewing stand.

Arbuk was on his feet by then, screaming obscenities at the beam of light, but to no avail. Dignitaries, including Hitho Mal, jumped off the platform and ran, each intent on saving him- or herself from the devastating weapon. But Arbuk was slow, *too* slow to make his escape, and there was a loud *pop* as the norm's bodily fluids burst through his skin and were incinerated a fraction of a second later. Then the rest of the platform disappeared as the ray of concentrated energy burned a hundred-foot-long trench into the rock and soil before suddenly ceasing to exist. A few moments later the entire area was empty of people as everyone who still could ran for cover. The rest lay where they had fallen. The locomotive was still a good fifteen feet from the log barrier when it finally screeched to a halt—and Rebo said what everyone else was thinking. "What the hell was *that?*"

"I don't know," a phib answered pragmatically, "but we're still a good five miles from the ocean. Let's move those logs and get the train going again before the norms can regroup." It was excellent advice, and Rebo took it. By easing the train forward they were able to nudge two timbers off the track—leaving the commandos to muscle the third out of the way.

Five minutes later Arbuk's soldiers began to emerge from hiding, but they were too disorganized to mount a coordinated attack, so could do little more than take potshots at the train as it pulled away from them. Meanwhile, having withdrawn to the top of a low-lying hill, Tepho eyed the scene via the raptor's optics. He was angry—no furious— and his voice quavered as he spoke. "Are we safe here?"

"We're safe," Logos allowed cautiously. "And now that I know Sogol is present, I can prevent her from taking control of Socket again. Unless she finds a way to get aboard before *we* do, that is—which would be extremely unfortunate."

"How very nice," the technologist said sarcastically. "I want to know everything there is to know about Sogol— and I want to know it *now.*"

The ensuing conversation was quite acrimonious, and still under way, when Tepho brought the raptor to a halt not far from all the carnage. Not to check on Lord Arbuk, as the nobleman might have hoped, but to secure the unexploded comets. Because even though the ironclads had been destroyed, and a second AI had appeared out of nowhere, Tepho was still in the race. And if Buru was the lock—then the comets were the key.

The island of Buru

During the hundreds of years since most of the star gates had been taken off-line, and humanity began the long, backward slide toward barbarity, the surrounding vegetation had closed in on what had been a two-lane highway until it was little more than a game trail. That meant Shaz, Phan, and the pirates they had engaged to accompany them were forced to whack at all manner of runners, vines, and branches as they fought their way up the path. All of them took turns, but it was exhausting work and left them soaked with sweat.

However, the same holes in the canopy that allowed sunlight to reach the jungle floor provided the small party with frequent glimpse of the sky and the wings that circled above. Sightings that would have been a lot more comforting had it not been for the lackadaisical commandant who welcomed the foursome ashore with what could only be described as unconcealed resentment. Because poor though the posting was, the wing was in charge and saw the mainlanders as a threat.

But orders were orders, and once the commandant read the instructions issued by Lord Arbuk himself, there had been little choice but to provide what assistance he could. That, after some discussion, turned out to be a succession of airborne guides who were to make sure that the party remained on course and report back should they run into trouble. A virtual certainty from the local's perspective, since the strangers had chosen to ignore his warnings regarding jungle sickness and enter the interior anyway. All of which had been documented, sealed into a pouch, and sent to the mainland. So that when Arbuk's agents turned up dead, as they almost certainly would, the commandant would be in the clear. The variant took pleasure in the thought and went to lunch.

The day after the raid on Prost dawned clear, and with only moderate winds, conditions were perfect for the relatively short trip to Buru. The norms didn't have any large ships to speak of, since the phibs were almost certain to sink anything that attempted to cross one of "their" oceans, thereby placing severe limits on the shipbuilding business.

But there were some sizeable coastal vessels, which were at the very heart of the so-called revenge fleet, still being assembled in Esperance Bay.

The concept, as put forward by Tepho, and subsequently communicated to Arbuk's functionaries by Hitho Mal, was to punish the enemy by attacking the phib stronghold of Buru. And, such was the anger at those who had come ashore to destroy the ironclads, and even gone so far as to unleash a secret weapon on Arbuk's troops, that no one in a position of power chose to question the plan. Even though every one who was familiar with Buru knew that while the waters around the island were thick with phibs, none of them lived ashore.

But only the most courageous wags gave voice to such doubts as the citizens of Esperance turned out to line the cobbled streets, threw flowers at the passing sailors, and cheer them on as the raggedly stalwarts rowed out to their ships.

There were no cheers for Tepho, however, thanks to the fact that he, along with his entire staff, had been loaded onto one of the smaller vessels during the dead of night. They stood in the stern and watched as the surviving members of Arbuk's personal staff were ferried out to the largest ship, which by virtue of its size and the colorful bunting that Tepho had purchased for it, would serve both as the flagship and the enemy's primary target. Meanwhile, lesser craft, such as the brig that the technologist had chosen for himself, were likely to be ignored. That was the plan at any rate—and the technologist saw no reason it wouldn't work.

Sunlight sparkled on the surface of the bay, and a band played atop the seawall as a puff of gray smoke appeared next to the gaily decorated flagship. The dull *boom* was like an afterthought as it rolled across the bay. That was the signal for the assemblage of fishing boats, coastal luggers, and other craft to get under way, and Tepho watched with considerable amusement as dingy sails were hoisted, boats collided with one another, and a tubby ketch ran aground.

It took more than an hour for the poorly organized fleet to sort itself out and finally leave the bay, with Tepho's vessel bringing up the rear. Word of the armada's departure, not to mention its well-publicized destination, arrived in Shimmer minutes later. The war for Buru, if that's what it could properly be called, was under way.

The island of Buru

The commandant didn't fly as much as he once had, which explained the small potbelly that hung over his belt and his somewhat labored breathing as his leathery wings beat at the air. But by nosing into one of thermals that rose off Buru, the administrator was able to get some additional lift. His scouts had warned him of an unusual amount of phib activity, and once the commandant reached an altitude of two hundred feet, he saw why. Phib warriors had always been easy to spot once they ventured into the shallows, and dozens of dark shadows could be seen patrolling offshore.

The question was why? Did the sudden interest in Buru have something to do with the combat variant and his emaciated companion? Or, and this seemed more likely, were they waiting for the so-called revenge fleet that was on the way? The whole notion of which made no sense to the wing—since Buru was the last place to go looking for large concentrations of phibs. Or was he wrong about that? Because the inshore waters were suddenly thick with phibs! So maybe the high muckety-mucks knew what they were doing for once.

Tired by then, and happy to glide most of the way to base, the commandant did what any successful bureaucrat would do. He dispatched a message to his superiors, told his subordinates to keep an eye on the situation, and went off to take a nap.

It was dark by the time the much-battered revenge fleet neared Buru island. Sadly for the citizens of Esperance, the once-proud armada was only half of its former size by the time it made landfall. Consistent with Tepho's predictions, *all* of the larger vessels had been sunk by enterprising phibs, who made use of their motorized sleds to get out in front of the oncoming fleet, where they could wait for the ships to pass overhead. Once a vessel obliged, it was a simple matter to attach a mine to the hull and detonate the explosive charge from a safe distance.

Not Tepho's brig, however, which because of its diminutive size, and position at the tail end of the armada, remained unharmed. That vessel's luck wasn't likely to hold however, both because it was increasingly visible as the size of the fleet was diminished, and because word had arrived that a large concentration of phibs was lying in wait just off Buru's harbor.

But, having been made aware of Sogol and her alliance with the variants, the technologist had anticipated such a move and made preparations to counter it. A dozen wings, all recruited with Hitho Mal's help, were waiting on the foredeck as the smudge of land appeared ahead. Each of the skeletal humans carried a bag made of netting as he or she flapped up into the air, and each container held a bomb, which, if the makeshift fuses worked like they were supposed to, would open a pathway through which Tepho's ship could pass. If that provided the norms with the revenge they sought, then so be it, although the technologist didn't care. He watched the wings until they were little more than dots, ordered the ship's master to hoist more sail, and went below to prepare. He was in radio contact with Shaz, and based on the reports received, the journey up to the transfer station was going to be tough.

Rebo and Norr were no more than half a mile away when the first wing let go of his lethal cargo and allowed it to fall. None of the phibs were aware of the comet until the ball of concentrated energy dropped through the ocean's surface and exploded underwater. The resulting shock wave sent a huge column of water up into the air, killed everything within a quarter-mile radius, and sent four-foot-high waves out in every direction.

Both of the off-worlders felt the force of the underwater concussion, and Norr "heard" a communal scream, as thousands of living organisms passed into the spirit world. Then came the *second* explosion, and the *third*, and more after that, until a total of *six* energy bombs had been detonated, hundreds of phib warriors lay facedown in the water, and what remained of the revenge fleet was free to enter the bay of Buru.

Rebo, Norr, and Sogol had surfaced by then, and were part of the much-diminished phib force that was about to invade the island. "Tepho survived," Norr said glumly. "At least that's what Lysander tells me."

"And so did Logos," Sogol added, having wrapped herself around the sensitive's neck. "And he's communicating with Socket."

"Can you stop him?" the runner wanted to know.

"I can *interfere* with his efforts," the AI replied. "Just as he can interfere with mine."

"Then let's go," Norr said grimly. "We need to reach Socket before they do."

The wings put up a fight, but not much of one, as hundreds of phibs marched up out of the light surf. That was partly because the winged warriors were badly outnumbered, partly because they were vulnerable to massed ground fire, and partly because they're hearts weren't in it. Given the absence of other leadership, it was the commandant's duty to lead a single mostly symbolic sortie, which he did. But having lost a quarter of his total force during first ten minutes of battle, and with no ground forces to provide support, the old soldier was soon forced to withdraw.

That left the way clear for the phibs to claim Buru as their own—and for the off-worlders to invade the jungle. A trip they would have to undertake alone, since the phibs had captured *their* objective and were still reeling from all the casualties they had suffered.

Rebo had supplemented his pistols with a phib energy rifle, along with a bag of grenades. And Norr, who had been reunited with her sword, carried the phib equivalent of a sawed-off shotgun plus a power pistol, which was strapped to her thigh.

With only light packs to burden them, the twosome marched up trail. And it wasn't very long before Rebo, Norr, and Sogol confirmed what they already suspected. Not only had Tepho preceded them, but judging from the deep pod prints, the technologist was behind the controls of his raptor. And, as if that wasn't disturbing enough, there were plenty of smaller footprints, some of which had been left by metal men.

Truth be told, Rebo might have called it a day right then had the runner been on his own, but Norr wasn't prepared to give up yet, nor was Sogol. So they continued the march, and thanks to the bushwhacking carried out by those who preceded them, made excellent progress. As if aware of their presence, and holding its breath to see what would happen next, the normally noisy jungle had lapsed into a brooding silence, broken only by the sound of their breathing, the occasional *clink* of metal, and the intermittent *splash* of water as they crossed a stream.

It made for a pleasant rhythm. But hours later, as the light began to fade, Sogol became increasingly agitated. Rather than wrap herself around Norr's biceps, as was her normal practice, the AI began to roam from one place to another. That was annoying enough—but the steady diet of intercepted intelligence was even worse. "Logos is communicating with Socket. . . ." "Two of Tepho's people have arrived at the transit station. . . ." "The main party is almost there. . . ."

Finally, unable to take any more, Norr ordered Sogol to, "Shut the hell up," and threatened to stuff the computer into her backpack. That served to silence the AI for a while, but eventually, as the vegetation-covered butte loomed ahead, Sogol broke her silence. Her snakelike body was wrapped around one of the sensitive's pack straps by that time—which put her triangular head only inches from Norr's ear. "Based on their radio traffic, it's clear that Tepho, Logos, and the rest of the party are standing directly outside the transfer station," the AI announced. "The gate appears to be operational—and they are about to make the jump."

That brought the sensitive to a momentary halt. And when Rebo heard the news, he said, "Damn!"

"I couldn't agree more," Norr added. "So, assuming the gate works, what will happen next?"

"They'll arrive on Socket," the AI predicted dispiritedly, "where they will transport Logos up to level three, where the nexus is located. Once in position, he will begin to reinstall himself."

"And how long will that take?" Rebo wanted to know.

"There's no way to know what conditions are like," Sogol answered. "If they're good, then the technos could reach nexus within a matter of minutes. But judging from *my* contacts with Socket, I get the impression that they may encounter problems. As for the *second* part of the process, well, I can be fairly precise about that. Given the fact that subsystems have to be conditioned while installation takes place, the process will take three hours, twelve minutes, and forty-two seconds. Give or take half a second."

The sensitive felt the full impact of Rebo's personality as his eyes made contact with hers. He was there because of her, because *she* believed in the star gates, and because he was sworn to protect her. Even if that meant dying for her. Something passed between them at that moment, as a promise made before either one of them had been born was kept and their fates forever joined. "Come on," Rebo said gruffly, as he reached out to take the sensitive's hand. "We're almost there."

The transit station was made of carefully joined blocks of limestone, which had been eroded by the weather and almost entirely hidden by a blanket of green foliage. The raptor, which Tepho had sealed against intruders, crouched off to one side. And right in front of the structure, where a parking lot had existed once, there was a flat area. And that was where the assassin stood as she looked out over the verdant jungle to the sparkling sea beyond. Phan had never been one to spend much time looking at nature, but as the light started to fade, and a golden glow settled over the island, even *she* had to take notice of the beauty that surrounded her.

Then, just as quickly as the moment came, it was gone. And when darkness fell, it fell quickly, as if eager to claim its full share of the day. And that was when the assassin was forced to confront the fact that while Tepho, Logos, Shaz, and the rest of the party had been transported to Socket, she along with two metal men, had been left to guard what the combat variant called, "the back door."

It shouldn't have mattered, not so long as she was being paid, but it was difficult to ignore the power-core-induced nausea, or the feeling of disappointment that resulted from having participated in a long, difficult journey only to be left behind just short of the final goal. But such maunderings were unprofessional, not to mention unproductive, and therefore dangerous. With that in mind, Phan forced herself to focus on the task at hand.

Logos claimed that the runner, the sensitive, and the second AI were not only present on the island of Buru, but determined to reach Socket. Having traveled with the humans, the assassin didn't doubt it. She knew from personal experience that Rebo and Norr were not only tough but tenacious. So they would come. . . . The question was when? Neither one of them liked to travel at night. She knew that, but what if they did? Phan could survive on very little sleep, but she couldn't go without any at all, and that suggested that some sort of early-warning system was in order.

Fortunately, the metal men were perfect for that role, because while the cudgel-toting robots had limited combat capabilities, they could literally see in the dark thanks to their sophisticated sensors. With that in mind, the human led the machines out to positions in front of the transfer station, where their sensors would overlap, thereby establishing an invisible wall between the jungle and herself.

Once the machines were properly positioned, Phan withdrew to the point where a flight of stone steps led up into the building and settled in for the night. Somewhere out in the jungle an animal made a strange, gibbering noise, Socket topped the eastern horizon, and ghosts roamed the land.

The transfer station was no more than a hundred feet ahead—and Sogol wanted to enter it with every atom of her electromechanical body. And, had she been equipped with a vehicle that could push buttons located approximately four feet off the floor, might have rushed to do so, even if that meant leaving the humans behind. The need to reach Socket and fulfill her purpose was that strong.

But, just as Emperor Hios and his engineers had been careful to craft Logos 1.1 so that he couldn't leave Socket without human assistance, the same limitation had been placed on her. Still, Sogol took satisfaction from the fact that she could assist the humans by snaking her way forward to discover what sort of defenses lay between them and the transfer station. Dead leaves rustled as the AI slipped between thickly growing plants, slithered over an enormous tree root, and "sensed" electromechanical activity ahead. That shouldn't have been a surprise, since Sogol knew that the Techno Society often made use of robots, but it was because the AI had been on the lookout for *human* sentries. There was barely enough time to electronically cloak herself before the android's sensors began to ping the area around her. But the metal man had been too slow, and after thirty seconds of intensive probing, reverted to standby.

Farther back, located about halfway between the androids, the AI "saw" a blob of heat and knew it to be of human origin. Sogol's first impulse was to return to the others, report what she had discovered, and wait for them to handle the problem. But then a more daring option occurred to the construct. One that, if successful, would not only be more efficient but save a significant amount of time as well.

Still protected from prying sensors, the snakelike AI slipped noiselessly along the ground, circled around behind one of the two androids, and coiled herself into the shape of a spring. Then, having launched herself into the air, Sogol managed to fall across a crooked arm. The reaction was almost instantaneous as the robot sought to shake off whatever it was. But the AI was already up on the machine's shoulder by then, searching for what she felt sure would be there. And the receptacle *was* there—right at the base of the metal man's alloy skull.

Sogol's head morphed to fit the hole, darted inside, and locked itself in place. For one brief moment the computer thought she might be able to take control of the robot and thereby secure a larger body for herself, but quickly discovered that the other machine's systems were too primitive for her architecture. That left the AI with no choice but to lock the robot's joints, erase most of its CPU, and withdraw.

There was only the faintest *thump* as Sogol hit the ground and wriggled her way over to the point where the second metal man stood gazing out into the darkness. Sixty seconds later *that* machine was off-line, too, and the AI was back on the ground, snaking her way back to the point where the humans were waiting.

Both Rebo and Norr listened intently as the construct delivered her report—and the runner was already in the process of rechecking his weapons when Norr touched his arm. "No, Jak. I can 'see' in the dark . . . Remember? And, given the fact that there's only one guard, I should be able to handle this one alone."

Rebo didn't like the proposal but, knowing what the sensitive said about being able to see the guard's aura was true, reluctantly agreed. "Okay, but be careful, and don't hesitate to call for help."

"I won't," Norr assured him, and proceeded to dump her pack along with the stubby shotgun. Then, having checked to ensure that none of her equipment would creak, rattle, or otherwise betray her, the sensitive planted a kiss on Rebo's whiskered cheek and vanished into the night.

Foliage slid past Norr's shoulder, a small animal scuttled away, and the light reflected off Socket seemed to glaze the area ahead. The robots were invisible, or would have been if the variant hadn't known where to look. But, thanks to Sogol's report, she could see a faint glint off to the right, and a place where the darkness seemed even darker over on the left.

Now, with her senses focused on the area between the machines, the sensitive crept forward. She perceived nothing at first, other than the multiple pinpoints of life force that represented a host of flying insects, but it wasn't long before a dim glow became visible. Based on the aura's size and shape Norr knew she was looking at a human. And not just *any* human—but one she knew quite well. It was Phan! Left to guard the star gate.

Norr felt a momentary surge of fear, because she knew what the female warrior was capable of and felt certain that Phan could best her. *But, not at night,* the variant told herself, not when the assassin couldn't see.

Phan was leaning against her pack, which was supported by the transfer station's door, when she awoke from a light sleep. A night sound perhaps? Or a surreptitious bug bite? It must have been something of that sort the assassin reasoned—or the metal men would have warned her. It was tempting to illuminate the machines with her cell-powered torch, but that would be childish, not to mention potentially fatal. Because if Rebo and Norr were lurking in the darkness, trying to spot her position, a single flash of light would provide them with everything they needed.

So Phan closed her fingers around the grip of her submachine gun and let her head rest on the door behind her. Sleep swept in and was just about to pull her down when a soft breeze touched her face. With it came a strange yet familiar scent. Strange, because it was foreign to that environment, yet familiar, because Norr wore that particular perfume every day!

The assassin rolled right, moonlight gleamed off the razor-sharp blade as it passed through the area just vacated, and the automatic weapon stuttered as Phan fired a quick burst. Not because it would hit Norr, but to intimidate the sensitive and prevent a follow-up. But that was a mistake, since the muzzle flash left afterimages dancing in front of the assassin's eyes, just when she needed her night vision the most. Where were the robots, Phan wondered? And why hadn't the machines given some sort of warning? But there was no time for further thought as the norm heard three soft footsteps and felt cold steel caress her right cheek.

The cut burned as Phan rolled again, slammed into a wall, and bounced to her feet. The stairs made for uncertain footing, but the norm soon regained her balance and was back in the fight. Having lost the advantage of surprise and missed her target twice, Norr felt a surge of fear as Phan activated the torch. The light pinned the sensitive to the stairs, feet planted, sword ready to strike.

The assassin saw the fear in Norr's eyes, paused to savor it, and felt something nudge her chest. Once, twice, then three times as an energy weapon winked at her from the jungle. *Rebo! How could I have forgotten Rebo?* Phan wondered. But the question went unanswered as what looked like a thick gray fog rolled in to engulf her—and the first of more than a hundred of Phan's victims arrived to greet the assassin.

Having holstered his weapon, Rebo emerged from the bush carrying both packs and Norr's shotgun. "Here you go," the runner said lightly. "And the next time you call for help—speak a little louder."

Norr was about to reply when Sogol interrupted. As before, the AI had wrapped herself around the sensitive's arm. "Tepho's party ran into trouble! We still have time! Let's go!"

Rebo wanted to ask, What kind of trouble? but was left to follow as Norr mounted the steps, took hold of the massive door handle, and pulled the slab of metal open. Hinges squealed as the rich odor of decay pushed out to greet the newcomers. Then, as the sensitive moved forward, she nearly tripped over a pile of bones. It was impossible to tell if the remains were human, but their very presence was cause for concern since the gate was supposed to be sealed against all intruders.

"Look at this," Rebo said, as he sent the light from Phan's torch down the tunnel in front of them.

That was when Norr saw that vines, some as thick as her wrist, had forced their way down through the ceiling and into the passageway. But why? Unless . . .

Having sensed their presence, a motion detector activated a long series of glow panels, some of which remained dark. Here was the light the creepers would need—but what would trigger the motion detector? And do so with sufficient regularity?

The answer became apparent as something dropped out of an overhead vent, landed on Rebo's right shoulder, and went for the runner's jugular. The norm felt needle-sharp teeth penetrate his skin and made an ineffectual grab for the creature. But it was Norr who got a grip on the attacker's pointy tail, jerked the reptilian beast free, and smashed it against the nearest wall.

Whatever it was fell, jerked spasmodically, and produced a tendril of black smoke. "It's some sort of machine!" Norr exclaimed, her shotgun at the ready.

"Not 'some sort,'" Sogol put in. "The guardian in question is a Porto Industries 8812-B specially enhanced mechanimal. Back when Socket was first commissioned, thousands of security robots were introduced to the satellite's crawl spaces and air ducts."

"Then why did it attack you?" Rebo wanted to know.

"It didn't attack *me*," Sogol replied tartly. "It attacked *you*. Which would explain why Tepho and his party are having so much trouble. Come on . . . let's make the jump!"

"Oh, goody," Rebo said, and he followed the other two down the corridor. "That should be fun."

Norr felt as if she was going to throw up as the radiation produced by the power core grew even stronger. Because the mechanimals were machines, they lacked auras, which meant the sensitive was just as vulnerable as Rebo was. But the shotgun imbued the variant with a sense of confidence and seemed to fire itself when a sleek body launched itself off a ledge, only to disintegrate in midair. The rotary magazine made a clacking sound as the next shell was advanced.

"Nice shooting," the runner said approvingly, as they entered what had once been a standard decontamination chamber but had long since been converted into what looked like a hothouse for exotic plants. The invaders lined both sides of the chamber, and judging from the bits of bone that stuck up out of the dirt, had originally been sustained by a corpse. Perhaps a wing, who, curious as to what might lie behind the outer door, had been so foolish as to venture inside.

Some of the plants glowed as if lit from within, some turned to track Norr's progress, and one of them sent a stream of fluid squirting into the air. It fell short of the sensitive, but made a sizzling sound as it hit, and left another burn mark on the filthy floor. Rebo gave the plants a wide berth, heard something move over his head, and fired three energy bolts into the ceiling. The noise stopped.

The star gate itself was no better. The actual platform had been cleared of debris, but all sorts of vegetation had grown in and around it, and Sogol didn't like the looks of what she saw. "I think other life-forms may have passed through long before Tepho and his party arrived," the AI warned. "Socket has been contaminated."

"Terrific," Rebo said sarcastically. "Just what I wanted to hear."

Norr pushed the only button there was to push, but it wouldn't budge. But then, as she stepped out onto the transfer platform, the now-familiar female voice started into its usual spiel. That meant *anything* could have passed through the gate over the years. The sensitive held the shotgun with one hand and extended the other to Rebo. "Come on, hon," Norr said, "we're almost there."

It was the first and only time that Norr had ever called Rebo "hon," and there was something about the way it felt that caused Rebo to step out onto the platform and take her hand. The recording was followed by a flash of light and a long fall into nothingness.

FIFTEEN

Aboard Socket

Those individuals who choose to use the Elior Industries IS472-B hyperspace transporter do so at their own risk, and by using said transporter agree not to hold Elior Industries or any of its subsidiary companies liable for incomplete transfers, traumatic injuries, radiation-induced illnesses, psychotic episodes, or death.

—Standard disclaimer engraved into durasteel plaques welded to each transport platform

Rebo absorbed the shock with his knees, nearly fell, but managed to keep his balance. Norr arrived on the platform a fraction of a second later, went facedown, but broke the fall with her hands. "Uh-oh," the sensitive said as she came to her feet. "Look at that!"

Rebo looked and didn't like what he saw. The body that lay sprawled in front of the blood-splashed platform had a machete clutched in its right hand. The corpse looked as though something, or a number of somethings, had been gnawing on it. "The guardians killed him," Sogol remarked. "Be careful, there are more of them."

"Words to live by," the runner said grimly, as he eyed the dismembered mechanimals that lay scattered about.

"This guy's dressed like a fisherman," Norr remarked, as she bent over the body.

"How much would you like to bet that Tepho sent him through first?" Rebo inquired cynically. "Just to see what would happen."

"I wouldn't be surprised," the sensitive agreed. "Look! There are some dead mechanimals over by the hatch . . . except they have bullet holes in them."

"Which suggests that Tepho and his crowd shot them," the runner concluded.

"I'm picking up some jumbled radio traffic," Sogol announced. "The technos are one level up. They're battling a group of enforcers."

"*Enforcers?*" Rebo asked. "How are they different from guardians?"

"They're larger, more heavily armed, and they can fly," the AI responded simply.

"I should have known," the runner commented darkly.

"Can you turn them off?" Norr inquired hopefully.

"Yes," Sogol responded. "But only if I control Socket . . . so let's go."

As Rebo and Norr stepped over the bodies heaped around the hatch, it was clear that the robots had been cut down as they attempted to enter the compartment. Reinforcements perhaps? Summoned after the fisherman had been killed? Yes, the runner thought that was likely. But, unfortunately for the robots, it looked as though they had arrived *after* the main party materialized on the platform.

Now, as Rebo entered the corridor, he found himself in an environment that was reminiscent of the great starships. Med kits, fire extinguishers, and emergency pressure suits could be found at regular intervals along the metal bulkhead, along with directional signs that pointed toward destinations like MAINTENANCE, PERSONNEL, and MEDICAL.

But unlike all of the starships that Rebo had been aboard, Socket had yet to be looted, and there was no graffiti to be seen. "Take the next left," Sogol ordered. "That hallway leads to the lift."

Rebo approached the intersection with care, paused to peek around the corner, and was glad that he had. Judging from the bullet-scarred bulkheads, and the burn marks that crisscrossed the decks, Tepho and his party had been attacked as they transited the hall. But based on heaps of dead mechanimals that littered the floor, it was clear that the technos had been able to successfully defend themselves. Except for a hapless metal man, that is, who lay with his arms outflung, sensors staring sightlessly at the overhead. It appeared that the mechanimals had been able to open the robot's belly, because the android's electronic entrails lay splayed across his waist, where many of the fiber-optic cables had been severed.

Norr "felt" a life force behind her, whirled, and fired. The shotgun went *boom*, *clack*, *boom*, *clack*, as a dozen of the chittering guardians rushed her. Green animatronic fluid splattered the bulkheads as the first wave of mechanimals came apart. But farther down the hall, beyond the scope of the present battle, *more* lithe bodies were spilling out of ducts, chittering madly as their claws fought for purchase on the metal deck, each robot communicating with all the rest by radio.

Having spotted the oncoming wave, Rebo readied one of the energy grenades that the phibs had given him, thumbed the fuse, and tossed the weapon down the corridor. The bomb bounced once, went off with a silent flash, and blew at least fifteen mechanimals to smithereens.

In the meantime Norr pulled the trigger again, heard

nothing more than a metallic *click*, and grabbed for the power pistol. There was no recoil as the bolts of blue energy struck the remaining robots and reduced most to little more than badly burned carcasses. But even though the rear portion of its body was missing, the front half of a guardian continued to drag itself toward the sensitive, its jaws snapping at empty air. Another energy bolt put the beast down for good, but the experience left Norr shaken, and the sensitive's hands trembled slightly as she reloaded her weapons. "Good job," Rebo said reassuringly, as he administered the coup de grace to a twitching robot. "Come on . . . Let's get down that next stretch of hallway before the little bastards can regroup."

Norr followed the runner as he turned the corner, glanced at a hatch marked EMERGENCY ACCESS LADDER, and made his way past the same metal man he'd seen before. Meanwhile, having been attacked from behind once, the sensitive didn't want the same thing to happen again, and was walking backward when she passed the robot. That's why the variant didn't realize the android was still alive until steely fingers wrapped themselves around her ankle. There was a single *boom-clack* combination as Norr blew the robot's head off.

Rebo whirled, ready to fight, but concluded that Norr was getting jumpy, and turned back again. The runner arrived at the end of the corridor, followed the MAIN LIFT sign to the right, and spotted the door ahead. A few seconds later he was standing in front of the polished metal door pushing on the UP button. Once the indicator light appeared, Rebo started to back away, and motioned for Norr to do likewise.

And it was a good thing, too, because when the lift chimed and doors parted, a Porto Industries 8813-B Enforcer opened fire on them. The sphere-shaped machine floated two feet off the deck and was armed with an energy cannon. A cluster of three energy bolts passed between the humans as they opened fire. Even though Rebo scored three hits with the energy rifle, and Norr blasted the robot with her shotgun, the machine remained unaffected. That was when the robot swiveled toward Rebo, and Norr stepped into the gap between them. There was a loud clatter as the shotgun hit the floor. Rebo shouted, *"No!"* and the sensitive went for her sword.

But, rather than blowing Norr in half, the enforcer moved as if to bypass the female. That was when the runner remembered what Sogol had said earlier—and realized that the construct *couldn't* attack the sensitive so long as the AI was wrapped around her arm. Come to think of it, the guardians they had encountered earlier had probably been after *him*.

There was a metallic flash as the sliver of steel fell, followed by a loud *ka-ching*, as the supersharp blade sliced down through the robot's armor casing to lodge itself somewhere inside. The sensitive tried to free her weapon, discovered it was locked in place, and was forced to place a foot on the enforcer's casing in order to pry the sword free.

Then, just as Norr was about to take another cut at the robot, sparks spurted out of the gash in its casing. The machine shuddered, hit the deck with a thud, and rolled for two feet before coming to a stop next to a bulkhead. The sensitive returned the sword to its sheath, bent to retrieve her shotgun, and broke the weapon open. "Damn," the runner said fervently, as he watched his companion pluck empties from the weapon's rotary cylinder. "That was close! You scared the hell out of me."

"I was never in any danger," the variant replied smugly.

"Yeah? Well, you soon will be," Rebo replied darkly. "Tepho and his people would be more than happy to shoot you."

"They are entering nexus!" Sogol hissed urgently. "Hurry!"

The humans entered the lift, the runner touched the button that said, LEVEL THREE, and felt the car jerk into motion. "Why *three*?" Norr wanted to know. "Nexus is on two."

"Which means they'll be waiting for us on two," the runner predicted. "By going up to three and going down the emergency access ladder to level two, we might be able to surprise them."

The elevator stopped, the doors parted, and the runner eyed the corridor. It was blessedly empty, for which Rebo gave thanks as he jogged down the hall to the point where the vertical emergency access ladder sign had been stenciled onto the bulkhead. He opened the hatch, heard a gentle *hiss* as pressures were equalized, and entered what amounted to a vertical tunnel. "I'll go first," the runner announced, as he positioned himself on the ladder. "And remember, we don't have friends down there, so shoot anything that moves."

Then Rebo was gone, his boots sliding along the outside surface of the rails, the energy rifle hanging across his chest. The runner braked when he saw the numeral 2 appear, transferred his weight to a small platform, and was already turning toward the hatch when Norr began her descent.

Cognizant of the fact that the hall was probably occupied, Rebo opened the hatch, tossed a grenade through the gap, and pulled the door closed again. There was a muffled scream, followed by the dull rattle of automatic fire and a series of unintelligible shouts.

That was Rebo's cue to toss a *second* energy bomb into the corridor. He pulled the door closed, counted to four, and pushed his way out into the hall. The badly pulped remains of at least three bodies were scattered about, and two humans plus a metal man were crouched not thirty feet up corridor. Judging from the way some of the norms held their weapons, they weren't too familiar with them. A couple of Tepho's attendants perhaps? There was no way to know. But when they fired, the runner fired back, and it was *his* bullets that struck home. The robot went down first, quickly followed by both humans, one of whom took a burst of bolts from behind.

That surprised the runner until he saw something shimmery was standing farther down the hall, weapon in hands, firing *through* his own men. And that was the *last* thing Rebo saw as Shaz shouted an order, the lights went out, and the combat variant made his way forward.

Norr had cleared the hatch by then, and even though the corridor was nearly pitch-black, the sensitive "saw" the man-shaped blob of color coming her way. The shotgun roared, the aura staggered, and the variant felt a moment of elation. But that was when the target recovered, changed course as if to avoid a potential follow-up shot, and continued to advance. Some sort of armor perhaps? Yes, the sensitive thought so, and suspected that the oncoming combatant could see her as well.

Everything appeared green through the night-vision goggles, but both of his opponents were clear to see as Shaz pulled the trigger. That was when the variant felt something cold slither up his right leg and make straight for his genitals. Shaz couldn't resist the urge to stop and attempt to grab whatever the thing was.

And it was then, as Shaz paused to deal with Sogol, that Norr removed her opponent's head. The combat variant felt something tug at his neck, "saw" his head bounce off the floor, and knew the rest of his body was in the process of falling. And that was when the man once known as Hoggles appeared in front of him. His form was different now, but powerful nonetheless, and there was nothing friendly about his smile. "Welcome to the spirit world, friend. . . . It turns out that there are worse things than dying . . . as *you* are about to find out."

In the meantime, the lights came back on as the surviving members of Tepho's force emerged to celebrate what they assumed to be the combat variant's victory. Except that it wasn't. All five of them were armed, but none was ready, and that was a mistake. One fell to Norr's sword and the rest of them were still fumbling with their weapons when Rebo cut them down. Sogol made her way back to Norr, the humans reloaded, and the entrance to nexus was clear.

The only way Tepho could obtain sex was to purchase it from the whores of Seros. But pleasurable though such encounters had been, they didn't even begin to compare with what the technologist felt as he sat in the thronelike chair and gazed at the 360-degree holo projection that encircled him.

The panorama had been conceived to look as it should when viewed from Zeen. All of the suns that had once been part of the Imperium were represented, complete with their planetary attendants, each orbiting exactly as it should. And some of those worlds, the ones fortunate enough to boast a star gate, were further identified by what looked like green jewels. One for each portal that remained operational. Sadly, in light of what had once been, such lights were few and far between. Although Tepho was pleased to see that the vast majority of remaining portals were under the Techno Society's control, which was to say *his* control, given that the organization belonged to him.

Still, the extent to which the once far-flung network of star gates had deteriorated meant that the opportunity before him was that much greater. As Tepho stared at the panorama he could envision himself as humanity's savior, the emperor who returned mankind to its rightful place in the galaxy and thereby earned himself a revered place in history. The sudden pressure of a gun barrel against the back of Tepho's head brought the glorious dream to an abrupt end. "Stand up," Rebo grated. "And remove the vest."

But Logos 1.1, who was busy downloading himself from the vest via a wired connection, didn't want to be interrupted. Especially given the fact that the transfer was 96 percent complete. "Remain where you are," the AI ordered tersely, his voice booming through the overhead speakers.

Fortunately, Rebo was standing so close to Tepho and Logos that when the hidden weapon pods began to fire it was impossible to score a direct hit on the runner without harming the AI as well. The norm felt a momentary sensation of heat as a ruby-red energy beam scorched his right sleeve, struck the deck beyond, and etched a black line into the steel plating.

"Stay close to Tepho!" Norr shouted, and was reaching for the power pistol when Sogol attempted to jump free. Not in an attempt to flee, but to reach the console, where the AI hoped to download herself into Socket's CPU.

But Norr managed to grab hold of the construct before she could escape, said, "Oh, no you don't," and took aim at the nearest laser pod. The automated weapons couldn't fire back, not so long as the sensitive had Sogol to protect her, which left the variant free to destroy the energy projectors one at a time. It typically required at least three energy bolts before a given turret would explode in a flash of yellow light. And that meant precious seconds were coming off the clock.

Once Norr had neutralized all the pods, and Rebo was able to step away form Tepho, the sensitive carried Logos 1.2 over to the console. There was a small metal-rimmed hole off to one side, which was intended for her, and the AI went in headfirst. The variant saw Sogol's tail wiggle for a moment, then disappear as the construct sought the evil twin within.

Tepho felt the gun barrel jab the base of his neck again. "Stand up," Rebo growled, "or I will blow what passes for your brains all over that console."

The technologist stood, mind racing, while the runner tugged at the vest. Never in his wildest imaginings had Tepho visualized a situation like this one. But there had to be a way out, some means to escape the couple who had caused him so much trouble, and return with reinforcements. What neither man realized was that by the time the technologist passed the vest over to Rebo, Logos was no longer resident within it, which made them vulnerable. A fact that quickly became apparent as the surround rippled and three of the spherical enforcers appeared. The first energy bolt punched a hole through the garment that dangled from Rebo's hand, the second took a chunk out of Tepho's left arm, and the third severed the top of the chairman's thronelike chair.

Tepho ducked behind the console while the others turned to engage the enforcers. Having already learned that the energy rifle didn't have the power required to punch holes in the robot's armor, Rebo dropped that weapon in favor of the dart gun, which he removed from its shoulder holster.

And, while Norr was ready with her sword, the sensitive was so busy ducking and dodging it was impossible to use it. The variant's opportunity only came when the runner fired—and the first explosive round hit the enforcer nearest him. There was a loud *boom*, the robot belched smoke, and the acrid stench of ozone filled the air.

Then, as the other machines turned to concentrate their fire on Rebo, Norr managed to roll under one of them. That turned out to be a mistake however, because the downward pressure generated by the enforcer's onboard repulsor unit was sufficient to pin her down, and the machine clearly intended to crush her.

But, thanks to the fact that the sensitive's sword was pointed upward, the enforcer wound up impaling itself on the supersharp sliver of steel rather than killing the human being it was after. Norr felt the pressure disappear as the repulsor went off-line, knew the robot would fall, and hurried to roll out of the way. The variant felt the machine's metal casing brush her arm as it fell. There was a loud *clang* as armor hit the steel deck followed by the gentle moan of released air.

Meanwhile, the battle between Rebo and the remaining enforcers continued. The good news was that the explosive darts were effective against the big spheres. The bad news was that the first unit the runner attacked sustained three separate hits before finally suffering significant damage to its onboard guidance system. A few moments later the construct powered its way through the surrounding holo curtain, smashed into the bulkhead beyond, and crashed to the deck.

Now, having taken cover behind the wreckage of the first enforcer, the runner was attempting to get a bead on the *third* robot. Unfortunately for Rebo, the machine had the capacity to learn. And, having observed what had happened to the other units, had taken evasive action. By going up to its maximum altitude of twelve feet, the robot had positioned itself against the dark overhead, making it difficult to see. Although Rebo could see the energy bolts as they flashed down at him, it was impossible to know which way the machine would move next. All of which explained why the last three shots had missed their mark.

But the enforcer's plan, good though it was, failed to take the second biological into account. A fact that became evident when the robot passed under a crossbeam and felt something land on top of it. Then, even as the machine readied an electric shock designed to counter that sort of attack, the weight dropped away. The enforcer bobbed upward, and was still in the process of analyzing what had occurred, when the phib energy grenade went off.

Since she knew next to nothing about the robot's design, and was eager to jump off the machine as quickly as possible, Norr had been content to shove the little bomb into any aperture she could find. Which, as it turned out, was an intake vent. And once the grenade detonated, the duct channeled hot gases directly into the enforcer's high-tech guts, where they triggered a secondary explosion. Rebo heard a dull *thump*, saw flames shoot out through multiple cracks in the machine's armor, and watched the construct as it fell on the far end of the kidney-shaped console.

Rebo's first thought was for Tepho. Had the technologist been killed? The runner sincerely hoped so, but crossed the room only to discover that the slippery bastard was nowhere to be found.

Meanwhile, deep within the surreal universe of Socket's CPU, an entirely different kind of war was being fought. A desperate conflict in which bolts of logical lightning illuminated a bleak landscape, multicolored lights glittered as they cascaded down tiers of memory into rivers of molten data, and mountainous subroutines vanished only to magically reappear as twin titans battled for control.

But dramatic though the contest was, there was never any doubt as to which AI would emerge victorious. By the time Sogol entered Socket's Central Processing Unit Logos was so firmly entrenched that a miracle would have been required to dislodge him. And there were no miracles within the space station's CPU, just calculations, which the older AI controlled. So, even as Sogol continued to fight, she knew what the ultimate outcome would have to be. And though not capable of human emotion, processed a sense of profound noncompletion, which was analogous to regret.

Norr had just learned of Tepho's escape when Sogol's voice came over the speakers. "I will hold out as long as I can, but Logos 1.1 will ultimately seize control of Socket, and therefore humanity itself."

"*No!*" The word was formed by Norr's lips and delivered from her mouth, but had been spoken by someone else. The sensitive felt a surge of something akin to electricity as the entity once known as Emperor Hios took control of her body. "This is Lysander. . . . Hold Logos 1.1 off as long as you can! There is a way to destroy Socket . . . a code that I took to my grave. Once I enter it into the console, my channel will have ten minutes to evacuate. Then, once the power core blows, the entire satellite will be destroyed."

Rebo watched Lysander walk Norr's body over the badly ravaged console. There was an audible *whir* as a section of seemingly solid material opened in response to her touch, and a keypad was revealed. Slim fingers danced over white buttons as a string of potentially lethal numbers were entered and Logos 1.1 immediately sought to neutralize them. But the AI *couldn't* interfere with the ultimate safeguard, not so long as his programming was intact, but was quick to express his frustration. "*No!* Are you insane? When Socket dies, everything you built, everything you worked for will die with it!"

"That's true," the onetime emperor intoned. "But it's better than allowing entities like Tepho and you to control humanity! Perhaps someone will reinvent the star gates one day. . . . If so, I can only hope that they do a better job of it than I did."

Then, as if to underline Lysander's words, a klaxon began to bleat. Norr staggered as the spirit entity released its grip on her, felt Rebo take her hand, and heard him yell, "Run!"

Tepho tripped, fell, and threw out his hands in a last- second attempt to protect himself. Having added still more bruises to the collection he already had, the technologist struggled to his feet and limped ahead. The shoulder wound was painful, but the flesh had been cauterized by the same bolt of energy that injured it, so there wasn't any blood. Of more concern were the robots that wanted to kill him. But not if he made it to the star gate first!

Armed with a pistol taken off Shaz's headless torso, the technologist was on level one, making his way down a long stretch of corridor, when a klaxon began to bleat. Emergency beacons began to flash soon after that, and it became obvious that something was wrong.

But the administrator was already running as fast as he could, so there was nothing more that he could do as a synthesized female voice began the final countdown. "Time remaining for evacuation nine minutes, thirty seconds. All personnel who wish to exit the station prior to detonation are ordered to leave Socket *now.* . . . Time remaining for evacuation nine minutes, twenty-five seconds. All personnel . . ."

Tepho lost track of the announcement as a loud *chittering* sound was heard, hundreds of guardians poured out into the hallway in front of him, and the technologist was forced to stop. The pistol jumped in the administrator's hand as he fired into the oncoming mob. Tepho had the momentary satisfaction of seeing more than a dozen robots go down. But then he was out of ammo, and with no backup clips to call on, the norm could do little more than throw the empty gun at the roiling mass of electromechanical bodies before him. Just as Tepho was about to surrender to the inevitable, a dart whizzed past his right ear, struck one of the mechanimals, and exploded.

"So, we meet again," Norr observed, as she stepped up to fire her shotgun.

The technologist felt something warm seep down along his legs, and looked down discover that he had peed himself, even as Rebo fired three explosive rounds into what remained of the horde. "Time remaining for evacuation, eight minutes, fifteen seconds," the voice announced calmly. "All personnel who wish to exit the station . . ."

"That would be *us!*" Rebo exclaimed, and reached out to help Norr through the electromechanical gore that covered the deck.

"But what about *me?*" Tepho wailed miserably, as the others left him behind.

"It looks like you're screwed!" Rebo shouted cheerfully, as Norr rounded the corner ahead, and he followed. The couple were in the final stretch by that time, and racing through the area where an earlier battle had been fought, when Sogol was forced to capitulate. There was a symbolic explosion deep within Socket's CPU, as the eternally shifting computational landscape was momentarily illuminated by a brilliant flash of light, and operating system 1.2 was eradicated.

And it was then, even as the countdown fell to six minutes, twenty seconds, that Logos chose to close all of the station's airtight, blastproof doors in hopes that he could trap Rebo and Norr in the main corridor. Rebo saw the steel barriers begin to deploy and urged Norr to greater speed, but knew it was hopeless. They were still fifteen feet away from the nearest hatch when metal clanged on metal. Socket was going to blow, the countdown continued, and the star gate lay on the other side of the hatch.

Rebo felt his spirits plummet as both he and the sensitive were forced to put on the brakes, and were still struggling to slow themselves, when they threw up their hands. "Damn," the runner exclaimed as his hands made contact with cold steel. "What now?"

"Time remaining for evacuation, five minutes, thirty seconds," the voice put in emotionlessly. "All personnel who wish . . ."

Norr had no answer, and was just about to say as much, when a third person spoke. "Perhaps I can help," Tepho said calmly. They turned to find that the technologist had approached them from behind. The front of his pants remained wet—but the technologist was otherwise composed. "As with any habitat of this size," Tepho continued carefully, "there is one more than one way off. Come . . . I'll show you."

So saying, the administrator turned and limped back the way he had come. Rebo looked at Norr, and the sensitive shrugged. With no other options to choose from, the twosome had very little choice but to follow Tepho a short distance to a newly opened hatch and the bright red decal located beside it. The sign was directly opposite the area where the first battle with the guardians had been fought—which explained why the runner failed to see it earlier. Simple though they were the words caused his heart to leap: ESCAPE POD THREE.

Norr peered through the opening and saw that a short ladder led up to another smaller hatch. The sensitive looked at Tepho and frowned. "Why come get us? You could be clear by now," the variant commented suspiciously.

"Because I can't climb the ladder by myself," the technologist answered honestly. "Please help me."

"You've got to be kidding," Rebo responded angrily. "After everything you've done? I don't think so. Come on, Lonni, let's get out of here."

"No," the sensitive objected stubbornly. "It wouldn't be right. Boost him up there . . . Or would you like to be standing there arguing with me when Socket blows?"

Rebo made a face, urged Tepho through the first hatch, and muscled the other man up the ladder. And it was there, on the escape pod's threshold, that the technologist launched his backward kick. The blow struck the runner in the face, which caused him to lose his grip, and fall backward into the corridor.

Tepho laughed triumphantly as he scooted into the four-person pod, and was reaching for the controls, when Norr fired the power pistol up through the open hatch. She wasn't an especially good shot, not by Rebo's standards, but the range was short. The energy bolt punched a neat little hole through the technologist's throat and left him gasping for air. Rebo had recovered by then. He scrambled up the ladder, grabbed the front of Tepho's shirt, and jerked him out through the hatch. There was a meaty *thump* as he hit the deck.

Norr felt no sense of guilt as she was forced to step on

Tepho in order to access the ladder and join Rebo inside the vehicle. They heard the voice begin to announce that one minute and twenty seconds remained, but the sound was cut off as the hatch cycled closed, and an even shorter countdown began. There was barely enough time to strap themselves in before the escape vehicle blew itself free of Socket, and the couple became weightless.

Meanwhile, back aboard the space station, Tepho struggled to breathe. He was still trying to come up with a plan to extend his life when Socket exploded into a million pieces. There was chaos on the surface of the planet as the tides ceased to exist, the phib tidal generators failed, and the oceans went on a rampage. Eventually, after all of the destruction, the phibs and norms might be forced to contemplate some sort of truce and find ways to cooperate with each other.

But for Rebo and Norr, there were other problems to consider. Would they travel to Esperance? And attempt to backtrack the technos to their hidden star gate? Or was that a waste of time without Socket to facilitate the transfer? And what about the great starships? Could they take passage aboard one of them? And thereby find their way back to Seros? That seemed like the best hope.

Finally, after a rough-and-tumble journey through the planetary atmosphere, a red chute deployed. The escape pod slowed and rocked back and forth before it finally smacked down on an azure ocean. Fresh air flooded the tiny cabin as the off-worlders opened the top hatch, stood on their seats, and eyed their surroundings. The escape pod rose as a huge swell rolled in to lift it up, and it managed to remain stubbornly upright as the mountain of water fell away. Days, if not weeks would pass before the ocean found its new equilibrium, and the tidal storms stopped. Rebo could see fluffy white clouds, a circling seabird, and a point of land off in the distance.

Norr thought about Seros, the hand-to-mouth existence she had led there, and wondered if she would see the planet again. Or even *wanted* to see the planet again. But then, as Rebo put his arm around her shoulders, the sensitive knew it didn't really matter. Finally, having wandered halfway across the galaxy, she was home.

DANGER FROM ABOVE!

The stone fell with surprising slowness. Meat imagined that this was because his heart had sped up a thousand times. He'd read about this. A person's whole life really could pass before his eyes when the heart sped up a thousand times.

The limbs of the trees around him were moved by a sudden gust of wind. Leaves rustled, branches cracked. The wind was so sudden it seemed unearthly, like the woman in the tower.

If the stone tried to go this way or that way, the wind would correct it and send it . . . to him!

Then the stone seemed to flutter as if it had suddenly sprouted wings. That would not have surprised Meat. Nothing would ever surprise him again. Wind, wings, whatever—that stone was going where it was intended to go.

Whoever had thrown the stone was shouting something, but Meat couldn't make it out.

A cry cut through the late afternoon air, drowning out all other sound.

Meat knew that cry even though he had never heard anything like it before. It was the cry of someone about to die.

And it had come from his throat.

A HERCULEAH JONES MYSTERY

THE BLACK TOWER

BY BETSY BYARS

SLEUTH
PUFFIN

PUFFIN BOOKS

Published by the Penguin Group

Penguin Group (USA) Inc., 345 Hudson Street, New York, New York 10014, U.S.A.

Penguin Group (Canada), 90 Eglinton Avenue East, Suite 700, Toronto, Ontario, Canada M4P 2Y3
(a division of Pearson Penguin Canada Inc.)

Penguin Books Ltd, 80 Strand, London WC2R 0RL, England

Penguin Ireland, 25 St Stephen's Green, Dublin 2, Ireland (a division of Penguin Books Ltd)

Penguin Group (Australia), 250 Camberwell Road, Camberwell, Victoria 3124, Australia
(a division of Pearson Australia Group Pty Ltd)

Penguin Books India Pvt Ltd, 11 Community Centre, Panchsheel Park, New Delhi - 110 017, India

Penguin Group (NZ), 67 Apollo Drive, Rosedale, North Shore 0745, Auckland, New Zealand
(a division of Pearson New Zealand Ltd.)

Penguin Books (South Africa) (Pty) Ltd, 24 Sturdee Avenue,
Rosebank, Johannesburg 2196, South Africa

Registered Offices: Penguin Books Ltd, 80 Strand, London WC2R 0RL, England

First published in the United States of America by Viking,
a division of Penguin Young Readers Group, 2006
This Sleuth edition published by Puffin Books, a division of Penguin Young Readers Group, 2007

1 3 5 7 9 10 8 6 4 2

THE LIBRARY OF CONGRESS HAS CATALOGED THE VIKING EDITION AS FOLLOWS:

Byars, Betsy Cromer.
The black tower / by Betsy Byars.
p.   cm.—(A Herculeah Jones mystery)
Summary: Herculeah Jones gets involved in another dangerous mystery when she
goes to visit old Mr. Shivers Hunt, resident of the forbidding Hunt House.
ISBN 0-670-06174-3 (hardcover)
[1. Mystery and detective stories.] I. Title.
PZ7.B9836Bit 2006   [Fic]—dc22   2005033317

Puffin Books ISBN 978-0-14-240937-4

Printed in the United States of America

Set in Minion
Book design by Sam Kim

CONTENTS

A HERCULEAH JONES MYSTERY

THE BLACK TOWER

THE TERROR IN BLACK TOWER

Slowly she climbed the circular stairs in the tower, drawn against her will to what waited at the top.

Halfway there, she paused. She heard the sound of the tower door close below her. Had it been a hand that closed it? She looked down. The thought that she might be trapped made her dizzy.

She touched the wall to steady herself. There was an eerie coldness to the stones beneath her hand.

She lifted her head. She listened.

She heard nothing, but she knew someone was up there, waiting for her.

And whoever it was knew she was coming.

Slowly she took another step and another. Higher . . . higher. With each step, her fear grew until it seemed to swirl around her like a cape that held no warmth.

Herculeah stopped reading and let the book fall to her lap. "Are you positive this is the book you want me to read?" she asked.

The old man on the bed blinked his eyes once. That meant "yes."

"Well, I'm getting spooked," Herculeah said. "Particularly because this house, your house, has a tower attached to it. It's exactly like this one, isn't it?"

One blink. Yes.

"Have you ever been up there?"

Yes.

"What's up there? Oh, I forgot. You can't answer that kind of question. Only yes or no. Is there a room up there?"

Yes.

"Does the tower have circular stairs?"

Yes.

"That was stupid of me. I guess all towers do. Either that or they have a ladder."

Herculeah glanced out the window. She could see the tower now. It rose, black and forbidding, part of the house and yet somehow separate. Halfway up the tower there were windows. They were slits so deep in the stone that no daylight could come through.

Herculeah paused in thought. Her hands tightened on the book in her lap. The silence continued.

Herculeah had come here to read to Mr. Hunt. Her mother,

a private detective, had asked her to do this. Mr. Hunt was, or had been, one of her mother's clients.

"Why was he a client?" Herculeah had asked, instantly curious. "What did he want you to do?"

"That doesn't concern you."

Herculeah had leaned forward, more interested than ever. "What did he want you to find? That's what all old people want you to do—find someone or something from their past."

Her mother's wry smile made Herculeah think she had hit the mark.

"So what could it have been?" she went on thoughtfully. "What could have happened? Murder? Was it a murder?" Her gray eyes lit up. "It was murder, wasn't it?"

"Whatever it was happened a long time ago."

"So it was murder."

Her mother lifted one hand to silence her. "If you're going to play detective—"

"Mom, I don't *play* detective. I have solved six murders." She began to count them on her fingers. "Mr. Crewell, Madame Rosa . . ."

Her mom sighed, and Herculeah discontinued her list. "Oh, all right, what do you want me to do?"

"Just read to him for an hour or so. The man is lonely. He can't move at all since his stroke. He can only blink his eyes— one blink for yes, two blinks for no."

"How awful! Sure, I'll do it. Actually, I enjoy reading to

people. What kind of book would an old man like? Something about old horses, old airplanes, or"—she grinned—"old women? I'll take a bunch of books so he'll have a choice. First thing tomorrow I'll go to the library and load up with books."

"Oh, there's a huge library at the house. You won't need to take anything."

"A huge library? This old man has a huge library in his house?"

Her mom hesitated a moment before she answered. "Have you ever heard of Shivers Hunt?"

"Mom! Not *the* Shivers Hunt!"

"There couldn't be but one."

"Mom, you mean I'd actually get to go inside Haunt House?"

"What?"

"Haunt House. That's what all the kids call it. And, Mom, nobody has ever been inside it. I cannot believe that I'm going to Haunt House."

"Well, you aren't going unless you stop calling it that."

"Right! Hunt House!"

"I won't let you go unless you promise you won't do anything to upset Mr. Hunt."

"I won't, I won't! I promise! But I can't help being excited. I, Herculeah Jones, am going inside"—she swallowed the word—"Hunt House."

But when Herculeah got there, she hadn't been taken to the

library to choose a book as she had expected. The nurse took her straight up the stairs to Mr. Hunt's bedroom. The book had already been chosen for her. It was waiting on the table by the old man's bed.

Herculeah picked up the book. She read the title aloud. "*The Terror in Black Tower*. This is what I'm supposed to read?" she asked the nurse.

"Yes, Herculeah. When I told Mr. Hunt that you were coming to read to him, I asked if there was any particular book he'd like. He blinked yes. I must have carried a hundred books up from the library before he finally saw this one and gave a very definite yes."

Herculeah picked up the book. On the cover, embossed in the black leather, was the silhouette of a tower. It was outlined in gold, but it looked as if someone had rubbed their fingers over the gold, as if to erase the whole tower from sight. It gave the book a sinister look. She rubbed her own fingers over the gold, then stopped abruptly.

"Well, let's get on with it." She opened the book. "Ready, Mr. Hunt?"

Yes.

Inside, the pages were thick and yellow with age. They smelled of mildew and dark passages and old secrets. Herculeah loved it.

Perhaps, she thought, Mr. Hunt had read the book as a boy,

and back then it had seemed scary, probably full of family madness and secret passages, and—who knows?—maybe some terror actually had been up in the black tower.

But those things didn't exist in modern times.

They didn't.

She paused.

Or did they?

THE TRAPDOOR

Herculeah glanced at Mr. Hunt. He was waiting for her to continue. She looked down at the page.

"Where was I? Oh, yes, she's going up the tower steps." Herculeah smiled. "Actually, this will probably sound foolish to you, Mr. Hunt, but I can understand the girl doing this. I mean, she knows she's not supposed to. She knows there's something up there, something dangerous. But she can't stop herself. That's the way I am. I would do the exact same thing. The only difference would be that at this point my hair would be frizzling. I have radar hair. It gets bigger when I'm in danger. Like this."

She laughed and fluffed out her hair. Mr. Hunt watched. His bright bird eyes never left her face.

At that moment, her hair actually seemed to be frizzling on its own, as if it were anticipating the day she would climb the tower, the day she—heart racing with fear—not the character in the book, would take those circular stairs.

She patted her hair into place and said, "Oh, here's where we were." She began to read.

Slowly she took another step and another. Higher . . . higher. With each step, her fear grew until it seemed to swirl around her like a cape that held no warmth.

In the distance came the sound of thunder. She glanced out the window. She could see nothing through the dense, chilling fog that circled the tower.

A storm was coming. She must hurry.

Still she hesitated before taking the next step. Only eight steps remained. She could see the heavy wooden door at the top now, a trapdoor.

Only seven steps.

Now she could hear it. The sound of breathing seemed to move from side to side behind the trapdoor. It was as if whoever, whatever was there, was trying to find a way out.

"I'm coming," she whispered.

The door to the bedroom opened behind Herculeah, and, startled, she spun around.

"Your hour's up, Herculeah," the nurse said.

"Already? I just started. I've hardly read two pages. I got

started talking about myself—I do that all the time. Plus I was getting to the good part. The girl in the book was hearing breathing. I've got to find out what's doing that breathing."

"Sorry. It'll keep. Tomorrow the print will still be right there waiting for you."

"I know." Herculeah sighed. "Actually I read a lot of books, and I've learned that authors save important things—things like what's waiting up in the tower, doing that heavy breathing—until the very end. If I know authors, this one will start a flashback just when she gets to the trapdoor. Then, on the last page—finally, finally—we'll find out what was in the tower."

"You must do a lot of reading."

"Yes."

"But we don't want to tire Mr. Hunt."

"No. Did I tire you, Mr. Hunt?"

Two blinks. No.

"But did I scare you?"

No.

She laughed. "Well, I scared myself."

Herculeah folded a ribbon into the book to hold her place. She closed the book and set it on the table.

"I'll be back tomorrow to pick up. Remember where we left off? It's getting ready to storm. The girl heard thunder. It'll be a dark and stormy night when anything can happen." She gave her words a dramatic reading.

He blinked a forceful yes.

"Dramatic things always happen during storms—though it's dramatic enough with something waiting for her at the top of the tower."

Another forceful yes.

"Do you know what's up there?"

Yes.

"Because you've read the book before?"

"Time," the nurse reminded her.

"I have to go." Herculeah smiled at the old man, his face pale against the pillows, his bright bird eyes trying to tell her something, something important.

The nurse said, "Your friend is waiting for you outside."

"Meat?"

"I think that's his name. I tried to get him to come inside, but he wouldn't."

"That's Meat."

Herculeah almost explained that Meat was afraid of this house, that he half believed the ghost stories that surrounded it, believed the stories that the portraits had holes in the eyes so that someone in a secret passage behind the wall could watch your every move.

"Meat . . . Herculeah . . ." the nurse said. "What wonderful names!"

"Meat got his because there's a lot of him. I got mine because my mom was watching a Hercules movie when she was waiting for me to be born. Mom was kidding around about naming me

Hercules if I was a boy. The nurse said, 'What about if it's a girl?' Mom said, 'She'll be Herculeah.' I guess I was lucky. The doctor got in the act and said, 'How about Samson?' He even sang it, 'Oh, Samson-ya!'" She laughed. "Anyway, everyone who knows me says it suits."

"I only met you this afternoon," the nurse said, "but I think it suits you, too."

As they moved into the hall, Herculeah said, "You know, I can't stop wondering why he chose this book." She smiled. "Although I'm always looking for the reasons people do things."

"I wondered about that, too."

"Really?"

"Because I've had other patients like Mr. Hunt, patients who have been deprived of everything but their minds. And it seems that another sense has been heightened. They seem to know what's ahead, the way an animal can sense a storm."

"Premonitions."

"Yes. If Mr. Hunt had some way of knowing there would be trouble in that tower, he would have picked this book. Well, I've got to get back to my patient."

"Right. I'll see you both tomorrow."

"Oh, I won't be here," the nurse said, smiling. "New grandchild. A Miss Wegman is taking over for me. Do you need me to show you the way out?"

"No, I remember the way."

"Because this house has a lot of halls that don't go anywhere and oddly shaped rooms. It's easy to get lost in here."

"I won't."

She started down the stairs. She was lost in thought until she glanced at the painting on the wall. It was a family portrait: old man Hunt—Lionus Hunt, who had built the house—his wife, and the four children. Mr. Shivers Hunt was the oldest of the children. Then there was a younger sister and twin girls.

Herculeah paused, half hoping to see someone peering at her through holes in the old man's eyes.

Oh, well, she told herself, it was too much to hope for.

She was turning to go when something about the twins caught her eye. The twins were dressed alike—in middy blouses—but there was something about the blouse of the smaller twin.

She bent closer. She rubbed her fingers over the painting. The figure of the smaller twin had been damaged in some way. It had been repaired, but not by the same artist who had done the original picture. Strange.

Strange, too, about Mr. Hunt's choosing the book. There was so much she didn't know, so much she would have to find out.

With a shiver of anticipation, she continued down the stairs.

3

HAUNT HOUSE

"I thought you were never coming out," Meat said. He got up from the steps and brushed off the back of his jeans.

Herculeah glanced at her watch. "Five o'clock. Right on time."

"I thought something had happened to you," he confessed. "I thought you were never coming out."

"Oh, Meat, that's silly. Just because you thought you saw me get stabbed that one time, now you think you have to protect me."

"It's the kind of house where things like that happen," he explained. "A person goes in and they never come out."

"You've listened to too many ghost stories."

"I have never trusted a house that has—well . . . that has a face," he finished in a rush.

"A face?"

"Yeah. That huge door is the mouth, and those windows seem to be eyes looking at us."

"You know what this reminds me of? The time we went to the amusement park and you wouldn't go in the funhouse because the front was like a clown face, and you were afraid to walk in his mouth."

"I was not afraid. I just prefer doors that look like doors." He decided to change the subject. "So, tell me everything."

"Well," Herculeah said, "first the nurse and I walked upstairs, and, Meat"—she lowered her voice—"eyes watched me from a portrait every step of the way."

"Get outta here," Meat said. He was proud that he hadn't sounded as if he believed her, but then he spoiled it by adding, "They didn't really, did they?"

"No, they didn't."

Meat said, "Let's go."

"What's your hurry?"

He glanced up at the house. With the sun setting behind it, the house cast deep shadows over the ground. A dense area of woods circled the house and seemed to be reaching for whoever was unfortunate enough to step off the drive.

Meat's first impression of the place had made him shudder. If he had not been with Herculeah, he would have turned and run for his life, but she had been beside him, giving him the history of the house.

"It was built over a hundred years ago by old Mr. Hunt, Lionus Hunt. See, Meat, Lionus Hunt had been like a field hand on this big estate in England, and when he got over here and struck it rich, he built the exact same house, only he'd never been inside the house so he had to make up the rooms. They're all crazy."

Meat didn't doubt that.

"And from the first day, Meat, the house was struck by tragedy."

Meat didn't doubt that, either.

As Meat had gotten closer, he had seen the tower. He had known there would be one. Herculeah had told him that and had said, "Guess what it's called."

"I can't."

"Shivers Tower."

Well, it made him shiver, all right.

"But the tower's been locked up," she had said, "because there was some terrible tragedy there. My mom claims she doesn't know what the tragedy was, but I'm going to find out. And, Meat, there's supposed to be money hidden somewhere in the house. Old man Hunt didn't trust banks so all the millions and millions are in the walls or the secret room or the tower."

"Can we change the subject?" Meat asked.

"Yes, but guess what happened today?" Herculeah said as they started for home down the long drive.

"What?"

"When I was reading to Mr. Hunt—"

Something cold seemed to touch Meat's neck, and he glanced over his shoulder. He gasped with fright.

In one of the upstairs windows, a face was framed, a face in a tangle of wild hair. The eyes stared down at him with a look of such wildness that it froze his blood.

He stopped. He couldn't move. He closed his eyes.

"What's wrong?" Herculeah asked. She had continued on a few steps and now turned to look at him.

"A face," he managed to say.

"What face?"

"In the window."

As he spoke, he saw the face again in his mind, and he felt the image was there permanently, the way looking at the sun can leave the eye scarred with the image.

"Which window?"

He pointed a trembling finger.

Herculeah shaded her eyes from the setting sun. "I don't see anything."

He forced himself to look. Of course there was nothing there now.

"It was a face—I don't know how to describe it—an evil face. There was a lot of wild hair—"

"Like mine?" she asked, grinning and fluffing her hair.

Herculeah wouldn't be serious. "No. No! This was hair that hadn't been combed in years—maybe never—and the face, well, it was like, like a bird of prey, and I was the prey. And the fingers were like talons and—"

"You saw the hands, too?"

"No, but those were the kind of terrible hands that would go with the face. . . ."

Herculeah smiled.

"It really isn't amusing," Meat said.

"I know. I was smiling at myself. It's just that this is the kind of house that makes you think you see things, makes you think you hear things. When I was reading about the girl going up the tower steps, I actually imaged I was the girl and—"

"This wasn't my imagination."

"All right." She looked thoughtful. "I think Mr. Hunt does have a couple of sisters. I don't even know if one of them lives in this house, but if she does, maybe that was who you saw."

"*What* I saw is more like it. That face might not even have been human."

She looked at him closely. His face was as pale as if he had seen a ghost.

"Let's go home."

"Gladly."

They walked through the open gates. On either gate, the figure of a lion was worked into the wrought iron. One paw was raised as if, Meat thought, to menace visitors as they passed through.

"And the owner, Lionus Hunt," Herculeah said, speaking as if she were reading from a guide book, "had these gates made in his likeness to guard the house. He wanted visitors to know the house was his and that they entered at their own peril."

"Did you read that somewhere?"

"No, I just made it up."

"Well, if he really wanted to menace people," Meat said, "he could have used that old woman's face."

4

MAN OR BEAST

"Let me," Meat said, reaching for the doorbell. Over his shoulder he said, "I hate this doorbell. It's like the ding-dong of doom."

It was the next day, and Meat had walked Herculeah to Hunt House for her second reading of *The Terror in Black Tower*.

It was one of those old-timey doorbells that had to be turned, and Meat gave it a manly twist. From deep within the house came the ding-dong.

They heard heavy footsteps. "It's a new nurse today," Herculeah said. "I think her name's Miss—"

The door opened then, stopping Herculeah's sentence. Herculeah and Meat looked up. The smiles on their faces faded.

Nurse Wegman was big. Meat had seen bodies like that on *World Class Wrestling*. She was not as big as his father, of course. Few people were. After all, his dad was Macho Man, a championship wrestler. Just the thought of his dad brought back the picture of him entering the ring, the crowd chanting, "Macho,

Macho, Macho Man." He could hear the music, feel the pride, the—

Meat's pleasant picture was shattered by one harsh word from the nurse. "Yes?"

"I'm Herculeah Jones."

Nurse Wegman said another word. "So?"

"Didn't anybody tell you? I read to Mr. Hunt every afternoon at four o'clock. It's four now." She lifted her arm to display her watch.

Meat thought Nurse Wegman looked as if she didn't trust Herculeah, so he came immediately to his friend's defense. "It's all right, Nurse. Her mom's a private investigator. She works for Mr. Hunt."

That seemed to help Nurse Wegman make up her mind. "You'd better come in."

Herculeah went inside, and Meat said, "I'll wait out here in case you need me."

"You aren't coming in?" Nurse Wegman asked.

"No, sir."

Meat turned away quickly, his face red with embarrassment. He hoped neither Miss Wegman nor Herculeah had heard that "sir."

Inside, Herculeah followed Nurse Wegman up the stairs. "Your mother is a private detective?" the nurse asked.

"Yes."

"What, exactly, is she investigating?"

"I don't know. She doesn't confide in me."

"I was only asking because I've heard rumors about this place. People seem to think it's kind of spooky." Her voice seemed to deepen. "I've even heard there's money hidden in here. Have you heard that?"

"Yes, I heard the Hunts didn't believe in banks."

"Are there any rumors where it might be hidden?"

"Not that I've heard. It could be anywhere."

"And this is a big house."

"Yes." Herculeah watched Miss Wegman's broad back, the ponytail that swung between her shoulder blades. At least, she thought, this nurse was big enough to take care of an invalid. "The book I'm reading to Mr. Hunt is *The Terror in Black Tower*, and this house even has a black tower, in case you didn't notice."

"I noticed."

Nurse Wegman opened the door to Mr. Hunt's bedroom. "I'll be around if you need me."

Herculeah approached the bed. "Hi," she told Mr. Hunt, "it's me again—Herculeah. Do you feel like hearing some more about the girl in the tower?"

For a moment Mr. Hunt didn't seem to recognize her. His eyes weren't as bright as yesterday.

"Do you want me to read?"

Three blinks.

What did that mean? Herculeah wondered. One blink meant "yes"; two meant "no." Three meant what?

"Are you trying to tell me something, Mr. Hunt?"

One blink. Yes.

"Is it about the book?"

No.

She had a sudden insight and she asked, "Is it about Nurse Wegman?"

Yes.

"Is she—?"

From the doorway Nurse Wegman said, "If you came to read, read!" It was a command.

"I'd better read," Herculeah said. "Don't you think?"

Yes.

"And I'll be sitting right out here to make sure everything's"—Nurse Wegman paused as if trying to find the right words—"all right."

Herculeah picked up the book, opened it, and glanced down at the page.

"Ah, yes," she said. Herculeah was smiling, but there was a false cheer in her voice. "The girl is still on the stairs. You know, people have climbed Everest in the time it's taken this girl to get to the top of the tower."

Although the man on the bed could not move or speak, he seemed on occasion to send off signals—brain waves, maybe. At any rate, sometimes Herculeah seemed to know what he was thinking. Maybe, as the nurse suggested yesterday, Mr. Hunt had developed special powers.

"Yes," she agreed, "that's true. People want to get to the top of Everest, and this girl definitely does not want to get to the top of the tower." She lifted the book to the light. "But I do admit I wish she'd hurry up." She began to read.

She took two more steps. The noise above her was unlike anything she had heard before. It was not a human sound, and it was not the sound of an animal—at least not any animal she had ever heard before.

Herculeah glanced up at the man on the bed. She grinned. "Man or beast?" she asked, trying to turn his attention to the book.

And the silent answer that seemed to come from the man on the bed was, "Beast."

5

A PREMONITION

"You're awfully quiet," Meat said.

He and Herculeah had left the grounds of Hunt House and were entering their own neighborhood. Now, in familiar surroundings, seeing familiar signs—BERNIE HOLDEN: ACCOUNTANT, BESSIE FLOWER: ALTERATIONS, CAKES BY CHERI, ONE-DAY DENTURES—Meat felt he was capable of holding an intelligent conversation.

"I'm thinking," she said.

"About the book? Is it getting better?"

"The book couldn't get any better. It started strong and scary. That's my kind of book."

Meat glanced at her quickly. "But why would you choose a book like that to read to someone who's sick?"

"I didn't have any choice."

"You always have a choice."

"Not this time. The book was chosen for me. Mr. Hunt picked it out himself."

"How could he? I thought he could only blink."

"The nurse—this was the other nurse, the one I liked, not Nurse Wegman—brought in hundreds of books, and he blinked at this one."

"I wonder why."

"Who knows. I tried to figure it out. It could be that he read the book a long time ago when he was a boy. And—this just occurred to me—in the book, there's somebody up in the tower, a prisoner maybe, and since Mr. Hunt probably feels like a prisoner himself . . . he's identifying with the prisoner."

"Yes, but you'd think, if he does feel like a prisoner, he'd want to hear a story about people outside doing things—climbing mountains and forging streams, looking for buried treasure."

"Or maybe," she said thoughtfully, "he's trying to warn us about the tower. The nurse said she'd had patients in Mr. Hunt's condition who got premonitions about the future. I hope that's not the case, because something terrible is going to happen and—"

She broke off and lifted her head. "That's strange," she said.

They were now at the front steps of Herculeah's house. Her face was lifted to the window.

"What?"

"The phone."

"What about it?"

"It's ringing."

"What's strange about that?" Meat asked. "That's what phones do."

Herculeah's face had that serious look, so he changed his question. "Why do you think it's strange?"

"Look at my hair."

"It's frizzling," he said.

"Yes! Exactly! As soon as I heard the phone ringing, my hair started doing this."

"The phone's stopped ringing now," Meat said. "Your hair can go back to normal."

Herculeah didn't answer. It was as if she were listening to something happening inside the house. Meat didn't hear a thing.

"Your mom probably answered," he said.

"Mom's not home."

"Then someone's leaving a message."

"That's what I'm thinking. The message is for me."

"You don't know that."

Herculeah reached for the banister and started quickly up the steps.

Meat followed. "This is what I don't get," he said to her back. "Your hair is frizzling, which means there's danger, and here you are hurrying into the house. If there's danger, why would you go to meet it?"

She turned and looked at him. Her gray eyes were dark with concern. "Because I might not be the one in danger. Someone may need me."

She unlocked the door and went inside, leaving Meat alone on the steps.

Well, *he* wasn't going inside. He'd never been foolish enough to rush to meet danger. Anyway, he knew Herculeah would tell him about it. She was very generous about sharing her danger.

He glanced across the street at his house. He could go home, but there wouldn't be anything to do there. He sat down on the steps.

Inside, Herculeah stood in the hallway for a moment. She listened. Someone was leaving a message on her mother's office answering machine.

The voice was old and shaky, but Herculeah could make out the message. Her blood froze.

"Meat!"

There was such urgency in her voice that Meat couldn't help himself. He jumped up and went to meet the danger, too.

When he entered the living room, he saw that Herculeah was standing by her mother's desk. She was bending over the answering machine. "You have to hear this," she said.

Meat had the childish urge to put his fingers in his ears, but he resisted.

"Something's wrong, isn't it?"

"Yes."

"Is it very wrong, medium wrong or"—he paused hopefully—"just some little thing?" He had asked Herculeah this question before, and he knew how she would answer. "It's very wrong, isn't it?"

"Dead wrong."

6

THE WARNING

Meat moved closer to the desk.

"Listen," Herculeah said. With quick, practiced motions, she rewound the message and played it. An old shaky voice came from the machine.

"—s a murderer. Stay away from the—"

"You must not have rewound it all the way. Try it again."

She rewound the tape and replayed it.

Again the old voice said, "—s a murderer. Stay away from the—"

Well, Meat thought, maybe he couldn't begin the message for the old caller, but he sure could end it.

In the silence that followed, he finished the sentence. "Tower."

For emphasis, to make sure Herculeah got the message, he said, "Stay away from the tower."

"I hate it when people do that," Herculeah said.

"Do what?" Meat asked. "Leave warning messages on the answering machine?"

"No, I hate it when they start their warning message before waiting for the beep. Half the message is lost."

"I can finish the last half," Meat said. "It's—"

"I heard you before. I'm going to play it again."

"Good idea," Meat said. Listening to the message had obviously become an instant addiction with Herculeah. He wouldn't mind hearing it again himself.

"Listen real carefully this time. In the beginning of the message, I think the person was saying either 'He's a murderer' or 'She's a murderer.'"

"That's all there are—'he's' and 'she's.'"

"But they could have said a specific name."

"Either way, it didn't sound good to me."

She rewound the tape. "Listen."

"—s a murderer. Stay away from the—"

Meat couldn't help himself. He said, "Tower."

Herculeah glanced at him with irritation. "You don't know that it was tower."

"Then why do I keep hearing it in my mind? You hear things in your mind and believe them completely."

"You just think it's 'tower' because you're afraid of towers."

"I am not afraid of towers. I just can't see any good reason for putting one on a house. Oh, maybe if you had a mad relative that you wanted to keep out of sight—a tower would be good for that. Or if a parent had bad kids. I mean, 'Go to your room,' is nothing compared to, 'Go to the tower.'"

Herculeah didn't seem that interested. She plopped down in her mother's chair. "I think it was a woman's voice, don't you? Give me your thoughts."

"My only thought," he said, "is that it *is* a warning. I think that you should never go back to that house again."

Herculeah frowned. That was obviously not what she wanted to hear. "Anyway," she said with a shrug, "we can't be sure the message is for me."

"It's for you."

"It could be a wrong number."

"It's no wrong number."

"It could be for my mom. And my mom has lots of cases she's working on. It could be a warning to her."

"Yeah, right."

Herculeah leaned back in her mother's chair. Her mother, Mim Jones, used this front room for her office. She saw her clients here. And Herculeah, sitting in her mother's chair, always felt more like a detective than she usually did.

"I wonder," she said, picking up a pencil and putting it behind her ear as her mother sometimes did, "if I should let my mom hear this."

"Of course."

"I don't know. She might take it seriously."

"I should hope so."

"And make me stop going."

"You *should* stop going. Remember your hair frizzling. And your hair is never wrong."

"I can't stop. Things are just starting to get interesting. Let's listen one more time, and this time try to see if there's any background noise—any clocks ticking or doorbells ringing or cars in the street outside."

She rewound the machine and the message came again.

"—s a murderer. Stay away from the—"

Meat clamped his lips together so he couldn't say "tower," but it was not necessary. A voice spoke from the doorway.

"What's going on here?"

Herculeah and Meat looked up to see Herculeah's mother.

"What is going on here?" she repeated, separating the words to show her displeasure.

"Nothing," Meat stammered, but he knew it was not going to satisfy her. It wouldn't have satisfied her daughter. He then said something that might satisfy them all.

He said, "I'd better be getting home."

SOME SILLY IDEA

Meat crossed the room quickly only to find that Herculeah's mother, looking very immovable, was blocking the doorway.

"Excuse me," he said.

She didn't even do him the courtesy of looking at him. He cleared his throat, but that didn't do any good, either.

"What's going on, Herculeah? I want an answer. Now."

"Mom, nothing's going on," Herculeah said.

Good start, Meat thought.

"Anyway, it's not what you're thinking," Herculeah continued.

"You have no idea what I'm thinking."

Meat thought he knew. He remembered the last time Herculeah's mother had caught them in her office. They had been listening to one of her private taped conversations with the Moloch, and he was sure that was going through her mind as well as his own.

"We weren't snooping this time," he said, hoping to ease the situation. He wished he hadn't said "this time," because if she hadn't been thinking about that, then she would be now.

"I'll handle it, Meat," Herculeah said.

"Thanks."

Herculeah took a deep breath and lifted her head. This caused the pencil behind her ear to fall onto the desk. She carefully put it beside the yellow legal pad where she found it.

"When Meat and I came in the front door, we heard someone leaving a message. I thought it might be important, so we came in here to listen. That's the entire story. You're too suspicious."

"Was the message for me?"

"We don't know. It was anonymous."

"I'd better be going," Meat said.

Herculeah said, "Well, it wasn't so much anonymous. It was just a piece of a message, Mom. *Whoever left it* started too soon and broke off in the middle. It was an old person, and some old people aren't used to using answering machines."

"Old people are impatient, too, and sometimes won't wait for the beep, or they might not even know what a beep is," Meat offered, though he could see at once that no one was interested in his knowledge of old people.

"Play it," Herculeah's mom said.

"I've already heard it, so I'll be going."

This time it worked, and Herculeah's mom stepped aside, allowing him to move through the doorway.

As soon as the front door closed behind him, he felt instant relief, but almost immediately he wished he were back inside. He could be hearing what Herculeah and her mom were saying. If only he had been slower opening the door.

What Herculeah was saying was, "Listen for yourself."

The message was played, and in the silence that followed, Herculeah said, "Meat has some silly idea that the message was to warn us to stay away from the tower at Haunt—I mean, Hunt—House."

"I had a silly idea, too."

"Oh, Mom, you never have silly ideas."

She kept her eyes on her daughter. "My silly idea was that I could trust you to read to Mr. Hunt without stirring up trouble."

RETURN TO HAUNT HOUSE

"I can't believe your mom is letting you go back to read to Mr. Hunt," Meat said.

Herculeah didn't answer.

It was three thirty in the afternoon, and Meat and Herculeah were on their way to Hunt House.

They had been walking in silence. Herculeah had been admiring the fall afternoon, the way the leaves fell from the old trees. Meat was trying not to sound like his mother, though his last statement—"I can't believe your mom is letting you go back"—came close.

"She *is* letting you go back, isn't she?"

Herculeah didn't answer. Meat thought she was avoiding questions by feigning interest in nature.

"Does she even know you're going?"

"Yes, she knows I'm going. She's giving me one last chance,

mainly because I convinced her that Mr. Hunt would be very disappointed if I didn't show."

"Did she have anything to say about the message?"

"Very little. She did let it slip that she thought it might be one of the Hunts."

"One of them! How many are there?"

"There's a portrait of the family in the hallway and it shows four children, but I could only recognize Shivers Hunt. Mom thinks it might be the older of the sisters. She's been loony for about fifty years."

"Your mom said 'loony'?"

"No, she actually said 'childlike,' but that's what she meant. If it was the sister, Mom said you can't rely on anything she says."

"Like phone messages," Meat said.

"Exactly. Mom said she knows our number and has left messages before—well, parts of messages."

"I don't suppose it could have been Mr. Hunt's voice, because he's paralyzed." A sudden thought crossed his mind. "He *is* paralyzed, isn't he?"

"Yes, he is paralyzed."

"Because you do read about things like this happening. Someone pretends to be paralyzed and then when nobody's looking, they get up and do things." He warmed to the thought. "For all we know, he could have made the threatening phone call."

"He didn't make the call."

"But think of this: He's lying there. You're engrossed in reading to him. You're completely off your guard because the man can't move. Then all of a sudden you hear a sound. You don't pay any attention because the man can't move. Then the sound is closer, but you still don't pay any attention. Then without warning you feel hands around your throat. Now you pay attention but it's too late. Gotcha!"

"Oh, Meat, don't be silly."

"If it's so silly, then why are you rubbing your neck?"

They rounded the corner, and Hunt House lay ahead. They passed through the gates and down the shaded drive.

Meat rang the ding-dong bell, and they waited for a long time before the door was opened.

"You again," Nurse Wegman said.

"Yes."

"Well, you'd better come in." She looked at Meat. "You wait."

Herculeah followed Nurse Wegman up the stairs and went directly to Mr. Hunt's bedroom. "Well, I'm not going to waste any time today," she said, crossing the room and picking up the book. "We are going to read!"

She spoke loudly for Nurse Wegman's benefit. Apparently satisfied by what she had heard, Nurse Wegman left the room.

Herculeah sat and opened the book. "Here's where we were . . . sound of breathing . . . she whispers that she's coming. . . ."

She turned the page. "Oh, I was right. A flashback is coming up." As she straightened, a yellowed piece of paper slipped from the book and fluttered to the floor.

Herculeah said, "Oh, what's this?" She bent and picked it up. "Why, it's a clipping from an old newspaper. Well, part of one. It's been folded in half and unfolded so many times that it's torn. Either that or somebody tore it deliberately."

She opened the book and riffled the pages gently to see if the rest of the clipping would drop out.

"No, I guess this is all there is. . . . Strange."

She held the clipping to the light and, without thinking, began to read aloud.

A family reunion turned to tragedy Saturday afternoon at the Hunt estate. Twenty-five members of the Hunt family had gathered to celebrate the birthday of Lionus Hunt when a children's game—

She broke off. "Oh, I'm so sorry, Mr. Hunt. I wasn't thinking. You probably don't want to hear this. This is your family, isn't it?" She didn't wait for a blink. "You were probably at this party. I'm sure you don't want to relive it."

She paused, and once again she had the feeling that Mr. Hunt was telling her something.

"Or do you?"

One blink. Yes.

"I mean, I know you don't want to relive it—nobody would—but I think you want to hear this, am I right?'

Blink.

"Then we might as well read the rest, or what there is of it. I'll be honest with you. I would like to know about the tragedy. It's not," she went on truthfully, "that I enjoy tragedies, but that I always, always have to know what really happened. Do you want me to read on?"

And although she knew the answer, she waited.

Blink.

"Here goes."

IT CAME FROM THE TOWER

Meat got up from the steps and stretched. He felt he had been sitting here on these stone steps for hours.

He looked at his watch. Only fifteen minutes had passed. Shaking his arm, he tried to rouse the watch and remind it that it had better keep the right time or else.

He walked a few steps away from the house. He bent and pretended to tie his shoe. His shoe did not need tying, of course—the straps were Velcro—but he needed to glance up and see if the scary lady was watching him from the window.

But the windows were empty. Even so, Meat thought, they had the look of eyes—blind eyes, perhaps. He shuddered.

The tower was to the right of the house. Meat glanced at it, examining it. Why, he wondered, was Herculeah so fascinated by it? He moved closer for a better look.

And, his thoughts continued, she really was fascinated. When she had first seen the tower today she had said, "When I see that tower, I feel as if I'm waiting for something to happen, something unknown, something I can't even imagine, something I can't understand." Then she added firmly, "That I can't understand yet!"

He still didn't understand why anyone would want to put one of these hideous things on their house. The house was hideous, too, of course, but that was no reason to put a tower on it.

Again he glanced up at the house, his eyes focusing on the window. He thought he saw a movement there; he waited for a long time, but no face appeared.

Turning his attention back to the tower, he thought about the tragedy that had happened here. It would be nice if he could discover what that tragedy was before Herculeah did.

He heard a noise overhead and looked up, startled.

Birds were flying out of the tower, through the slotted windows, their wings beating fast. They were struggling for their lives as if something were after them.

The sun was in Meat's eyes, and he put one hand up to shield them. Now it seemed that the last of the birds were free from the tower. They had gotten away from whatever had startled them.

Meat took one step closer. Something else was coming out of the tower, but he couldn't make it out. What was that? A stick? Surely it couldn't be an arm.

Then he heard a laugh. It was faint, muted by the thick tower walls, but it could only have come from one throat—that of the woman who had looked down at him from the window.

In his mind he saw it again, the face that had haunted his dreams for two nights, even appearing in his bathroom window, which was a double shock since his bathroom had no window. No wonder the birds were frightened.

Now he could make out that other object coming out of the tower. It was an arm, and at the end of the arm was a hand that was just as he had described to Herculeah. Talons—the hand had talons instead of fingers.

And something was clutched in those terrible talons. It was something round. A stone? Could it be a stone? Why hold a stone out the tower window? Was she going to throw it? The only person she could possibly want to hit with a stone was—

He looked around the empty yard. Him. Him!

Meat gasped. He wanted to run. It was the only sensible thing to do. But he seemed to be rooted to the spot, as unable to move as Mr. Hunt was upstairs in his bed.

The arm lifted. It was the movement a pitcher might make to test the weight of the ball.

Then, in a movement so quick that he almost missed it, the stone left the hand. It was on its way to—to him!

Still he could not move. He was like a rabbit frozen in the headlights of an oncoming car.

The stone fell with surprising slowness. Meat imagined that this was because his heart had sped up a thousand times. He'd read about this. A person's whole life really could pass before his eyes when the heart sped up a thousand times.

The limbs of the trees around him were moved by a sudden gust of wind. Leaves rustled, branches cracked. The wind was so sudden it seemed unearthly, like the woman in the tower.

If the stone tried to go this way or that way, the wind would correct it and send it . . . to him!

Then the stone seemed to flutter as if it had suddenly sprouted wings. That would not have surprised Meat. Nothing would ever surprise him again. Wind, wings, whatever—that stone was going where it was intended to go.

Whoever had thrown the stone was shouting something, but Meat couldn't make it out.

A cry cut through the late afternoon air, drowning out all other sound.

Meat knew that cry even though he had never heard anything like it before. It was the cry of someone about to die.

And it had come from his throat.

HALF A TRAGEDY

Herculeah lifted her head.

"Did you hear something?"

She glanced at Mr. Hunt. He was staring at the ceiling, eyes open. There was no response.

"I thought I heard a scream."

Still no response.

Herculeah smiled. "I guess I'm hearing things now." She lifted the clipping.

"Okay, here goes." But she paused a moment, listening. She knew she had heard a scream, and the scream had been somehow familiar. Now there was nothing.

"Well, on to the clipping."

She felt the thrill she always felt when she was on the edge of discovery. Also, there was something about old newspaper clippings that excited her. The writing was more polished back when this piece was written. People respected the news back then and so did the writers who recorded it.

She showed her respect by clearing her throat. She read in a voice that would have won her an audition on prime-time evening news.

A family reunion turned to tragedy Saturday afternoon at the Hunt estate. Twenty-five members of the Hunt family had gathered to celebrate the birthday of Lionus Hunt when a children's game of hide-and-seek ended in death. According to a family spokesman, the adults were in the dining room when they heard screams. They rushed outside and discovered the body of Eleanor Pitman, the children's governess, at the base of the tower. She had been struck on the head by a stone from the tower. Speculation was that the stone had worked loose over the years. No children were hiding in the tower at the time, as the tower door is always locked. This is the second time tragedy has struck the Hunt tower—

"And that's all there is," Herculeah said.

She looked closely at the man on the bed. His eyes were bright with intelligence and . . . something else Herculeah did not understand. Slyness? Cruelty? Interest?

At any rate, Herculeah was sure he knew far more about the story than the newspaper reporter had.

"Were you there at the party?"

Yes.

"Were you part of the game?"

Yes.

"You could tell me what the rest of the clipping said. I know you could—probably word for word. But you know what? I can go to the library. I can look this up. I can find the other half of the tragedy and—"

At that moment Herculeah heard a noise outside in the hallway. It was too soon for the nurse, wasn't it?

She listened. Someone was running in the hallway. The footsteps were light, too soft to be from Nurse Wegman's heavy shoes. The footsteps stopped outside the door.

Herculeah glanced at the man on the bed. She could tell that he recognized the footsteps and knew who waited in the hall.

"Who's there?" Herculeah called.

Then the door to the bedroom opened slowly, creaking on its hinges. Herculeah swirled in her chair.

The face looking at her from the doorway, the face framed in wild hair, was the face of an old woman—something out of a Greek tragedy, something out of a nightmare. Excitement burned in the dark eyes. The cheeks were flushed with something like triumph.

Herculeah knew instantly that this was the face Meat had seen at the window the other day. And she knew instantly why it had filled him with dread.

The woman took one step into the room. Her body was small

and frail. Her hair flew about her head. Her skeletal arms flapped excitedly at her sides.

"It happened again," she said. She punctuated her sentence with a nervous giggle.

"What? What's happened again?"

"Death from the tower."

"What are you talking about? Tell me!"

The woman in the doorway seemed to be smiling, although Herculeah knew this was nothing to smile about. The woman's teeth were dark and as pointed as an animal's. Herculeah's anxiety grew.

Herculeah glanced down at the clipping in her hand. "Are you talking about this?"

She lifted the clipping and showed it to the woman.

The woman shook her head. She had not come here to read a piece of paper. "Again," she said.

"Today? Now?"

Herculeah tried to calm herself with the thought that her mother said you couldn't rely on this old woman, but it didn't work.

The woman took one quick breath before she explained.

"Death fell from the tower." Then as if she was saving the best for last, she added, "The body lies in its shadow."

THE BODY IN THE SHADOWS

For a moment Herculeah stared at the old woman, hoping to make sense of the situation. She turned to the man lying so still on the bed, as if he could help her.

She was struck by the fact that their faces were almost identical. Both resembled birds of prey. Their eyes seemed to be looking for something weaker to devour. Her feeling of impending doom heightened.

Then the woman spoke again, her voice rising with excitement. "A body! A body!"

"Whose body?"

"The boy."

Now Herculeah remembered the scream. There had been something familiar about it.

"Meat! Meat!"

Herculeah leaped to her feet. The book dropped to the floor unnoticed.

In the doorway, the woman—childlike—clapped her hands together as if in triumph.

Herculeah ran to the door. The old woman stood there, her hawklike eyes gleaming, her hands clasped together in delight, but Herculeah slipped past her in one quick move.

She ran out into the hall. She crossed quickly to the stairs.

Behind her the old woman let out a squeal of success. Her cackle of delight followed Herculeah down the long stairs.

Nurse Wegman came out of a room down the hall, bringing with her the faint odor of tobacco. "What's wrong?" she asked. "Mr. Hunt?"

"No! Meat!"

She was taking the steps two, three at a time, pulling herself along by the banister. Nurse Wegman was right behind her, matching her speed.

"Your friend?"

"Yes. That old woman said something fell on him from the tower."

"That old fool."

"I thought the tower was locked."

"It is, but there are keys around if you know where to look."

"She said there was a body."

Nurse Wegman was fast, but not as fast as Herculeah, in crossing the hallway. It was Herculeah who got to the front door first. She threw it open and burst out into the late afternoon sun. She turned immediately toward the tower and broke into a run.

"In the shadow of the tower," the old woman had said. Herculeah's eyes scanned the shadows.

"There," said Nurse Wegman.

She passed Herculeah. Herculeah continued to run, but her pace was slowed by her increasing dread.

Meat lay facedown on the ground. His pale face was pressed into what had once been a lawn. He was not moving. He did not even seem to be breathing.

"Oh, no," Herculeah sighed.

"I'll turn him over."

"Maybe you shouldn't move him," Herculeah began, forgetting she was talking to a nurse.

Nurse Wegman turned him over in a quick, unnurselike way, and Meat's face was turned to the sky. The shadow of the tower lay across his pale cheeks.

"Resuscitation!" Herculeah cried, gaining strength. "Mouth-to-mouth resuscitation! Let me! I've had a course. You go call for an ambulance and the police."

"That will not be necessary."

"It is necessary. Get out of my way. We've got to save him! Go call for an ambulance!"

But Nurse Wegman's hands were firm on Herculeah's shoulders, and she could not break free.

"Trust me," Nurse Wegman said, "that will not be necessary."

12

THE KISS OF DEATH

"What do you mean it's not necessary? What do you mean?"

"Don't get hysterical."

"But what do you mean?"

"I mean he's not dead."

These were the most beautiful words Meat had ever heard in his life. He had been lying there wondering about that very thing. He didn't know where he was except that it was somewhere he didn't want to be.

His face had been pressed into grass that had seen better days when he felt himself being turned over. Bits and pieces of memory began to come to him. He had heard Herculeah's voice, so she was here. Also that nurse—whatever her name was—and then he remembered hearing Herculeah saying something about mouth-to-mouth resuscitation.

That had been a sort of fantasy of Meat's. He could not imagine kissing Herculeah, but he could, in a particularly wild dream, imagine something like mouth-to-mouth as an emergency measure. The kiss of death, he thought of it, not unpleasantly.

Then he remembered Nurse Wegman. She had flipped him over—he thought with her foot—and he realized with a real sense of horror that if any lips were going to come in contact with his, they would be Nurse Wegman's.

Meat opened his eyes.

"Hello," he said.

"He *is* alive!" Herculeah cried. There was such joy in her voice that, despite all the horror he had endured, his spirits rose like sun breaking through black clouds.

"I think he just fainted," Nurse Wegman said. "His pulse is normal. I see no injuries. I'll elevate his legs."

"No, no, I'm all right," Meat said. He wanted his legs to stay right where they were—stretched out on the ground. "Just let me lie here for a moment."

"What happened, Meat? Can you tell us?"

"I was walking toward the tower, just checking things out, and all of a sudden, birds came flying out of the windows, like they'd been startled."

"Take it easy," Nurse Wegman advised, as if she was making an effort to be a nurse. "Take deep breaths. Speak slowly."

"And I saw an arm—"

Now Nurse Wegman stopped sounding like a disinterested nurse. "You saw an arm? An arm in the tower?"

"Well, it was like an arm—a skeleton arm. Maybe it was a stick, but it looked like an arm."

"So someone was in the tower."

"Yes."

Herculeah thought of the old woman. She remembered the thin, sticklike arms, fluttering in the air, clapping with delight.

"And then there was something in the hand—so it had to be an arm if there was a hand attached."

"Death fell from the tower," Herculeah said, remembering the old woman's words. She glanced at Nurse Wegman. "That's what the old woman said it was."

"It looked like a stone to me," Meat said.

"Go on," Nurse Wegman ordered.

"And then she threw the stone, or whatever it was, at me. I wasn't worried at first because I was standing back here. And I knew that nobody could throw a stone that far, especially an old woman."

Nurse Wegman took a deep breath. "I've got to get back to my patient." She turned quickly, crossed the yard, and disappeared into the house.

"I'm glad she's gone," Meat said. "I don't think she likes me."

"She doesn't like anybody. Go on."

"Only whatever she threw came at me, like, in slow motion. It was as if it were on a radar course or something and I knew it was going to hit me. I knew I was going to die."

"Why didn't you run?"

"I couldn't."

"What did you do?"

"I screamed."

"And then?"

"You know the rest?"

"I don't! And then what?"

"Then I fainted."

FLYING FINISH

"It has to be here somewhere," Herculeah said.

She was walking up and down in front of the tower. Meat was sitting where he had fallen, watching her.

"Because, Meat, stones do not just disappear."

"No," Meat agreed.

Herculeah's sharp eyes went over every inch of the ground. "If it rolled," she said, more to herself than to Meat, "then it would have ended up here. But"—she shrugged—"there's nothing."

Meat was beginning to feel uneasy. In thinking back to the moment when the stone—and he had thought it was a stone, then; at any rate, it had been round—had appeared, Meat realized he didn't know exactly what he had seen.

"The sun was in my eyes," he explained.

"Well, yeah, but you saw her throw something, right?"

"Right."

Herculeah moved closer. Her gray eyes had that look that seemed to penetrate right into his brain.

"Go over it again. Describe what you saw."

"Well, it was round. When it left her hand, it was round—I'm sure of that. And then it was as if, I don't know, it sort of sprouted wings."

"Wings! Like a bird?"

Meat drew in a deep, unhappy breath. "I know you wouldn't understand."

"I want to understand. I've got to, because I know that whatever she threw had some meaning and that if we could find it, we would know—"

She broke off. Meat glanced quickly up at the tower, thinking Herculeah had seen something at one of the windows. He struggled to his feet and took a few unsteady steps backward.

"Is the old woman back?" he asked.

"No," Herculeah answered. "But I just remembered where she probably is. She was outside Mr. Hunt's room, and I bet she went inside. I ran off and left Mr. Hunt at the mercy of that woman. Nurse Wegman did, too."

Meat felt a pang of sympathy for the man. Being in the same world with that loony woman was bad enough; being in the same room would be unbearable. And the man was paralyzed. He couldn't protect himself. Meat took another backward step to get away from the thought.

"I've got to make sure he's all right. You keep looking for the—whatever it is we're looking for. Don't leave."

Meat could not have gone anywhere if he had wanted to, and he did want very much to go somewhere—home. But he would settle for any place that didn't have a tower. He glanced around without enthusiasm at his possibilities.

Herculeah ran to the house. The front door stood open as if Nurse Wegman had had the same thought as Herculeah—Mr. Hunt's safety.

Herculeah ran into the hallway and up the stairs. She took them three at a time. She crossed the hall and came to a stop in the doorway to Mr. Hunt's bedroom.

Nurse Wegman was beside the bed. She was leaning over Mr. Hunt's body, a pillow in one hand.

"Is he all right?" Herculeah asked.

Nurse Wegman straightened abruptly. She looked around, obviously startled. She punched the pillow with one hand, as if to make it more comfortable, and then settled it under Mr. Hunt's head.

"He's fine. The old woman was in here. She was by the bed, holding this pillow. I thought she was getting ready to smother him."

Herculeah crossed to the bed and stood beside the nurse. She looked down into the bright hawklike eyes.

"I'm sorry I ran out like that," she said, speaking to Mr. Hunt. "My friend fainted outside and that . . . that woman who was in here—your sister, I guess—must have thought he was dead. I don't know if you want me to come back or not, after the way I've acted."

The blink came forcefully. Yes.

"Good. I want to come back. I'm going to redeem myself." She picked up the book, slipped the newspaper clipping inside, and put it on the bedside table. "Next time we will do nothing but read."

Herculeah paused. One hand still rested on the book. She had the feeling that Mr. Hunt wanted to tell her something, needed to tell her something important. He needs my help, she thought abruptly, and not just to read him books.

Nurse Wegman coughed to remind her to leave. When that didn't work, she said, "Go on now. Look after your friend. Mr. Hunt needs to rest."

"I'm on my way." At the doorway she paused. "I wonder if I could use the phone. I need to call my mom."

"We don't need any private detectives around here."

"No, but Meat and I are going to need a ride home. I don't think he can make it on foot."

"The phone's downstairs in the hall."

"Thanks. I'll see you both tomorrow?"

She glanced at Nurse Wegman, hoping for many reasons that it wouldn't be Nurse Wegman's day to be on duty.

But to her disappointment, Nurse Wegman said firmly, "I'll be here," and then added, "from now on."

MIRROR IMAGE

"I'm phoning my mom to come pick us up," Herculeah called to Meat from the front door.

Meat turned toward her. His lips moved, and although she could not quite make out his words, Herculeah suspected they were something like, "That's the first good idea you've had all day."

With one quick glance at the tower she disappeared back into the house.

Meat watched her go. Then with slow steps he began to make his way to the porch.

Herculeah glanced around the hall for the telephone. The hall was large, high-ceilinged, and dark. All the rooms in Hunt House, she thought, seemed to be shadowed in gloom, as if they had secrets to hide.

There. Herculeah found the phone at the back of the hall, in one of those gloomy shadows.

It was an old-timey black rotary phone, and as she picked it up, she shook her head. She had to dial the number. Dial! This was probably the first time she had ever not punched in the numbers.

She dialed and shifted from one foot to the other, waiting impatiently for the phone to be answered.

All of a sudden Herculeah had the feeling she was being watched. It was such a strong feeling that she glanced first at the portrait of Lionus Hunt. She smiled at her foolishness. Of course no hawklike eyes peered at her through slits in the painted eyes.

She turned slowly. She thought her hair was beginning to frizzle. She found herself looking into an old mirror. The glass was wavery with age, and so at first all she could make out was her own hair. Yes, it was definitely frizzling. Then she noticed a figure crouching behind her on the stairs.

She tried to breathe slowly, deeply to calm herself. The phone rang twice. Pick up, Mom, she said to herself. I'm in trouble here.

Now she could hear, above the ringing of the phone, the beginning of a childish giggle. It was low, broken by mutterings of the woman reminding herself to be more quiet.

Pick up, Mom. I need you.

A hand came through the banisters, reaching for her. The long-taloned fingers curled as if to grab. "Pretty," she said. The fingers brushed her hair, and the old woman said, "Come closer."

No way, Herculeah said to herself, and she moved away from the stairs. She was almost against the wall now. But she was in a better position to make a beeline for the door if that became necessary.

Answer me, Mom. Answer.

On the fourth ring, as if in answer to Herculeah's pleas, her mother's voice came on the line.

"Hello. You have reached the office of Mim Jones. I cannot take your call right now, but if you leave a message and phone number at the beep, I'll get back to you as soon as I can."

The beep came and Herculeah said, "Mom, it's me. I'm at Hunt House. We've had a bit of excitement. I'm fine but Meat fainted, and I need you to come out and pick us up. Now."

She waited because sometimes, when her mother was busy, she wouldn't answer her phone, but she always answered when she heard Herculeah's voice, especially when it was something urgent.

Her mother did not answer now, and Herculeah reluctantly hung up the phone.

"I've got to make one more quick call," she said. She glanced up at the woman and then toward the front porch where Meat sat on the steps. "You aren't going to like this one, Meat," she predicted as she dialed.

The phone was answered on the second ring this time, and Herculeah gave her message.

She glanced at the stairs. "Well, our ride is on the way; it'll probably be here any minute."

The skeleton arm still reached through the banisters, the long fingers stretching for Herculeah's hair. And if it frizzled any more, Herculeah thought, she'd get it.

Quickly she returned the phone to the table and backed away from the stairs. "I'll wait outside."

The fingers closed on air, and then the old woman spoke. It was as if she had awakened from a dream, as if she had been so dazzled by Herculeah's hair that she had forgotten her mission.

"Did you find it?" she asked in a tired whisper.

"What?"

"Did you?"

"Did I find what you threw from the tower? Is that what you want to know?"

"Yes."

"No. What did you throw? Why?"

But the woman seemed to be fading, to be shrinking.

"I don't know." Then she had one final burst of energy. "When you find it, you will know," she said.

She got to her feet and, holding the banister, began to pull herself up the stairs.

"Wait." Now it was Herculeah who reached through the banisters, her fingers brushing the worn fabric of the woman's dress as she moved out of range. "Wait."

The woman shook her head. She chuckled to herself and disappeared onto the landing.

"It's not funny," Herculeah said to the empty hallway. Then she sighed and walked to the door.

THE FOURTH FAINT

"I just had a talk with the woman who threw something at you from the tower," Herculeah told Meat.

"You actually talked to her?"

"Yes."

"She admitted she threw something?"

"Yes."

"So what was it?"

"The most intelligent thing I got out of her was that when we find it, we will know what it is."

"Great. So is your mom coming?" Meat asked.

"Our ride is on the way, Meat. Sit down." She patted the step beside her.

"Your mom is coming, right? You didn't—"

To divert Meat, Herculeah said quickly, "You know, Meat, you really ought to do something about your fainting. You faint all the time."

He was diverted. "I do not."

"Well," Herculeah said, "you fainted that time at Madame Rosa's."

Meat said, "Yes," quickly, hoping that would end the story.

"You were sitting out in the hall," Herculeah recounted, "and you thought the murderer was coming down the stairs—"

"The murderer *was* coming down the stairs."

"Yes, it was the murderer, but you thought it was Madame Rosa's ghost. That's why you fainted."

Meat said, "Getting back to our ride . . ."

Herculeah said, "Then there was that time you were in the park and you thought some boys were going to punch you in the stomach."

"They *were* going to punch me in the stomach."

"But they didn't have to, because you fainted."

Why was she doing this, Meat wondered, bringing up his fainting? Was she trying to divert him? Oh, yes—the ride!

He heard a car turn into the driveway, looked up, and gave a gasp of dismay.

"Oh, here she is," Herculeah said cheerfully.

"It's my mom. You said you were calling *your* mom."

"I couldn't get her."

"You didn't tell Mom I fainted."

"I had to, or she wouldn't have come. Hi, Mrs. Mac," Herculeah called as she went down the steps. "Thanks for coming."

As he followed, Meat hissed, "Let me tell it."

Meat flung the door open. He said, "I don't care what she said, Mom, I did not faint." He got into the backseat and slammed the door.

Herculeah had known he wouldn't be pleased, but he had never slammed the door in her face before. She opened the door and said, "Scoot over."

At least he wasn't too mad to scoot over, and Herculeah climbed in beside him. Meat's mom turned around and gave her son a hard look. "So," she said, "if you didn't faint, what did happen?"

"Nothing! I was standing outside looking up at the tower and birds started flying out the windows. And then an arm came and threw something and somebody yelled something and—"

"You didn't tell me she yelled something," Herculeah interrupted.

"I couldn't hear what it was—probably something stupid like 'Look up here!' Where else would anybody be looking?" He paused. "Anyway, I got dizzy. Looking up like that always makes me dizzy. I sat down, put my head between my knees, and was fine."

Mrs. Mac's gaze turned to Herculeah, so she knew it was her turn.

"I was in the house when this happened, Mrs. Mac, so I didn't see it. I had found this old newspaper clipping. It was in the back of the book I was reading to Mr. Hunt. It was a clipping about a tragedy years ago at Hunt House and guess what the tragedy was?"

"Someone threw a stone from the tower and killed the governess," Mrs. McMannis said.

"Yes! Exactly! But nobody threw it. It was a loose stone and it fell."

"It was thrown."

"How do you know? The clipping said no one was in the tower."

"Someone was in the tower. There had to have been. My great uncle Ben was the stonemason who worked on the tower. He laid those stones, and he said those stones were laid to stay laid."

"Why would anyone want to kill a governess?"

"Maybe the killer was aiming at someone else. I don't know."

Herculeah looked at Mrs. McMannis sharply. "Who was close to the governess at the time?"

"I have no idea."

"Probably one of the twins," Herculeah said thoughtfully. "The smaller one." Her mind turned back to the family portrait on the stairs, to the figure of the smaller twin that had been damaged somehow.

"Did the article mention that this was the second tragedy?" Mrs. McMannis continued.

"Yes, I was going to the library to look that up."

"A man working on the tower was killed. Ben was there when he fell. No big deal."

"Except to the man who fell," Herculeah said, "and his family."

Mrs. Mac didn't care for the comment. "No good can come from that tower or that house. You stay away from that place, Albert." She turned the key and started the car.

"He has to come, Mrs. Mac," Herculeah told the back of her head. "It wouldn't be any fun without him."

Meat looked at her in amazement. Fun? Hunt House was fun? He read the answer in her face. She thought it was fun, like something in an amusement park where no danger is real.

As if the matter was settled Herculeah said, "Here's what we've got to do tomorrow. Something was thrown at you from the tower, and it wasn't a stone."

"No."

"And," Herculeah continued, "I don't think it was anything that would have done you harm. I think the old woman was trying to tell you something or warn you of something."

"Why me?"

"Maybe because she needed someone and you were there. We're getting close. Whatever fell from the tower is the answer to the mystery. We've got to find it."

Mrs. McMannis glanced at Herculeah in the rearview mirror and smiled sweetly. Herculeh never trusted Mrs. Mac when she smiled like that.

"Oh, Albert won't be able to go with you tomorrow."

Herculeah said quickly, "You don't have to worry about him, Mrs. Mac, I'll be with him every second."

"No, I won't worry about him." Now her smile changed as she looked at Meat, but Herculeah didn't trust that smile, either. "Albert, guess who called this afternoon. And it wasn't Steffie."

Now she looked at Herculeah. They were stopped at a red light now, so Meat's mom was free to smile triumphantly without causing a wreck. "I'm not sure you remember Steffie, Herculeah. She's that girl that was visiting and was so crazy about Albert."

"I remember Steffie."

"Anyway, it wasn't Steffie this time. Albert, it was your dad. You need to stay home tomorrow so you won't miss the call."

The light changed. The car moved forward, but the three people inside had nothing more to say.

16

THE THINK COCOON

Herculeah took out her granny glasses. She put them on, hooking the thin metal wires behind her ears.

Herculeah had gotten these glasses at Hidden Treasures, a secondhand store where she often shopped. Herculeah bought some of her clothes there, and other useful things. Once when she had been in Hidden Treasures, she had tried on these glasses. She couldn't see anything out of them, but she discovered she could think better. The world seemed to blur into a mist, making her ideas stand out. "It's like being in a think cocoon," she had explained to Meat.

She was sitting on her bed, waiting for her thoughts to clear when her mother came and stood in the doorway.

"Have you got on those ridiculous glasses again?" her mother said. "You're going to ruin your eyes."

Herculeah couldn't see her mom, but she knew she was there. She pushed the glasses to the top of her head.

"Hi, Mom."

"So what was the phone message about? Why did you need me to come pick you up?"

"Oh, that. I meant to erase it. Meat's mom came and got us. It was nothing. Meat fainted."

"Fainted?"

"Oh, Mom, he faints all the time."

"I didn't know that. So what was the excitement you mentioned?"

"Meat was standing out in the yard and someone threw something out of the tower window, and Meat got dizzy watching it and fainted. End of story."

Herculeah sincerely hoped it was.

"Someone was in the tower?"

"Yes, the sister."

"I thought it was locked."

"The new nurse said there are keys if you know where to look."

"How would she know that? The woman's only been there one day."

"Good question."

"I'll have to talk to the lawyer. There's been enough tragedy connected with that tower."

"I know. Meat's mom told us. Someone threw a stone from the tower and killed the governess." She eyed her mother, pretending to be critical. "You could take some lessons from Mrs. Mac."

Her mom knew Herculeah's opinion of Mrs. Mac. She smiled. "How so?"

"She tells us things. For example, if she knew what you were working on for Mr. Hunt, she would tell us. She doesn't treat everything as a big secret."

Her mom seemed to think that over. "Mr. Randolph, the lawyer, was drawing up a will for Mr. Hunt. This was before his stroke, and he wanted some investigative work done. He contacted me. I was to find the other sister. That was the extent of my involvement, but I became interested in the old man. I felt sorry for him. I used to drop in and see him from time to time."

"This sister you were going to find. It's not the old crazy one who left the message on your machine."

"No. There were younger sisters—twins. Only one of them is alive now, and that was who I was to find."

Herculeah had her mom talking now, and she didn't want her to stop. "Everybody says there's money hidden in the house—even Nurse Wegman. By the way, I don't trust her. She's weird."

"Mr. Randolph hired the nurses himself. They're the same team that nursed his invalid mother, so you don't have to worry about them."

"So is there money hidden in the house?"

"I hope you haven't been poking around the house looking for it."

"Of course not. Give me some credit. I'm smarter than that."

"Too smart sometimes." Her mother changed the subject. "Did you get supper?"

"I ordered pizza. There's some left if you want it."

"I grabbed a bite on the way home. Incidentally, I'll be leaving early in the morning."

"Don't work too hard."

"I won't."

She left and Herculeah put her granny glasses on again. "Think," she told her brain. "Think about what could have been thrown from the tower. What could have sprouted wings? What—?"

Before her brain had a chance to work, the phone rang. "I'll get it, Mom, it's probably Meat.

"Oh, hi, Meat," she said, "I was hoping it was you. Also, I'm hoping that you'll go to Hunt House with me tomorrow. It won't be any fun without you."

"Didn't you hear what Mom said in the car? My dad's going to call."

"I heard, but if he calls early . . ."

"Maybe."

"Don't you want to find out what was thrown at you?"

"I guess."

"Remember that old song 'Blowin' in the Wind'?" She tried

to make her voice mysterious so he would be interested.

"Yes."

"Well, something was blowin' in the wind at Hunt House."

"And you're going to find out what it was."

"I've got to."

"Call me when you get back."

"I will. Maybe I'll call before I go—try to change your mind. I gotta go now. Good night, Meat."

"Good night."

Herculeah sighed. Maybe she could compete with a phone call from an airhead like Steffie, but not a call from Macho Man. She adjusted her granny glasses and waited, hoping to get an idea of what had been blowin' in the wind.

17

HERCULEAH ON HER OWN

This was the first time Herculeah had come to Hunt House without Meat at her side. She missed him. Being with Meat always made her feel she had to be brave and protective. She didn't want anything to happen to him. And she knew she was going to have to be especially brave today.

The night before, when her mom came in to say a final good night, she had said, "I'd rather you didn't go back to Hunt House to read to Mr. Hunt."

"Mom!"

"At least not until I've had a chance to talk to Mr. Randolph about the situation."

"Mom!"

"And I'll do that tomorrow. Good night, Herculeah."

Her mother had not, Herculeah reminded herself, said, "I forbid you to go to Hunt House." She had said, "I'd rather you didn't go back to Hunt House to read to Mr. Hunt." And she wasn't going to read. She wasn't even going into the house. She was going to clear up a mystery.

The house came into view, and Herculeah had to admit that the house did have a face, and not a welcoming one. She paused inside the open gate. Which was not welcoming, either. It was rather like a Venus flytrap, open to lure in the unwary. See, she told herself, if Meat were here and said something like that, I would make a joke of it.

She continued up the drive to the house.

The day matched her mood—gloomy. The gray arch of the sky overhead was lower today. She felt she could almost reach up and touch the dark patches of clouds.

"It's going to rain," she told herself. Hurrying, she left the gate behind and, as if on cue, something hit the dry ground at her feet. It hit with such a sharp sound that Herculeah thought at first of a bullet.

She glanced down. A raindrop. She smiled at herself.

Meat, I could really use you, she said to herself. This house is getting to me.

The single raindrop was followed by a smattering of them. Herculeah crossed the drive quickly and took shelter in a grove of trees.

She paused. She hadn't heard thunder or seen any lightning, so it didn't seem reckless or unsafe to wait for a few minutes under the trees.

As she waited, she moved slowly toward the tower, keeping

under the protective branches. She felt an odd tingling as she got closer. It was as if she were moving not just closer to the tower but to the solution of its mystery.

And there was a mystery.

She turned her eyes from the tower to the house. There were no signs of life around Hunt House today. There were no lights in the windows, no smoke in the chimney. It reminded Herculeah of the vacation houses at the beach that had been closed for the winter.

Herculeah continued to move closer. Now she could see the very spot where Meat had stood when he had seen something coming toward him from the tower, the exact spot where his body had lain after he had fainted.

Her eyes narrowed in concentration. She began to calculate distances.

But wait a minute, she cautioned herself. Meat had said something about wind. He'd told her that a sudden gust of wind had come up and sent the missile straight toward him.

But nothing had touched him. So whatever it was had to have been carried farther by the wind. Perhaps it had gone over his head.

Her gaze swept over the ground behind where Meat had fallen.

And, she remembered, the missile had been light. It was not stone; Herculeah was sure of that. So if something light was thrown from the tower—a ball of fabric or a balled-up garment, and this ball became unfolded or unwrapped by the wind in the process, well it might have looked like it sprouted wings, as Meat described. . . .

Her thoughts were going so well, Herculeah thought it was as if she had on her granny glasses.

And, her thoughts raced, if this something came unwrapped and was caught by the wind, then it could have gone much, much farther than she had thought.

She began to retrace her steps, keeping close to the trees. The brief rain had stopped, but she somehow sensed that she still needed the protection of the trees.

She glanced at the house. There was still no sign of life there.

These grounds had once been tended and cared for. This had been a beautiful lawn with birdbaths and statues. She came to an overgrown clearing.

In the center of the clearing she could see the ruins of an old fountain. Stones had fallen from the sides. The statue that had once graced the center of the fountain had fallen on its side.

There! She saw what she had been looking for.

It was a brown, stone-colored bundle blown against the fallen statue. It was so much the color of the statue that it was as if it had been deliberately camouflaged.

She approached carefully, looking over her shoulder at the house. No one seemed to be watching, so she bent and picked up the bundle.

It was a large piece of fabric, a garment of some kind, slightly damp now from the recent rain shower. She gathered it up and moved back into the shelter of the trees.

She unfolded the garment and held it up. It was a coat. It was one of those practical all-purpose coats that Herculeah's mother was always after her to buy.

She drew in her breath and peered closer. There were dark stains on the fabric. Brown stains. And Herculeah knew instantly what the stains were.

Blood.

DRAGON-LADY RED AND
TICKLE-ME PINK

Herculeah felt an instant and deep concern for the owner of this coat. And, at the same time, she felt a deep determination to find out what had happened to the owner.

The belt of the coat hung loosely to the ground. She ran her fingers over it thoughtfully as if seeking a clue.

She realized that if the raincoat had been wrapped and tied with the belt before being thrown from the tower, it would look exactly as Meat had described it. First it would appear to be round, even a stone, and then as it unfolded and was blown by the wind it might seem to have wings.

But whose coat was it?

She held it against her, checking the size. It was a small coat, too small to fit her. And way too small for Nurse Wegman.

She eyed it. And it couldn't belong to the sister. She hadn't been out of the house for fifty years. The style of clothing she wore was so old that even Hidden Treasures wouldn't carry it.

She patted the pockets.

Yes! Now at last she would learn something about the owner of the coat. What people kept in their pockets was often revealing.

She was reaching into the left pocket when she saw movement at the house. Instinctively she drew back deeper into the trees.

The front door opened and Nurse Wegman came out. She was wearing a down jacket and a cap. The peak of the cap hid her eyes.

She paused on the steps and looked to the right and left. Her eyes seemed to linger on the grove of trees where Herculeah was hiding. Herculeah clutched the coat tightly against her as if for protection. To her great relief, the eyes moved on.

Nurse Wegman came down the steps. She turned away from the direction of the tower. Anyway, she couldn't have been headed there. The tower had no outside door. She circled the house and walked to the large stone garage at the rear. Herculeah had not noticed the garage before. Nurse Wegman entered the garage by a side door and closed it behind her.

Herculeah sighed with relief. Now she could get back to the pockets. She reached into the left pocket and took out the contents. There wasn't as much there as she had hoped—a crumpled tissue, a small comb, and a lipstick.

Well, there was one other pocket to search. She was disappointed in what she found there, too—a scarf and a single white glove.

The scarf was white silk. The lipstick was Coty. Herculeah took off the cap and twisted the base. The lipstick was pale pink.

She glanced at the bottom of the tube. In the little red circle, in white letters, was the shade: Petal Rose.

Herculeah didn't know much about lipsticks—she didn't bother with the stuff herself—but she did know that a lipstick called Petal Rose would never have appealed to Nurse Wegman. She'd want something like Dragon-Lady Red.

And the old sister, she'd want something like Tickle-Me Pink. Herculeah grinned. Maybe, she thought, I'll go into the cosmetics business and think of names for them.

She broke off quickly.

She noticed the garage door was being opened. She noticed one other thing: Her hair was beginning to frizzle.

DEAD PHONE, DEAD MAN?

The garage door was not one of those modern, remote-controlled garage doors. This door required manpower, but Nurse Wegman was up to the job. She shoved the door with such force that it not only opened but rattled overhead in its tracks as if it didn't want to stop. Herculeah could hear the noise from where she stood in the trees.

A car shot out of the garage. Nurse Wegman was at the wheel.

She backed the car onto the grass and turned onto the drive with such speed that gravel flew. She did not glance in Herculeah's direction. Nurse Wegman seemed to be in a hurry.

Herculeah moved out of the trees to make sure Nurse Wegman drove through the gates. She watched the car disappear around the bend and out of sight.

Herculeah's mind then turned to Mr. Hunt. Had Nurse Wegman left him alone? Was the housekeeper there? The housekeeper usually parked her car—an old Buick—by the kitchen door.

Holding the coat against her, Herculeah went around the house. As she had feared, there was no car parked by the door.

I've got to call Mom, Herculeah thought. This situation has gotten out of hand. Mr. Hunt has been abandoned.

She tried the kitchen door. It was locked. She knocked and peered through the glass. She saw no one, and no one came to the door.

She went quickly around the house. She paused at the window of the library. The curtains had been opened, and she looked in. She saw a scene of destruction. All the books lay on the floor. Pictures had been torn from the walls.

With a sinking feeling, Herculeah continued to the front of the house. She went up the steps, draped the raincoat over a porch chair, and turned the doorbell. The ding-dong of doom—as Meat called it—sounded, but no one came to answer. She turned the doorknob, but the door was locked.

"Hello, is anybody home?"

She had turned to go when suddenly she heard a faint click. It was as if someone had done something to the lock of the door. Herculeah reached out and took the doorknob a second time. Now it turned in her hand.

She pushed, and the huge door opened. The hall inside was empty. No one was in sight. Perhaps, Herculeah thought, the door had been unlocked all along.

She was not satisfied with this explanation, but she couldn't waste time wondering about it. She went directly to the phone at the back of the hall. She would call her mom, and then she would leave Hunt House. She would take herself out of what was becoming an increasingly frightening situation.

She put one hand up to her hair. My hair is too frightened to even frizzle, she thought, trying to make herself smile.

She stopped at the telephone table where yesterday she had called her mom. The phone was not there. It had been overturned and lay beneath the table on the floor. Herculeah picked up the phone and listened. The line was dead.

She glanced around in confusion. Maybe, she thought, that was why Nurse Wegman had left in such a hurry. Maybe something had happened upstairs and Mr. Hunt needed attention. Nurse Wegman had had to go and phone for the doctor. Or an ambulance!

Herculeah glanced overhead at the ceiling as if she could find the answer there. Then, making a quick decision, she ran to the stairs. Taking them in twos, then threes, she was soon at the top.

"Mr. Hunt!"

She ran to his bedroom. The door was open.

"Mr. Hunt!"

Herculeah rushed into the room. Today the air was stale with the odor of sickness. As she crossed to the high bed, she saw that the sheets had not been changed. Mr. Hunt wore the same stained gown from yesterday.

She glanced around. The curtains had been drawn over the windows. It seemed more like a funeral parlor than a sick room.

Mr. Hunt lay without moving. His eyes were dull and listless and stared up at the ceiling. Herculeah saw no sign of life.

"Mr. Hunt, it's me, Herculeah Jones."

His thin arms lay palm-up on either side of his body. Gently she reached out and touched the inside of his wrist. She had a moment of relief as she felt his faint pulse. He was not dead.

She bent closer, and now she could hear him breathing. It was shallow, however, and his face was pale.

"Mr. Hunt, can you hear me?"

She froze. For in that moment, when her guard was down, she heard a noise in the hallway behind her.

A footstep.

Someone was there.

The softness, the stealth of the footstep told Herculeah that whoever was outside did not want her to know they were there.

Herculeah waited. Her heart pounded with fear. She was frozen in place at Mr. Hunt's bedside. She listened with increasing dread for the next, closer footstep.

THE KEY

Minutes passed, clicked off audibly by the old clock in the hall downstairs.

Herculeah did not move. She listened, her face turned toward the doorway, her heart in her throat.

She heard no more footsteps.

Moving carefully, quietly, Herculeah crossed to the door. She peered out. The hall was empty. She stepped outside the door and looked both ways. There was no one in sight. As she turned to go back into the room, she glanced down at her feet.

There lay a key.

It was an old iron key, heavy. It was the kind of key that would open a basement door, a garage door, or—she drew in her breath—the door to a tower.

She tried to remember if the key had been there when she had come up the stairs. She didn't think so, but it could have been. She had been in such a hurry, she could have stepped right over it and not noticed.

She picked up the key and held it in her hand, feeling the weight of it. Her fingers curled around the metal as she reentered Mr. Hunt's bedroom.

Mr. Hunt's eyes still stared blindly at the ceiling.

"I need your help, Mr. Hunt," she said.

She opened her fingers and held the key in front of his unseeing eyes.

"Mr. Hunt," she said. Her voice was low with urgency. "I need your help, Mr. Hunt. I need to know if this is the key to the tower."

No answer.

"Just blink once if it is. I have to know."

No answer.

"Mr. Hunt, please try to help me. I found this key outside the door to your room. It was on the floor. I think someone put it there deliberately. I think someone wanted me to find it."

No answer.

"Because if this is the key to the tower, I think it means that someone wants me to go there. There's something there that I'm supposed to see, something important."

She was talking to herself now. "And there's no door to the tower outside, so this key opens a door that's somewhere inside the house." She turned back to Mr. Hunt.

"Is there something in the tower, Mr. Hunt? Something I ought to see?"

She glanced at the drawn curtains as if to see beyond them to the tower. Then she looked over her shoulder at the door.

"Because this is beginning to make sense to me. When I tried the front door, it was locked. Then there was a faint click and the door opened. It was as if someone wanted to me to come in. Then when I was beside your bed, I heard a footstep. No one appeared, but this key was left where I would find it. Someone is telling me to go to the tower."

She continued to hold the key in front of Mr. Hunt's unblinking, unseeing eyes.

"Is this the key to the tower, Mr. Hunt? And if so, should I go there?"

His eyes closed, then opened.

"Oh, that was stupid. I asked two questions. You'll have to do it again because I don't know if that was just a reflex or if you were telling me, yes, this is the key to the tower and, yes, I should go there."

Mr. Hunt had no more answers to give, and Herculeah wasn't sure that one blink had been an answer.

"Mr. Hunt, I know it's your sister who is trying to lead us to the tower. Yesterday she threw a woman's coat from the tower. Today, this key. She is determined that someone will go there. And there is no one left to go but me."

Herculeah made her decision.

"I'll be back," she told Mr. Hunt. She started for the doorway, crossed the hall, and ran down the stairs.

She paused for a moment at the foot of the stairs and glanced at the front door. All her instincts told her that she should leave now. She should go out the door while she still could. She should get help.

But the key. The key!

Mr. Hunt's sister had given her this key as surely as if she had put it directly into her hands. The sister had wanted her to come into the house and now wanted her to unlock the door to the tower.

And if she left, her thoughts continued, whatever was in the tower might disappear. If she left, she would never know the secret it held. That was something Herculeah could not bear.

She didn't know where the door to the tower was, but she knew the direction. She ran through the hall, through an old parlor, into another hallway. The first nurse had said a person could get lost in the house. She said there were odd-shaped rooms and halls that led nowhere.

This was one of those halls that led nowhere. Herculeah turned. There was a small storage room on the left, then another hallway. It was like a maze. The door had to be here somewhere.

With the key clasped tightly in her hand, she continued her frantic search for the tower's entrance.

AT THE WINDOW

Meat was standing at his living-room window. He had been standing here ever since Herculeah had left for Hunt House. His dad had not called, and Meat was not free to leave until he did.

He had already been uneasy about her going, but there had been something in her early morning phone call that had made him even more uneasy. "I wish you were going with me," she had said. The voice had not sounded like Herculeah at all.

"I wish I could, too," he had said. It wasn't true; what he really wanted was for neither of them to go again—ever. He'd blurted out, "Don't go!"

And she had answered, as he had known she would, "I have to."

There at the window, Meat would occasionally rub his hands nervously up and down his sweatshirt. As he did this, he thought of all the dangers, all the things that could harm her.

There was Mr. Hunt. Meat wasn't at all sure the man was

really paralyzed. The thought of Herculeah sitting there, unaware, reading that terrible book when suddenly . . . gotcha!

Meat swallowed.

The sound was loud enough to reach his mother in the kitchen. "Are you all right, Albert?" she called.

"I'm fine."

Then there was the old woman. He had looked into her face and seen madness and evil, and the thought of Herculeah being trapped by her in one of those dark rooms . . .

He swallowed again. Immediately he called out, "I'm still fine," to his mother.

He realized then that he was trying to swallow his fear. He knew from past experience that fear was an object that could not be swallowed.

Then there was Nurse Wegman. Meat had only seen her for a moment or two at the front door and when he was recovering from a faint, but there had been a look in her eyes that he hadn't liked. It reminded him of a newspaper picture he'd seen of a nurse who went around killing old people, putting them out of their misery.

What was it they had called her? Oh, yes—"The Angel of Death."

Meat didn't even try to swallow that thought. He just pressed his fingers against his throat to hold the terror from rising any higher.

And then there was the tower.

The tower was a place where tragedy happened. It had happened twice before, and it would happen again. He himself had almost been the victim, but a tower like that would not be satisfied with only two victims.

Meat's mom came and stood in the doorway to the living room. She smelled nicely of barbecued pork chops, but Meat, whose throat was blocked, could not have eaten anything.

"If you're so worried about Herculeah . . ." she began.

Meat didn't let her finish. "I didn't say I was worried about her."

"You didn't have to. If you're so worried about Herculeah, why don't you call her?"

"She's at Hunt House."

"Well. Hunt House has a phone, doesn't it? She called me on it yesterday to ask for a ride."

"Mom, that's not a bad idea." He sighed. "Only it's probably an unlisted number."

"It's not. I looked it up." She handed him a Post-it note with a number on it.

"Why are you doing this?" he asked, genuinely puzzled by this unexpected kindness.

"Sometimes I think I'm a little hard on the girl. I actually felt sorry for her yesterday when we were talking about Steffie. She isn't entirely to blame for the way she is. She's got a private detective for a mother and a police detective for a father. I'm not saying a word against the father—we owe a debt of gratitude to him. He saved your uncle Neiman."

"And he found my father," Meat added.

She gave him a sharp look. "A phone call to Hunt House is one thing. I don't want you to go back there. Is that clear?" It was.

He went directly to the telephone. He didn't know exactly what he would say when the phone was answered. It didn't matter. It was just an I-know-Herculeah's-there-and-she'd-better-be-all-right call.

With trembling fingers he punched in the numbers. The line was not busy. It was ringing. He was expecting to hear the voice of the housekeeper, or Nurse Wegman, maybe even Herculeah herself. It was none of these.

"Pizza, pizza," a young male voice said. "Our special today is—"

"Sorry, wrong number," Meat said. He hung up the phone even though he was a little curious about the special. He dialed more carefully this time. The line was busy. He dialed several more times. Busy. He dialed the operator. He did not like to speak to operators, but this was an emergency.

"I've been dialing and dialing this number," Meat told her, "and I keep getting a busy signal. It's very important that I get through. A girl's life might depend upon it."

"I'll check the line."

Meat waited for an eternity.

"Sir?"

"Yes."

"That line appears to be out of order."

"Can you do something? Can you send somebody out there to fix it?"

"Probably not till Monday."

"But a girl's life might be at stake."

"I'll report it to customer service."

"But the girl is Herculeah," he told the operator as if that would make a difference. It should. "Herculeah's my best friend—actually she's pretty much my only real friend, but if Herculeah is your friend, you don't need any others."

"I'll tell customer service. Have a nice day."

And she was gone.

22

TERROR IN THE TOWER

Herculeah stood in front of the door that led to the tower. She listened. The house around her was quiet. The tower in front of her was quiet. Only the beating of her own heart broke the stillness.

The hallway was dark. There were no windows, and Herculeah wished for a flashlight. Or a candle. The book she had been reading to Mr. Hunt flashed into her mind. The girl in the book had also stood at the tower door. She had not had a flashlight or a candle. She had managed to proceed. So would Herculeah.

With one hand she felt for the keyhole. Her fingers found the opening, and her heart raced.

There was nothing like getting to the end of a mystery, Herculeah thought. Nothing like finding the last piece of the puzzle and setting it in place.

She took a deep breath, put the key in the lock, and turned. It resisted.

Another deep breath and a quick glance over her shoulder, and she turned the key the other way. With a click, the old lock yielded. Herculeah pulled the narrow, surprisingly heavy door toward her.

The hinges creaked loudly and Herculeah paused. She knew that anyone who was in the house would have heard that creak and known where she was.

As she waited to be discovered, she peered inside. The air that met her face was dank and cold. She could still turn back, she reminded herself, yet—just like the girl in the book—she could not. She stepped into the dark, unwelcoming interior of the tower.

She crossed the stone floor to the first of the circular stairs and looked up. Above her, the stairs twisted, snakelike, up the walls. They stopped at what appeared to be a trapdoor. Slowly Herculeah began to climb. She knew now that she had no control over the matter.

She continued up the stairs slowly, taking them one by one. Halfway up the stairs, she paused. She heard the sound of the tower door closing below her. Had it been a hand that closed it? She looked down. The thought that she might be trapped made her dizzy.

She touched the wall to steady herself. There was an eerie coldness to the stone beneath her hand.

She lifted her head. She listened.

She heard nothing, but she knew someone was up there, waiting for her.

And whoever it was knew she was coming. The creaking of the tower door would have given her away.

Slowly she took another step and another. Higher . . . higher. With each step, her fear grew until it seemed to swirl around her like a dark cape that held no warmth.

Herculeah continued to move slowly, deliberately up the stone stairs. Her steps were silent.

Suddenly she froze. She had heard a noise from the tower room above. She listened.

The noise was unlike anything she had heard before. It was not a human sound, nor was it the sound of an animal—at least no animal Herculeah had heard of.

It was breathing, and yet not ordinary breathing. It was a labored, troubling sound, almost a moan.

Herculeah glanced at one of the slotted windows. She could not see outside, but maybe the sound she had heard was the wind. A storm was coming. She knew that. She had seen the dark clouds. She had felt the rain. And now she could feel the wind moving around the tower.

What was it she had said to Mr. Hunt? "Dramatic things always happen during storms—though it's dramatic enough with something waiting for her at the top of the tower."

But, no, what she was hearing was not the wind around the tower. It was inside the tower.

Seven steps remained now.

It was just as it had been in the book, she thought, just as she had known it would be. But there would be no Meat waiting outside Hunt House to walk her home and make her laugh.

Six steps remained.

The trapdoor was overhead. Herculeah looked at it for a moment, trying to judge its weight. The wood was heavy. Perhaps it would take all her strength to open it.

She decided she would open it just a crack, just wide enough so she could see what was in the room. Then she could close it if she saw. . . . Her thoughts trailed off because she had no idea what she would see.

Five steps remained.

What was it she had said to Mr. Hunt? "People have climbed Everest in the time it's taken this girl to get to the top of the tower."

Four.

But then people want to get to the top of Everest.

Three.

She could go no higher without opening the trapdoor. She brushed her hands together, raised them, and, with all her strength, she pushed on the trapdoor.

Herculeah had misjudged. The trapdoor was not heavy at all.

Perhaps it was even on some sort of pulley, because the trapdoor sprang open.

Herculeah did not have time to see what awaited her in the tower room and to close the door if she didn't like what she saw.

The trapdoor seemed to pull her with it. Her momentum carried her into the tower room and left her sprawled across the dusty floor.

She lifted her head. She was not alone.

23

THE ANGEL OF DEATH

Meat walked slowly toward Haunt House. His mother had not wanted him to come here, but he had said, "I have to go, Mom, even though I may be in danger myself. I'm sorry if that causes you discomfort, but Herculeah needs me."

Well, actually, he had not said that. He had written it.

Well, actually he had not written those exact words. The note he had left pinned by a magnet to the refrigerator door said, "I've gone out—save me some pork chops."

The gate loomed ahead. He could make out the lions with their lifted claws.

He was still standing there, planning what he was going to do and say at the front door of Hunt House when he heard a car approach.

Meat closed his eyes. He knew it was his mother. It would be just like her. She treated him like a child! Probably as soon as she discovered he had left the house, she had grabbed her car keys.

He heard the window roll down. He waited for his mother's voice to say, "Albert Ambrose McMannis, you get in this car this minute." And he would get in the car like a good little boy—No, he would not!

He opened his eyes, turned and stared into the stony face of the Angel of Death herself—Nurse Wegman.

Meat had never particularly cared for nurses. They were mainly used, in Meat's experience, for carrying out orders too unpleasant for doctors to do themselves, like give shots.

Although Meat would rather it be Nurse Wegman than his mother, he still could not help noticing that Nurse Wegman was the kind of nurse who would carry out the most unpleasant orders with joy.

"What are you doing here?" Nurse Wegman asked.

"I tried to call, but—"

"I know. The phone's out."

Nurse Wegman waited, looking at him so fiercely that Meat wished car windows could be rolled up from the outside. If any engineer ever found himself being looked at by Nurse Wegman like that, he'd invent one.

"So what are you doing here?"

"I came about Herculeah."

"Who?"

"Herculeah, the girl who reads to Mr. Hunt."

"Oh, her." Nurse Wegman's look got even more unpleasant. "She's here?"

"I think so."

"In the house?"

"I think so."

"She couldn't be. There's nobody to let her in. I've fired the housekeeper."

"If Herculeah wanted to get in, she'd find a way."

Nurse Wegman's hands—they were big hands—hit the steering wheel in frustration. The horn, as if startled, gave a quick honk.

Nurse Wegman took a breath. "You go home. I had to leave to make a call . . . the . . . doctor. Mr. Hunt needs the doctor, and the doctor should be arriving any minute. The girl will have to be taken care of."

"Taken care of?" Meat asked. He didn't like the sound of that.

"She will have to—to go home."

"Oh."

"If she hasn't already gone, I mean."

"I guess she could've, though I didn't pass her on the way."

Nurse Wegman continued to stare at him. "Well, go on! Go!"

He continued to stand by the car. He couldn't leave. Herculeah was inside Hunt House—he knew that now—and she needed him.

As if reading his mind, Nurse Wegman said, "You aren't needed here."

Meat wished he could be sure of that.

"Go! Go!"

Still he could not move.

"May I give you some nursely advice?" Her tone was sweet now, but the same cold, bird-of-prey eyes watched him, as if swooping in for the kill.

"I guess."

"You need to lose some weight."

Meat drew in his breath. Nurse Wegman rolled up the window. Not until the car was halfway down the drive was Meat able to turn and take a few steps toward home.

When he was out of sight of the house, he stopped. He breathed deeply. He thought.

If I had not just thought about my dad . . . if I had not been reminded that my dad was my exact size at this age . . . if I had not been the son of Macho Man and a gentleman, I would have said, "And you, madam, need a shave."

But Son of Macho Man did not stoop to petty insults. He was a man of action.

Maybe he himself could not handle Nurse Wegman, but Son of Macho Man knew someone who could.

IN THE DEATH GRIP OF
A HUNDRED MEN

On the floor of the tower room, Herculeah lay where she had
fallen, but only for a moment.

Then she scrambled to her feet. Her hands were fists. She was
ready to do battle. What she saw caused her arms to sag. She
took a step forward, moving away from the trapdoor.

Lying in front of her was a small woman. She lay on her side,
curled toward Herculeah. Her face was streaked with blood and
tears.

Around her lay—like remnants of an old picnic—crusts of
bread, empty cups, a half-eaten apple, cake crumbs in an old
napkin. Perhaps these offerings were what had been keeping the
woman alive.

"Help me," the woman whispered. She reached out for
Herculeah with a hand that trembled.

"What happened to you?"

"Help me."

"Yes, yes, of course I'll help you. Who are you?"

The woman spoke so softly Herculeah could not make out the words.

"Who?"

This time the words were clearer. "I'm Ida Wegman."

Herculeah took in a deep breath. "Wegman?"

"Yes."

"Nurse Wegman?"

"Yes. This man hit me on the head. . . ." Her eyes focused on Herculeah's for the first time. "It's coming back to me now. The man stopped me at the gate to ask directions, and before I knew what was happening, he struck me here." She raised her hand to the side of her head.

"Do you remember anything else?"

"He was a strong man. I remember he carried me up the circular stairs. He left me here . . . like this."

"Oh, my," Herculeah said. As she knelt beside the woman, her thoughts raced.

The man who hit her on the head is the man pretending to be Nurse Wegman. Nurse Wegman is a man! I should have known that. The first time we met him, he was dressed like a woman, but when he asked Meat a question, Meat answered, "Yes, sir." Sir! Meat sensed it, and I—like an idiot—

She broke off her thoughts.

"Listen, we've got to get out of here. The fake Nurse Wegman drove off in a car about an hour ago—I saw him leave—but he may come back, and we don't want to be up here in this tower if he does. We'd be trapped."

"Yes."

"Can you sit up?"

"If you help me."

Herculeah bent to put one arm around the woman's shoulder and raised her into a sitting position. The woman's head sagged against Herculeah.

"I'm dizzy."

"Take deep breaths," Herculeah advised. "Can you stand?"

"I don't think so."

"Then I'd better go for help."

"No, no, don't leave me. I'll stand. Just don't let go of me."

Herculeah lifted the woman into a standing position, but her legs crumpled and she sank back to the floor.

"I'll go for help."

"You won't come back."

"I will."

"Someone went for help before."

"Who?" Herculeah's thoughts lifted with the hope that help might already be on the way.

"An old woman. Very old. She brought me food. I asked her to call the police. She said Papa wouldn't like it."

"Oh." Herculeah realized that she meant Miss Hunt. She realized, too, that Miss Hunt's way of helping was by throwing a blood-stained coat out of the tower, by leaving phone messages, by opening the front door to let Herculeah inside, by leaving the key to the tower where she would find it. The old woman was like a child. She wouldn't call the police because Papa wouldn't like it.

"I've got to go for help."

"Don't leave me."

The woman's arms encircled Herculeah's legs with surprising strength. Her face was pressed against Herculeah's knees. Herculeah tried to move her legs, but she couldn't even take a step.

"If I don't go for help, we might—" She didn't want to say the word "die." That would upset the woman even more. "We might be trapped here."

The woman lifted her head. "Was that a car?'

"You heard a car?"

"I don't know. I heard something."

"Maybe it was the storm. I hope that's what it was, but I've got to get out of here. You have to let go of my legs."

"No! No! You'll leave me!" she wailed.

Herculeah pulled at the woman's arms, but her grip was like steel.

Herculeah had heard of something like this. It was called a

death grip. It happened when people who were dying suddenly got enormous strength and could hold on to someone so tightly a hundred men couldn't break the grip.

Herculeah didn't think the woman was dying, but she did think she had a death grip a hundred men couldn't break.

"Look," Herculeah said in her most reasonable and, she hoped, reassuring voice, "at least loosen your grip a little, just enough so that I can get over to the trapdoor and close it."

"No, it's a trick. As soon as you get over there you'll go down the stairs and leave. I won't be left again. I won't. I'll die if I'm left again."

"Look, let's inch over to the trapdoor. You can be with me every step of the way. We'll go over slowly. I'll close the door and we'll sit on it. That way, if the man does come back, he won't be able to get up here, and sooner or later my mom will come to see what's wrong and—"

She didn't finish because at that moment she heard something that froze her blood.

She heard the creaking of the tower door as it opened. Then she heard a heavy footstep on the stairs.

It's too late, she told herself, he's here.

25

A MURDERER'S CHILD

Herculeah lunged toward the trapdoor. She was determined to get there even if she had to crawl, dragging this wounded woman with her. The woman screamed with pain as they fell to the floor, but she did not loosen her grip.

The footsteps on the circular stairs were coming closer. Herculeah was on her stomach now, pulling herself along with her elbows, but the woman was a terrible burden. She reached for the trapdoor, but there was not enough time.

A huge hand reached in the opening, holding the trapdoor in place, and Nurse Wegman's—the wrong Nurse Wegman's—face appeared in the opening. Then his chest. With his weight on his arms, he pulled himself up and sat in the opening, his feet swinging down over the circular stairs. The look on his face told Herculeah he was enjoying himself.

The woman moaned. Herculeah felt her arms go limp. She had fainted, and now—too late—Herculeah was free.

"It's you," she said. She got to her feet and began to move away from the trapdoor.

"You should have stayed away," the man said. "This was no concern of yours."

"I guess I made it my concern."

"That was a mistake."

"You're no nurse."

"Never have been."

"No woman."

Another cruel smile. "Never have been."

"You're one of the Hunt family, though, aren't you?"

"Lionus Hunt the Second, at your service."

"I thought so. You've got the Hunt eyes." Herculeah did not intend that as a compliment.

Herculeah took another step back. The man stood and glanced down at the unconscious woman at his feet. Herculeah thought he was going to step over her body and come after her, but he did not.

Herculeah said, "Does all this"—she made a gesture that took in his disguise, the woman's body, the whole house—"have to do with that family reunion?"

"That was a long time ago. How did you find out about that?"

"I read about it in a news clipping." Herculeah kept talking. She knew from past experience that when you were facing a killer, you kept talking. "There was a game at the reunion— hide-and-seek, I believe."

"Yes, a child's game."

"The governess was killed. A stone was thrown from this tower, I believe."

"The stone wasn't meant for the governess."

"Who then?"

"My mother's twin sister."

"And who threw the stone?"

"My mother."

Herculeah said, "Your mother hated her own twin that much—enough to try to kill her?"

"Oh, yes. Her twin was the good one. Everyone loved her twin. It started as jealousy, I guess—normal in sisters. It was petty things at first. She'd hide her twin's toys, spill her milk, make her cry."

He paused, and Herculeah said quickly, "But it didn't stop there."

"No, it got physical. She would shove her twin, push her down the stairs. Once she even stabbed her twin's portrait with a knife."

"That should have been a warning to the family."

"Oh, my mother was punished all right, but that only made her hate her twin more."

"What happened then?"

"There were several accidents—near misses, like the stone from the tower. I believe it was the poison mushrooms that finally did her in."

"Your mother gave her poison mushrooms?"

"The family thought so. They kicked her out. She was only seventeen." He glanced down at the unconscious woman at his feet before he continued. "But my mother is dying now, half out of her mind with pain. I just went out to call her for more instructions and only got babbling. Earlier I managed to piece the story together. I didn't even know she had a twin. She had never even mentioned her family. Now I learn that not only is there a family, but a family with a great deal of money. And this money is quite probably hidden in the family house."

"And you had to get inside."

"Yes."

"But you're family. Why couldn't you just come for a visit?"

"The family made my mother an offer she couldn't refuse. They wouldn't contact the police if she would leave. The old man didn't trust the police, but he mistrusted her even more. She left, and I—a murderer's child—would not have been welcome." He gave that cruel smile that Herculeah was beginning to hate. "Because a murderer's child could also turn out to be a murderer, don't you think?"

"But you haven't murdered anybody. The nurse is still alive."

"I just wanted her out of the way. So you're right. I haven't killed anyone. Not yet." Another smile, and then he changed the subject. "Once I came here and saw the situation, it wasn't hard to make plans. It was simple. I'd take the place of one of the nurses. I'd find the money. I'd leave with nobody the wiser."

"But how did you get the nurse up here? I almost got lost just finding the tower door."

"I slipped in the house through the side door. So convenient. The door led directly into the hall and the tower door. My mother told me a lot of shortcuts. She knew how to get around in the house without being noticed."

"The tower door was locked, wasn't it?"

"Anybody could open these old locks, if"—he touched his pocket—"if he had the right knife."

Herculeah drew in her breath. He had a knife! To divert him, she said quickly, "You haven't found the money! There may not even be any money."

"I think there is. All I have to do . . ." He trailed off.

Herculeah could sense a subtle change in him. His body was no longer relaxed; he was ready in a way he had not been before.

"Listen," she said, stepping back, "my friend knows I'm here. He'll tell my father. My father's a police detective."

"I've taken care of your friend."

"What? You did something to Meat? What?"

Now Herculeah was also ready in a way she had not been before.

"If you hurt Meat . . ."

She stepped forward, prepared for battle. Now the unconscious body of the woman was all that lay between them.

The woman stirred. She lifted her head. It came to her that

just before she lost consciousness, she had held on to legs. Those legs had been all that lay between her and death.

With a cry, she reached out for the only legs she saw—the wrong Nurse Wegman's.

"What?" he cried. "What are you doing? Get off, you fool."

He took a step back, trying to escape the clutching hands, but his heel caught in the opening of the trapdoor.

"Push!" Herculeah cried.

She waited with her heart in her throat to see if the woman had the strength to obey.

26

SON OF MACHO MAN

Meat rubbed his hands over his sweatshirt to dry them of sweat. He tried to calm himself by humming "Macho Man." When his hands were as dry as they were going to get, he turned to the pay phone. He deposited the coins in the slot, dialed the number, and waited for three rings.

A voice said, "Police Department. Zone three. This is Sergeant Rossini. Can I help you?"

Meat cleared his throat. "I sure hope so," he said. "I need to speak to Detective Chico Jones. It's important."

"What's the problem?"

"It's about his daughter. She's—"

"Herculeah?"

Meat sighed with relief. Everyone in the county—in the United States, probably—knew Herculeah. "Yes, sir. There's something he needs to know. Herculeah may be in trouble."

"Is this, er, some kind of personal problem? I've met Mrs.

Jones, Herculeah's mom, and she seems to be the kind of woman who can handle most anything."

"I can't get her—just her answering machine—and I believe this is a matter for the police. Also, I'm at a pay phone and I'm running out of coins."

"I'll see if he's in." There was a pause.

Meat waited. When the police put you on hold, they didn't bother piping in soothing music to ease the wait. You just had to hold the phone and hope for the best.

Since there was nothing else to do, Meat let his thoughts continue. The chorus of "Macho Man" would have been a perfect waiting song for him.

Other callers, of course, might like something different, something to lift their spirits. What was the name of that song that went, "When you walk through a storm, hold your head up," or something like that? A lady sang it in an old movie.

Anybody calling the police was bound to be in some kind of storm. That was a given. You wouldn't want to walk through them with your head up, however, because—

"Chico Jones," a voice said.

"Oh, hi." Meat was brought back from his musical interlude abruptly. "Thank you for taking the call, Mr. Jones. It's me from across the street."

"Albert?"

"Yes."

"What's up?"

"Herculeah's at a place called Hunt House, and I think she may be in trouble."

"I spoke with her mom this morning, and she assured me Herculeah wasn't going back there anymore to read to Mr. Hunt."

"I don't think she went there to read."

"I'll check into it. Where are you?"

"I'm at a gas station. It's not far from the house. I could meet you at the gate to Hunt House, if you don't mind. I'm worried."

"I'm on my way. See you there."

Meat hung up the phone.

A customer had heard Meat's side of the conversation and gotten interested. She said, "Is everything all right?"

"I hope so," Meat said, then added what was causing him to continue sweating, "if we're not too late."

27

ON THE TOWER STAIRS

"Push!" Herculeah shouted again.

The woman did not seem to hear her. She seemed intent on only one thing—not being left alone in the tower again.

"Help me! Help!" She was pleading with the man now. "Please!" He was no longer the man who had wounded her; he was her salvation.

"Let go of me, you fool!"

She managed to get to her knees, but she had no intention of letting go. The struggle to her knees was too much. She fell forward, and as she fell forward, the man fell backward.

Herculeah gasped. She saw what was going to happen. The man was going to fall down the tower stairs, and his momentum would take the woman with him.

Herculeah rushed forward. In two strides she was there. She encircled the woman's body with her arms.

For one terrible moment the three of them were locked together at the top of the stairs.

"Push!" Herculeah cried, and this time, the woman had a moment of clarity. She understood. This was the man who had hurt her. This was the man who wanted to kill her. This was the man they were trying to get away from. She pushed.

The three of them fell at the same time. Herculeah fell backward. She sat down hard on the tower floor. The woman fell with her, landing on Herculeah's lap like a child.

The man teetered for a moment on the edge of the stone steps. Then, with a terrible scream, he went over the edge, hitting his head hard on the edge of the trapdoor as he disappeared.

The nurse moaned. "What happened?"

"You saved our lives. That's what happened."

Herculeah lost no time. She shifted the woman's body to the floor and got to her feet. She moved quickly to the opening of the trapdoor and peered down the stairs. She was prepared to slam the trapdoor shut if the man was conscious and likely to come up to the tower room again.

She didn't think he was going anywhere. He lay halfway down the stairs. He was not moving. His eyes stared blindly up at her.

As she looked at his thick features, the shadow of stubble on his face, she wondered how she had ever mistaken him for a woman.

"He was the man at the gate, the man who hit me," the woman said, speaking as if she was trying to get the facts straight in her mind.

"Oh, yes," said Herculeah.

"He would have killed us."

"That, too," Herculeah said.

"Is he gone now?"

"Yes. He's on the stairs. He's unconscious, though, so he won't be bothering us anymore. I'm going for help."

She kept her distance because she was afraid the woman might try again to restrain her, but the woman seemed to be lucid now. Herculeah went down one step without incident.

"Will you see the old woman who tried to help me?"

"I don't know. Miss Hunt comes and goes. She did try to help you, but in her own way. She couldn't call the police. . . ."

"Papa wouldn't have liked it," the woman said with a faint smile.

Herculeah smiled back. "Exactly. But she did the best she could. Did you know she threw your coat from the tower to let us know you were here?"

"I remember her calling to someone, 'She's up here, up here,' but nobody came."

"Finally, I got the message and I came. Now I do have to go. You need a doctor. That man needs a doctor, and Mr. Hunt does, too. You'll be fine now."

The sound of the woman's voice followed Herculeah down three more steps, though Herculeah couldn't make out her words. She knew the woman was remembering more and more of her ordeal.

Halfway down the stairs lay the man's body. It blocked Herculeah's way. The stairs were narrow. There was no room between his body and the stone wall, but there was a small space to the outside of the steps. She would have to be very careful.

She paused for a moment, examining the man. He had not moved. His eyes were blank. But he was breathing. He was still alive.

She took one more step, then one more. The man's shoulders were broad and blocked the next two stairs. She would have to step over him, but then the danger would be over. She could fly down the rest of the steps and be on her way.

Just this one long step.

She took a deep breath. She was lifting her foot when the man's eyes focused. She did not see this, but she knew something had happened by a sudden twitch in his shoulder muscle. She must move quickly.

At that exact moment, she felt his fingers encircle her other foot. Not another death grip! she screamed to herself. Then she let out a real scream. It echoed within the circular walls, and seemed to go on and on.

"Let me go!"

Then from the bottom of the stairs came an old quavering voice. "Let her go or I'll shoot."

Both Herculeah and the man looked down the stairs. At the bottom, gun in hand, stood old Miss Hunt. In her trembling hands was a gun.

28

AT GUNPOINT

This was the oldest gun Herculeah had ever seen in her life. This gun would probably have been outdated in the Civil War.

Herculeah knew instantly that she was in much more danger from Miss Hunt with a gun than she was from the man lying beside her. Already his hand was losing its grip on her ankle.

"Don't shoot, Miss Hunt," Herculeah said.

"Wants to kill us."

"Put the gun down. We're fine."

"I'll kill him first."

"Miss Hunt—"

"His mother killed my sister."

"Maybe she did or maybe it was an accident."

"No accident." The gun was waving back and forth, and Miss Hunt held it with both hands to steady it. One finger was on the trigger.

"He's sly."

"Yes," Herculeah agreed.

"He pretended to be a nurse. Didn't fool me."

"No." Herculeah's ankle was free now, and she went down one step. "He's hurt now. He can't harm us."

"Pretending to be hurt."

"He's not pretending. He's unconscious. Look at him." Herculeah reached down and touched his shoulder. "See? Now put the gun down."

Herculeah straightened. She came down the rest of the stairs slowly. Her hands were raised in the classic gesture of having no weapon.

She paused at the bottom of the stairs. Miss Hunt backed away from the tower, through the open door, and into the hallway beyond. The gun was still pointed in Herculeah's direction.

"Please put the gun down. I have so much I want to tell you, but I can't tell you with that gun pointed at me."

"This is an old gun. Won't hurt anyone."

"I'm afraid of *all* guns," Herculeah said truthfully.

"This was Papa's gun. It's never been shot. It's not even loaded."

She pointed the gun upward, pulled the trigger, and blew a hole in the ceiling.

"Well, I'll be," she said.

There was a moment of silence while the smoke cleared, and then a voice broke the silence. "I'll take that gun."

It was the voice of a man, a man of authority.

Herculeah had covered her ears with her hands when the gun went off. She lowered her hands now and saw Meat.

She couldn't believe that Meat had spoken in such a manly way. She had always thought he had the same aversion to guns as she did.

Then she looked behind Meat and saw her father.

Miss Hunt was eyeing her father's outstretched hand with suspicion. She looked at his face. "Are you the police?" she asked.

"I am."

"Papa never wanted the police here."

"But your papa would have wanted you to give me the gun." Her father's voice was kind, reassuring, forceful.

"Here," Miss Hunt said. She thrust the gun on him. Then in a moment she disappeared down the hall with only a wisp of smoke from the old gun to show she had ever been there.

Her father handed the gun to an officer behind him.

"You'll never, never know how glad I am to see you!" Herculeah cried. She opened her arms and rushed forward.

Meat thought for one glorious moment she was coming to throw her arms around him. He was just getting his hands out of his jacket pockets so he could participate in the hug when she rushed past him and threw her arms around her father.

"Dad! Dad! How did you know I was in trouble? How did you know to come?"

"You can thank your friend for that. Albert called me. Then I got your mom on her cell phone. She's been worried about you—obviously with good reason. You're all right?"

"Yes, now that you're here I'm fine."

"Let's go where we can talk."

"There's a man on the stairs." She nodded toward the stairs behind her without leaving the safety of her dad's arms. "And up in the tower room there's the real Nurse Wegman. She has a head injury, and . . . oh, it was too much for me." She buried her head in her father's chest.

"It's not your problem anymore. I'll get some officers to see about them. I've got half the police force here with me."

She lifted her head. "And old Mr. Hunt—the man I was reading to upstairs—was unconscious when I left him."

"Check upstairs, too," he told an officer.

Herculeah glanced over her shoulder and saw Meat. "And Meat!" she said, acknowledging him at last. "How did you get here?"

"I was waiting out by the gate, and your dad gave me a lift the rest of the way." He did not mention that the only good way to arrive at Haunt House was in a police car with two policemen in the front seat.

"Meat filled me in on some of what happened, but you'll have to tell me the rest."

They walked down the hall, and Herculeah was gracious enough to call over her shoulder, "You come, too, Meat. I need you."

He came.

OH, MOM

"I see now that I absolutely cannot trust you," Herculeah's mother said.

Herculeah said, "Oh, Mom."

"You're worse than an infant. I ought to have my head examined for asking you to read to Mr. Hunt. I should have known you'd go poking your nose in where it didn't belong."

Herculeah and her mom were driving home through the black gates of Hunt House. They were in the front seat of the car, talking. Meat sat alone in the backseat, listening.

They had seen the two Nurse Wegmans and Mr. Hunt loaded into ambulances and on their way to the hospital. They had waited for the housekeeper to arrive and look after the sister. "I knew something was wrong about that nurse as soon as she fired me," the housekeeper had said. Now the three of them were on their way home.

Herculeah glanced at her mom's profile. Sometimes her mom really looked like a private detective.

"If you'd tell me things, then I wouldn't have to poke my nose in, as you put it. Well, can I ask you one thing?"

"You can ask."

"You were hired to find the sister, right? And you had located her when all this happened?"

"I had located her address. The lawyer was going to contact her."

"Why did they need the sister? They kicked her out a long time ago. For the mushrooms."

"Mushrooms?"

"The poison ones. It's a long story, Mom."

"They did kick her out, but they need her now. They want to sell the house—there's going to be a mall there—and they can't sell without consent of all parties. The sister is one of the parties."

"So what's going to happen to the nurses?"

"There's only one real nurse."

"I know that."

Her mother sighed. "Your dad thinks that neither of them has injuries that are life-threatening, although the man who impersonated a nurse is going to face serious charges—attempted murder for one. And it was all for nothing."

"Why do you say that?"

"He came to Hunt House thinking there was money hidden

in the house, when the only thing of value is the property itself. He and his mother would have gotten a third of that."

Herculeah glanced out the window to see if she could get a final glimpse of Hunt House. Only the tip of the tower rose above the trees. "I guess I'll never come back to Hunt House."

"Why would you want to?"

"The book, Mom! To finish the book. I know what I found at the top of the tower, but I don't know what the girl in the book found."

"Maybe I can get the book for you, but if you go to the hospital to read to Mr. Hunt, I suggest you take another book."

"Of course, Mom."

Meat spoke from the backseat. "Tell your mom what your dad said about the end of the book."

Herculeah glanced around as if surprised to see him there. It had been so long since anyone noticed him that he was surprised to find himself there. "I was just getting ready to," she said.

She turned back to her mom. "I was puzzled about why Mr. Hunt chose the book. I mean, maybe he read it as a child, or maybe he wanted me to see the clipping, or maybe he sensed danger in the tower. I said I was mainly curious about the end of the book and what was up in the tower, and he said, 'Oh, I can tell you what was at the top of the tower if that's all you want to know—Batman.'"

Herculeah laughed. "I thought he meant like Batman and

Robin, but he meant 'Batman' like Dracula. He admitted he hadn't read the book, of course, but he claimed to have seen the movie. It was very funny. I wish I could imitate him so—"

"Don't bother."

There was silence, broken only by an uneasy cough from the backseat. Meat felt that the front seat could take a lesson from him. When you were about to say something wrong, cough.

Herculeah's mom didn't believe in coughs. She said, "Your dad picked an inappropriate time to be amusing."

"Mom, you don't understand Dad at all!"

"Oh?"

"It was the perfect time. I was upset and it helped me. At least he didn't say I was worse than an infant. You know what he said?"

"No."

"He said that whatever the girl in the book found in the tower, she couldn't possibly have handled it any better than I did."

In the backseat, Meat waited for Mrs. Jones's reply, but apparently she had used up all of her one-word sentences. They drove the rest of the way home in a blessed silence.

30

A MIDNIGHT CALLER

The phone rang and Herculeah picked it up on the first ring. She said, "Hi, Meat."

"How did you know it was me? Has your mom gotten caller ID?"

"I don't need caller ID to know when it's you. And," she went on, "you always call when we've solved a case."

"I didn't do much to solve this one."

"Yes, you did. You recognized right away that Nurse Wegman was a man. And I didn't pick up on that at all. I was an idiot. I thought she was just an unattractive woman. Sometimes I think I don't deserve to be a detective."

"Oh, yes, you do. You manage to get people to confess things, like Lionus Hunt telling you all about his mother killing her twin sister, about his plans to get into Hunt House in the disguise of a nurse. He would have thought it was a waste of time to tell me stuff like that. He would have just killed me."

"If I've learned one thing about criminals, it's that they think they're so clever, they want to talk about how they did it."

There was a silence, and then Herculeah said, "You know what I was thinking about when you called?"

"What?"

"I was thinking about the connection between this case and the labors of the real Hercules."

"It had to be the Nemean lion. Remember Hercules killed him? There were wrought-iron lions on the gate? Did you notice them? And the old man's name was Lionus."

"Yes, I noticed the lions. I saw them the first day I went to read."

"Did your hair frizzle?"

"No, but I got a this-is-it feeling. When I get that feeling—it's hard to describe. I just know . . ." She took a deep breath, searching for the right words. "I just know . . ."

"This is it," Meat supplied.

"Exactly!" She hesitated. "Why are you laughing at my feeling?"

"I'm not laughing at that. I just thought of another Hercules connection."

"What?"

"Remember the girdle of Hippo-something? I forget what her name was."

"Hippolyte. But I don't get what that's got to do with it."

"The girdle. The imposter Nurse Wegman wore one to help

him look like a woman. I saw it when they were putting him in the ambulance."

Herculeah laughed, too.

Meat waited and then got to the real reason he had called. "You haven't asked me about the phone call from my dad."

"Meat! I'm sorry! I can't believe I forgot. How was the phone call from your dad?"

"It was great. He's going to be here next weekend."

"I hope I get to see him. I only saw him that one night, and he was dressed like Macho Man."

"He even looks like Macho Man in his everyday clothes, too."

"So what are you and your dad going to do? Anything special?"

Meat hesitated, trying to decide whether to say, "Oh, nothing special, just hang out," or tell the truth. He decided on the truth. "My dad has this friend who runs a health club here. My dad trained there when he was getting started. He's getting me a membership, and I'm going there every weekend."

"Lucky! I wish my dad would get me a membership. What's the name of it?"

"I forgot," he said. Meat didn't want to seem unfriendly, but he did hope that he and Herculeah would not be in training together. This was something between two Macho Men.

To change the subject he said, "Have you got any idea yet about what your next mystery will be?"

"I not only have an idea, I know."

"How?"

"Well, when I was searching Ida Wegman's coat, I reached in the pocket and pulled out a lipstick. It was Summer Rose or something like that. And I knew it wasn't the fake Nurse Wegman's lipstick because she'd wear something like Dragon-Lady Red. And as soon as I thought, Dragon, I knew that would be part of my next case."

"One of those this-is-it feelings?"

"Yes."

Meat said, "Dragon . . . dragon. . . . There are no live dragons, of course. Maybe this has something to do with that Chinese martial arts place or that Chinese restaurant on Peachtree. Both of them have dragons in their windows."

"No. This will not be a dragon advertisement. This will be a dragon."

She yawned. Meat always dreaded that sound because it meant the conversation was over. He tried to think of some way to keep it going, but before he could, she spoke again.

"I've got to go. It's been a long day. I'll see you tomorrow. Good night, Meat."

There were only three words left to say, so he said them.

"Good night, Herculeah."